SO-BIL-209

PRAISE FOR *TORN*

She Reads Romance Best Age Gap Romances

"Well-written tension and forbidden longing. The angst in this was incredible! Loved every second!"
—Penelope Douglas, *New York Times* bestselling author

"A captivating journey of forbidden romance. *Torn* is unputdownable and unforgettable."
—Meredith Wild, #1 *New York Times* bestselling author

"Soulmates tangled in a forbidden, twisted situation. Every word is painfully beautiful. *Torn* shattered me and put me back together again. It's not a story—it's a ride that I never wanted to end. It takes forbidden love and angst to an entirely new level."
—Abbi Glines, #1 *New York Times* bestselling author

"*Torn* won my heart so fiercely." —Addicted to Romance

Aram Public Library
404 E Walworth Ave
Delavan, WI 53115

TORN

ALSO BY CARIAN COLE

TORN

CARIAN COLE

FOREVER

NEW YORK   BOSTON

This book is a work of fiction. Names, characters, places, and incidents are the product of the author's imagination or are used fictitiously. Any resemblance to actual events, locales, or persons, living or dead, is coincidental.

Copyright © 2023 by Carian Cole

Cover art and design by Daniela Medina. Cover images © Trevillion; Shutterstock. Cover copyright © 2024 by Hachette Book Group, Inc.

Hachette Book Group supports the right to free expression and the value of copyright. The purpose of copyright is to encourage writers and artists to produce the creative works that enrich our culture.

The scanning, uploading, and distribution of this book without permission is a theft of the author's intellectual property. If you would like permission to use material from the book (other than for review purposes), please contact permissions@hbgusa.com. Thank you for your support of the author's rights.

Forever
Hachette Book Group
1290 Avenue of the Americas, New York, NY 10104
read-forever.com

Originally published in ebook by Forever in July 2023
First trade paperback edition: February 2024

Forever is an imprint of Grand Central Publishing. The Forever name and logo are registered trademarks of Hachette Book Group, Inc.

The publisher is not responsible for websites (or their content) that are not owned by the publisher.

The Hachette Speakers Bureau provides a wide range of authors for speaking events. To find out more, go to hachettespeakersbureau.com or email HachetteSpeakers@hbgusa.com.

Forever books may be purchased in bulk for business, educational, or promotional use. For information, please contact your local bookseller or the Hachette Book Group Special Markets Department at special.markets@hbgusa.com.

Print book interior design by Emily Baker

Library of Congress Control Number: 2023947726

ISBNs: 9781538765982 (trade paperback), 9781538765999 (ebook)

Printed in the United States of America

LSC-C

Printing 1, 2023

To all the amazing readers who have changed my life.

TORN

PROLOGUE

Kenzi

> *My love,*
> *Walk in the rain with me. Kiss me in the misty fog.*
> *Let me hold you all night under the hush of the wind.*
> *I'm waiting for you. Throwing pennies ... making wishes.*
> *I'm wishing only for you. Always for you.*
> *Come back to me.*
> *I'll fight for you. I'll fight for us.*
> *Wish for me, too ... and I'll make it come true.*

The frayed parchment paper is soft in my fingers, perfectly worn and aged, and I'm very aware that he chose this texture of paper, this color of ink, with careful consideration. Because he knows how much it means to me. Because he knows *me*. Like no one else ever has or ever could.

I read his words over and over again, long after I have them memorized and they're burned into my heart and soul, yet I still hold the handwritten note and stare at the words until they blur. I can hear his voice saying them—deep, yet soft and sensual. *Raw.*

I like touching the paper that I know he held in his hands. The hands that had once held me. Caressed me. Ignited passion and desire in me so deep that I still can't forget.

And I don't ever want to.

The faint scent of his cologne drifts from the paper. Or maybe I've just wished for it so much that I've imagined it. Either way, it's comforting and stirs memories.

So many memories...

Reading his words, all the feelings rush back like acid on a wound that won't heal. He's my other half, the one who makes my heart beat. The man who makes me feel every feeling that could possibly be felt—and then some. The man who held me and loved me through almost every moment of my life. I have no past without him and no future without him. Quite simply, he is my world. There's no way I will ever move on from a love like ours. We belong to each other. I've always known it, and I am utterly exhausted from fighting it, denying it, keeping myself from it, and hiding it—as I'm sure he must be, too.

And now after the distance... he still loves me. He still believes in us, and his words assure me he's willing to take on the world for me. For us.

It's time for me to go back home to my love and to my heart. Time is precious, and I don't want to give any more up.

I lift the lid of the small antique wooden trunk on my desk and pull out a sheet of sky-blue paper and my favorite rose-gold calligraphy pen.

Tor, my love...

My wishes have always been, and always will be, for you.

I'm coming home with a clear mind and a strong heart. We'll fight our battles together from now on.

I love you. I've loved you in so many different ways, and I want to continue to love you in all the beautiful ways we've yet to discover. I refuse to hide anymore. If there are some who cannot accept our age difference, then that is their choice, but I will not let their opinions or thoughts keep me from you—the love of my life. All I ask is that we tread gently with my father, as his heart is just as precious to me as yours is. I know you feel the same.

I will call you as soon as I'm settled in my new place. I cannot wait to be in your arms, and I promise we will never be apart again.

I love you the most,

Kenzi

I fold the letter into an envelope, write Tor's address on it, and slip it into the mailbox on the corner. On my way back to the Inn, I walk down the beach to the water's edge, and I toss in the penny that Tor sent with his note.

I wish for all the things that would heal our hearts and give us—and everyone we love—a happily-ever-after.

CHAPTER 1

Kenzi—one day old

Toren—fifteen years old

"We want you to be her godfather," Asher says as he gently lays his newborn baby into my arms. I have to tear my gaze away from her spellbinding eyes to look up at him from the chair I'm cradling the baby in.

"Me?" I repeat, glancing over at the hospital bed, where Ember beams back at me with a tired, yet genuine smile.

"Yes, you," they both say at the same time. "If it wasn't for you, we probably never would've met," Ember adds, grabbing Asher's hand. "And we wouldn't have this beautiful little baby. We know you'll always protect her."

"That's right, man. You're Uncle Tor now."

I'm an uncle. And my two best friends are parents. And we're all fuckin' under sixteen.

But Kenzi Allyster Valentine would change us all forever. She needed us.

"Wow. I'm honored, guys. No doubt, I'll always be here for her."

I kick back the pang that hits my stomach. I didn't get the girl...but I got something better that I never expected. A gift in the form of a little tiny hand wrapped tightly around my finger, huge eyes like gems staring up into mine like I was the most amazing person in the friggin' world, and the first glimpse of what I could already tell was going to be a heart-stopping smile.

At that moment, a connection was born.

That was it.
She owned me.
My niece.
My goddaughter.
The love of my life.

💗 💗 💗

KENZI

I hop off the back of the motorcycle and run my fingers through my shoulder-length hair, trying to detangle the mess. The wind is brutal on my hair and turns it into a tumbleweed in less than five minutes of being on the bike. Grabbing my hips, he pulls me against him and plants a dry kiss on my lips that tastes like dirt from the road.

"Kenzi!" A deep male voice bellows from the top of my driveway, making us both jump. "If I see your ass on the back of that bike again, we're gonna have some fuckin' issues."

Jason quickly pulls away his hands, which had inched their way down to my ass. "Holy shit, is that your father?" he asks under his breath.

I let out a sigh and shake my head. My father is not one to raise his voice. Unless he's singing onstage, of course. But never out in the driveway. And never at me. "No, it's just my uncle."

Jason squints at Toren before his eyes dart back to mine. "Isn't that the guy who owns the motorcycle place in town? I think I bought my bike from him."

"Yeah...we're not really related, though. He's my dad's best friend."

Tor is coming farther down the driveway toward us, his black leather boots thumping heavily along the stone, his eyes riveted on the boy who just had his hands on me. "You hear me?" He points a finger at Jason, his inked arm muscles bulging menacingly. "I don't want her on that fuckin' bike again."

"Yes, sir," Jason calls back, visibly paling.

"I better go inside before he starts foaming at the mouth." I throw my purse strap over my shoulder. "Have fun tonight at the party."

"You could come to the party with me." The teasing glint in his eye and his slightly raised eyebrow hints at more than just a party, and while I should be jumping up and down at the chance since he's one of the hottest guys in my class, he seemed way more interesting from afar. Before he proved he can't kiss and has zero conversation skills. I'd much rather stay home and read a book or hang out with my father's friends who are coming over tonight for a bonfire.

"I really can't, Jase. I'm sorry." *Not sorry.* "I'll call you."

Before Jason has a chance to reply, I head up the long cobblestone driveway, glaring daggers at Toren as I walk by him.

"Hey, listen to me." He turns and catches up to me as Jason speeds off down the street. "That kid just got his motorcycle license. You don't get on a bike with someone who barely knows how to ride. He's way too squirrely. You could get killed. You can ride with me or your dad or your uncles, but not some fucking kid."

"I was only on it for like six miles to get home from school. Stop yelling at me. You're not my father," I throw back.

"I'm close enough. I mean it, stay off that bike."

"Fine, Uncle Tor. Don't get all rabid."

"I'm not even close to rabid. Yet." He rushes ahead as we approach the house and climbs the stairs of the back deck to open the French doors that lead into the kitchen for me. Inside, bags of groceries are lined up on the granite-topped center island. Twice a month, my father likes to have his friends and the members of his band over to hang out in the backyard, eat, have a few drinks, take a dip in the pool, and jam a little. Toren usually brings over the food and alcohol and sets everything up.

I should help him put the food away, but I'm not in the best of moods. I just want to be alone, so I disappear down the hall and up the stairs to my bedroom, closing the door behind me. After kicking off my shoes, I collapse onto the bed and stare up at the vaulted ceiling. Just one more month till my high school graduation and then I can get away from the drama, fake friends, drunken parties, and groping boys who don't know how to kiss.

What will I do then? Not a freakin' clue. I just know I want to get away from school and the people in it.

I don't fit in with them. I never have. My parents were only fifteen years old when they had me. Still in high school themselves, attending the very school I'm graduating from, in fact. Some of my teachers were also their teachers, and of course, the entire faculty knows this. It's a bit bizarre to think that my mother was pregnant with me, sitting in the same classrooms I sit in now. Maybe that's why I'm so smart—I was in high school in utero.

I was born into a family of rather famous people. My grandfather is a popular singer and songwriter, and my grandmother is a best-selling romance author who has written over one hundred books, twenty of them turned into television movies. My parents started a rock band when they were seventeen, and both went on to become well-known musicians. My father's band, Ashes & Embers, now consists of his three brothers and two cousins. I grew up right in the middle of all of this. By the time I was ten years old, I was certainly no stranger to tour buses, loud concerts, drugs, and drama. But despite all that, I was loved and adored. I was everyone's baby, really. Everyone took care of me. I wasn't hidden from much that went on, and that wasn't because my parents were negligent or irresponsible. They just wanted me to be a part of everything they were doing. They exposed me to things in life way before I could truly understand them, but in time it all caught up and sank in. I think that made me older and wiser than I should be, which has made me feel out of step with everyone else my age.

It didn't take me long to figure out there were people who only wanted to be around me because of who I was related to. Kids pretended to be my friend to get concert tickets, T-shirts, an autograph, or to try to see the inside of our house—which might be big and have a small recording studio downstairs, but there's nothing overly exciting going on here. Boys pretended to like me to get me to slip demo tapes to my father or to meet the sexy women of my mom's band, Sugar Kiss. And the high school girls hoped they could meet my hot rock star uncles or, even worse, my dad. I never know who I can trust or who wants to be friends with me just for *me*. So other than spending time with my best friend, Chloe, and my dad's younger sister, Rayne, I mostly stay home and hang out with my family, the band, and their friends. They're the only ones I feel comfortable with.

My pocket vibrates and I pull out my phone to read a text message.

Chloe

Jason said you're not coming tonight?

> No, I'm not in the mood for a party.

Chloe

Come on! It's Friday night! :) Jason really likes you.

> Eh...

Chloe

> Don't mess this up! You can totally lose your V-card with him!
> He's hot as fark!

I don't know what the heck fark is and why Chloe can't just text the word *fuck*. But whatever. I accept her because I love her. We initially attached ourselves to each other in third grade, when she was dropped off on the first day of school by her two moms and I was dropped off by my father who was already covered in tattoos and had hair almost to his waist. *And he still does.* Chloe and I bonded over our mutual outsiderness while the other kids avoided us like we were circus freaks.

> Stop with the V-card. You're obsessed.

Chloe

> Fine. Come to the party. I'll be there. It will be fun.
> You can't sit home all the time.

> I'm really not into it tonight.

Chloe

> Every single girl at the party is going to try to hook up with Jason.

> We've only been seeing each other for two weeks.
> I don't care what or who he does.

Chloe

> You should and you will! I'll text you later. Love ya, girl!

> Love ya too

I have zero interest in joining the race to lose my virginity before graduation and I definitely don't want to be a notch on some guy's belt before he goes off to college, either. So far, Jason's kisses haven't made me feel any feels. For now, I'm happy enough

living through the romance books my grandmother sends to my
e-reader. It's pretty sad that the kisses in the books are way more
exciting than the ones in real life. At least for me.

Music, laughter, and voices rouse me from the nap I slipped into
after I texted with Chloe—almost four hours ago. I'm surprised
my father didn't wake me when he came out of the studio, but I
guess he's finally learning to respect my closed door.

Sitting up, I glance at my phone and see I have another text
message that came through an hour ago.

Jason

> I'm at the party. Want me to come get you? In the car,
> of course. ;) It'll be fun.

I type a quick reply:

> Thanks but I'm good. Kinda tired tonight.
> I'll call you tomorrow.

Jason

> ;-(K. You better call ;-)

I'm not sure why I'm going out of my way to avoid him and
can't just attempt to have fun with him. He's cute and mostly
nice. He's popular. Everyone likes him. I don't think he's using
me for concert tickets, which is a big plus. Whether he's trying to
make me a notch or really likes me is still a mystery to me. His
kisses are hella boring, but he could get better at that in time, I
suppose. Maybe he's just nervous?

Or maybe it's me.

After slipping my sneakers on, I head downstairs, through the kitchen, and out the French doors to the deck leading to our backyard. The sun has set, but the yard is lit up with various lights hidden in the landscaping, scattered tiki torches, the fire pit that's blazing, and the cool blue glow from the in-ground pool.

It's no secret my father has a lot of money because his band is super successful, and it's well deserved. I've never once been embarrassed by my father or how he acts onstage. He doesn't drink, do drugs, or screw around. My uncles in the band have had their moments of crazy over the years, but not my dad. He's all business.

Am I spoiled? Not really. My father won't even buy me a car until after I graduate—*if* I maintain my good grades until graduation and work to pay for my own gas and insurance. I have a gold card with a limit that would probably allow me to buy a small island, but I don't abuse it. I respect my dad and the trust he puts in me to not go crazy at the mall and buy five thousand dollars' worth of makeup and shoes. I believe trust is a gift from someone, just like love is. Trusting and loving someone says *I have faith in you.* And I appreciate the depth of that way more than I do material things. I'll take faith over shoes any day of the week.

There are about twenty people mingling around our yard—some by the bonfire, others at the tables on the deck, some sitting in the gazebo playing acoustic instruments and singing. I find my dad standing at the monstrous grill built into the stone patio, turning steaks and hamburgers.

"Hey, kiddo, you hungry?" he asks when he sees me.

"Nah, maybe later."

"There's salad." He gestures over to the table where assorted fruits and salads are spread out in serving bowls.

"I'll grab some later. I'm not really hungry."

He blinks at me for a few seconds. "You feel okay?" His face takes on that *I have no idea what to do with a female teenager who might not feel good or might be in a mood* expression.

Smiling, I touch his arm and lean close to kiss his cheek. "I'm fine, Daddy. I had ice cream on the way home from school."

He backs away from the heat of the grill and pushes his long wavy brown hair out of his face. "With that kid Jason? On a motorcycle?"

Damn Toren and his big mouth. "Yeah. It was just from school, though. It's not that far. And what the hell? Tor has to tell you everything I do?"

"No, only the dumb things." He grins at me. "He's right, though. Stay off the bike. We don't want anything to happen to you."

We. I'm being raised by everyone and no one.

My dad's not *with* Toren. He's one million percent committed and in love with his wife. My mother—his teen sweetheart. But she's gone now, and my father is a thirty-two-year-old rock star with a seventeen-year-old daughter trying to act like he's not broken and lost and on the verge of losing the very definition of his *shit*. But I know better. He's afraid something's going to happen to me, too. That I'll be here one moment and gone the next. And I don't blame him for feeling that way at all because I feel it, too.

Once you've lost someone you love with no explanation, no closure, no end—you're stuck in a torturous limbo. You don't know if you should hang on to that ray of hope that they might come back or give in to your grief and accept that they're gone. So you teeter between both until you slowly go insane.

I let out a breath. I can't think or talk about my mom much without having a meltdown myself, so I put myself in denial and don't face any of it. *She's just away. Like a long vacation with no mobile phone access.* It's easier that way.

"Okay. No more bikes, Dad. I promise." I don't mind calming

his overprotectiveness because he doesn't deserve to have any more stress in his life.

His broad shoulders relax again and he gives me a smile that lights up his face and softens his eyes. It's the smile that's reserved for me and my mother, and it makes my heart melt. My father is an incredibly beautiful man, possessing the kind of good looks that women will actually stop and stare at, eyes wide, mouth parted, heart pitter-pattering. Some even ask to touch his long hair or his tattooed arms, while others just want him to look at them so they can catch a glimpse of his soulful eyes. You don't just *see* his beauty; you can *feel* it, like a warm breeze that caresses your soul. At least that's how a journalist described him after doing an interview with him.

I fill a small dish with fruit to make him happy and then spy Tor sitting on the edge of the pool by himself. I cross the yard, stopping at one of the coolers to grab a beer on the way. One of the guitarists from another local band is sitting on a lawn chair right next to the cooler. Probably so he doesn't have to get up to get another drink.

"What's up, Finn?" I shake the ice off the bottle.

He tips his drink at me in reply. "Kensington."

"Are you guarding the beer?" I tease.

"I might be. You're not drinking that, are ya?" He eyes me suspiciously. "Last time I checked, you weren't twenty-one, little girl."

"No, it's for Toren."

A smirk crosses his lips. "Well, if you're playing waitress, I'll take a steak, rare, with some fries."

"Nice try, Finn."

He laughs and throws a potato chip at me as I walk away.

Toren is still sitting on the ground staring into the pool when I sit next to him, tucking my legs beneath me. The pool is heated, but no one's gone in yet. It's still early spring, so the air is a bit too cold for most people to want to swim. A few stray leaves are floating along the surface, and I like how peaceful they look, not going under the water, and not blowing away either. Just floating, weightless and effortless. *I want to be a leaf.*

I hand Tor the cold bottle and he takes it from me, using his keychain to pop the cap off.

"I thought you were mad at me." He takes a long drink before glancing sideways at me. I can see why Jason was scared of him—on the outside, Tor looks like a badass. He's a beast of a man, not an ounce of fat on him, broad and hard as a rock with ink covering both arms from neck to knuckle. Wavy brown hair falls to the tops of his shoulders. It's usually tied back in a short ponytail to keep it out of his face when he's working and from tangling up when he's riding. He notoriously wears dark sunglasses to shade his even darker eyes, and his ride of choice is an old custom Harley that roars down the road so loud that you can barely hear yourself think if he's near. But on the inside, he's quiet. Thoughtful. Amazingly caring and giving. Unlike my dad, he's good-looking in a rugged, almost scary way. Chloe has nicknamed him the walking orgasm. I think she's way too fixated on sex lately.

I put my bowl of fruit off to the side. "You know me better than that."

"I shouldn't have embarrassed you in front of your boyfriend."

He passes the bottle to me and I take a sip. I don't like the taste of beer at all but I take sips every now and then, thinking maybe someday that will change and I'll enjoy it like everyone else. *Nope. Still tastes gross.*

"He's not my boyfriend."

"Really? You were pretty excited about him a few weeks ago. I distinctly remember a bunch of squealing and a happy dance when he asked you out."

Sighing with slight embarrassment over that colorful flashback, I hand the beer back to him, our fingers touching against the cold, damp bottle. "I was, until I got to know him. There's nothing there. I don't feel anything. There's nothing interesting about him. He's just…blah." I feign a shudder.

He laughs and shakes his head. "That shit must be contagious, then. That's exactly what Lisa said to me a few days ago."

"You guys broke up?"

"We weren't really together, Kenz. Just kinda seeing where it was gonna go. Testing the waters."

I pick a big, juicy strawberry from my bowl and bite it in half. "What did she say?"

He looks up at the sky for a moment before answering. "Well, let's see. She had a whole list, actually. She said I don't give enough. I don't communicate enough. I'm too cold and closed off. I'm too quiet. I work too much. I don't smile enough. I don't dress nice enough." He shrugs. "I've heard it all before."

"You're not cold, Uncle Tor. Not at all. You're just not the type to talk for the sake of talking. You talk when you have something to say. And maybe she's just mad because you're not saying what she wants to hear."

"Apparently I never have much to say, and it's never what they want to hear. *She* said pretty much the same things to me." He raises his chin and nods across the yard, his eyes zeroing in on Sydni, who's talking to my dad, her long fire-engine-red hair cascading down her back like a mermaid. Aunt Sydni is the bass player in my mom's band, and is my mom's best friend. She's also been Toren's on-again-off-again girlfriend for the past twelve years or so. Mostly off.

But lately I see her as the woman who's in love with my dad, and she isn't very good at hiding it.

Welcome to the soap opera that is my life.

"Sydni said that, too?" I ask.

"Sydni's said a lot of things over the years, but we both know what it all comes down to. *I'm not him.* I don't smile like him, I don't talk like him, I don't make her laugh like him, I'm not rich like him. I'll never be as good as him. Blah, blah, blah. To her I'm just a dirty mechanic who chases animals around." He gulps down his beer and I wish I hadn't given it to him.

"He doesn't want her, Uncle Tor," I say softly, trying to defuse him. "He has zero interest in her other than as a friend."

"I know that. Fuck, everyone knows that. But it doesn't change how *she* feels."

"Maybe you two can work it out? It's been a few months since you broke up; maybe she feels different now. Sometimes you have to lose something to appreciate it, ya know? She knows you were seeing Lisa. Maybe that made her open her eyes a little. Jealousy can be a great motivator."

A grin spreads across his face. "You're pretty smart, Kenz. But that ship has sailed and sunk. I don't want someone who's in love with someone else. Fuck that."

Agreed. "I don't blame you. You deserve way better than that. She's stupid."

It's hard to love so many people, want to see them happy, but also not like them for the things they do. My mom would be disappointed in Sydni for chasing after my dad and for making Tor feel like he's not good enough. I want to see my dad happy again, and while I admire him for staying committed to my mom, I wonder how long he'll torture himself by not letting himself move on. I don't want him to move on with Sydni, though. Not because I don't like her, I do. But because it's just too twisted. She's his wife's best friend *and* his best friend's ex.

I live in a deep, dark, perplexing sea of people. Some might be starfish, and some might be sharks. I just bob along on my little raft, watching and learning.

Rubbing my bare arms, I pull my knees up to my chest and watch as my father walks away from Sydni and takes his acoustic guitar to the gazebo to join the others playing some old rock songs. She doesn't follow him. *Good.*

"You cold?"

"A little," I answer. "Just when the breeze blows, it's kinda chilly."

He pulls off the gray hoodie he's wearing over his T-shirt and hands it to me. "Here, put this on."

I hesitate before accepting. "Then you'll be cold."

He frowns, like he's too cool to feel the chill. "I'm fine. Put it on."

Taking it from him, I slip it over my head, and shiver, but not from the cold. The heat from his body is still in the fabric of the sweatshirt, and it warms me like a hug. I push my hands through the sleeves that are way too long for me and roll up the cuffs.

"It's huge. But thank you."

"You look cute. Keep it. Add it to your growing collection."

Laughing, I lean against his shoulder and he rests his head against mine for a few seconds before pulling away to finish off his beer.

I've been hoarding Tor's things since I was a little girl. Mostly shirts, mugs, his old lighters, the faded denim jacket he wore in high school, a switchblade, some baseball caps, a leather belt, and other random stuff. I've taken all sorts of odd things that I fixated on and wanted to have, just because they were his. And he always let me have them.

He's been collecting parts of me, too. I just didn't know it yet.

CHAPTER 2

Kenzi—age five

Toren—age twenty

I can hear her crying before I even step through the door. And when I do, she bolts to me and I catch her as she throws herself into my arms. Her face is red, stained with tears, her green eyes bloodshot.

"Uncle Tor..." She gasps for breath between each word, tearing my heart out.

I wipe her cheeks with my thumbs. "What's wrong, Angelcake?"

"My bunny! I looked everywhere and he's gone. I think he's on that fucking tour bus!"

Ah. The coveted stuffed bunny I gave her for her last birthday. She drags it everywhere with her.

I try not to laugh at her epic use of the word fucking.

"Whoa. Kenzi...that's a very bad word." Her eyes meet mine defiantly and she says she doesn't care.

I love her fire.

"I wonder where she learned that," Ember says, glaring at me.

Kenzi pulls on my hair. "He's gone, Uncle Tor. That's all that matters."

"He's not gone, Angel. He's just on a journey. But ya know what? There's another bunny out there that needs you. Do you think we should go find him?"

She nods solemnly and sniffles. "Yes. Right now."

Ash and Ember just shake their heads when Kenzi and I come back hours later with a new stuffed bunny... and a real live bunny equipped with a deluxe cage I set up by the window in her bedroom. Kenzi is over the moon with the little rabbit we named Snuggles, and I feel like a hero for saving the day and bringing her smile back.

"She's got you wrapped around her little finger, man," Asher says.

"And you're gonna take care of that rabbit, Tor," Ember warns. "I'm not cleaning that cage every week."

I shrug. "I don't mind. Pets are good for kids. It teaches them responsibility."

"She's five, Tor."

"So? Age doesn't mean shit."

I wink at Kenzi, who's cradling her new bunny across the room, an adorable smile on her face, tears long forgotten. It's the best high I've ever felt.

💜 💜 💜

TOR

Asher hands me a cup of black coffee and falls into the chair across from me at his kitchen table, zeroing in on me with his dark eyes.

"Sydni thinks you're avoiding her."

My head hurts too much from drinking last night to deal with Asher's probing into my life today. He's always trying to play shrink, and sometimes he has great advice, but other times his philosophical ramblings grate on my nerves. Now is one of those times.

"That's because I am." I vaguely remember her following me to the couch last night and me telling her to go fuck herself.

"You think she deserves that? She just wants you to talk to her."

"I have nothing to say to a chick who tells me she wants to get married one second and then admits she's in love with you the next."

He shifts in his chair. "She's not in love with me, Tor."

Something comes out of me that is half laugh and half snort. "Oh, trust me, she is. And ya know what? I don't give a fuck. I'm done. You can have her."

"I don't want her. I'm married." He fingers his platinum wedding band, turning it in circles. It's a habit he does often, and I'm not sure he even realizes he's doing it.

As I sip my bitter coffee, I decide to let him stay in his delusion. Trying to make him see that Ember is never coming back is a feat I can't tackle. And if Sydni's attempts to do so haven't worked, then nothing will. Not many men can say no to Syd with her legs for days, flaming red hair, double Ds, endless talent, and overactive sex drive. We'd all be better off if he would just hook up with her and move on with his life. Then they'd both be happy and I can lock the revolving door that she keeps trying to creep through every time she realizes she can't have him.

I'm not going to be anyone's second choice.

But somehow, I always am. I should just get the number 2 tattooed onto my forehead.

"What are you two doing up so early?"

Kenzi interrupts our silent stare-off as she comes into the kitchen—still wearing my sweatshirt from last night, no pants, and fuzzy purple socks. As she reaches up into the cabinet, she goes up on her toes to grab one of her favorite mugs that once was mine and the sweatshirt rides up, uncovering half her ass and exposing her white panties with red hearts. I quickly look away and bring my coffee cup to my lips. *I didn't just see that. I didn't just see that...*

"I have a meeting and Uncle Tor had too much to drink, so he slept here. And where are your clothes? I know we can afford pants. You shouldn't be walking around half naked when we have company."

She runs her hand through her rumpled hair. "How was I supposed to know anyone was here? I just woke up. And it's only Tor. Since when is he company? He used to live with us." She opens the refrigerator and pulls out milk, eggs, cheese, and a container of diced veggies, then bends over to take a frying pan out from one of the lower cabinets.

I divert my eyes again as Asher downs the last of his coffee and stands. "I'm outta here." He nods to me. "See ya later, man. You up for a ride tomorrow? It's supposed to be warm."

I'm always up for a ride. "Hell yeah."

"Dad, I'm making omelets. Don't you want one before you go?"

"I don't have time today. I'm sure Tor will eat one, though." He kisses her forehead. "I'll be home around four. We'll have dinner together."

I'm not about to turn away food. "Actually, I could use something to eat." Kenzi makes wicked omelets, expertly folded like they serve you at a diner. When I try to make one myself, it ends up looking like roadkill.

As soon as Asher's gone, I get up and dump the coffee he made and start a new pot. He always makes this expensive crap that's way too strong and it makes my heart jump around for the rest of the morning.

"Did you sleep in my shirt?" I ask.

She flips the omelet in the pan and peeks at me from behind the veil of messy golden hair falling over her face.

"Maybe..."

Scowling, I take two plates out of the cabinet and set them next to the stove for her. "Kenz...I had that on while I was working on a bike yesterday. It's probably got grease on it. And sweat."

Shrugging, she transfers a perfect omelet onto one of the plates. "You can have that one. And so what? I like it. It's cozy."

"It's dirty."

She laughs. "Cozy. Dirty. What's the difference? I like how it feels and smells."

Her liking the feel and smell of cozy and dirty while she's wearing nothing but *my* shirt is not something I should be thinking about. But I do, for a quick second, before I bury it deep in that place in my chest with the other thoughts I don't let myself think about.

Like the thought that I wish I'd had a chance to say goodbye to my father.

And the thought that I should have been there to help my brother.

And the thought that I should have tried harder with Sydni years ago.

And let's not forget the thought that I should have stayed in the band.

So many regrets.

I wait for her to sit with me at the table before I cut into the omelet, because my mom raised me with manners, and high on that list is you don't start eating until everyone is seated at the table.

"So...you had yourself a little binge last night?" Her eyes dance as she chews and swallows. "What brought that on?"

"Just a bad mood, I guess. It's not going to be a habit."

"A bad mood named Sydni or a bad mood named Lisa?"

"Eat your breakfast. And both."

"Neither one of them is worth drinking over, Uncle Tor. You want to turn into a drunken mess again?"

I glare at her for bringing that up. A few years ago, I had what you might call a drinking problem, but I'll never go down that road again.

"Not gonna happen."

"Good. Because I'm older now and I'm armed with a camera and social media. I'll document all your embarrassing drunk moments."

"I'm sure you would, brat."

She tilts her head at me, chewing her lip, and I know that look all too well. It means she's thinking about asking or telling me something. I brace myself, because Kenzi saves all her deepest and craziest conversations for me.

"Chloe thinks I should give up my V-card to Jason," she finally says.

I choke on my coffee.

"Chloe should keep her mouth shut. And her legs." *Christ.* I'm totally not prepared for this conversation, especially hungover. I was expecting her to want tattoos or nose piercings, or maybe purple hair to match her socks. But not sex.

"Why? I'm seventeen. Almost eighteen. Maybe she's right."

I wipe my mouth. "She's not."

"How old were you?"

"When?"

"Your first time."

"That's different, I'm a guy."

"Well, how old was she, then? The girl you did it with?"

Fuck.

"Kenz, you should only be doing that when the time is right. With the right guy."

"I know . . . but what if the right guy never comes?"

"He will." *As I sit here still single at thirty-two.* "You're young, just enjoy your life and don't worry about sleeping with guys. Your father will have a shit fit if he hears you talking like this. You want to give him a heart attack?"

She rolls her eyes. "He still thinks I'm five."

"So do I."

She kicks me under the table. "No, you don't. You're not nearly as bad as him. And my mom had to be about fourteen, obviously, when she started having sex."

"I think you should talk to your grandmother about this. Or your aunt? Maybe Rayne? Someone of the female persuasion?"

Her nose crinkles. "Nah. I'd be too uncomfortable talking to them."

"But not with me?"

She shakes her head. "I like talking to you. You listen to me and you don't judge me."

"I'm flattered. But I'm the last fucking person to be giving relationship or sex advice."

I lean back in the chair and push my empty plate away. I can't think about Kenzi having sex. My brain is way too mangled up with visions of her as a little girl and the glimpse of her half-naked ass I saw a few minutes ago. She's growing up too fast. It seems like just yesterday I was babysitting her. Now she's asking me questions about sex and looking less like a little girl and more like a woman. It's confusing as hell, and I have no idea how Asher is dealing with this shit.

"Most of the girls I know have had sex already, way before they were seventeen. With a few guys, even. Not at the same time... at least I don't think so. You know what I'm saying, right?" She pauses and I nod, dumbfounded and at a loss for words. "I don't feel that way about any of the guys I've dated, though. I don't even like kissing them." She plays with her napkin and doesn't look up at me. "Do you think maybe there's something wrong with me? Why don't I feel anything yet?"

I suppress the laugh and relief I feel. "No, Angel. I think you're fine."

"Really?"

"Really. You'll feel it when you're ready and when it's the right guy. You can't force it. It should mean something. Especially your first time. Don't do it just because fuckin' Chloe says to. Just be you, like you've always been. Don't cave to pressure now. That's never been you."

She nods slowly. "I just hate always being the weird one that isn't doing what everyone else is doing. I want to fit in for once."

"Trust me, you're not the weird one. You're unique. You've always had your own mind and your own plan. I'd hate to see you change and end up like everyone else out there. That would be a shame."

She fidgets with her fork, pushing a small piece of ham around on her plate. "I'm on the pill," she says softly, still looking at her plate.

I blink at her. "Come again?"

"The pill. Birth control."

"I know what it is, Kenzi. Why?"

"I was having a lot of cramps every month, so Rayne took me to her doctor for a checkup. The doctor said it would help, and it has. I didn't tell my dad, though, and I'm afraid he's going to find them and go ballistic."

"Well, yeah, of course he will."

"Chloe says it's a good idea anyway, though, because guys don't like to wear condoms."

My jaw clenches so hard I'm afraid I'm going to crack a molar. "Listen to me, Kenzi. There's a lot more to sex than just getting pregnant. There're all sorts of diseases you can get." She stares at me, wide-eyed. "When you start having sex, you better make the guy wear a condom until you're damn sure you can trust him. I don't give a fuck if some little douchebag doesn't like the way it feels. You stand your ground and make him, okay?"

"Okay."

"If anyone tries to pull that shit with you, I'll put them in a fucking hole, Kenzi."

I end the conversation by standing and taking our plates over to the sink. "I better get going. I should have been at the shop hours ago. I'll see you tonight? About six?"

"Sounds good." She stares out the window, lost in her thoughts.

"And wash my sweatshirt!" I yell over my shoulder on my way out the door.

As I drive to the bike shop, my mind keeps wandering back to the conversation I just had with Kenzi. Maybe I should have said more. Or nothing at all. I've always tried to be there for her, but I sure as hell don't know how to give sex advice to a teenage girl who's on the verge of giving up her virginity. The mere thought of it makes me feel sick. I can't even get my own shit together when it comes to dating.

She always comes to me when she needs to talk, though. Or when she's scared. Or has something exciting to share.

It really should come as no surprise since my name was the first word she ever said.

Now it's like we're verbally bonded.

The motorcycle shop is already open and blaring with the racket of heavy metal music and air tools when I get there. My brother Tanner usually opens the shop and I close, because he's a morning person and I'm usually up late at night rescuing lost pets. You think I'm kidding? I'm not.

The shop belonged to my father, Thomas Grace, who lived, breathed, and ate bikes, and he passed that passion down to his boys. The only thing he loved more than riding was my mom.

And his kids, of course. But Mom came first, and that's the way it should be.

That changed twelve years ago when my dad dropped dead of a heart attack. *Bam. Gone.*

Being the oldest, I had no choice but to step up and take care of the family business, my mom, my four younger brothers, and my little sister. Six sets of eyes all looking at me to put us back together again. This went down just two months before the band's big break, first major tour, and a record deal. I had to bail out of the band that Asher, Ember, and I started years before and watch from the sidelines as they became rich, famous rock stars. Meanwhile, my guitar ended up in a closet collecting dust and my dreams slowly faded away. But hey, I get a royalty check since I wrote some of the songs on the first album.

In the blink of an eye, I went from being a wild musician living on the road out of an old suitcase, partying hard without a care in the world, to having to be the responsible one.

Life is funny like that.

I enter through the back door of the shop, where my brothers Tanner, Taran, and Tristan are busy working in their areas. Tanner and Taran mostly do engine rebuilds, and Tristan does all our custom airbrushing and pinstriping. We have another mechanic, Sled, who works part-time. I mostly work on the older, vintage bike restorations. Dad's strict rule was we only sell and work on cruisers—no racing bikes. To this day, I've made sure we held up that rule. No race bikes. No scooters. Ever.

And yeah, my mom had a thing about the letter T and giving us unique names when she named all of us.

Every day starts the same for me at the shop, and it's the part I hate the most because I have to hole up in my office and go through the mail, sort out the bills and purchase orders, and set the schedule for the upcoming work. I fucking despise paperwork, but my dad did this all himself, so I figure I should, too.

After I finish the paperwork bullshit, I switch gears and focus on my role as head of Devils' Wolves MC and Pet Rescue—run by myself, my brothers, and a few other bikers. Devils' Wolves was my brainchild about five years ago, fueled by my deep respect for two things that my parents instilled in us: the love of pets and motorcycles. That, and a bout of insomnia, is how I came up with the perfect plan to actually do something with my life that made me feel like I had some purpose again.

My mother runs Wolfy's Place, a pet shelter and sanctuary in town that operates twenty-four hours a day, seven days a week. And while taking in strays, getting them medical attention, and adopting them out is great, I wanted to find the ones that were too lost to be seen, save the ones that were being abused, and basically fuck up the people who were hurting them. Like the assholes who run underground dogfighting rings. Or the old ladies who go out of their minds and hoard two hundred cats in their dilapidated houses. Okay, so I don't fuck up old ladies, but I do go in there and use my charm to get those cats out before they start eating each other.

We use the club to run charity events and rides to raise money to support our rescue equipment, and we donate a portion of the funds to Wolfy's Place. So, it's a win-win.

It also coaxes Tyler to come out of his house hidden in the woods. Just like the lost, scared, and abused dogs, he'll only come out in the dark when no one can see him. Or hear him. My brother Ty has a special gift for being able to creep around the woods unheard and unseen. Stalking, hunting, and capturing are his specialty, second to his ability to get in and out of houses without making a sound or getting caught. And that's how my brother has saved over fifty pets—and how he's put several animal offenders in the hospital after nearly beating them to death. To say he likes to inflict pain and suffering would be an understatement.

I haven't seen Ty in the daylight in years, and he's said less than ten words in that time. We communicate solely through text messages and meet in the parking lot of the shelter late at night when he has a captured dog or cat to drop off.

Every month I deposit money into his bank account. Partly because he deserves profits from the family business, and partly from my own guilt over what happened to him.

I shove that thought down into my chest with the rest of my mistakes and regrets.

Last night's recorded video feeds from my night-vision cameras on the trails didn't catch anything and neither did my feeding traps. A few weeks ago, a limping dog was seen several times roaming that area by the river. I've caught him on the feeds a few times, sniffing at the cage, wanting to go in and grab that food, but he's leery and won't go in. Sometimes they'd rather starve than give in and get caught, and that's a position I can respect. Freedom to do what we want, even for a short time, can be worth the pain and suffering we have to endure to have it.

Just as I'm about to go out to the shop to start doing some real work, my phone rings.

Lisa.

I swipe the screen and hold the phone to my ear. "Yeah?"

"I figured if I didn't call you, you'd never call me." She's right about that. I don't chase. If you choose to walk out that door, you can keep fuckin' going.

"As you pointed out, I don't have much to say. Remember?"

"Tor, I'm trying. I heard you were with Sydni last night. Are you back together?"

"I wasn't *with* Sydni. We were at Asher's house with about twenty other people. I didn't go with her or leave with her. We talked for a few minutes and that was it. Tell your gossip hounds not to quit their day job. They suck."

She sighs a mixture of relief and annoyance. "Maybe we could try again? What are you doing tonight?"

"After work I'm going to refill my feeding traps. You can come with me, if you want. It's right by the river. We could sit there and talk." If she wants to talk, I'll try to talk. The truth is, I like Lisa. She's attractive, with long dark hair, almond-shaped Bambi eyes, and a nice body. She works at the bank, has no kids, and doesn't party. In theory, she's the perfect kind of woman to settle down with. She's the kind of woman I could bring home to my mother and not be embarrassed of or have to worry about her flirting it up with my brothers.

"Trekking out into the woods with a pile of meat really isn't my idea of a date. Can't you skip it tonight? Let's go out to dinner to a real restaurant. I want to see you out of jeans for once. If things go well, we can go back to my place..." She trails off, her intention clear.

My eyes close for a long moment. I was hoping she would agree, and that for once a woman would walk through the door I was holding open and step into my world to get to know *me*. I want her to care enough about me to get involved just a little in what's important to me. I thought maybe Lisa could be that woman, especially after her speech a few nights ago about me being cold, uncaring, disconnected, and all that other shit. Here I am asking her to help me do something that's a huge part of my life, something I built out of nothing and is evidence of the care and giving she claims I don't have in me, and now she doesn't want it.

"I can't do that, Lisa. Not tonight. Ty watches the live video

feeds at night, or sits out in the woods, especially on the weekends, so if he sees one of the dogs, he can get an idea of the shape
it's in or go pick it up if it goes in the cage. I have to set out the
food to lure them."

"Can't he do that?"

"No. He doesn't like to handle the food, and he only goes out
at night. The food has to be set out before it's dark."

"That's stupid," she says flippantly. "I'm sure he can do it if you
told him you have plans."

The urge to end the call wafts up in me, but she doesn't know
Ty or his story and why he is the way he is. Her use of the word
stupid has pissed me right the fuck off, though.

"He can't. I gotta go. I have work to do."

"As usual." Disappointment is heavy in her voice and I'm sure
it matches mine. "Maybe when you're done playing in the woods
you can stop by. I'd still like to see you. Just take a shower first so
you don't smell like grease and chicken, okay?"

"Yeah. I'll do that."

I hit end on my phone and shove it in my back pocket with
zero intention of showing up at her house tonight for a late-night
sexfest. No thanks. I have this thing called self-respect. I'm disappointed in Lisa, though. I thought she may have been the one to
see that underneath the muscles, ink, and grease, beyond the loud
bike, past the long hair and dirty fingers, is a man who wants the
whole fucking package. Not just the fucking.

Been there, done that.

She's waiting for me at the end of the driveway, her earbuds in,
shaking her head back and forth to the music. I pull my truck up
to the curb and lean across the front seat to open the door for her.

"You're twelve minutes late." She slams the door shut and pulls the seat belt across her, fastening it before giving me an accusing look.

I give her a sideways glance as I shift the truck. "Twelve? Really?"

"Yup. You know how I feel about punctuality. Lateness is a sign of disrespect and it gives the person waiting for you time to think about your other shortcomings."

"Is that right?" Kenzi has a thing for quotes lately.

"Yes."

"I'm fairly confident I don't have any shortcomings, Kenz."

"Except lateness."

"I can live with that. There're a lot worse things a person can be."

She nods. "Yeah, like a bad kisser."

I let out a laugh. "Now, that would suck."

She takes out her earbuds and shoves them into her pocket. "You have no idea."

Poor Jason. That kid doesn't have a chance with her. Kenzi's going to be a hard girl for a guy to snag, and I kinda like that. She deserves to have someone work to get her love and respect.

Kenzi has been helping me set up the cameras and the feeding traps for as long as I can remember. When she was younger, she used to beg to go. After about a hundred tantrums, Ember agreed to let her come with me. I never minded having her come along because she's always fun to have around and she soaks up everything like a sponge. I've never met a kid as smart as her, or one who was so content hanging around with her parents and their third wheel. Aka me.

She sighs and looks out the window as we drive. "This dog is getting on my last nerve. What's it been...a month we've been offering food to him? What's his deal? There are people starving out in the world and he's turning away fresh chicken and beef."

"He's not ready yet. That's all."

"Maybe we should start feeding people. At least they'll be grateful. Don't get me wrong, I love dogs, and I want to help him, but *damn*. Right?"

"We're not doing this just to feed him, Kenz. We're trying to save him, get him out of the woods and hopefully into a good home before he becomes completely feral or dies out there."

She blows her hair out of her face. "I know. I'm just frustrated with him. I want him to just get in that cage already. He's wasting a lot of good food. Isn't he hungry? He must be. What's he eating out there?"

I shrug, but I'm intrigued by her intense interest. "Maybe squirrels and other rodents."

"Like rabbits?" she asks in horror.

"Maybe..."

She looks like she's going to start to cry. "He better not be eating rabbits, Tor. Or we're gonna leave his ass out there."

"Rabbits are fast. I doubt he could catch one," I lie. "Maybe he's a vegetarian."

Giggling, she turns up the radio. "You're such a nut sometimes."

It takes us about fifteen minutes to get to the dirt road that leads us halfway to the river; then we have to park the truck and walk the rest of the way. I grab the small cooler filled with fresh meat from the back seat and she grabs her backpack and we hike about a quarter mile to the first cage. We put on disposable gloves to remove the old meat and put it in a trash bag and then refill the cage. I check the hidden night-vision camera to make sure it's still working while she takes a small box wrapped in brown paper out of her backpack and puts it on top of the cage.

"A book. I think he'll like it," she says when she notices me watching her. Nodding, I reach out and grab her hand while we climb over a fallen tree to get to the next cage. Kenzi likes to leave gifts for Ty for when he checks the cages. She leaves him books, CDs, little statues. I've seen him on the recorded feeds when he finds them. He holds whatever it is in his hands for a long time, just staring at it, sometimes gliding his fingers over it, before he shoves it in his coat pocket. I don't have to show her what I see on camera for her to know he appreciates it, because she doesn't care about that part. She just wants to give. Even though she hasn't seen him in a very long time, it means a lot to me that she's never forgotten him.

My two best friends gave me my third best friend. Kenzi is the greatest parts of her parents combined. She's got Asher's philosophical *I-want-to-fix-everyone* outlook and Ember's happy, free, no-bullshit spirit.

Lately I've been wondering how she sees me. Now that she's older, I'm sure I don't come off as the hero who wipes tears and brings home bunnies like when she was little, and I kinda miss that. It was a cool feeling to have this little person view me as the one who made everything better for them.

After we check the second cage, we make our way up the trail a ways to sit on a big rock next to the river, where we watch the water for a few minutes before she pulls a penny out of her pocket and grins at me before tossing it into the water. This has become a little tradition with us—making wishes.

"What did you wish for?" I ask her.

"Direction."

I narrow my eyes at her in confusion. "Direction? For what?"

"My future."

My fingers twirl my own penny between my thumb and forefinger. I can't throw mine until we talk about hers. That's the rule.

"I'm not sure what I should be doing, Tor."

"That's simple, Angelcake. Do whatever you want to do."

"But it's not that simple. I don't think I want to go to college."

"So don't. Your parents have never cared if you went to college or not. That's not important to them; they just want you to be happy."

She chews her lip. "I know. Dad says I can do whatever will make me happiest and give me *peace of mind* as he calls it."

"He means that, Kenz. Within reason, of course. You can't go off and be a stripper."

She smiles weakly, still stuck in her serious mode.

She touches her pink work boot to my black one. "I like the little bit of modeling I've done, but I really don't want that to be what I do with my life. And I really do love to write, like my grandmother. But again, I don't know if I could do that day in and day out for the rest of my life. And I love my calligraphy, but not many people will pay for handwritten wedding invitations and stuff like that anymore."

"You could do some modeling, *and* some writing, *and* your calligraphy. You don't have to do just one thing. You can do lots of things. You can figure it out as you go. You don't have to make a plan right now. That's a lot to decide at your age."

"I know. I just feel like I want a goal, something to shoot for. Otherwise I feel lost."

"That makes sense."

She pushes her hair out of her face. "Can I tell you what I really want?"

"Of course."

She hesitates before she answers, her eyes cast down. "I want to get married and have a family. I want to have a cute little house— not something big like Dad's house. Something small and cozy, with a porch so I can watch the kids play in the yard with the dog."

"A dog, too?" I tease.

"Of course. And I want to cook dinner and have a husband who comes home every night and sits at the table with me and the kids, and snuggles on the couch with me. I want that to be my future, Tor. I don't want a 'job.'" She puts her hands up and makes air quotes. "I want to spend all my time loving my family. And I'd really like to keep volunteering at the pet shelter with your mom. That makes my heart happy." She peeks up at me, trying to gauge what I'm thinking. "Is all of that dumb? Is it too fifties to want to get married and have kids?"

I laugh, but mostly to hide how she's got me choked up. She just described exactly what Ember told me she wanted a few years ago one night when we were up late talking while Asher was asleep. She didn't want the band life for either of them anymore. She wanted them both to be home, with Kenzi, and not be on the road all the time being separated so much. She even wanted another baby, but mostly she just wanted them all to be happy and together.

Swallowing hard, I lean a little closer to her. "I don't think it's dumb at all, Angel. In fact, I think your mom is watching over you, helping you choose your direction." I wait for her to pull away and shut me out, because that's what she always does when we talk about Ember in the present tense. Kenzi can handle talking about her mother in the past, but not in the present or the future. This time she surprises me, her head snapping up, her eyes wide to meet mine.

"Really? You think she would want me to have that?"

"I definitely do."

Her eyes glisten with tears as she smiles. "That makes me feel better. Chloe thinks it's stupid and nobody wants to be a wife and mother anymore. At least not as their main goal in life."

"Do me a favor. Stop listening to Chloe and listen to your heart."

She throws her arms around me and hugs me. "You always make me feel better," she whispers into my neck. "No matter what, you say the right thing every time."

When she doesn't let go, I put my arm around her and hug her back.

"I try," I say softly, my fingers touching the ends of her silky hair. I've touched her hair many times, even brushed it and braided it when she was small, but I don't remember it feeling so soft.

Her breath is warm against the side of my throat, and for a moment I think I feel her lips against me. "You always smell so good. I don't want to let go," she says wistfully.

I hold her tighter, because lately she says all the right things, too. There's no way she could know that the innocent little comments she makes sometimes are everything I need to hear, but I hang on to the words anyway. Fuck it if they don't mean what I need them to mean, or don't come from the right person.

Four seconds. That's what I give myself. And then I slowly pull away.

"Your turn," she says, reminding me to throw my penny into the river and make my wish.

"It's getting dark. We should go." I move to jump off the rock but she grabs my arm.

"No, you have to make your wish first. Then we'll go."

Shaking my head, I toss my penny into the river. "Happy now? Let's go."

I jump off the rock and hold my hand out to her as she climbs down; then I grab the cooler and her backpack and throw it over my shoulder.

She brushes off the back of her jeans. "What did you wish for?"

"The same thing you did."

"Direction?" she asks as we walk down the trail. "What do you need direction for? You have the business and the rescue. You have your house and your bikes. Your life is together."

"It's not as together as you think. Maybe I want what you want."

"A wife and kids? You?" She says it like it's the most shocking thing she's ever heard.

"Yeah. Why is that so hard to believe?"

She looks down at the trail as we walk. "I don't know. Not hard to believe, really. But if you had those things, you wouldn't have been around as much. I can't even imagine that. I guess I always thought *we* were your family." She stumbles on a rock and grabs on to my hand. "I never knew you wanted more."

I squeeze her hand in mine. "Surprise. I did. I *do*."

"Well, then you should get it. Your wishes should come true, too. Not just mine."

"Yeah, maybe someday." I sigh and look around the woods. I'm not sure that's ever going to happen for me.

"So how come you never married Sydni? Or got more seriously involved with any of the other girls you've dated?"

"I have a hard time committing."

Her face flashes a look of distaste. "You mean you're a cheater? That's awful."

"No, I'm not a cheater, Kenz. I'm just waiting for the one who makes me feel like forever wouldn't be long enough."

"And you've never felt like that? Not even with Sydni?" She swats a bug out of her face. "Maybe that feeling just doesn't exist."

"I think it exists. I just think sometimes fate fucks it all up for us."

"Like what happened to my parents?"

"Exactly. Your parents had everything. And fate fucked them

hard. I don't know what's worse—never finding the one or finding them and then fuckin' losing them."

Her teeth work her bottom lip as she thinks that over. "I think losing them is worse than never knowing them at all."

"You might be right. Anyway, after a few months of dating, women start to want more. They start gawking at rings in the mall, talking about kids, moving their shit into my closet. And then I back off 'cause I don't want to lead them on, ya know? I don't want them to think something's there that might not be. But I don't want to lose them, either. I just never felt like I was ready to take the dive into more than just dating. Then, when they sense that, they get all fuckin' pissed off, call me an asshole, and it's all downhill from there, Angelcake."

She sighs and doesn't speak for a few moments as we walk along the trail. "You paint a grim picture, Tor. But I think your forever girl is out there. You just have to find her."

"Thanks for the vote of confidence."

"Remember when I was little I used to tell everyone I was going to marry you?"

"Yup. It's the first thing you told every girlfriend I had."

Her hand covers her mouth as she laughs, her cheeks turning pink. "Oh shit. I'm sorry, Tor. I was a pain in the ass, huh?"

I wink at her affectionately. "Kinda. At least you don't do that now."

"Maybe next time you bring a girl over I'll do it just to make you laugh and see the look on her face," she teases.

I don't say anything, because a part of me wants her to do just that. It was nice to have a girl stake a claim on me and be all prepared to go to battle for my heart. Even if she was only five.

CHAPTER 3

Kenzi—age four

Toren—age nineteen

I put on one of my old Elvis CDs while I boil water for ravioli. It's one of the few things Kenzi will eat since she's going through a weird picky eating phase.

"When are Mommy and Daddy coming back home?" She tugs on the leg of my jeans and stares up at me.

"Tomorrow."

She points to the stereo. "Is this my daddy singing?"

"No, Angel. It's Elvis. Do you like it?"

"Uh-huh. Will you dance me?"

I smile down at her. I did her pigtails lopsided again, but I think it adds to her cuteness. "You wanna dance?"

She raises her arms up to me and I take her hands in mine. "Okay . . . step on," I tell her, and she puts her tiny feet on top of mine, and we dance around the kitchen, with her giggling wildly.

"We're dancin'!" she squeals.

💜 💜 💜

KENZI

Almost my entire family has congregated at our house to see me all dressed up to go to my senior prom. My father, my grandparents, my great-grandmother, Rayne, Sydni, and Toren are all here to gawk at me. I'm so embarrassed with all the attention that I want to fall through the floor. They make Jason and me pose all over the house for pictures, and Jason has actually gained a few points for being so tolerant of the whole embarrassing ordeal.

"Okay, we really have to go or the limo is going to leave," I finally say when I can't stand it anymore. "We still have to pick up Chloe and her date."

"The driver will wait," my father says, pulling me in for a hug as we walk toward the foyer to make our exit. "You look beautiful. Have a good time. And no drinking. Or drugs."

"Dad. Please."

Behind my dad, Tor is glaring at Jason with his *You better not mess with our girl or I'll kill you* face and I make a warning expression back at him to stop.

"We're going!" I announce, grabbing my bag. "I love you guys."

Taking Jason's hand, we make for the door and practically run to the limo waiting in the driveway.

"My God. I'm so sorry," I say when we get inside, and the driver closes the door behind us.

"It's all right. Your family is cool."

"Yeah. A little overbearing sometimes, though."

"Be glad my parents are out of town or they'd want to be doing the same thing."

We stop to pick up Chloe and her boyfriend, Brendan, who's also good friends with Jason, and she squeals when she sees me, gushing over how beautiful we both look.

I'm not a dress girl at all. I feel completely awkward and, honestly, not very beautiful wearing this purple dress and insanely high heels that Chloe and Rayne talked me into when we went dress shopping a few weeks ago. I really want to go home and throw on an old faded T-shirt and ripped jeans and curl up on the couch with a book or maybe watch a movie and binge on chocolate and ice cream.

We had a plan to go to the prom, then go to Hampton Beach for the night and spend the day on the beach tomorrow, as most of our graduating class is doing. One of Jason's friends is supposed to drive us back home tomorrow night. We have two rooms booked, one for Chloe and me and one for the guys. But earlier today, Chloe threw a surprise change at me and made it clear that she and Brendan are taking one room for themselves so they can go at it all night like rabbits. This obviously leaves me alone in a room with Jason, which I'm trying to get myself mentally prepared for because I'm not sure if I'm ready. All day I wanted to call Jason and tell him I was sick and bail out of the prom completely, but I knew that would be unfair to him and then Chloe would get all crazy mad at me. Now it seems like everyone is looking forward to the prom and the beach and a nighttime rendezvous with their date. *Except me.*

I've never been alone in a bedroom with a guy before, let alone a hotel room, which is basically just code for sex room. Even though we've fooled around a few times over the past few weeks, I still don't feel like I want to rip Jason's clothes off or have him rip mine off. I've tried to get in the mood with him and turn my brain *off* and my body *on*, but so far my body hasn't gotten on board with his groping and nipple manhandling. To me it all feels like a really impatient doctor is giving me an examination, and I can tell Jason is getting impatient with me stopping him every time he tries to go further. I'm not sure if him not dumping me by now is due to him actually liking me, or because now I've become a conquest for him.

The ballroom of the hotel has been turned into a magical dance floor surrounded by tables that each have seating for six. We find our table, and just as I'm wishing I was a better dancer, Jason and Brendan are approached by a friend of theirs who flashes a bag of weed and a flask, and they disappear with him.

Chloe shrugs. "Don't worry. They'll be back."

Dinner comes and goes. Then dessert, and the guys still haven't come back. Our class president starts to announce the winners for things like most likely to succeed, best couple, prom king and queen, and I'm surprised when I hear that I was voted female with the prettiest eyes.

"Way to go, honey," Chloe cheers.

"Thanks." I look around the room, wondering if the guys are ever coming back. "This kinda sucks. We haven't even danced. You and I could have just come together. What did we need the guys for if they were going to ditch us anyway?"

"I'll dance with you."

I shake my head at her and laugh. "My feet hurt way too much to dance now. These shoes are awful."

"Guys hate the prom, Kenz. They just come to party. The real fun is after the prom." She takes a few sips of her red punch. "Are you going to be okay tonight?"

Letting out an aggravated sigh, I slip my shoes off under the table before answering her. "You could have told me this was your plan, Chloe. I really didn't want to be trapped with him alone in a hotel room."

"God. You make it sound like it's terrible. Why can't you just enjoy yourself? Just let it happen and get it over with. I figured this was the best way to do it, like pushing you into the deep end of the pool."

"I didn't want my first time to be with some guy who's drunk and high."

She rolls her eyes. "I'm pretty sure it's like that for ninety per-cent of the population, Kenzi. You've been reading too many books. Trust me, your first time is not going to be some epic earth-shattering experience. Drink a little first, or smoke a joint. It'll be easier if you're loosened up." She giggles at her own words. "Loose in several ways!" She laughs.

I shake my head and look away from her to watch a couple whose names I can't remember dance in the center of the dim dance floor. She's smiling up at him, and him down at her, their arms wrapped tightly around each other. They look happy and in love. *That's what I want.*

"I think I'll pass on being loose," I say.

When my parents used to bring me on tour with them, I was around drunk and stoned people all the time, and those memories have snuffed out any interest for me to ever drink or do drugs for any reason. I like to be in control of how I'm acting and the deci-sions I'm making.

Another half hour goes by before the guys finally show up, their eyes bloodshot, both of them laughing at nothing remotely funny.

"You ladies ready to get out of here?" Brendan asks, pulling Chloe out of her chair.

"We thought you'd never ask," she replies, winding herself around him.

"Sorry I missed the dinner, babe," Jason says, putting his arm around me as we walk out of the hotel.

I'm not sure when I became "babe."

"And I'm a pretty sucky dancer anyway," he adds.

"It's okay. The food wasn't that great, so you didn't miss much."

His arm tightens around my waist, and he leans into my neck, his breath reeking of alcohol. "I'll make it up to you at the hotel."

Nerves turn my stomach as we climb into the back of the limo. I'm grateful the driver is not one of my father's usuals. Initially, my dad wanted to pay for the limo and have one of his drivers take us, but Jason and Brendan insisted on paying, and now I know why. Chloe must have told them that they had to get the limo out of my father's control to make sure that word didn't get back to him that we ended up in a hotel for the night. I'm annoyed at Chloe's orchestration to ensure she tricked me into spending the night with Jason, even though I know her intentions are for me to have fun. I don't like being manipulated.

The boys resume drinking once we hit the road, and Chloe joins them. I decline when Jason offers the bottle to me. Smiling, he pulls me against his chest. "You don't have to be a good girl all the time, Kenzi," he whispers, his lips against my ear.

I know I don't *have* to be, but I want to be. Why is being good considered bad? Just a few hours ago half my family stood in my living room, proud of me and happy for me, telling me how beautiful I looked and how handsome Jason was. They thought they were sending me off to experience one of the happiest nights of my teen life. I feel ashamed that now I'm on my way to a hotel, about to lose my virginity to a drunk guy who probably won't even remember me by the end of the summer. My mother would be incredibly disappointed.

I feel sick and trapped, and not excited in any way about what's to come.

When we reach the hotel, Jason and Brendan go to the office to check us in while Chloe and I wait outside. I watch the limo pull away, wishing I had asked the driver to take me home. Now my ride is gone, and I have no way to get home until tomorrow.

"I feel kinda sick," Chloe says, grabbing on to my arm.

"Are you okay?" Under the parking lot lights, she looks like a mess. The makeup she paid someone a hundred dollars earlier today to apply is smeared, and her perfect updo is now very much down. The bodice of her black dress is stretched from Brendan's groping. I want to drag my best friend out of here, take her home, and scrub her face.

"I think I'm gonna be si—" She turns toward the bushes and vomits.

Ugh.

The guys join us a few minutes later and laugh at Chloe, who's bent over in the bushes, but immediately vaults into Brendan's arms when she's done. I have an immense urge to shove a piece of minty gum into her mouth as they lean into each other for a kiss.

"You two have fun," she drawls as Brendan leads her away to their room.

Jason grabs our duffel bags and eyes me suggestively. "Well, at least you're not puking in the parking lot," he jokes. "Let's go find our room and get this party started."

Our room is just like any other hotel room, with the usual stiff bed, ugly orange comforter, and generic pictures on the walls. I've been in literally hundreds of these rooms over the years with my parents. I make a beeline for the bathroom, which always seems to be in the same place. I blot my face, fix my hair, and rinse my mouth with the tiny bottle of mouthwash provided by the hotel.

Calm down, I tell my reflection. *Stop being a loser prude. Relax, have fun, and get this milestone out of the way. Stop being the class weirdo.*

I open the door, prepared to attempt to have some fun, to find Jason right outside.

"Hey. I was just going to ask if you were coming out." His blue eyes are glazed, his voice slightly slurred. He doesn't move from the doorway to let me by. Instead, his gaze drifts down to my chest before he leans in to kiss me, his hands circling my waist, pulling me against him.

"You're so fuckin' hot, Kenzi..." His hands move down my body to paw my ass through the thin material of my dress.

"Jason..." I try to squirm from his touch, but he backs me up against the sink, his lips coming down hard on mine again.

"I've been waiting weeks to get you like this..." His hands slide up and squeeze my breasts, his fingers pulling the delicate fabric aside. "God, your tits are fucking amazing..."

His head bows down to dive into my cleavage and I take that as an opportunity to grab his hands and push him away.

"I'm sorry...can we kinda slow down...?" My heart rate picks up speed, but not from desire. I'm panicking, not sure how to get away from him. The way he's touching me is making me feel dirty and scared.

His hand snakes around my neck and a grin flashes across his face. "I'll go as slow as you want, baby." He kisses me again and the taste of alcohol on him makes me queasy. "You've got the body of a fuckin' porn star, Kenzi." His hands are everywhere, on my ass, on my breasts, trying to pull my dress up my thighs.

"What?" I try to pull away from him, feeling my face flush. I don't even know what he's talking about but it doesn't sound like a compliment I want.

"This ass and these huge tits." He nips at my neck. "All these fucking curves." He slides his hands from my breasts down to my ass, then brings one hand between us, shoving it between my legs, bunching the fabric of my dress up against me. "All the guys want to fuck you, and half the girls, too. You're hot as fucking hell."

Disgusted, I push him off me, and he stumbles, feeling the effects of the alcohol. "Stop. I don't want to do this."

He comes back at me. "No, no, no. We're not playing this game anymore, Kenzi. For weeks you've been teasing me and I can't take any more." He tries to kiss me again, but I duck away from him and slam my hands into his chest.

"Jason, stop. I mean it."

His eyes go dark. "What the fuck? You think I paid all this money for this room so we can sit here and talk?"

I bite back tears. "I'm sorry. I'll give you the money for the room."

"You think your little rich spoiled ass is too good to be fucked by me?"

"No, not at all." I swallow hard, his anger feeding my fear. "I'm just not ready for this."

He sneers at me. "Not ready? Your body was made to get fucked, Kenzi. The faster you accept it, the better off we'll be. Now shut up and let's have some fun."

"Fuck you, Jason. You're a drunk asshole."

I push past him and get myself out of the tiny bathroom, but he follows me, grabbing my arm and spinning me around. "Come on, Kenzi. Stop being a cock tease."

"I'm not trying to be one!"

"Why the hell do you think you're here?" He slams his fist against the wall.

"I didn't agree to be here with you, Jason. This was Chloe's idea, not mine. Why are you acting like this? I'll give you your money back, I just want to go home."

His lip actually curls at me. "Fuck off, Kenzi. I'm outta here. There are plenty of chicks here who aren't stuck-up bitches. Too bad your body's wasted on such a cold, stupid bitch." He storms out of the room, slamming the door hard behind him.

Deep breaths aren't doing much to calm me. No one's ever talked to me like that before or said such ugly things to me. Sitting on the bed, I try to gather my wits. I could lock the door and stay here till morning, tell Chloe what happened, and get a ride home. But what if Jason comes back? He still has his room key. I can't sleep in this room knowing he could come back in at any time.

I pick up my bag and head for the lobby, trying to figure out where I can go. I could call a cab, but they'll have to bring me home and then my dad will know something went wrong. One look at me and he'll know, and I can't do that to him now when he's right in the midst of working on a new album. If I get him all distracted with my drama, it will interfere with his creativity because he'll immediately feel like he has to do something to fix this for me. I refuse to do that to him.

Rayne would come get me, but she'll want to track Jason down and tell him off and make a big crazy scene.

There's only one other person I know who will come get me in the middle of the night without question.

I count to ten and press his contact image on my phone screen, and it rings four times before he answers.

"Kenzi?"

"Hi..."

"What's up? You okay?"

"Yeah...I just kinda need a ride. Do you think you can come get me? Are you busy?"

"You know I will. I just got home. Where are you?"

I clutch the phone, knowing he's going to blow a gasket. "At the Blue Robin down at Hampton Beach."

"A fucking hotel? I thought you were spending the night at Chloe's?"

"That's what I told my father."

"Kenzi..." Disappointment laces his voice.

"Tor, come on. Please don't make this harder."

His keys jingle in the background, then the distinct sound of his front door opening and closing. "I'm on my way. It's gonna take me about an hour to get there, though. Are you okay? You're not hurt or anything?"

"No, I'm fine. Just humiliated."

"That's fixable. Are you in a room?"

"No, I left the room to get away from Jason."

"Then stay in the lobby, okay? Don't be wandering around in the dark by yourself. The beach can get weird at night. The last thing we need is you getting picked up by a sex trafficker."

"What? What the hell, Tor?" Sex trafficker? As if I wasn't nervous enough already, now I have to sit here and worry about being thrown into the back of a van and sold to someone.

"Just stay in the lobby."

After we get off the phone, I huddle in the corner of the lobby with a magazine hoping the manager doesn't come and kick me out or make me go back to the room. The last thing I want is another run-in with Jason.

Tor's truck pulls into the parking lot of the hotel a little over an hour later. I'm so glad to see him that I don't make any of my usual funny comments about him being late. He looks me up and down when I climb into his truck but doesn't say anything until after we've been driving for about ten minutes.

"I'll fuck that kid up if he did anything to hurt you, Kenz," he finally says, his hand tightening on the steering wheel, his eyes not leaving the road.

"He didn't hurt me. He was drinking all night, and I didn't want to put out. He got mad, we argued a little bit, and then he left to go to a party in someone else's room. I didn't want to be there alone after that."

"*Put out?*" He practically spits the words. "Jesus Christ. I can't stand hearing that shit come out of your mouth. It's fucking degrading."

"Well, what do you want me to say? That I wouldn't sleep with him? Is that better?"

"No."

"He called me a cock tease, too. I never even once hinted that I wanted to have sex with him. I haven't teased him at all."

Tor's jaw clenches and he shakes his head. "I'm gonna turn this truck around and put that kid in the fucking ground. Does that little shit think he can treat you like that and get away with it? Does he have any fucking idea who he's messing with?"

I touch his arm. "Tor, stop. Do you want to go to jail for assault again? Please just take me home. I want to forget all the filthy things he said to me."

"If I hear any more of this, I'll fucking kill him."

"Fine." I cross my arms in front of me, wishing I had changed my clothes and gotten out of this ridiculous dress.

He glances over at me. "I didn't mean you couldn't talk. I just meant I can't hear any more of how he treated you without going back to teach that scumbag a lesson on how to treat a woman. And how not to."

"I really don't want to talk at all," I reply, trying not to cry. "Can we just listen to some music?"

"If that's what you want." He connects his phone via Bluetooth to the stereo and starts up my favorite Eagles playlist that he made just for me a few months ago.

"Better?" he asks.

"Better."

I rest my head back against the seat back and close my eyes, letting the music ease away the stress of the night. Music has always been a huge part of my life. I may not be a musician like the rest of my family, but the love of music is embedded in my bones and lives deep in my soul. Nothing makes me feel more content than my favorite songs.

While I love my parents' bands and their music, I have lots of other favorite bands I listen to. A favorite song or melody can be so therapeutic and take you back to a better time and place, almost make you feel like you're really back there again. These songs on Tor's playlist remind me of when my mom was still here, and she and Dad would sit on the back porch and talk, drink wine, and listen to the Eagles. I'd get comfy in my beanbag chair with my favorite books, and we'd sit out there for hours. It didn't happen often since both my parents traveled a lot, but those nights were always my favorites. I'd do anything to have just one more night like that again with my mom and dad.

"Can I stay at your place until tomorrow afternoon?" I ask Tor when we get near the exit to our town. "If you take me home now, my dad is going to know something happened."

"Where the hell is Chloe?"

"Probably under Brendan."

"Terrific." He sighs.

"Yup."

"You can stay at my place, and I'm not going to tell your father about this. He'll lose his mind if he knows you lied to him to stay at a hotel with a guy. So now we're both lying to your dad."

"I'm sorry, Tor. Really. And I didn't know about this. Chloe and I were supposed to share a room. She switched everything up when we got there and there was nothing I could do."

"Let's just get home. What's done is done, and I'm too tired to fight about teen drama."

I'm half asleep by the time we pull into Toren's driveway, and

I feel bad, as he must be utterly exhausted after working all day, probably chasing dogs around all night, and then driving almost three hours for me.

"I really do appreciate you doing all this for me," I say when we get inside his house. "I didn't mean to piss you off and ruin your night."

He lets out a deep sigh. "I'm not mad at you, Kenz. I'm glad you called me. You can always come to me. You know that."

"I know. And I appreciate it. I'm sorry if I disappointed you. That bothers me more than anything else that happened tonight."

"You didn't." He throws his car keys on the kitchen table. "You can't get through life without making mistakes, right? It's how we learn."

I nod and pull the clip out of my hair, letting it fall around my shoulders. "True." I kick off my shoes, relieved to be out of them. "Jason started to drink and hang out with his friends as soon as we got there. I just sat there getting blisters. I didn't even get to dance or anything; it was a total waste of time and money."

He tilts his head and smiles at me. "I can fix that." He crosses the living room to his MP3 player that's hooked up to his speaker system, hits the play button, and Elvis's smooth voice fills the room.

My mouth falls open in surprise. "Wow. I remember this."

"Do you?"

"Yes. You danced with me standing on your feet when I was little. I used to love that."

He moves to stand in front of me and takes my hand in his. "Let's try it without you standing on my feet."

Laughing, I put my hand on his shoulder as he lightly touches my waist. "Okay," I reply. "But I'm afraid I'm not much better than I was when I was five. Your feet still aren't safe."

He laces his fingers through mine. "Don't worry about it. I'm not any better, either."

As we sway together, our bodies a few inches apart, I realize my forehead comes to his chin. I don't know why I like that, but I do. Jason and I are the same height, and it felt awkward to me when we kissed—as if we were sorta unbalanced even though we were even in height. I think the man should be taller than the woman; it looks better to me. And now I know it *feels* better.

"I always loved when you played these songs for me when I was little."

"That's because you thought it was your dad singing. Actually, you thought every guy singer you heard was him."

I laugh because that's true. It took me a long time to understand that not every man on the radio was him singing. "I've just always loved his voice."

"He does have a good voice, but he can't compare to the King."

Letting go of his hand, I reach behind his head, pull the black rubber band out of his ponytail, and wrap it around my wrist. With a shy smile, I clasp my fingers together at the back of his neck while he gives his head a little shake, his hair landing in an oddly alluring shaggy mess.

"Why'd you do that?" he asks, his warm hands circling my waist, pulling me a little closer to him.

"I like how it looks when it's messy." His hands tighten around me, and he turns us toward the window, where the blue glow of the moon is shining through, revealing his devilish grin in the dim light of his living room.

"I think you just want to steal my rubber band," he accuses.

"It's not stealing if you *let* me have it."

His smile widens. "You're right. Should I be worried about you hoarding all my stuff? I thought you would have outgrown this by now. You're not gonna start clipping pieces of my hair, are ya?"

Tilting my head, I finger the ends of his hair, pretending I'm contemplating that. "I *do* like your hair," I tease playfully, but on the inside, I've started to shake like a leaf. I haven't stood this close to him since I was a little girl, and I can feel his body heat mingling with mine. It's exhilarating and frightening at the same time. I slide my hands down to his shoulders, thinking it will ground me to hold on to him, but instead, the inner jittering amplifies. His shoulders are wide and hard, so different from the boys I've touched. Where they were athletic and lean, he's like a rock wall. The solidity of him is incredibly powerful, almost commanding me to get closer, to touch him more.

"I kinda want your shoulders," I say with a light laugh to mask my nervousness as I move my hands hesitantly down to his chest.

He leans his forehead against mine, still swaying us slowly back and forth to the music, and laughs softly. "Unfortunately, you can't take those home and put them in your box. They're stuck to me."

Suddenly I'm overtaken with the notion of taking him home with me, putting him in my box of cherished things, and keeping him for my very own.

I've lost my mind.

I peek up at him through my bangs to find his eyes just inches from mine, hidden behind his impossibly long dark lashes.

"I could get a bigger box," I whisper, my heart fluttering.

His eyes open and lock onto mine, and somehow the space between us is diminished, our bodies leaning into each other, my breasts against his chest. I'm not sure which one of us moved or if we moved at the same time. All I know is I don't want to ever move again.

"Yeah...you could."

My breath catches at the soft deepness of his voice and the unexpected brush of his hand across my cheek. My gaze drifts to his lips, so close to mine, but not nearly close enough.

Oh God, I want him to kiss me.

As if he can read my mind, he quickly pulls away from me, clearing his throat as he walks across the room to turn off the music.

"Tor..."

"It's late. We should go to bed," he says, looking at the MP3 player like it's the most fascinating thing he's ever seen and very obviously *not* looking at me.

My heart is pounding so hard I can't find the strength or air to speak. I nod slowly to his back and bend down to pick up my shoes and bag, glancing over at him questioningly.

Wow. My very first cold shoulder. This night just keeps getting better and better.

"You can sleep in the guest room," he says, still turned away. "You know where everything is."

"Okay." My voice is squeaky and strange and doesn't sound like mine at all. "Thank you for picking me up. I'm sorry—"

"Don't apologize, Kenz. You did the right thing calling me."

Did I?

"Could I borrow a T-shirt to sleep in?"

The look on his face when he turns burns right through me. "I'm not even going to ask why you didn't bring anything to sleep in when you were staying at a hotel with someone."

"I did," I say, following him to his bedroom. "But I'd rather sleep in yours like I did when I slept here when I was little. It makes me feel cozy."

He's just shaking his head at me as he pulls a big black T-shirt out of his dresser and hands it to me without looking at me.

"Thank you."

Once behind the closed door of the guest room, I let out a deep, shaky breath. I have no idea what just happened, but it was definitely something new. I felt it. And I'm pretty sure he did, too.

I think all relationships start with an invisible line, and even though we can't see it, we all know it's there because we can feel it. We respect that line because it keeps the bounds of the relationship intact. The line guides us within our relationships and dictates who is our friend, who is our family, who is our lover, who is someone we can or can't trust. The line between Tor and me is somewhat unique, because it crisscrosses between family and friend, and just now it blurred into something I can't quite describe. I'm not sure where our line is anymore, or if I even want a line at all.

I quickly change out of my prom dress, into Tor's T-shirt, and climb into the bed I've slept in many times before. The purple comforter with a big gothic sugar skull on it that Tor bought for me a few years ago is still on the bed and its softness and familiarity calm me. He said he wanted me to have something girly, but cool, here. His house has always been like a second home to me and I stayed here a lot when my parents were on tour. Since Tor lives closer to my dad than my grandparents do, it wasn't unusual for me to stay with him so he could bring me to school every day. For the past two years, I've come here twice a week to clean and do his laundry because he usually doesn't have time to do it himself and he pays me fifty dollars a week, which I stash away for when I can have my own car. Tonight, though, I don't really feel like I'm staying over at my father's best friend's house. Something feels different.

How can one little moment, one tiny touch, one quickening breath change so much?

It didn't.

I'm being ridiculous and hypersensitive because Jason was nasty to me. I wanted to feel pretty—maybe even wanted and cared about—tonight and when that didn't happen, I must have just projected that onto poor Toren. No wonder he couldn't wait to make me go to bed.

And telling him I want to put him in a box! *Gawd.* So awkward and borderline psychotic.

Cringing at myself, I grab my phone from the nightstand to see ten text messages. Eight are from Chloe and two are from Jason. All ten asking if I'm okay and where the hell am I? I'm surprised Jason even bothered after the way he treated me.

I text them both that I'm home and put the phone back so I can bury myself under the comforter, where I toss and turn. It's 4:00 a.m. and I should be exhausted, but I can't get my mind to turn off and let me sleep. It keeps shifting back to Tor and how his hand felt on my cheek, and how warm his chest felt against my hands through his thin shirt. When our bodies leaned against each other for those few moments, it was like a silent *click* into place. It's exactly the type of feeling I read about in all my romance novels. This proves that crazy butterfly moment really does exist after all, and it's not a myth.

The only problem is, it's all wrong. Very wrong.

Toren can't make me feel that way. He's old. Okay, not *old*, but way older than me. He's practically family. He freakin' babysat me. He's been to all my birthday parties and all my school events. He's taken care of me when I was sick. He taught me how to ride a bicycle. He held me when I cried for my mom. He knows all my secrets and dreams. He's...

...everything.

♥ ♥ ♥

I have no idea when I finally fell asleep, but I'm woken up by the scent of coffee. The clock on the wall reads 7:00 a.m. *Great*. Not getting enough sleep is going to make me cranky all day.

After using the restroom and making sure I look somewhat presentable, I follow the aroma to the kitchen to find Tor standing at the kitchen window, wearing old faded jeans and no shirt. I'm surprised to see his entire back covered in tattoos now, because he didn't have all those last summer when he was in our pool. That funny feeling returns to my chest and stomach as my eyes rake over not just the new artwork, but also the muscles and definition beneath the ink. When did Tor get so hot? Have I been living under a rock?

"Hi . . . ," I finally say, stepping farther into the kitchen.

He turns with a look of surprise, and I notice how his eyes quickly take in that I'm still wearing his shirt, which comes down to my thighs. I've dressed like this a hundred times in front of him and never felt self-conscious, but today I do. My legs feel incredibly naked and I'm so glad I shaved them yesterday before the prom.

"Hey, I didn't think you'd be up this early."

"The smell of the coffee woke me up." If coffee were a person, it would be my best friend. I'm definitely addicted in a bad way.

"You want some? You look pretty tired." He steps over to the counter and grabs the coffeepot, pouring some into a mug before I have a chance to answer. "I don't have any of that caramel milk stuff you like, though."

"That's okay; I'll drink it with regular milk."

"And about twenty sugars?" He flashes me a teasing grin as he adds milk and sugar just the way I like it and then hands it to me.

"Thanks. Are you working today?"

He steps closer to me and grabs my hand, his eyes twinkling with that sparkling diamond glint he sometimes gets, and pulls his hair tie off my wrist.

My heart does an odd clench. "You're taking it back?" I ask.

"I'm borrowing it."

"Oh. Okay…" He's never taken back anything I've lifted off him before. Maybe he's finally fed up with my silly little game. I remind myself that I'm not five anymore, and collecting items from him is probably immensely annoying and possibly perceived as stealing and not cute.

"Hey, don't look all wounded, Kenz. It's the last one I have. I'll pick some up today and you can have this one back. I promise."

I sip my coffee, feeling idiotic for letting myself get upset over something so ridiculous as a rubber band. *But it's his. It's special.*

Shaking my head, I pretend to be nonchalant. "You don't have to do that. It's just a stupid little game."

"I know I don't have to. I *want* to. And it's not stupid, it's *our* game, and I'd miss it if you stopped." He leans back against the kitchen counter, crosses his arms, and studies my face for a moment with a faint smirk. "I was thinking, though, maybe I should take something of yours for once. Kind of like a trade."

Warmth floods through my body in a swift wave. It starts in my chest and scatters down between my thighs, intensifying with every passing second. I grip my coffee cup and hope I don't fall over into the wall.

"Oh," I reply, surprised. "I guess that's fair, huh?"

He nods slowly, his eyes dark and intent. Mesmerizing. "I want that black beanie you wear all the time," he says without hesitation, and I wonder when he decided *that's* the thing he wants.

"It has a little purple heart on it," I protest. And it's my favorite, but I don't care anymore. I'll love it even more once it's on his head.

"So? I can rock a purple heart, Angel."

No doubt he can rock anything. But him rocking my favorite beanie is something I can't wait to see.

I smile at him. "Consider it yours, then. Next time you see me, you can have it."

"Don't forget or next time you try to take something of mine, I'm not gonna let ya."

He wants something of mine. I'm pretty sure I've got a fever. Maybe even the flu. My body is on fire, and my insides are shaking again. My head feels buzzy and floaty. My lips feel stuck in a demented smile. I wish I had pants on.

"Deal," I manage to say.

He pushes himself off the counter. "I gotta get going. I have to go to work and pick up Tanner; then we're busting some douchebags with fighting dogs."

The excited nervousness I felt a second ago quickly turns into worry. The whole dogfighting thing scares the hell out of me. Usually the guys who run them are drug dealers or worse, and most of the dogs are dangerous. I've seen the dogs they rescue and bring to Tor's mother's shelter to evaluate for training and veterinary care. Most of them are either all torn up and bloody, or totally aggressive from fear and starvation. Or both.

"Be careful, Tor. Those guys are crazy." It's hard to believe that people who run dogfighting rings exist right here in our cozy little New England towns, but they do.

"I'm always careful." He goes to the laundry room down the hall and comes back pulling a heather-gray T-shirt on. "Do you need a ride home? Or you can stay here for the day, do the stuff you do, and I'll take you home later?"

"Can I stay here? I'll clean up for you. I could make dinner if you have food."

"Yeah, I got some stuff in the fridge. I'll be home around five. Make anything you find, I'm easy." He grabs his keys off the table. "Get in touch with your dad and let him know you're okay. I'm sure he's wondering how your night went."

"I will. I'm not going to tell him what happened with Jason. If he knows I had a sucky time, he'll get upset and he doesn't need that now."

"Your call. I'm not going to tell him anything, but if he asks, we'll just tell him you were here cleaning like you always do, and you came here from Chloe's after the prom."

I nod gratefully. "Thanks, Tor."

"Don't thank me. I don't like lying to Asher, though, so I don't want any more shit like this going on. I'll always help you if you need it, but I don't like keeping things about you from him."

I nod again, knowing if I apologize it will just make him angry. I feel terrible that I put him in a bad position of having to lie to my father because that's something he would normally never do. Tor is a good guy with strong values, especially when it comes to his family and friends, and I hate that my bad decision has now affected him.

He pauses at the door and turns to me before he leaves. "Go take a nap, Kenz. You know how you get when you're overtired. You don't even have to clean today if you don't want to, and I'll still pay you. I'll be happy with a dinner that didn't come out of the microwave and hasn't been frozen for the past four years."

I shake my head. "No. I'm not letting you pay me this week. You drove three hours for me in the middle of the night. So forget it."

He waves his hand in my direction. "Fine. I'm going. Get some sleep."

CHAPTER 4

Kenzi—age two

Toren—age seventeen

She's slamming one of the kitchen cabinets open and closed while I'm trying to read a magazine. Babysitting on a Friday night isn't exactly my idea of fun, but Ash and Ember wanted to get away for a night to see a movie. So Uncle Tor said yes and stayed home. As usual.

Slam. Slam.

"Kenzi," I warn. "You better stop slamming that door."

She looks over at me, giggles, and slams it again. Harder.

"I mean it, I'm gonna put you to bed early if you don't stop."

She looks at me, then the cabinet, then at me again.

Slam.

Pushing the chair back, I stand and she tries to toddle off, falls, and starts to cry. I kneel down and pick her up.

"Where does it hurt, Angel?" *I ask, knowing she didn't get hurt.*

She holds out her palm, sniffling. "Here..."

"Should I kiss it and make it better? Do you think that'll work?"

She nods, her hair falling over her eyes. I grab her hand and plant a big noisy kiss on her palm.

"All better now?"

Nodding, she wraps her little arms around my neck and rests her head against mine.

"Uh-huh."

All she wanted was for me to chase her and hug her. It's what she does. And I melt every time.

TOR

As I drive to the shop, I'm still exhausted and pissed off from the night before. Sleep never came last night, fury racing through my veins for hours, along with something else I can't find the words to explain.

That asshole put his hands on her and had the nerve to call her a cock tease. He ruined a night that was supposed to be special and memorable, and now I want to wring his skinny neck. He's an idiot for even thinking he could ever have a girl like her, and I'm proud of her for saying no to him. If I ever cross paths with Jason again, I'm going to beat some respect into him. He'll be wearing the imprint of my silver skull rings on his pretty-boy face for a long time.

I tell myself my rage stems from some punk pawing my niece like a twenty-buck whore. I'd feel the same way if someone treated my little sister like that and my reaction would be the same.

But not quite the same, right, Tor?

The feelings that surfaced later, when her hands slowly crept down my shoulders to my chest and her eyes fixated on my mouth, her own lips parting and practically begging...I don't know what the fuck that was.

I tell myself the way our bodies melted perfectly into each other for what could only have been mere seconds, and how her voice took on a sweet, sensual wistfulness when she told me she wanted to hide me away in her box of cherished possessions, all meant nothing and were due to exhaustion.

I lie.

I'd live in that box for the rest of my life just to make her happy.

At the next stoplight, I close my eyes and lean my forehead against the steering wheel, then pull back slightly and bang my head against it. Hard. And again. And again. And again. Until blood trickles down my face.

I did not just think that. I did not feel any of that. I did not pull her closer. I did not silently beg her to never take her hands off me. I did not want to touch her face and promise her the world. I did not love seeing her in nothing but my shirt in the middle of my kitchen.

I will never, ever let my mind wander to her again.

I will never, ever wish for what I can never have.

The car behind me blares its horn for me to move, rousing me from my thoughts and brain-banging.

"All right, all right...," I mutter into the rearview mirror, gunning the gas and wiping my hand across my bloody forehead.

My mood today could not be more perfect for the task at hand. Tanner and our buddy Sled don't say a word as we drive to the address given to us by an anonymous tipster. I barely have to look at the address to know where the house is. Nine times out of ten, they're in the same neighborhood, and this one's no exception. It's a seedy part of a nearby town, home to drug dealers, addicts, and assorted derelicts. At one point, I spent way too much time in this part of town, fighting underground and engaging in other activities I'm not proud of. Watching my brothers follow me down that same destructive path forced me to get out, and I convinced them to get out of it, too, before one of us ended up in prison or dead.

So now we build custom bikes, and we rescue lost and abused pets. And on some days, like today, we might just get the chance to fight and give some asshole a well-deserved ass kicking. That's always a bonus, especially when I'm in a bad mood.

I park the truck across the street from the house in question and we take a quick inventory of our surroundings as we make our way to the front door. A large garage in the back has the telltale boarded-up windows. Several rusty dog cages are stacked next to the garage, partially hidden in the bushes. We've been doing this for years with a decent success rate, but there's always the chance we could get shot or stabbed by someone strung out on drugs or just unwilling to comply. All of us know how to disarm someone, but that doesn't make the risk any less real. We're not cops, and these guys don't have to go along with our plan; even though we're giving them the easy way out, they don't always see it that way.

Knocking on the door is my preference over the doorbell, and after three knocks the door opens and a guy wearing nothing but sweatpants squints at us.

"Sup?" he says.

Most of these guys aren't too nervous when they see us at the door. When three guys show up at the door covered in tats, wearing leather vests and dark sunglasses, two with long hair and one with a half-shaved, tattooed head, they usually think we're here to buy drugs or get in on their action.

"Can we come inside?" I ask.

He swings the door open. "Okay, bro. You lookin' for something special?"

I've already noticed the white lines on the coffee table, the pill bottles, and the drug paraphernalia littering the house. A fawn pit bull is sitting beside the ratty mustard yellow couch, watching our every move. She has no visible scars, so she's most likely a pet or a guard dog.

"We heard you have fighting dogs," Tanner says, moving to my right.

The guy nods, and his suspicious expression shows he's not quite sure how he wants to react to us. "I might. You lookin' to buy or to bet? Shit goes down on Friday and Saturday."

My teeth clench. "Does that all happen here?"

His eyes shift from me to my boys and it's evident he's not sure he can trust us. "Mostly, yeah."

"How much you asking for a fighter?" Tanner asks, lighting up a cigar.

"Depends on the dog. We got puppies you can train yourself or we got experienced dogs that will fight to the death and win every ring. They're fucking gnarly terrors, man, and they go for a few grand if you're serious."

"Oh, we're very serious," I say calmly. "We're with Devils' Wolves dog rescue."

"What the fuck is that?"

"We rescue abused dogs," I answer. "Dogfighting is illegal."

"You the fuckin' cops?" He steps back, almost tripping over one of the several beer bottles on the stained carpet.

"No, but we work with them and could have them here in about ten minutes if you don't cooperate," Tanner says. "And it looks to me like you might not want the cops here. Unless you're snorting baby powder over there."

His nostrils flare at us. "Fuck you guys. Get out of my house."

I shake my head. "Not without the dogs."

His eyes shift over to the dog. *"Achtung!"* he commands, and the dog jumps to its feet, its eyes riveted on me.

"Sitz!" I meet the dog's brown eyes, unwavering, and she obeys my command and sits. *"Bleib!"* I tell the dog to stay and turn my hard gaze to its owner after I'm convinced the dog will stay put.

"You think I don't know German?" For some reason, these guys teach the dogs commands in foreign languages. I only know about ten words, but he doesn't need to know that.

"You're gonna regret that, asshole." His arm swings up and I quickly block him. I deliver a hard punch to his face, and he goes down fast to the floor.

Sled flashes me an evil grin. "Nice."

"Thanks." Hitting him felt good. *Too good.* It's eased some of my anger from last night, at least for the moment.

I kick the guy on the floor with my boot and he rolls over, holding his bleeding face. "Get up, buddy. We're not done. Unless you like lying in your own garbage?"

"What the fuck do you assholes want?" He stands slowly, wiping the blood from his broken, crooked nose with the back of his hand.

"We just want the dogs, that's it. We don't want your drugs or your money. We won't even tell the cops what we saw here. The deal is we take the dogs and you agree to never fight dogs again. Simple as that. You can sit here for the rest of your life and get stoned, man, we don't care. We just want the dogs."

He attempts to talk but I raise my hand, making him flinch. "There's no debate. Either you let us take the dogs, calm and quiet, or we're calling the police, and that's gonna go way worse for you. Your choice on how much you want to lose."

Tanner leans down and pets the dog, which is still in the stay position, and it wags its tail at his gentle touch.

"Take the fucking dogs," the guy mumbles, his voice thick and nasally.

"Good choice. How many you got?"

"Eight adults and four puppies downstairs and there's four bait dogs out in the garage."

Puppies and bait dogs. What a scumbag.

I haul my arm back and crash my fist into his face again, knocking him back down onto the floor. "That's for the puppies and bait dogs, asshole. You might want to stay down there after all."

My brother nudges my arm. "You in a bad mood today, Tor?"

"You could say that."

It takes us an hour to load the dogs up into the transport cages and into the back of my truck. Three of the dogs are in bad shape with fresh open wounds and ripped, oozing ears. The puppies are young, maybe eight weeks old, kept in the basement on the cold bloodstained floor but still wagging their tails. The bait dogs are assorted breeds, timid and shaking, and were most likely strays or picked up on Craigslist ads from "free to good home" offers. Luckily, the puppies are young enough where they'll forget the horrors they must have witnessed the first few weeks of their lives, but the bait dogs will need rehabilitation.

On our way out, we take the pretty fawn pittie that was in the living room because I don't trust that asshole with any dog—pet or otherwise. Once an abuser, *always* an abuser.

My mother and a local vet who volunteers for situations like this are waiting for us when we arrive at the shelter to triage the dogs that need medical attention first. While they're doing that, we bring the other dogs to the quarantine area and set them up in their kennels with fresh food, water, and beds. Most of them seem pretty friendly, which is a good sign they'll be able to be put in foster homes and retrained. My guess is the guy who had these dogs was new to this sick hobby and hadn't had them for very long. I pet each dog softly on the head before we leave. It's a new beginning for them, and I always feel like a small part of my soul goes with each one.

My father used to tell us to try to make a difference in someone's

life every day. Even if it's only to make them smile. Today I made
a difference. It was just for a bunch of dogs, but it still counts.

♥ ♥ ♥

After dropping Tanner and Sled back off at the shop, I decide to
take the rest of the day off to unwind and get some sleep. Lisa
calls me just as I'm turning down my street. She has the uncanny
ability to always call me when I don't want to talk to anyone.

"Yeah?" I say into my phone, not doing much to hide my
irritation.

"Hey. You didn't answer your phone earlier, so I called the shop
and they said you went home."

"We took fighting dogs out of some guy's place this morning.
I'm in a shit mood, so I just wanted to go home and sleep it off."

"Isn't that something the cops should be doing?"

My teeth grind together. "We have an arrangement. We go in
first to get the dogs out."

"Oh. Do you think you'll be in a better mood tonight?"

"Maybe." *Let me check my crystal ball first.* "Why?"

"I was thinking we could meet at the bar, maybe play some
pool? I'll be there with one of my girlfriends and thought it would
be nice if you hung out with us."

Lisa either wants to show me off or let her friend psychoana-
lyze me. Neither of those options sits well with me but I feel like
seeing Lisa will be a good distraction after the weirdness of last
night, so I relent and agree.

"All right. I have to load my feeding traps but after that I can
stop by. First I'm going home to shower and nap."

"Great. I can't wait to see you."

I wish I felt that way, too, but I don't. Lisa seems to want something I can't give her, although I've yet to figure out what that

actually is, and I'm starting to wonder if even she knows. Story of my life. After spending almost twelve years of my life back and forth with Sydni, I'm in no rush to get seriously involved or become another second best to someone. I'm totally done with that bullshit.

♥ ♥ ♥

My stereo system is blasting when I walk through the back door, and Kenzi is pushing the vacuum across the floor, dancing, completely oblivious that I'm even in the house. I watch her in amusement for a few minutes before she finally sees me and jumps about a foot in the air.

"Tor!" She turns off the vacuum. "You scared the hell out of me."

"Aren't you supposed to be napping?"

"I couldn't sleep. And I felt bad for making you drive around last night, so I wanted to make it up to you by cleaning."

Shaking my head, I cross the kitchen to the sink and remove my sterling silver rings, revealing bloody knuckles underneath. I douse my hand with dish soap, wincing at the sting, and rinse with warm water.

"What happened?" She's next to me now, peering into the sink at my hand, and then up at my face. "You're bleeding. And you have a cut on your head." She lightly touches my forehead.

"I hit the guy with the dogs."

She pulls about two feet of paper towels off the roll and hands it to me. "The dogfighting guy?"

"Yeah. We got the dogs, though. That's all that matters."

She crosses her arms and leans her hip against the counter. "I thought you weren't going to hit people anymore after your stint in the clink?"

I glare at her. "Drop it. He deserved it."

Ignoring me, she grabs my hand and inspects it. "You should put some antibiotic cream on this."

"I will."

"Want me to kiss it better like you used to do for me?" she teases.

Fuck yes.

Pulling my hand out of hers, I bite my tongue to make sure my thoughts don't escape out of my mouth.

"Did you text or call your dad?" I ask, changing the subject. "I'm sure he's wondering how your night went."

"Yes. I told him the prom was boring and that I was at your house cleaning and making you dinner. Jason had the nerve to text me, do you believe that?"

My old friend anger has returned. "What the hell did he say?"

She follows me down the hall to the bathroom and watches me put ointment on my hand.

"He said he was sorry for being a douche."

"He fucking should be."

She chews her lip. "Chloe told me that Julie told her that while Jason was still drunk last night, he was telling everyone at the party that my porn star body was wasted on a prude like me and I was a big tease. I'm afraid everyone is talking about me now. So his apology doesn't mean much."

Porn star body? That's it. Jason is going to eat my fist.

"Kenzi, he's an asshole punk who's pissed because he didn't get laid. I bet everyone at the party was equally wasted. No one will even remember this in a few days."

Her blinking watery eyes crush my heart. "I hate that people might be saying bad things about me. I don't bother anyone; I'm nice to everyone. I just stay in my own little bubble. And they always find something to start with me about. First Dad's band, then my mom, then having money, being too quiet, and now this. I can't wait to graduate and get away from all of them."

I stick a bandage over my knuckle, wishing I could put one on what's hurting her, too. "They're immature and jealous, Kenzi. Unfortunately, it won't change much as you get older. There's always going to be people who will treat us badly because they're jealous or just unhappy with their own damn lives. You have to rise above it and do your best to ignore them and focus on your own life and happiness." She gives me a sad little nod. "You're a beautiful girl, Angel. You're smart and you have a great personality. You have an awesome family that loves you, you have Chloe, and you're getting a huge inheritance when you turn twenty-five. You can do whatever you want with your life. You're going to be just fine, trust me."

"What about you?"

I frown at her. "What about me?"

She runs her finger along the edge of the sink, her eyes following it intently. "You said I have my family and Chloe, but you didn't mention you."

"Oh." I rub the back of my neck, unsure of what to say. "I'll always be here for you. But you're getting older now. I'm sure you'll have a boyfriend soon who isn't a dickhead. You'll be doing your modeling and calligraphy and chasing after all your dreams, making new friends...all that stuff. You're not going to be wanting to be hanging around with an old boring guy like me."

"You're not boring, Tor."

"I promised your dad I'd look out for you when your mom had the accident. You won't be needing me around much anymore."

"Oh...I guess you're right."

I ruffle her hair and step out of the bathroom; uncomfortable with the feelings I'm having over not spending as much time with her in the future. Why should it matter? She's just my best friend's kid that I helped take care of.

In my bedroom, I pull off my shirt and toss it at the laundry basket in the corner, and I'm surprised when I turn around to see her standing in the doorway, still with a sad, worried expression in her eyes.

"Don't worry about the idiots at school, Kenzi. Just ignore them. What's left, like two weeks of school?"

"That's not what I'm thinking about." She watches me pull clean clothes out of my dresser and lay them out on my bed.

"Then what's wrong?"

"I never imagined there would be a time when I would see you less. I'll miss you."

"I'll miss you, too, but you can see me anytime you want, or call me. You know where to find me."

"I hope so." She sniffles. "I talked to your mom about continuing to volunteer at the shelter, too. She said she would love it. And I want to keep helping you with your rescues, if you still want me to."

"Of course I do. You can still clean my house after you graduate if you want to, and I'll still pay you. Nothing has to change, Kenzi. I just figured you'd be moving on, wanting to do different things with your life and not hanging around with me all the time."

"I like hanging around with you." The soft tone of her voice, and the way her eyes are roving over my chest is making me feel like all the air has been sucked out of my lungs. My house suddenly feels insanely small and lacking oxygen.

"Then you can. Anytime." I refuse to let my eyes lock with hers. I don't want to see what's there, or what might *not* be there.

"Good."

"Actually, there was something else I wanted to ask you but I was going to talk to Ash about it first. But since we're already talking, I'll just ask you directly. The girl who works the front register at the shop and greets our customers and books appointments is leaving in September."

"Gretchen?"

"Yeah. Her husband is getting transferred to Connecticut, so they're moving. I wanted to ask you if you wanted the job. It doesn't pay much, but you at least know about bikes and you know—"

"Yes. I want to," she says without hesitation, before I can finish. "I would love that."

"You're sure? It's not very exciting."

"I don't care."

"I just kinda feel like you're doing everything for me. The house cleaning, volunteering with my mom, and now this. I don't want you to think I'm turning you into my own personal assistant."

Her tongue slides across her bottom lip. "I don't mind at all. I love all of it."

I tear my eyes off her mouth and walk across my room to open the window. I need air. Lots of it. Badly.

"Okay, then it's settled. Now I'm going to take a shower, grab a quick nap, we'll load the traps, and then I'll take you home. Sound good?"

"Yes, of course. I made lasagna. I just have to put it in the oven when you're ready to eat."

Damn. I figured she would have just blown that idea off, but she really made me dinner. And one of my favorite dishes to boot. When was the last time anyone cooked for me who wasn't my mother? I can't remember.

"That sounds great. Wake me up around four and we'll eat."

"Okay. I'm going to nap on your couch. I'll set the alarm on my phone so we don't end up sleeping till tomorrow." She finally smiles at me, some of the sadness in her eyes fading.

I close my door when she leaves, which I've never done before. When she stayed here when she was little, she would leave the guest room in the middle of the night, drag about ten stuffed animals and her favorite blanket up onto my bed, and sleep on my king-sized bed with me. I'd usually wake up with a teddy bear or two rammed into my back.

I'm worried with her feeling sad she might try to crawl into my bed with me again.

And I'm not sure I wouldn't like it.

CHAPTER 5

Kenzi—age five

Toren—age twenty

"Can we do anything for you, bro?" Asher asks.

I shake my head. "No . . . I just needed to get away from my family."

He puts his hand on my shoulder and squeezes. "Understood. Anything you need, just let us know."

"Thanks."

Ember stands in front of me, concern all over her face. "Tor, please sit. You look like you're going to drop." Dazed, I sit in the chair I always sit in, and she kneels in front of me and pulls off my shoes. "Ash, honey, go get him some water." She smiles up at me as he goes off to the kitchen. "You just need to rest. It's been a long few days; you're exhausted and mentally drained."

Ash comes back with a glass of water and hands it to me. "It's okay to let yourself grieve, Tor. You've been like a fucking rock since it happened."

"My family needs me to be strong for them. I can't fall apart."

"I get that, man. But you need to let yourself feel. Cry if you have to. You're safe here with us, you know that. You can act all tough in front of them, but here you don't have to."

I sip my water slowly. I'm afraid to fall apart. I'm afraid I'll never go back together again.

"We love you," Ember says, having no idea how much her words are killing me.

"I know."

"We're gonna go in the other room and leave you alone for a while. Just yell if you need us."

"Thanks . . . for everything you guys have done for me and my family."

"Tor, don't thank us. You're our best friend. We'd do anything for you."

Closing my eyes, I nod.

A small hand touches mine, and I open my eyes to see Kenzi standing next to the chair, a tiny mirror image of her parents, watching me with grave concern.

Ember tries to pull her away. "Come on, Kenzi, it's time for bed. Uncle Tor needs some time alone."

"No . . ." She climbs up onto my lap and hugs me. "He can't be alone, Mommy."

Asher reaches for her but I stop him. "She can stay. I don't mind."

Ember sighs. "All right, but if she bugs you, just yell down the hall and I'll come get her."

"I will."

I put my glass on the table next to the chair and put my arm around her, comforted by her closeness.

"Uncle Tor?" she whispers when her parents are gone.

"Yeah?"

"Your daddy went to heaven?"

I take a deep breath. "That's right, Angel. He did."

She hugs me tighter. "Don't be sad. We can share my daddy."

I can't help but smile. "Thank you, Kenzi. That's very sweet."

She soon falls asleep against my chest like she always does. The sound of her breathing is calming, and not wanting to wake her prevents me from getting up to raid the liquor cabinet and get drunk off my ass to numb the pain.

My father is gone. I didn't get to say goodbye or thank him for being such a great father and supporting all my dreams.

Dreams that I now have to let go, to take care of his family and his shop. It's what he would want and expect, and I owe him that.

Kenzi stirs and I look down at her peaceful sleeping face. She's a little younger than my sister, Tesla. I should probably be with her, comforting her, telling her everything will be okay, but I don't have it in me to be there for all of them tonight.

Tonight, I just need someone to comfort me for once.

💜 💜 💜

KENZI

His door is closed.

I stand outside it in the hallway, in a state of utter confusion. He's never closed his door before.

Why today?

I have to believe it means something, this suddenly closed door. Is he trying to tell me something? Did I do or say something to make him mad? Have I been too clingy?

Is he drawing a line where there never was one before?

The scent of the lasagna cooking in the oven makes my stomach growl in protest as I stare at the door for a long time, contemplating its meaning.

I knock softly and wait. I don't hear a sound on the other side, so I knock harder. Still nothing. I bang harder.

"Tor?"

I press my ear against the door and the sound of his light snoring is all I can hear.

Screw it.

I open the door and step inside his room, feeling slightly guilty, but that quickly turns into something entirely different when my eyes land on him, lying on top of his white down comforter in nothing but black shorts. I literally freeze midstep and just stare at him, my breath caught in my throat as a swarm of feelings I've never felt before possess me.

I've seen Toren practically every day of my entire life. I've seen him as a teen and I've seen him as a man. I've seen him happy, sad, sick, drunk, behind bars, on a motorcycle, in a truck, grieving, pissed off, loving, playful, and serious. But I've never seen him look like he just fell out of some magical portal of hotness.

I knew he started working out a lot again over the winter, but I had no idea how big and muscular his entire body had become. Or maybe he was always like this? The ink I noticed earlier and tried not to look at spans across his defined abs—words in Gothic script that I can't read from where I'm still frozen, and a portrait of a female warrior takes up most of his torso and rib cage. A black raven covers one of his pecs, its wings seeming to flutter with his breathing.

Inching closer to the bed, I notice his hair is untied and damp, falling across half his face. I desperately want to reach out and push it away because he hates his hair in his face, but a little voice inside me says touching him right now, while he's lying in bed nearly naked, would be crossing a line.

Another new line has mysteriously popped up. I've touched Tor a million times. But today, now, like this...it feels wrong because something about it also feels so right, so needed, so demanded, so naturally instinctive that it shakes me right down to my toes. And that can only mean something really, really good, or really, really bad.

Swallowing, I say his name softly. "Tor?"

He doesn't move or wake.

The man sleeps like the dead.

I gently nudge his shoulder, warm and hard under my hand. "Tor? Wake up."

His eyes open and slowly focus on me, and goose bumps sprinkle across my flesh when he smiles sleepily at me. It feels faintly sensual, knowing I am the first thing he saw when he opened his eyes.

"I'm . . . I'm sorry . . . I knocked but it didn't wake you," I stammer, feeling even more exposed than he is. Can he tell I was looking at him while he was sleeping?

He sits up and stretches his arms over his head, flexing his fingers, and my stomach does the flippies again at the sight of his chiseled chest and abs straining as he arches his back.

"It's okay," he says groggily. "Shit. Something smells great."

"Dinner is ready. If you're hungry?"

"You kidding? I'm starving."

"Well, get up, sleepyhead. I'll go set the table."

I make a quick exit out of his room. He joins me in the kitchen a few minutes later, dressed and much more awake, and throws a pair of purple sweatpants at me.

"What's this for?" I ask.

"To wear when we check the traps after dinner. I don't want you to wear shorts walking in the woods; you might get a tick on you."

"Thank you. Whose are these? Is there a woman without pants running around town?" I joke, not sure I even want to know the answer to that.

"Sydni left them here months ago. She won't mind if you borrow them. You can burn them if you want. I don't want her stuff in my house anymore."

I fold them and put them off to the side. "Duly noted. Let's eat."

He raves over my lasagna, telling me it's just as good as his mom's and he'd love for me to make him dinner on the days I'm here cleaning his house. He'll throw me some more money to cook. I agree, not because I want the money, but because I want to cook for him. I have no idea why I'm so drawn to domestic activities, but

I am, and now I'm incredibly excited about cooking for him a few times a week. My mind starts to churn with meal ideas.

"Hey," I say as I'm cleaning up our dishes after dinner. "After we check on the food stations, do you want to hang out and watch a movie in Dad's theater room? He's not coming home tonight; he's staying in the city meeting with some friends, and I'm still mad at Chloe, so I don't want to see her yet."

"I can't tonight. I have a date with Lisa."

I almost drop the towel I'm drying my hands with. I didn't know he was seeing Lisa again.

"Oh." I try to hide my disappointment behind a smile. "Maybe another time."

"Are you okay to be alone all night?"

"Of course. You know my father and his crazy security system. I'll just read and watch the bunny hop around my room. I'm still kinda tired anyway."

"If I had known you wanted to hang out, I would have told Lisa I couldn't see her."

"Don't be silly. I'll be fine. I want you to have fun on your date. I'm glad you're giving her another chance." I honestly want to be happy for him, but I feel like Lisa doesn't deserve or appreciate him. How could she when she called him cold and uncaring? She clearly doesn't get him at all.

Tor is unusually quiet and distracted when we check on the food traps, and he opts out of our ritual of sitting on the rock and making wishes. I'm disappointed, because I love our little rituals, but I assume he wants to get to his date and I've probably worn out my welcome by now. An unexpected call from me for a ride home has turned into me spending the entire day at his house.

When he brings me home, he insists on walking me inside and then tells me he has to wash his hands before heading back out to meet Lisa because she thinks he smells like motorcycle grease and meat. I've actually always liked the faint smell of motorcycle grease because it's such a part of *him*, but I suppose most women may not feel the same way.

As he leaves, I watch his truck back out of our long driveway before I engage the security system and retreat to my room. As I'm running water for a bath, my phone rings.

"Hi, Dad," I answer. "I'm getting ready to take a bath. Tor just dropped me off."

"I know, he called me. I wanted to say good night and tell you I love you."

I smile into the phone. "I love you, too."

"You okay? I could call Rayne for you and have her stay the night."

"Dad, no. Why does everyone think I need a babysitter? I'm almost eighteen."

"You'll always be a little girl to me, Kenzi. I can't help it."

"I know..."

"I worry about you. That's what fathers do."

"I get it. And it's sweet. I'm going to just chill and read for a while and probably go to bed early. So, what's going on in Boston?"

"Just meeting with a friend who opened a club out here. We're going to have dinner and talk about setting up some shows. I'll be home tomorrow afternoon."

"Okay, I'll be here. Have a good night, Daddy."

"You too, sunshine."

I sit in the bathtub until the water turns cold, and then I let my dwarf rabbit, Snuggles, out of her cage to hop around my room while I sit on the floor with her and read. She's twelve years old, so she doesn't hop around as much as she used to in her younger days, but sometimes she'll get a spurt of energy and bounce around. She mostly just likes to sit on my fuzzy throw rug and stretch out like a little dog. Tor bought her for me when I was only five years old and taught me how to clean her cage, make her fresh salads, and hold her without spooking her. My parents didn't think it was a great idea to bring her with us when I traveled with them, so Tor would bunny-sit for me and I would call him every night and make him let me "talk" to the bunny on the phone. And in typical Tor fashion, he would do it and even tell me what she was "saying" back.

The memory brings a smile to my lips, and speak of the devil, my cell phone buzzes next to me and there's a text from him.

Uncle Tor

I just wanted to check on you.

I'm great. Just invited five guys over for an orgy.

Uncle Tor

Not funny.

I'm okay, just hanging out with Snuggles :-)

Uncle Tor

Aww. Give her a little kiss for me.

LOL I will. Are you still on your date?

Uncle Tor

Yes. Playing pool.

Did she approve of your soft, clean hands? ;-)

Uncle Tor

Barely. She's mad about me ripping my knuckles on that guy's face.

Geez. Isn't she turned on by you beating up bad guys?
That's how it works in all of Gram's books.

Uncle Tor
Apparently not.

Sucks to be you ;-)

Uncle Tor
Thanks. Ok. I'm going now.

LOL good night.

Uncle Tor
'Night, Angel.

CHAPTER 6

Kenzi—age seven

Toren—age twenty-two

I let go of her hand for one second to pay the guy in the ice cream truck, and when I turn around, she's gone. I stare around wildly, trying to find her in the crowded park. She was right next to me a second ago.

"Kenzi!"

My heart pounds faster and my chest tightens when she doesn't come to me. She's nowhere. She's gone.

I run to the other side of the truck, but she's not there.

"Kenzi!" The wind whips my hair into my face and when I shake it back, there she is, standing innocently right in front of me.

"Where were you? You can't do that, Kenzi. You have to stay by me."

She takes the ice cream cone from me and gives it a lick. "I just went over there for a second. There was a man with a cat on a leash."

"I don't care if it was a monkey driving a car. You don't run away from me. Ever. Okay?"

She puts her hand on her hip and rolls her eyes. "Monkeys can't drive, Uncle Tor."

The way she's staring up at me, I swear she can see right into my soul and it rattles the hell out of me.

"You look like you need to sit for a minute and handle your shit," she finally says matter-of-factly.

Fuck. She's been hanging around all of us for way too long. She has the vocabulary of a twenty-year-old.

"Don't say 'shit,' Kenzi. And I'm fine. You just scared me. I thought I lost you."

"You can't ever lose me, Uncle Tor. You're my favorite person in the whole world."

I've never been anyone's favorite anything.

♥ ♥ ♥

TOR

"What are you doing there, handsome?" Lisa sidles up to me, pool stick in her hand, and glances down at the cell phone in my hand.

"Texting my niece."

"The rock star's kid?"

"Yup."

"She's cute."

Nodding, I shove my phone back in my pocket. "Yeah, she is."

She leans closer to me, her breasts pressing against my arm. "You want to head out of here?" Her voice is low, riddled with unspoken but undeniably clear offers.

I search the crowded bar for her friend, whose name I can't remember, and find her making out with some guy in a dark booth near the back of the bar.

"What about your friend?"

She glances over in their direction. "Something tells me she'll be busy for a while. She'll be all right. I'd rather you drive me home."

I put our sticks back on the rack, mulling it over in my mind. The loud music and people yelling to be heard are starting to make my head throb. "Yeah. Let's go."

After paying our tab, I lead her out to my truck, my hand on the small of her back, and she beams at me when I open the passenger door for her.

"I'm glad you came tonight," she says when I get behind the wheel. "I know I've been a little...harsh on you."

"I wouldn't say harsh, Lisa. You're just speaking your mind. Nothing wrong with that."

She lets out a laugh. "I'm kinda known for doing that a little too much."

I throw her a grin. "Trust me, you could be a lot worse."

She tucks her long black hair behind her ear and smiles across the truck at me. "I'll try not to be worse."

"Just be yourself. That's all any of us should be."

I hate when women try to change to be what they think a guy wants. Eventually, they slip and the real them will come crashing through, and it's usually not as good as the person they were pretending to be. I have no time or tolerance for fake people or trying to figure out who they really are.

We talk casually on the drive across town and then sit in silence for a few awkward moments when I pull into her driveway. I'm not good at starting or ending dates. At all.

"I'll walk you to the door," I finally say, and jump out to open her door for her.

"You really have the best manners, Toren," she remarks as she steps out of the truck and takes the arm I'm holding out to her. "Opening doors seems to be a lost art."

"My father taught us how to treat a woman right."

"Well, it shows. I can't remember the last time a man opened a door for me."

"That's pretty sad."

"You have no idea," she agrees.

At her door, she looks up at me expectedly and lays her hand on my shoulder, her finger moving back and forth at the edge of my collar.

"You want to come inside? Have a glass of wine? Or a beer?"

I waver between wanting to fuck out my frustration and wanting to *not* be that kind of guy anymore. She's been giving me the green light all night, so there's no question she wants me. One touch, and I'm pretty sure I can have her melting right through this door and dragging me to her bedroom. And it's tempting, especially after six months and counting of no sex.

"Hmm?" she coaxes, running her hand up to the back of my neck and pulling my lips down to hers.

I let her press my lips to hers for a moment and then slowly pull away. "Not tonight."

Disappointment curves her mouth into a frown and her cheeks redden. She's embarrassed, being turned down, and I feel bad for her.

She takes a deep breath to recover. "Tor, we've dated a bunch of times, and I really like you."

"I like you, too." I chew the inside of my cheek.

"Then I don't understand why you've never done anything more than kiss me. Is there something wrong with me?"

"Fuck no, you're beautiful."

"Then what's the problem?" she asks, glancing down toward my dick. "Is there something wrong with *you*?"

"Fuck no, again."

She leans her back against her front door and makes a face at me like I just landed here from Mars. "Then what the hell is going on? I'm confused."

"Lisa, I was in a relationship for twelve years—"

"You're still in love with her?" she interrupts. "Is that it?"

I shake my head. "No, that's not it at all. I'm just not into casual fucking."

"Casual fucking?" she repeats.

"Yeah...fooling around with no commitment."

"I know what it means, Toren. And if that's the issue, I have no problem committing to you. I'm not seeing anyone else."

Oh shit, no. "Neither am I, but that's not quite what I meant."

"Then what *do* you mean?"

"I mean I don't want to get physically involved unless I'm mentally involved. I'm not lookin' to just get laid, Lisa. I pretty much spent twelve years of my life on someone who couldn't commit to me one hundred percent physically or mentally, and I'm not doing that shit again. She only came around when she wanted me to fuck her silly or she needed something from me. You want to be friends and see where it goes? Then I'm down for that. But I'm not getting my dick or my heart involved until I feel like it's gonna go someplace worthwhile for both of us, in every way."

I'm met with a glazed, unblinking brown-eyed stare. "You're serious?"

"Do I look like I'm joking?"

"No, not at all." She shakes her head slowly, studying my face. "I'm just a little shocked. I mean, come on, Tor. You don't exactly look like the kind of guy who would abstain by your own choice. You practically ooze sex."

"I know." I smirk, half joking. I'm not clueless as to how women look at me.

"Well, I'm not going to lie, I'm surprised but also impressed. I didn't think men like you actually existed." A seductive smile crosses her lips. "But it does make you even more intriguing and more of a catch."

A vision of me in a lake with a fishhook in my mouth comes to mind and it's not how I want to be thought of.

"I don't want to be a catch. I just want to be with someone for the right reasons. And I want them to be with *me* for the right reasons, too. I can't deal with bullshit or games or people who don't know what they want or who can't commit to it when they *do* know."

Her expression softens. "I wasn't expecting such a serious conversation tonight. This is the most you've ever talked about yourself. But since we're being honest...I'm not into games, either. I guess now is the time for me to tell you I'm separated."

Her admission comes out of left field and causes me to take a short involuntary step back.

"You're married?"

"Separated for about a year. The divorce is almost final. It's totally over between us—no lingering feelings at all."

I wonder, how can two people be married and not have any feelings left?

"What happened?" I know I'm picky, but I always pictured myself marrying someone who wasn't someone's ex-wife.

She shrugs and stares off someplace behind me. "We grew apart. We got bored. We stopped wanting it. It just wasn't meant to be."

So much for till death do us part.

"Okay. I'm glad you told me. I had no idea."

"Do you think there's any possibility of us going further? Or am I wasting my time? I don't mind being friends and taking things slow, but I definitely want more than that. I'm not sure I can date you and not get physically or mentally interested."

Who am I to judge what's a waste of someone else's time? If we don't end up screwing or in love, does that constitute a waste? In some ways yes, in some ways no.

"I don't really know. You've already made comments about me

being too quiet and cold, and I know you don't agree with all the things I do. I guess you have to ask yourself if you really do want more. And yeah, I ask myself does this chick like me for me, or because I ooze sex, as you put it?"

"I guess it's a little of both. But in my defense, you're a hard guy to get to know, Tor."

I can't argue with that. "True enough. But I'm trying."

"I can see that you are." She takes a deep breath. "So now that we've talked about all that, can we see each other again? Now that I understand you more?"

"We can. Just as long as we're clear there're no promises."

"That's fine. I don't need promises. But if you get…lonely…I wouldn't say no," she hints, raising her perfect eyebrow up at me.

Lisa just lost a point.

"I surpassed lonely a long time ago, honey. But thanks."

Her cheeks turn crimson. "On that note, I'm going to go inside. But I'd really like to see you again."

"I'll call you." I give her a quick kiss before she unlocks her door and disappears into her house.

Maybe I'm stupid, looking for something I'll never find, and I should've continued this date like a normal guy would have instead of going back home to my empty house and empty bed alone. I just want that magical feeling I wrote about years ago when I used to write the lyrics for the band's rock ballads. I want crazy fucking love. I want someone who'll never let me go. I want to wake up to my best friend every day.

CHAPTER 7

Kenzi—age twelve

Toren—age twenty-seven

"What's wrong?" He's towering over my bed, his faded leather jacket dusty from the ride he just came back from.

I roll over onto my side, away from his stare, and pull my blanket up higher, almost covering my head.

"It's just my stomach."

The side of the bed sinks under the weight of his body as he sits beside me. His hand lightly touches my shoulder.

"Kenzi? Are you sick?"

Another cramp tears through my stomach. I'm pretty sure I'm dying. I want my mom. The last thing I want to do is talk about this with him.

Grinding my teeth, I force myself to answer him. "I'm fine. My stomach just hurts."

"Did you eat something bad? Have you been throwing up?"

"No, Uncle Tor. Go away."

A frustrated sigh comes from behind me. "I'm the only one here, remember? I can't go away. Stop being like this and tell me what's wrong. Do you want me to take you to a doctor? I could call your grandmother…"

"Tor, no. Just leave me alone." I want to cry from the pain in my stomach and the unexplained sorrow and irritability that's taking over my life.

"I'm not leaving. Your parents are gone for two more days, so you're stuck with me unless you want me to call your grandmother."

"Please don't. I don't want to bother her."

Another cramp rips through my uterus and I scrunch myself up further into the fetal position.

He clears his throat. "Do you have your period?" His voice is soft, tentative, and caring, and I want to kick him.

"Oh my God . . . did you seriously just ask me that? Get out of my room."

"It's nothing to be embarrassed about, Kenz. Do you need anything? Have you had this before or . . . ?" His voice fades off awkwardly.

"Just leave me alone!" God. Could my life be any more embarrassing?

The sound of his boots thudding along my carpet and down the hall is a relief. Good. Now I can suffer in peace. I'm furious with my parents right now for being gone all the time and not being here when I'm having some kind of crisis. It's not fair.

A few minutes later, he's back in my room and throws a small pink bag on the bed. I peer into it to see a bunch of tampons and napkins. I rally between throwing up and crawling under the bed for the rest of my life. My dad's best friend just touched period stuff. There must be some kind of law against this.

"I got those from your mom's bathroom. Since you won't answer me, I hope you know how to use them because that goes way beyond my realm of responsibility."

I think I grow fangs when I glare up at him. "I hate you right now. I want to die." I pull the blanket over my head.

He tugs the blanket back down off my head. "Hate me all you want, I don't fucking care. I got you all this, too. Be glad I know where your parents keep everything in this place." A pile of stuff lands on my bed. A bottle of Midol, a heating pad, and a chocolate bar.

I start to cry. "Please go away. You're not supposed to know this stuff!"

He rubs his forehead and shoves his hand through his long hair. "I've lived with women, Kenzi. I know about this stuff, and it's nothing to be ashamed of. It's part of life and being an adult."

I try to burrow into my pillow. "I don't want to be an adult. It hurts."

He laughs. "No shit."

"Fuck all this."

"It doesn't get any easier, Angel."

"I hate you."

He leans down and kisses my messy head. "No, you don't. And I love you no matter how evil you try to act." He straightens up. "I'll be downstairs if you need me or want to hurl more obscenities at me. I kinda like it."

I smile behind the blanket as he walks toward my door.

"Uncle Tor?"

Halting, he turns back. "Yeah?"

"Thank you."

He winks at me and finally leaves me alone to wallow in my feelings of yuck.

I decide right there that even though I yelled at him like a raging bitch, he's pretty much the coolest guy in the world.

KENZI

After a shitty week at school and sitting in my bedroom every night immersing myself in a book trying to forget the outside world exists, I'm glad tonight is bonfire night at our house. I need to be around some humans who aren't high school asshole bitches.

"Kenzi!" Rayne yells as soon as she sees me come out of the house and onto the back deck.

Grabbing a soda first, I make my way across the yard, past small groups of chatting people to where she's standing with a guy I've never met but looks vaguely familiar. Rayne is gorgeous as ever, her long hair recently dyed black with purple and blond highlights and the start of a light golden tan touching her skin.

Her winged eyeliner is perfect and on point, enhancing her feline green eyes.

"I want you to meet Sailor," she says, smiling from ear to ear. "He's a local guitarist. This is Asher's daughter, Kenzi."

"Nice to meet you," he says. "I've been friends with your dad for a while. He's an amazing mentor."

"Hi…and thank you. He's pretty great." Sailor is too cute for words with wavy brown hair that touches his shoulders, eyes the color of the sea, and an adorable smile that reminds me of a five-year-old boy who got caught doing something naughty. He looks like 1992 Eddie Vedder.

"Are you a musician, too?" he inquires.

I shake my head with a laugh. Everyone asks me that once they realize who I am. "No…sadly that talent seems to have skipped me in this family."

"She models," Rayne adds. "And she does this amazing calligraphy. She wrote the words tattooed on my back in calligraphy for me, and my artist copied it. And she wrote the lettering for the title on my brother's last CD."

Sailor makes an impressed face and his smile widens, showing off his perfect white teeth. "Wow. I didn't think anyone wrote in calligraphy anymore."

My smile agrees with him. "Exactly. It's kinda useless, I guess. I just like the way it looks. I love paper and ink."

He tilts his head, his eyes squinting just a bit, and I think both Rayne and I drool a little. "I think it's incredibly cool. Not useless at all. I'm sure there are a lot of people who would want that. I love the tattoo idea. I may just hit you up on that myself."

"That would be awesome." I wonder if he and Rayne are dating or if she called me over here in an attempt to set us up. I can't say I mind if that's her plan, especially after the disaster with Jason.

My question is answered by Rayne's attention zeroing in elsewhere. "Tristan is here. I haven't seen him in a while." She gestures over to a group of people across the yard, where Tristan is hanging out with Tor. "Is he single now?"

Hmm. So she's hawking on Tor's brother. "I'm not sure," I reply. "I see him at the shop all the time but I've never seen him with a girl."

Rayne continues to stare, her green eyes sparkly with interest. "He's hot as hell just like the rest of that clan. Find out for me, Kenzi. Tor will tell you anything."

"Okay . . . I guess I could ask him."

Sailor laughs. "Why don't you just go talk to him? Don't make her do your dirty work."

Rayne playfully smacks him on the arm. "You be quiet. I'm too shy to just walk up to him."

"You've known him forever. It's not like he's a stranger," I remind her.

"I know . . . but I haven't seen him in about two years. He probably won't even remember me."

Sailor and I exchange a glance and smile. There's no way Tristan won't recognize her. She's not the kind of girl who's easily forgettable, even though she's oblivious to it.

Rayne grabs Sailor's hand, diverting his attention from me. "Let's go get some food. My brother makes a mean burger. You want to come, Kenzi?"

"No, I'm good," I reply. "Nice meeting you, Sailor."

"You too. I'm sure I'll be seeing you around."

I nod hopefully as Rayne drags him up to the patio where my dad is manning the grill. After the stress of dealing with rumors about prom night all week at school, I still have no appetite for food. My stomach has been in knots from dealing with the whispers and judgmental glances.

I cross the yard and sit on a bench overlooking a stone water fountain my dad had installed last summer after I told him I love the sound of water. It's right below my bedroom window, and being able to hear it when my windows are open is incredibly soothing. My father has always tried to create a calm, quiet, almost Zen-like atmosphere for us, which is odd considering he's in a loud rock band and immersed in noise of some sort most of the time.

"I hope you wore that because you remembered."

His voice startles me, and at first I can barely see him leaning against a tree about five feet away.

"Huh?"

He nods his head up and shifts his eyes to my head. "The hat."

Oh yeah. My hand reaches up to touch the black beanie covering my head. I did remember, actually, that he said he wanted it, but I was expecting him to forget all about that conversation. Apparently, he didn't. My heart twinges.

"Come over here, Angel." His voice is transformed by the dusky night, familiar but tinged with a deeper, gravelly tone that makes my legs wobbly as I stand and walk over to him.

"What are you doing over here in the trees?"

"Watching you. You say you like being around everyone on bonfire night, but you always end up sitting off by yourself."

"So do you."

He smiles. "Guilty as charged."

What we don't say is we usually end up sitting alone together, one of us eventually going to the other.

"I came to get the hat you owe me for all the stuff of mine you've taken. Hand it over," he says playfully.

"It doesn't work that way. You have to take it yourself."

"Fair enough." He steps toward me and when he takes the knit beanie off my head, a halo of staticky hair surrounds my face. His signature snarly but sexy grin takes over his face as he pulls my hat over his dark messy hair, which I've just noticed is not in a ponytail tonight, and I want to believe he left it loose for me.

"How do I look?"

He looks less like the man I've known my entire life and more like a dangerous stranger with eyes and a smile that could melt a glacier in two seconds flat.

"It looks good on you."

Cocking his head, he frowns like he doesn't believe me. "You hesitated before you answered. What was your first thought? Spit it out."

"That you look hot as fucking hell." The words tumble out of my mouth before I can stop them, and we stand there as he takes them in and I try to wish them back. *Oops.*

He coughs into his fist. "Well. I wasn't expecting that."

Me either.

I swallow hard over the anxiety that's suddenly bubbling up inside me.

"You were right, though," I say nervously. "You can definitely rock a purple heart."

"I told you I could." His hands capture my head and smooth down my flyaway hair. "I made your hair all messy."

"Is Tristan single?" I blurt out, attempting to distract myself from how his fingers feel in my hair, strong and electrifying.

"Tristan? Why would you want to know that?"

"Rayne was asking. She saw him with you earlier."

He shoves his hands into his front pockets. "I think he is... but I thought she came here with Drifter."

"Sailor," I correct. "And she did but I think she was trying to set us up. They must just be friends."

I notice him biting the inside of his cheek as he contemplates this. "Your dad doesn't want you to date musicians."

Here we go again. "Jason turned out to be an epic asshole, so maybe a musician would be better after all."

He rocks on his heels. "Maybe. You won't get that picture-perfect little life you said you wanted with a musician. With the kids and the dogs and the dinners."

"Jesus, Tor. I'm talking about dating, not marriage. I just want to have some fun like everyone else. He's really cute."

"Just be careful. He's older than you, probably has lots of experience...I don't want you to get hurt again."

I shake my head and step away from him, heading back to my bench. "Why do you always have to switch back into uncle mode?"

"What's wrong with that?" he asks, following me. "I worry about you."

Why is everyone always worried about me? Do they think I'm going to spontaneously combust someday?

"Well, don't. I just want you to be my friend."

"Aren't I?"

"Yeah...mostly. I think."

He touches my arm and I turn to face him. "I'm always your friend, Kenzi. Not mostly. Always."

I've wondered about that a lot lately, especially since he mentioned us not seeing each other as much once I graduate, like his work with me was done. That's been slowly eating at me, planting seeds of doubt.

"Are you?" I ask. "Or do you just hang out with me and give me things to do as a favor to my parents?"

"Why are you being so moody? You've never doubted me before."

"I don't know," I admit. "I guess I'm just nervous about

graduating and things changing. And I've had a shit week with the kids at school calling me a slutty prude."

"Slutty prude?" he repeats. "How is that even a thing?"

I throw my hands up. "I have no idea! Leave it to me to create some new form of loser. It's been total hell."

"Let's sit." He leads me to the bench and I fall onto it with a big sigh of frustration. "I know it's hard growing up, Kenz. Change can suck, but it can be good, too. You've had a rough couple years."

"That's an understatement."

"And fuck those idiots at your school. They don't know you."

"I guess…"

"I just want you to be happy." He says it like it should be so simple.

"I'm trying to be. Life just keeps getting in my way."

We watch the water splash in the fountain for a few minutes, and then he digs into his front jeans pocket.

"Here." He holds his hand out to me and drops a penny into my hand. "We can make wishes here in your fountain," he says.

"I never thought of that." My smile returns. "You go first."

He cocks his head as he thinks for a moment; then he tosses his penny into the water.

I watch the shiny copper coin sink to the bottom of the fountain. "Okay…tell me what you wished for."

"I wished you would never doubt me again. I've spent almost eighteen years being here for you, Angel. Because I *want* to. No one ever made me or expected me to. You're just where I always wanted to be."

My heart nearly stops.

I close my eyes for a long moment as his words echo through me, bouncing off the walls of my soul before settling into my heart, where they'll live forever.

"Tor..."

"Don't." His voice is low, a subtle warning. "Just make your wish."

My hand shakes as I throw my penny. I miss, and it lands in the grass somewhere, lost in the dark.

"Shit," I mutter. My wish lies in the lawn someplace, unspoken. And maybe that's for the best right now.

"I'll get it."

I can't take my eyes from him as he kneels over in the dark, hunting for my penny like it's a buried treasure. His inked arm flexes with hard muscle as he runs his hand through the grass, and my insides flutter in response. I shouldn't be looking at him this way, or thinking of him this way, but I can't tear my attention from him.

You're where I always wanted to be.

It was obvious he didn't want to say those words. But something inside him made him say it, like he *had* to say it, like they were eating at him, threatening him to let them out. The taboo of what could be hiding in the depths of him awakens a part of me that feels like it's been waiting, patiently, silently for him to come.

Warmth starts in my stomach and spreads like a slow fire, down between my thighs and up to my chest. My pulse speeds up as I watch him, my head becoming light.

I can't think.

I should be scared. I should recognize this as wrong. I should go inside.

But I'm not, and I don't, and I can't, because he suddenly looks over at me and smiles, holding my lost penny up triumphantly like my eternal hero, and it chases all those doubts away, leaving the truth staring me right in the face.

We are an us.

CHAPTER 8

Kenzi—age five

Toren—age twenty

My little sister leans over the princess-shaped cake with a big smile and blows out her seven candles. Mom's dining room is filled with people—my aunts, uncles, cousins, and brothers, and a few little kids from Tesla's class. It's been six months since my father passed away, and this is the first I've seen most of the people in this room smile in a long time. Including myself.

Tessie starts to open her presents, with Kenzi sitting at her side, taking the discarded wrapping paper from her and shoving it in a big garbage bag, always the little neat freak. I wink at her across the room, and she waves at me.

"Tesla seems better," I say to my mom when I bring some plates into the kitchen to help her clean up.

"She's doing much better, but she still cries at night sometimes. She misses him a lot."

"I know," I agree softly. "We all do."

I help her load the dishwasher. "We should be going soon. Sydni has a class in the morning, and I have to get Kenzi to kindergarten on time for once."

"You two are babysitting again?" she asks with a slight emphasis on the "again."

"Yeah, just for a few days."

"It's nice you and Sydni help out so much." She wipes her hands on a dish towel and folds it neatly before putting it back on the counter.

"We don't mind. She's a good kid, like Tessie."

"Toren...," she starts, and then stops for a moment. "I'm going to ask you something, and I just want you to tell me the truth. I'm your mother, and I love you. I won't judge you."

I raise my eyebrows and take a step back. "Whoa, Mom. That sounds heavy."

"Is she yours?"

I stare at her in shock, the smile fading from my face. "What?"

"Just answer me. Is that my granddaughter in there?"

"Shit, Mom. Is that what you think?"

"She looks like you..."

"I look like him. Everyone says we look like brothers. Even you said it when we were young. We've always looked alike."

She nods. "Yes...that's true."

Her eyes bore into me, waiting.

"I can't believe you're asking me this after all these years, Mom. You really think I'd let someone else raise my own kid?"

"She's with you all the time."

"Because her family is never around. They're all wrapped up in their own shit, being famous people. She can't live out of a damn suitcase all the time. She needs some stability sometimes, and she likes staying with me. They're our best friends. What's the big deal?"

"It's not a big deal, hon. Your devotion to her is sweet. You're a good friend to them. I just wondered if there was more to it than you just doing your friends a favor."

I shake my head, my hair falling into my face. I push it away with annoyance. She could have been mine, if I hadn't introduced my best friend to the girl I was crazy about but too shy to ask out.

"No, Mom. She's not mine. I've never slept with Ember."

♥ ♥ ♥

TOR

My fourth beer goes down too fast. I'm itching for another but I know if I keep drinking I won't stop. I sure as hell don't want to be drunk tonight. I've already proved I can't control my mouth sober, so there's no telling what I'll say if I get wasted off my ass.

I'm doing a good job of pretending to have a conversation with this girl named Heather, but my eyes keep drifting back to Kenzi, who's talking to Sailor on the other side of the property, but she also keeps looking over at me and quickly looking away when I catch her.

The wish she made after I found her penny in the grass earlier keeps echoing in my head.

"I wish you weren't who you are . . . ," she'd whispered.

We laughed at it awkwardly, trying to make something funny that wasn't, and then I made an equally riddling joke about it before I forced myself to get away from her, running to the nearest good-looking woman at the party, like that was going to cover up what just happened.

I think I knew what Kenzi was trying to say with her wish, though, and I don't like it.

That's a fucking lie. I like it a lot.

I'm pretty sure she's got a crush on me. Lots of Tessie's friends flirted with me when they were in high school. They giggled at me, said crazy things to me, paraded around trying to make me notice them, and then giggled some more. It's the same thing and normal for girls her age. *That's all it is.*

My own feelings, however, are completely not normal. In any way. I shouldn't be flirting back with her. Or feeling all fucking giddy stupid over her hat on my head. But I do. I might never take this thing off.

"I'd love to go for a ride on your bike someday," Heather is saying. I've known her for a while, and she says this every time we talk, even though I continue to never call her.

"Sure... when I get a free day, we'll go for a ride." I say the lie well. It sounds legit.

It's my canned reply when a woman thinks she's just going to hop on the back of my ride like I'm some kind of pony. I like to ride alone. If I ever stick a woman on the back of my bike, there's a good reason for her to be back there.

Kenzi's laugh floats across the yard, even over the acoustic music Asher and his friends are playing. I can tell she likes Sailor, and judging from the attention he's giving her, he feels the same, which is no surprise. I'm not normally the jealous type, but I can feel a shade of green coming over me.

Sailor is me twelve years ago. A young, good-looking musician on the cusp of a kick-ass music career. I've heard him play, and he's good. His riffs are fast, furious, and flawless. *Like I once was.*

Now my fingers fly over wrenches. And the occasional text message.

What I really want and need is my fingers on the warm flesh of a woman. This self-imposed celibacy is making me question my own sanity. Shutting out Kenzi's laughter, I focus on Heather like I should be doing. She's telling me she's a fitness instructor now, and it shows. Her body is tight, lean, and lacking the curves I prefer, but she's very easy on the eyes and hasn't shown any signs of being a psycho freak yet. Always a plus.

I'm not surprised when she reaches toward me and lifts my shirt, her eyes widening in appreciation as she takes in my abs. When you have lots of muscles and ink and hair that's longer than the norm, people think they can touch you. Pet you. Like it's okay.

"Wow, Toren. You've been hitting the gym hard. I noticed a difference as soon as I saw you tonight. Are you fighting again?"

Raising my beer to my mouth, I shake my head before taking a drink. "No, I'm done with that. Just been working out a lot."

She nods and licks her glossy lips. "It shows. Abs and eyes are my favorite parts of a man."

I grin at her. "I'll keep that in mind."

"I hope you do." Her smile is sexy and inviting, and I wonder how I always seem to get here. I only wanted a conversation.

I consider taking her home and breaking my sexual leave of absence. A long night with her would put me out of this self-imposed misery and maybe I'll stop reading nonexistent signs from my best friend's seventeen-year-old daughter.

Heather runs her finger along the waistband of my jeans, her fingernail grazing over my skin. "I don't have anywhere to be tomorrow," she hints.

My stomach muscles twitch under her touch, begging for more. My body isn't exactly on the same page as my brain.

"Is that right?"

Her hand slides a bit farther into my pants. "I'll do all the work," she coos. "You can just lie there and enjoy the ride."

I grab her hand and pull it out of my jeans. "That's not how I like it, sweetheart."

"How *do* you like it?"

"Not easy."

I'm not sure if she gets the double meaning of my answer, but she tries one more time.

"I don't mind it rough."

Most women say that without having any idea what they're

asking for. Cheap sheets are rough. An unpaved road is rough. A slap on the ass, some handcuffs, a hard pounding—that's not rough. That's fun.

I can feel Kenzi's eyes on me without even having to look over at her, and I wonder if she saw Heather attempting to do a cock dive into my jeans.

"I'm on a break," I finally say.

"A what?"

"A break," I repeat, finishing my beer. I want to go home. Alone. Heather might be fun for a few hours, but in the morning, I'd have to find a way to get rid of her and not see her again. I don't want to be a douche like that.

"What does that mean, exactly?"

"It means my dick is on a vacation."

Heather scratches her head and looks around us, trying to find someone else to do *all the work on*, most likely. "Well...that's a new one, and I think I'll pass on asking for the details of what that might mean and why. Have a good one, Toren."

As I watch her practically run away from me, I wonder what the hell I'm doing to myself. I'm on a path to sure social suicide.

CHAPTER 9

Kenzi—age ten

Toren—age twenty-five (in jail for assault)

Dear Uncle Tor,

I miss you and hope you come home soon. Daddy said I can write to you every week. I'm using the special pen and ink you gave me.

I am cleaning the bunny cage every Saturday just like I promised.

I threw a penny in a puddle and wished you to be back, but it didn't work. I think it only works with deeper waters.

Don't forget me while you are gone.

I love you the most,
Kenzi

♥ ♥ ♥

Dear Kenzi,

I'll be home soon, I promise. Your writing is beautiful, and the parchment paper was very nice. A letter from you every week would make me happy. I'm sorry I'm not there to help you with Snuggles. I'll be back in a few months. Save some pennies for when I get there and we'll make wishes together. I don't think puddles will work, but thanks for trying.

I could never forget you, Angel.
Be good for Mommy and Daddy.

I love you forever and longer,
Uncle Tor

♥ ♥ ♥

KENZI

I always thought the last day of school would be exciting and I'd walk out the school doors for the last time with a huge smile, hugging Chloe, and we'd race off to get Frappuccinos to discuss our plans for an amazing summer together.

But instead, I'm standing under a tree on the front lawn of the school with my hoodie over my head, alone, in the rain. Chloe took off with Brendan to celebrate, and now I don't have a ride home. Six miles is going to feel like twelve in this weather if I walk.

I call my father on his mobile, but it goes straight to voice mail. I frown, vaguely remembering him telling me he was going to the city today for a grief-counseling meetup.

Rayne is working, so she won't be able to come get me. I quickly flip through my contacts on my cell phone. I have Sailor's number saved, but I don't know him well enough to beg for a ride and I don't want him to see me looking like a gutter rat. Aunt Sydni isn't good at last-minute plans and probably isn't even awake yet. I don't want to bother any of my dad's brothers, as they're all usually pretty busy.

I hit Tor's number, and he picks up on the second ring.

"Hey, you. Happy last day."

"Thanks. I seem to be without a ride home. What a great way for me to launch into adulting."

"You're in luck. I'm in the truck on my way to pick up a stray. I'll grab you first if you don't mind coming with me?"

"Not at all. Now you can pick up two strays. I'm out front."

Ten minutes later, he pulls in front of the school, and I climb into his truck wearing a big grateful smile.

"You're a lifesaver." I lean across the front seat to kiss his cheek. "I'm talking to Dad tonight about getting a car. This is stupid."

"Truth. Ask for something cool, like a Mustang. Or a Corvette."

"I'll take anything with four wheels and a roof at this point."

"Be careful or he'll get you a golf cart."

Laughing, I run my fingers through my damp hair, which is starting to frizz. "So, where are we going?"

"I just got a call about a dog on the highway; they said he almost got hit a few times."

"On the highway? Where? How are you even going to find him?"

He makes a left turn and turns the radio off. "They gave me a mile marker. They said he's not moving, just huddled up against the cement divider."

This doesn't sound like it's going to go well. "Oh no. Tor, he's probably hurt."

Nodding, he pulls the truck onto the onramp of the highway. "Can you climb in back and find one of my leashes? And there's some treats back there; I'll need those."

I lean over the seat into the back and find everything he mentioned and then spread an old blanket over the back seat. The dog's paws and coat will be wet from the rain and I don't want Tor's truck to get all muddy. I grab an old towel so we can dry the dog off.

"There he is."

I turn back into my seat as he pulls the truck over onto the bumpy shoulder of the highway and throws it in park. He grabs the leash and the treats, shoving a handful into his pocket, and we both stare across the two-lane busy road at the large off-white dog who's got himself smashed up against the divider, his uncontrollable shaking visible from here.

Tor turns his attention to me. "Kenzi, listen to me. I want you to stay right here. No matter what, do *not* try to follow me onto that highway, okay?"

I look at him, to the dog on the other side of all that traffic, and then back at him. "Tor, you're scaring me. This is dangerous. It's pouring rain."

"I can't leave him there. He'll get killed."

"So could you," I point out. It's raining and foggy, and the cars are flying past us nonstop. He's crazy if he thinks he's going to reach that dog.

"I'll be fine. If one of these assholes hits me, call nine-one-one and stay in this truck."

My heart seizes at his words. How can he say he'll be fine and then talk about calling 911 all in the same breath?

"What? Tor, maybe you should let animal control come. Let's just wait here for them."

"And do what? Watch that poor dog scared out of its mind in the middle of a four-lane highway? It'll take AC too long to get here. I'm here now."

"I know, but—"

He interrupts me, not hearing any of it. "Don't worry. Stay here and wait for me."

Before I can say anything else, he's jumped out of the truck and is standing on the edge of the road, waiting for a gap in the traffic. I gasp when he runs across the first lane and then he's forced to stop right in the middle of the two lanes, to wait for another break in the traffic. Cars continue to fly by him, blaring their horns. I hold my breath as he makes another mad dash across the next lane and ends up about ten feet behind the dog. My hand clutches my phone, ready to dial 911 immediately if anything happens to him.

The shivering dog peers behind him warily and starts to belly-crawl farther away, obviously petrified of not only the cars and trucks whizzing by but also by the very large stranger creeping up behind him. Tor crouches to his knees and holds out his hand, offering treats, his lips moving. I know he's talking softly to the dog, attempting to gain the tiniest amount of trust. Animals can always sense he's a good person and they warm up to him quickly, but between the downpour and the traffic, the dog looks like it's on the verge of mania.

Tor inches closer, and the dog's ears perk up with a slight amount of interest. The leash is grasped in Tor's other hand at his side, the end in a noose-style loop so he can throw it quickly over the dog's head.

"Please stay, please stay," I whisper in desperation as Toren moves slowly closer to the dog, just inches from being able to pet him, when an eighteen-wheeler flies by, spooking the dog.

My body goes cold with fear as I watch the dog stand and attempt to move farther away from Tor, dragging one of its back legs, its eyes wild and darting from the stranger creeping up on him to the busy road. The feeling of entrapment is bringing on a fight-or-flight reaction. Obviously the dog got where he is by running through cars, and he's thinking about doing it again.

Tor moves closer, and the dog suddenly lurches into traffic, attempting to run away. Cars honk and swerve and the dog freezes—right in the middle of the fast lane. My heart jumps into my throat as Tor dives at the dog, landing on top of him, then scoops him up into his arms and somehow manages to get both of them out of oncoming traffic.

"Oh my God." Tears stream down my cheeks as I watch,

completely stricken with panic as Tor stands between the lanes, the huge dog in his arms, trying to cross back to the shoulder where I'm waiting.

I can't take this anymore. I leave the truck and run out to the edge of the highway and wave my arms at the oncoming traffic, trying to get the cars to slow down or stop. Why does no one care or stop to help? Can't they see a person is standing in the middle of the highway with an injured dog?

No one stops.

My tears mix with the rain as I stand there helplessly, begging cars to slow down.

Finally, there's about two car lengths of space in the traffic and Tor runs toward me, kneeling to the ground with the dog as soon as he reaches the side of the road next to his truck. I fall to my knees with him and grab the leash from his hand, looping it over the dog's huge furry neck.

"You're insane," I scold with relief and frustration, wiping at the tears on my face.

"Hey, my insanity just saved this dog."

"Is your leg okay?" His jeans are ripped at the knee from skidding across the wet pavement and blood has started to seep into the edge of the fabric. "I was so scared something was going to happen to you," I say shakily, but he's ignoring his own injury, checking the dog instead, gently running his hands over the dog's trembling body and down its legs.

"I'm fine, Angel."

As he checks over the dog, I notice blood on his hand and grab it, turning it over in my own. The flesh of his palm is torn up with road rash from when he jumped for the dog.

"You're bleeding." My voice cracks as I choke back new tears and dab at his hand with the sleeve of my sweatshirt.

His hand closes over mine on top of the big furry dog's back, and his gaze drifts from our joined hands, up to my face. For the first time, I don't recognize the deep, dark eyes staring into mine, but I fall right into them willingly as our lips meet. My eyes flutter closed as I tumble farther into him, but he quickly jerks away, and we simultaneously suck in a startled breath, staring at each other with wide-eyed shock.

Dropping my hand, he grabs the back of my neck, yanking my mouth back to his hungrily, and I clutch his arm to keep from falling backward onto my ass. His lips are warm and demanding, his tongue pushing past my teeth, coaxing my mouth open. My heartbeats turn into soaring butterflies. *Nothing has ever felt like this.* He steals my breath, making me dizzy as his mouth claims mine, his fingers tightening at the back of my neck. I tilt my head slightly to deepen the kiss, and a low, guttural growl sounds in his throat, turning my sweet butterflies into fireflies and sparking heat from my stomach to my thighs. He pulls away slightly, stares into my eyes with a lusty gaze, then comes back for more, his kiss much softer now, his hand moving from my neck to gently touch my damp cheek. My body and heart reel from his sudden shift from fierce demand in one moment to soft and loving the next.

The scared dog moves between us, breaking the spell. Tor lets go, pulling away from me, his eyes darker, wilder, and avoiding mine.

Oh shit.

Oh shit.

He clears his throat and grabs the dog's leash again before he stands.

"Let's get him in the back of the truck and to the emergency vet. I'm pretty sure his leg is broken." Fake normalcy courses through his words, trying to erase the last ten seconds, but the shaking of his hand as he holds the leash totally betrays his efforts.

Dazed, I quietly help him maneuver the large dog into the back seat, where he's calmer now, tail wagging slightly as we talk softly to him and wipe him down with the old towel. He looks like a polar bear with his thick white fur and jet-black eyes and nose.

We're both soaking wet as we climb into the front seat, and I'm still trembling from head to toe from the anxiety of watching Tor cross that busy highway coupled with what just happened between us.

Did that really happen?

That couldn't have happened. I must have blacked out or had a delusional episode.

Nervously, I peek over at him, but his eyes are glued to the road as he pulls out onto the busy highway. I gulp some air and shove my hands into the front pocket of my hoodie.

"Tor...?" I whisper.

He shakes his head, fast, as if he's trying to deny hearing my voice, then takes a few deep breaths, like he's about to be sick or pass out.

"Check the dog," he says softly. "Please."

I climb over the front seat and settle myself in the back next to the dog, who immediately lays his head on my lap and whimpers when he tries to move his body closer to me. If not so wet and dirty, he would be a beautiful animal and I hope he's not hurt too badly inside. Even though he's scared and in pain, he's friendly, soaking up the attention I'm lavishing on him. He's most likely someone's lost family dog; he's way too pretty and sweet to be a stray. I pet him softly and tell him how brave he is and how he's going to be okay, and his tail thumps a few times while he licks my hand. When I look up, I catch Tor watching me in the rearview mirror. My heart immediately starts to beat faster in response, my lips tingling at the memory of his on mine. I'm disappointed when he quickly averts his eyes from mine and back to the road.

He kissed me.

Tor kissed me.

I keep chanting it over and over in my head, weighing the reality of it, as half of me believes it was a hallucination and the other half believes it was indeed very real.

After we take the dog to the animal hospital and wait for him to be admitted, Tor drives me home. Wordlessly. It's clear he's uncomfortable, and I'm confused, unsure what to do or say. Shouldn't we talk about what happened?

What *did* happen?

"Tor...should we...talk, maybe?" I ask tentatively.

His body goes rigid, his jaw clenches, and several incredibly long moments drag on before he finally speaks.

"I'm sorry."

Sorry? Those words could mean anything, and everything—but I haven't a clue what he wants them to mean.

I start to speak, but he puts his hand up, stopping me. "Please, Kenzi. I can't."

The torturous tone of his voice shreds my insides, rendering me utterly speechless and even more confused. I've never seen him like this before. All I want to do is reach out to him, make him talk to me like we always do, but he's making it very clear that he *can't*. Or won't. He's put a wall up, and I don't know if I'm supposed to knock it down or let it stay there. Some walls need to be taken down to get to a resolution. But other walls...those walls have to stay up to protect us.

When he drops me off at home, I jump out of his truck without so much as a goodbye. I go straight up to my room, grateful that my father isn't home yet because I don't want to see or talk to anyone right now. I need to be alone with my feelings and try to calm my racing thoughts and shaking insides.

Everything's suddenly been turned upside down.

He kissed me.

A real kiss, with passion and desire.

He growled at me.

A feral, lusty sound that I can still hear. And I want more.

A lot more.

CHAPTER 10

Kenzi—age thirteen

Toren—age twenty-eight

It's a beautiful, warm spring day as I ride my bicycle to his house. My basket is filled with milk, bread, some cans of soup, orange juice, and chocolate chip cookies because they're his favorite.

I frown with worry when I see his truck in the driveway because it's Wednesday afternoon and he should be at the shop working. After letting myself in with my key, I empty the shopping bag onto the counter and throw out the old food in his fridge before I put the new groceries in.

"Uncle Tor?" I call down the hall. "I'm here. It's my cleaning day."

He doesn't answer. I quickly check out the door to his backyard and his bedroom turns up empty, but his bathroom door is partly closed.

"Tor?" I hesitate before I push the door farther open, and it hits his body, which is sprawled out on the bathroom floor. My heart slams into my throat as I kneel down next to him on the tile. Relief washes over me when I see his chest moving up and down. He's not dead.

"Tor!" I shake him harder than I should and he mumbles and grumbles at me. The stench of alcohol coming off him is overpowering.

"You're drunk," I observe, disgusted. "Get off the floor. You're lying in your own puke."

I want to be sick myself seeing him this way, wasted on the floor. This is not the man I grew up adoring.

He grabs on to my leg. "You're such a good kid, Kenzi," he slurs.

"You're a mess."

He rolls over, away from me. "I'll never be good enough."

Grabbing his arm, I try to tug him up, but he's way too heavy for me. "I don't know what you're babbling about, but you're getting off this floor and taking a shower. Now."

I manage to heave him up into a sitting position and he slumps against the wall, trying to focus on me. His eyes are bloodshot, his hair a mess, and he's gone at least a week without shaving.

"You're the only one who really loves me, Angel," he says sadly.

Turning the shower on, I pull the curtain closed so the floor doesn't get drenched.

"That's not true at all. Get your ass in that shower and then into bed so I can clean this mess you made. If I catch you like this again, I'm telling my father. We're not going to let you do this to yourself."

💗 💗 💗

TOR

She hauled ass out of my truck like a cyclone and slammed the door so hard behind her I'm surprised the airbag didn't blow.

Fuck.

Fuck. Fuck. Fuck.

I fucked up huge.

I've fucked up a lot in my life. And that, my friends, was the biggest fuckup ever.

I've been sitting on my couch for over an hour, in complete darkness and silence, volleying between wanting to get drunk off my ass on some hardcore liquor, calling up Sydni or Lisa and screwing the shit out of them to make myself forget what I just did, or puking my guts out. But what I really want to do is call her and hear her voice. Or better yet, see her again. After what happened, I have an intense need to know if I've affected her. Will her voice sound shaky and nervous or will it have that new wistfulness I've caught glimpses of in the past few weeks? Is she hiding in her room like I am, ashamed and confused? Or is she lying on her bed wearing one of my many shirts, with rainbow fuzzy socks on her feet, a faint smile on her lips, thinking about me? Possibly wanting me?

Fuck me. *I want to kiss her again.*

Kenzi.

My niece-by-association. My best friend's daughter. My little partner in crime for the past seventeen years.

I kissed her like a deranged animal and she *let* me. In fact, it felt an awful lot like she enjoyed it.

She welcomed it.

I lean my head into my hands and push my fingers into my skull.

No, asshole. She didn't want it. She couldn't want it. You scared the shit out of her. She's just a kid.

It was an accident, conjured up by the emotions of the situation. She was scared after watching me running through traffic and I was high on adrenaline and it all created some wacked-out reaction between us. That's all it was.

Nothing else.

Nothing. Else.

I stand and pace the dark room like a caged bear. What if she tells Asher? He'll fucking kill me. And if he does? I deserve it. *I'll let him kill me.* I won't even fight back.

She won't tell him, though. She would talk to me first. Which she tried to do, and I wouldn't let her. *I couldn't.* Because I'm a douche, just like Sydni and Lisa told me I was. I don't communicate. And here's a big reminder of how true that is staring me right in the face.

There's a bottle of whiskey hidden in my closet in case of emergencies and major fuckups like this. My skin is crawling with the intense need to drink the entire thing and pass out cold to forget what I did.

Instead, I yank my phone out of my back pocket and hover my finger over the keyboard. I can't avoid her like I've done to others in the past. If I'm this messed up in the head right now, what the hell is she feeling? I probably scared her to death, and I can't let her feel that way.

I type out a quick, nervous text:

> Angel...you okay?

Five agonizing minutes pass while I sit on my bedroom floor and stare at my closet door.

Kenzi

> Yes. Are you? I hope you washed that road rash on your hand and leg so you don't get infected.

God. Why does she always try to take care of me?

> I will.

Kenzi

> Have you heard any news on the big fluffy dog?

> Not yet.

Kenzi

> I like him a lot. He just wanted love, even though he was hurt and lost. He reminds me of you.

My chest contracts.

Ya think?

Kenzi
Yup.

I'm sorry I scared you.

Kenzi
You never scare me, Tor.

Shit. Wrong answer, little girl. Wrong. Fucking. Answer.

Kenzi
Maybe you're scared.

I want to throw my phone against the wall. I don't know what to say to that. I'm afraid to say anything because I don't trust anything about myself right now. This kid has always had a microscope right into my soul and it's driving me mad.

Am I scared?

Yes. I'm petrified of what she's made me feel.

Kenzi
Everything is okay, Tor.

My fingers shake as I type back on the tiny keyboard.

Is it?

Kenzi
Yes. It is.

Her words convey comfort and confidence—not fear as I expected.

I don't reply and a few minutes later, a text message comes through with a picture of a penny, and she's typed the words *I wish you wouldn't worry* across it. The last thing I feel like doing is smiling, but I do, because that's what she does to me.

> Thanks, Angel.

Kenzi
> No drinking. Promise me?

I shake my head at the phone. She knows me too well. Better than she really should.

> I promise.

Kenzi
> Good.

I breathe a deep sigh of relief as I toss my phone off to the side. We've silently agreed to pretend the kiss never happened.
Bullshit.

For the past two weeks, I've been lying low, working on my bike, landscaping my yard, and training this goofy white dog who almost got me killed and then led to me kissing someone my lips had no right to be on. When my mom told me no one ever came to claim the dog, I went over and adopted him and he stuck his head out the truck window on the way home with the wind in his face as we drove right past the place I saved him. I couldn't let a beautiful dog like this sit in a concrete kennel recuperating with a broken leg, right? At least that's what I told Mom.

We know the real reason, though. Because Kenzi fell in love with him in the back seat that day and now he has sentimental value. He witnessed our first kiss.

First and last kiss, I remind myself. *First and last.*

I haven't talked to her since that day due to her having her wisdom teeth pulled out and then she came down with "the worst friggin' cold ever." At least that's what her text message told me. I did go to her graduation and stood with her family like I always have, watching her take steps into adulthood. She didn't say one word to me at the ceremony. In fact, she barely looked at me. I declined the invitation of going back to Asher's house for a small party afterward. I felt too guilty being near her and all her loved ones, afraid someone would notice a difference between us or that I'd have a meltdown and admit what I did to all of them while we stood around eating cake.

Is she avoiding me? The possibility has crossed my mind several thousand times, and it hurts me in a way I can't describe, but it's the way it should be. I kissed a fucking seventeen-year-old girl. *Seventeen.* That little fact turns my stomach every time I think of it. She thinks of me as her uncle. I'm closer to her than her *own* uncles are. I've never once been even remotely attracted to anyone under twenty-one before, unless I was that age myself. But something about Kenzi is different. She doesn't act or look her age at all. I've come to think of her as more of a friend than anything else over the past few years, and I have no idea how that even happened. Up until now, I never thought about our relationship as unhealthy or wrong. Now I'm second-guessing everything.

I've texted her pictures of the newly groomed and incredibly white fluffy dog, who I've named Diogee. She texted back that as soon as she feels better, she's coming right over to play with him and vacuum up all the white fur that's accumulating in places of my house that I never thought dog fur could end up.

I have mixed feelings about seeing her again, and I try to convince myself it will be a good way to prove to myself that what happened was just a one-time mistake that will never happen again. But mixed in with that is hidden excitement and longing. I want to see her smile at me with those lips that tasted so delicious. *Even if I can never taste them again.*

I feel guilty as I'm walking into Asher's house on this sunny Sunday morning. Today we've got a ride planned and we always meet up at his house. But now that I'm here, I feel like I have a big red mark on my face in the shape of his daughter's lips.

"Hey, man, it's a perfect day for a ride," he says when I walk into the kitchen. "You want some coffee before we head out?"

"Nah, I'm trying to quit. It makes me jittery."

He pulls two bottles of water out of the refrigerator and tosses one at me. "Let's ride up to Cathedral Ledge. I got a new camera and I want to take some pictures."

"Dude, every year you buy a new camera."

"I know. I think I have some bizarre camera fetish. Do you want one of my old ones? I've got about five I think."

"Thanks, but I'm good. If I want a picture of something, I'll just use my cell phone. I can't deal with all those buttons and settings." I wander across the kitchen to look out the window while I wait for him to put his boots on, and that's when I see Kenzi, Chloe, and Rayne sitting out by the pool, laughing like girls do. I have to force myself not to stare at Kenzi in cutoff faded denim shorts, bright apple-red bikini top, sunglasses on top of her head pushing her hair off her face, and black motorcycle boots on her feet. It's the little black leather boots that get to me the most and make my body twitch in ways it definitely shouldn't be.

Fuck. I can't escape this shit.

She looks like she just stepped right out of one of Tristan's biker chick calendars he's got hanging in his work area. As hard as I try, my eyes disobey me and take in the swell of her breasts cradled in the thin material, the perfect curve of her waist, to her belly button just above the hem of her low-cut shorts.

She's not hot. She's not hot. She's not hot.

"She's cute, but way too young, man," Asher says, coming up behind me and slapping my back.

I blink rapidly. "Huh? Who?"

"Chloe."

Shit. "I wasn't looking at her. She's got the body of a twelve-year-old." Unlike Kenzi, who suddenly has the body of a twenty-something who's got my blood pumping wildly.

Why can't she be one of those giggly, annoying teens with a horrible attitude who hates everyone? Why does she have to be so sweet and smart and beautiful and caring and independent and such a great listener and—

"Well, you better not be looking at my little sister."

—and everything I want.

I quickly turn away from the window. "I wasn't looking at anyone. I was spacing out wondering if that dog is trashing my house. Can we go? You take longer than a chick to get ready." A thin sheen of sweat has covered my body as I fight my physical and emotional reaction to her. I've got a Kenzi-induced fever and I need to get out of here and away from her before I pass out.

Riding all day helps settle my mind and body. Something about the mountain air, the roar of my engine, and the endless clear blue sky always puts me in a good mood. Asher rides in front and I follow a few lengths behind. About three hours into the ride, we stop for lunch at an old roadside burger place, and I come damn close to coming clean and spilling my guts to Asher about what happened with Kenzi. I feel like pure scum betraying the trust of the guy who's been my best friend for twenty-five years, who's done more for me than anyone else, and trusted me with the most precious thing in his life. It's eating at me day and night and I want this monster out of me.

"How's the shop doing?" he asks.

"Great. The past two years have been the best we've ever done for profits. I was actually able to give my brothers a raise for once, so they're happy."

He nods around his burger. "Good deal. I think the new sign out front and painting the building really helped; it kinda breathed new life into it. People like that."

"You're right, it made a big difference. Pop never thought about things like that."

"Marketing can be a bitch. Our PR team is on us to change our logo. I told them to go get fucked. I'm not changing it."

Ash and I designed the scrolling A&E Ashes & Embers logo when we first started the band way back in high school. I never cared that the band name was a play on his and Ember's names. It fit perfectly.

"I don't blame ya. It's been the brand since day one. The fans recognize it. Shit, how many people have it tattooed on them that we've seen?"

"Exactly. The logo stays. It's us."

"It's you."

He leans back in his chair and shakes his head. "No, man. It's always us. Just because you and Ember aren't in the band anymore doesn't mean shit to me. We started it. It's our baby. I'd have none of this without you. Don't think I ever forget that, because I don't."

"We're equal, Ash. Where would I be without you? Broke? In prison? Dead, maybe? I wrote some songs. Big deal. You've bailed me out of a mess a hundred times. You don't owe me anything."

"I know I don't. I helped you because you needed it and you deserved it. People fall, we pick them up, right?"

"Right." I finish my soda, still feeling sick. I don't think Asher will understand my fall for his daughter.

By the time we're done with lunch, I still haven't told him about kissing her and I know I'm not going to because he'll fucking despise me and I'll never see him or Kenzi again. He'll never forgive me or believe it was just a random heat-of-the-moment thing. Maybe I'm a coward or just a bigger selfish asshole than I ever thought I was, but I don't think I can deal with losing them. The void that would leave in my life would be huge.

So I don't tell him, and instead I promise myself that I'll never give in to a moment of weakness or insanity around Kenzi again. *Ever.*

I'll learn to destroy the monster myself.

CHAPTER 11

My love,
I wished for you a thousand times,
and finally, you're mine.

KENZI

The past two weeks have felt like an eternity. Longer than an eternity, if that's even possible. I Googled *what is longer than eternity* out of curiosity and boredom, but it came up inconclusive, with the only real answer being *eternity means lasting forever.* I liked how that sounded word-wise but not time-wise in relation to the unsettled feelings I was experiencing.

I spent the days and nights in bed, recovering from the torture known as oral surgery and then getting a cold. My father, my grandmother, and Chloe each took turns visiting me and bringing me soft food. My grandmother dropped off a bag of new romance paperbacks to keep me busy—some her own books, others by her favorite authors. Buried under my cuddliest comforter, I spent those two weeks napping, reading, and thinking about Tor. And missing Tor more than I should. We texted a few times when he said he hoped I felt better soon, and told me he adopted the dog. I replied back that I wanted to come see the dog, to which he replied "anytime." And that was it. At first, I thought it was best for us to just ignore the fact that we kissed, go about our lives as if it never happened, and accept that it was an accident of sorts.

But then I dreamed of him. I'm not sure if it was the painkillers from the surgery making me crazy, the cold meds making me loopy, or if reading erotica romance books every night had my imagination in overdrive, but whatever the reason, this was a dream like no other. It was one of those super-special dreams that feel so incredibly real that when you wake up, you're not quite sure if it was a dream or if it actually *did* happen. And then you want to try to fall asleep really fast again and somehow find your way back into that dream and live in it. *Make it real.*

He kissed me in the dream like he did that day on the side of the road, rough and demanding, overpowering all of my senses. Only in the dream kiss, he didn't stop there. His lips moved down to my throat, and his hands gripped my waist, pulling my body against his. And in the dream I wasn't afraid to touch him. I wrapped my arms around him and let my hands roam all over those beautiful muscles he has, and every inch of me that his lips touched burned and tingled and begged for more. And now I *do* want more. I want that dream to not be a dream at all.

"What are you doing?"

My dad's voice startles me out of my daydream and I realize I'm staring at myself in my bathroom mirror with my toothbrush hanging out of my mouth, blue foamy gel all over my lips. I quickly rinse my mouth and wipe it with a washcloth.

"Dad...I was just getting ready to leave." *Jesus.* I can feel heat rising to my face, and I'm sure I'm blushing.

His eyes narrow at me like he does when he's trying to read me, his hand reaching out to touch my forehead. "You look weird. Are you still feeling sick?"

Yes. I'm sick. I can't stop thinking about Toren and his lips and his hands and his muscles and his voice and his—

"Kenzi?"

I shake my muddled head and force a smile before putting a quick coat of lip gloss on.

"I'm fine, I was just thinking."

"You looked like you were on another planet."

"I'm just excited to finally drive my new car today!" I do a little happy hop and give him a hug. "Thank you so much for getting it for me."

His face is still all concern and worry as he follows me into my room and watches me put my shoes on. "Are you sure you feel okay? I'm worried about you driving after you've been sick."

I cock my head at him. "Dad. This has nothing to do with me having a cold and everything to do with you worried about me being in a car alone."

"Driving is dangerous."

"So is walking. And stairs. People die in their sleep! Or choking on food!"

He rubs his head and stares at me. "Yeah...true. I knew that bubble I wanted to put you in was a good idea. It's not too late, ya know," he says with a smirk.

"Dad, stop. I'll be fine. You said yourself all the times you took me out to practice that I'm a good driver."

Sighing, he crosses his arms and leans against my dresser. "You're right. Just pay attention. I want your phone on the passenger seat next to you and not in your hand. At all. Don't even look at it."

"I promise."

"And don't blast the music too loud; you won't be able to hear the cars around you."

I quirk an eyebrow at him. "Seriously? This coming from a rock god? Loud music is in my blood."

"Fine. Just not *too* loud, then. And make sure it's good music and not shit."

Laughing, I agree. "Okay. I promise. Please don't worry. I won't embarrass you with any bad music choices."

"Where are you going? I don't want you to go too far your first time alone. And make sure you have a full tank of gas."

"I'm only going to Tor's to see the dog. I'm so glad he kept him; he's the sweetest dog ever. Do you think we can get a dog?" I ask for what must be the millionth time since I was about ten years old. "There are so many at Mrs. Grace's shelter..."

"No, you have a rabbit that's almost a hundred years old." He glances over at Snuggles in her cage. "I travel too much to have a dog and I don't want you strapped down with another pet right now while you're figuring out what you want to do next. I want you to be free to do whatever you want. You can go and love on Tor's dog anytime you want."

What *do* I want to do next? I still have no idea.

I snatch up my phone and my new shiny keyring and head downstairs with him right behind me. When we reach the foyer, I turn to face him and he practically slams right into me. He's severely hovering.

"Dad, I'll be fine. Stop being a helicopter. I've been riding my bicycle to Tor's house and all over town since I was eleven years old. I think the car is probably much safer. I'll text you when I get there, and when I leave, and when I get home."

That gets me his famous smile. "Deal. I'll be in the studio most of the day working some new vocals, so I'll be able to focus better if I know you're safe and sound."

"Don't work too hard. And I can't wait to hear your new stuff.

I know it's going to be amazing. As always." I kiss his cheek. "I'll see you in a little while."

As soon as I get in my new Jeep, I'm tempted to take a selfie to send to Chloe but I stop myself. I promised Dad no phone shenanigans in the car, and even though I'm technically still parked in the driveway, I'm going to stick to my word.

At least about the phone. I *do* blast my favorite music pretty damn loud on the fifteen-minute drive over to Tor's house. What's the point of having a kick-ass stereo system if you don't use it?

Usually I let myself into his house with my own key but I feel odd doing that now, so I knock. Hearing the dog bark makes me smile and I wonder if he'll remember me.

The door opens a few seconds later and when he's smiling down at me, everything feels normal again. He's wearing my purple heart beanie, and I'm wearing his old Guns N' Roses T-shirt I stole last year. We're us again. His gaze shifts behind me to his driveway and he breaks out into a bigger grin.

"You finally got your car. Jeeps are nice. Good choice."

"Yup! I love it."

"It's cool. White suits you, Angel. I could hear you coming from way down the street, though. I figured Ash would make sure you had the best sound system."

"Don't even start," I tease, nudging by him, where I'm immediately greeted by a mass of white fur and a tongue. I kneel and the dog is all happy wiggles, wagging his huge plume of a tail and licking my face. His back leg is in a blue cast, but he seems to be getting around okay with it.

"Wow, Tor! He's so white! And fluffy! He almost looks like a different dog!"

"Tell me about it. Who knew under that wet muddy dog was a cloud with paws."

"He's gorgeous!" The dog is beautiful, like a show dog you'd see on television, and he's obviously very happy, with an immense love for people. He's prancing around the room, going from me to Toren to get patted, and he almost looks like he's smiling.

"I love him! How has he been since you brought him home?"

"He's been really good. He's house trained, and except for gnawing on the legs of the coffee table, he hasn't done anything bad. The vet thinks he's about two years old. His back leg is healing up nice."

I look up at him as I hug the dog's neck. "And nobody came for him? No postings about a lost dog matching his description?"

He shakes his head. "Nope, nothing. Ty checked all the databases, going back three years, and there's nothing within a hundred-mile radius listing an all-white dog. I can't believe his owners aren't missing him. It's messed up."

"It is." I don't know how someone could have such a great dog and not even report him missing. I hope nothing horrible happened to his owner.

"You'll have to do a lot more vacuuming now," he jokes. "The fur that comes off him on a daily basis is crazy. It sucks for me since almost all my shirts are black. I can't get out of the house without having white fur on me."

I stand up and smooth down my T-shirt, which is covered in fur now, too. "I'll get you one of those lint roller things if you don't have one."

"I've been using masking tape and went through a roll already. Pick me up a bunch of those lint things." He reaches into his wallet and hands me a fifty-dollar bill. "You're still going to clean and stuff, right?"

I nod, taking the bill from him. "Yes, and make you dinner."

"Wicked cool. That's the best news I've heard in a long time."

We watch as Diogee grabs a big white bone off the floor and carts it over to a dog bed in the corner of the living room to chew on.

"He seems really happy, Tor. I'm so glad you kept him. I'm looking forward to seeing him now when I come over. I could brush him for you, too, if you want."

"That would be awesome. He obviously loves you. He's a little high maintenance, so I'll take all the help you want to give."

"I don't mind at all. I asked Dad for a dog again but he said no, that I can basically come over here and hang out with yours."

"I'm good with that. Anytime you want to come over is fine. You know that by now. Since he's all settled on his bed, you want to see what I've done to the backyard?"

"Of course."

A few weeks ago, he told me he wanted to do some landscaping in his yard and plant some new flowers and shrubs because he was sick of looking at nothing but grass and rocks. When we step outside the sliding glass doors to his patio, I'm completely unprepared to see what he's done. He fenced in the entire yard with white fencing and planted different-shaped shrubs, a myriad of colorful flowers that I can't even name, a birdbath, and a hummingbird feeder, along with various birdhouses nailed to the trees. But the part that blows me away is a stone walkway that leads to a tiny pond with an old wrought-iron bench nearby. He's watching me with a grin on his face, waiting for my reaction.

"A pond?" I exclaim. "You did this?"

We walk over to it and I'm shocked again when I see three koi swimming in the clear water that's being circulated by a small waterfall.

"Yeah, Tanner helped, though. We watched about fifty You-Tube videos. It took a few days just to do the pond but it came out pretty cool. We used rock from the river down in the woods. Tanner power-washed everything; then we arranged it all in here. It's almost three feet deep."

"Are you kidding? This is amazing."

"Thanks. The dog keeps trying to stick his head in it, but I think he'll get bored of it. Tristan gave me some training tips to work with him."

"Tor, it's all beautiful. My dad's going to be jealous of this, though," I tease. "This is kinda better than his water fountain. I mean, there's *fish*."

He winks at me. "We won't tell him."

"Can we sit?" I ask. "I want to watch the fish swim around. They're so pretty and peaceful looking."

"Sure. I haven't sat back here at all, actually. Just been busy working on it but not really enjoying it yet."

"Then it's time you did."

We sit on the bench together and he stretches his long legs out, proudly looks around his beautiful new yard.

"It's seriously amazing, Tor. So much better than just all that boring grass you had before. The fence is a good idea."

"Yeah, I was afraid the dog would wander off and get lost again." He stares around the yard some more. "I really like it. It feels more like home now, ya know? I should have done this years ago."

"I think so, too. I love everything you did. This is what I want when I have my own house someday. I could sit back here all day."

We share a smile and my heart dances. I've missed him and our talks, and now as my eyes discreetly take in his muscular jean-clad legs, flashbacks of my dream make my heart beat even faster. I wonder if he's thought about me differently at all, like I've been thinking about him.

"How have you been feeling?" he asks.

"Huh?"

"You were sick. And had four teeth ripped out of your head. Your dad said you were in a lot of pain."

"Oh. Yeah, it hurt a lot afterward. My face got all swollen and I looked like a chipmunk."

He laughs. "Aww...I'm sure you looked adorable."

I shake my head. "I don't think so. I was all bruised, too."

"It's better now, though, right?"

Yes. It's much better because you just pretty much called me adorable.

"Yeah. I can open my mouth all the way now." I demonstrate by opening my mouth wide and snapping it closed several times.

"Please don't do that." He sits forward and leans his elbows on his knees.

"Okay..." *Hmm.* Is it possible he *has* been thinking about me?

He clears his throat and points over to the fountain. "Did you see that? I left a surprise there for you."

I follow his finger to a small painted glass mason jar on the edge of the pond that's filled with pennies.

"Hey," I say excitedly. "Is that for our wishes?"

"Of course. I don't sit here and make wishes alone."

I jump up and run over to grab the bottle. "Can we throw pennies in the pond? Or will it hurt the fish?"

"We can. I washed them all first to make sure there was nothin' on them."

"You're awesome." I shake out two pennies, put the jar back, and join him on the bench again, handing him one of the copper coins.

"You go first," he says. "You've been sick."

I laugh at him. "It was just a cold."

"You called it the worst friggin' cold ever."

"It felt pretty bad at the time."

"They always do."

I hang on to my penny for a second and then toss it in the water, making sure it doesn't bonk one of the fish on the head. We're quiet for a few minutes as I think about my wish and how best to word it. I knew what I was going to wish for long before I threw my penny in, but now I'm not sure I have the courage to say it out loud.

"So?" he urges. "What did you wish for this time? It should be a big one—you just graduated high school and have a whole new slate in front of you."

I take a deep breath and watch the koi circle slowly over my penny as if they know what's about to happen.

"I wish you'd kiss me again," I say softly, grateful for the breeze blowing my hair across my face at that exact moment, hopefully hiding the yearning that I'm sure is overly evident in my eyes.

He doesn't look at me. In fact, he goes completely still and I'm not even sure he's breathing, to be honest. My pulse quickens as I wait, and a swirling warmth manifests in the pit of my stomach.

"I didn't kiss you, Kenzi," he finally says. I can't see his eyes, because he's still leaning on his knees with his chin resting on his hands, so I'm left staring at the back of his head.

"Yes, you did." Does he think I imagined the most epic kiss of my life thus far?

"It was an accident." Again, with the emotionless tone that's totally foreign to me.

"Are you kidding?" I say, my voice rising slightly.

"No," he says simply. "I'm not."

No way. I'm not going to let him put himself in denial over this.

"How do you accidentally kiss someone, exactly?"

Now I can hear him breathing, and he lets out a deep sigh. "I don't want to talk about this." He moves to stand but I quickly grab his arm and pull him back down on the bench.

"Please don't walk away."

He turns his face up to the sky and takes another deep breath, shaking his head. "Fine, Kenzi. It never should have happened. It was a fucked-up, spur-of-the moment thing because we were both all ramped up about saving the dog and we just kinda...collided."

"Collided?" I repeat. Is he serious?

"Yeah, and I'm sorry it happened. My mind was just fucked for a few seconds. I would never touch you, Kenzi. Not like that. You know that, right?" He turns sideways to look at me and his eyes are troubled, searching mine like he's lost and confused and needs me to set him back straight again.

I swallow hard over the lump growing in my throat. "Of course I know that, but I don't want it to be a mistake. I liked it."

His eyes close for a long moment before he opens them to meet mine again. "Kenzi, no. It was wrong on about a thousand levels. It didn't mean anything."

I slowly shake my head, refusing to let that be true. "No. I thought it meant a lot, actually."

He stands up and hurls his penny into the woods, and that just deepens the blow of what he's saying to me. Our little wish moments have always been special to us and he just threw one away like it meant nothing.

"We're not talking about this, Kenzi. This subject is over, you got it? Just drop it."

I stand and grab his arm again, forcing him to look at me, and he glares down, his dark eyes narrowing at me.

"No, Tor. I don't *got it*. What if I don't want to drop it? You going to spank me and take me home like a little baby? I'm a little old for that now, don't you think? Can't we sit here and talk about our *collision* like adults?"

"Stop taunting me," he says through clenched teeth. "We're done with this. I want you to forget it happened."

"I want to talk about it."

His eyes flash at me, his mouth set in a tight line. "Did you tell anyone?"

"No, of course not. I'm not stupid."

"I hope not. This isn't funny, Kenzi. It's serious. I'm not some fucking high school kid. You're a teenager and I'm an adult. I own a respectable business in this town. I can't have people spreading rumors about me."

"Don't you think I know all that? Why are you acting like this? We didn't do anything wrong. Please stop being so mad at me and talk to me."

He shakes his head vigorously. "No. I want you to forget it happened. That's exactly what I'm doing."

"I can't," I confess with a shaky voice.

"Then try harder." His voice is deep and spiked with venom. He's never spoken to me like this, and I ache for the man who's been nothing but sweet and comforting to me for the past seventeen years. I've never been the target of his anger, and I'm not liking this side of him at all.

Tears start to roll down my cheeks and I wipe at them, annoyed that I can't control my emotions. I don't want him to perceive me as a little girl having a tantrum.

"Wow. Maybe Sydni and Lisa were right about what they said to you. You can't communicate at all."

He takes a few steps away, his fists clenched at his sides, then comes back to face me.

"Don't even throw that shit in my face. This is completely fucking different. You better watch where you're treading, Kenzi. You may not like where you end up."

I cringe away from his fury. "I'm sorry. I just want you to talk to me."

"Look, what happened was a mistake and I'm sorry it's got your head all messed up, but we both need to just forget it. It was wrong and it's making me sick thinking about it, let alone talking about it."

His words are like a slap to my face and a knife straight through my heart. "I make you feel sick?" I ask in disbelief.

"No, Angel, not like that." His voice softens as he realizes how harsh he's acting. "It's just *wrong*. You're only seventeen for God's sake."

"So?" I sniffle.

He smiles in wonder at me. "So?" he repeats, letting out a little laugh.

I nod. "Yeah, so?"

Pulling me into his chest, he hugs me and kisses the top of my head, just as he did when I was a little girl. "That's such a *you* answer. I don't want to fight, Kenzi. Not with you, not ever. But you gotta let this go. I'm sorry I let this happen. I'm just fucked up sometimes."

"You're not fucked up," I say defensively into his chest.

He slowly pulls away and looks down into my eyes, his full of turmoil. "I am. And now you're seeing it firsthand, and I hate it. I liked it when you looked at me like I was some kind of hero who made everything in the world all better for you."

"But you do. You always have."

Smiling weakly, he shakes his head and swipes his thumbs across my damp cheeks. "I can't stand to see you cry. Please let this go, I'm begging you. Can you do that? For me?"

Nodding tearfully, I say yes. Because I'll do anything for him.

But I know I'm not going to be able to let this go. I'll never forget how it felt to be kissed by him. If I live to be a hundred, I still won't forget or let it go.

CHAPTER 12

Kenzi—age seven

Toren—age twenty-two

Sydni is sitting on my lap and we're making out in a dark corner of Asher's apartment when I feel something tugging on my leg. Pulling away from Sydni's lips, I look down to see Kenzi staring at me with wide eyes.

I wipe Sydni's red lipstick off my lips with the back of my hand as I'm being scrutinized by a seven-year-old. "Hey, kiddo, shouldn't you be in bed?"

"Why?"

"Because it's late and your mom and dad have friends over."

"So?"

"I know I saw your mom put you to bed."

"I couldn't sleep." She turns her narrowed gaze on Sydni. "Why is she on your lap? I sit on your lap. Nobody else."

Sydni laughs and snakes her arm around my neck. "Kenzi, honey, you should go back to bed. Do you want me to find your mommy? I think she's in the kitchen."

Kenzi glares at her. "No. Thank you." She holds a piece of paper out to me. "I drew this for you, Uncle Tor."

Smiling, I shift Sydni off me and take the piece of paper from Kenzi's hand. She's drawn a black heart with a scribble in the middle. With the new calligraphy pen I gave her, she's written "Uncle Tor, I love you the most. Love, Kenzi" and her words actually look really good even though they're a little crooked. I can tell she's been practicing.

"This is beautiful, Angel. Look how pretty your letters came out."
She beams at me. "I did the swash like you showed me in the book."
"I see that. I'm going to keep it forever."
"Really? You promise?"
"I promise."

🤍 🖤 🤍

KENZI

"Why do I need a website? I have Facebook."

Chloe sighs at me and doesn't take her eyes off her laptop screen. I'm perched next to her at the desk in her bedroom, watching her fingers fly over the keyboard.

"Facebook isn't the internet, Kenzi. I mean, yeah, it's great for socializing and you can use it as a place for customers to find you and see your work, but you really want a website to showcase your portfolio so you look like a real professional. I can even add an order form."

I chew my lip as I stare at her screen. "Are you sure? I doubt I'll get many orders, Chloe."

"I think you're wrong. Look at this list we made of things you can do with your calligraphy instead of just handwritten invitations. The tattoos and the custom handwritten wall art is awesome. Trust me, it'll start out slow and then it will take off."

"If you say so." I appreciate her confidence in me. I'm just not sure myself yet if people will actually pay for my calligraphy. It's taken her two weeks to convince me to let her design a website for me. She seems excited to have the project to work on since she's going to college soon for marketing and graphic design. So in a way, I'm sorta her guinea pig, which I don't mind at all.

"By the end of the week, I'll have this all up and running for you," she assures me. "You'll love it. It will look great."

"I trust you. In the meantime, I'll send you some pictures of my work so you can add them when you're ready."

She shuts her laptop lid and turns to me. "Okay, girl. Tell me what your plans are for the summer. Are you going to Maine to stay with your aunt? I really wish you were coming to New York with me. I just don't get why you won't go to college. You're smart, and it'd be crazy fun. Do you have any idea how many new people you'd meet? New York City is freakin' amazing. And with your dad's connections, we could get into all the cool clubs."

I push my hair out of my face, tired of having this same conversation with everyone for the past two months. "I just don't think it's for me. I don't have that inner drive to go to college, or party, or start some kind of career, or get away from my family. I honestly don't know why."

She tilts her head at me thoughtfully. "Maybe your parents dragged you around too much when you were younger. I think that made you just want to stay in one place. For some people, it would do the opposite, where they'd want to keep traveling as much as possible since that's what they're used to. It seems like it had the opposite effect on you. I think you need to feel settled. There's nothing wrong with that, though, Kenz."

I nod slowly, taking that in. "I think you're right. I just want calm and quiet, and a sense of security and home."

"You better at least come visit me. You can't just stay in this tiny town and wither away. You have to get out sometimes."

"Of course I'll visit. I'm going to miss you like crazy. It's not that far, though. I could drive, or even fly."

"We can shop our asses off when you visit."

"We definitely will," I agree. I don't know anyone who loves to shop as much as Chloe does, and every time we go shopping, she insists on buying some ridiculously random thing that she will never, ever use, and then she'll wrap one of those things up in the gaudiest wrapping paper she can find and give it to me on my birthday. It's a silly joke she started when we were younger, and now I look forward to it every year.

"I'm not sure if I'm going to Maine this year or not," I say as Chloe starts to put bright pink nail polish on her nails. She'll probably want to do mine next, and I will inevitably smudge at least three nails by the time I get home.

"Why? I thought you loved going there."

Every year for the past six years, I've spent summer break in Maine with my mom's older sister, Katherine, who owns and runs a bed-and-breakfast in a beautiful Victorian house right by the water. This year I'm just not sure I want to be away for almost three months, especially since Chloe will be leaving for college soon, and my father will be going on tour in the fall.

My cell phone beeps with a text, and when I see his name on my screen, my heart jumps in that new way that it does every time he texts me.

It's been a week since the talk we had in his backyard about the *collision*, and that night I changed his name in my contacts from Uncle Tor to Tor. I knew in my heart I was never going to call him my uncle again. Not after I knew what it felt like to be kissed by him, and not after the daydreams I've been having about him. Seeing the dream version of us was like looking into a crystal ball, and I saw our relationship in a new way that now I can't forget.

It also forced me to face several unexpected truths. I'm insanely attracted to him physically and mentally. I want to take care of him, and I want to be the person who makes him smile every day. I don't want him to be any sort of uncle to me or be my dad's best friend. I want him to be *mine*. Thinking back, I can't deny that some of these feelings started to grow in me a very long time ago, like a seed that's been slowly blossoming over the years, growing as we grew together. For as far back as I can remember, I've always wanted to be close to him and now it's evolved into something far beyond friendship and guardianship.

I'm not entirely delusional. I know I shouldn't be thinking of him in that way. I was raised thinking of him as my uncle and he is my godfather. Those memories can't be wiped away from our history. He's my dad's best friend. He's almost twice my age. But with each day that passes, those facts seem less valid to me, and the feelings I'm having for him are becoming much stronger than fake titles and age differences. It's undeniable—our feelings for each other have changed. I know it, and I know he knows it. I just don't know what to do about it.

I swipe my finger across the screen to read his text, and it's a photo of a penny lying among some dirt and leaves.

Tor

> I found the penny I threw in the woods the other day.

> It hurt that you did that :(

Tor

> I know. I'm sorry.

> It's okay. Put it back in the jar.

Tor

> Some things we can't wish for. I need you to understand that.

Tears well in my eyes reading his words and I type a quick reply.

> I do understand. I just don't like it.

A few minutes go by and I focus on Chloe painting little flowers on my nails until my phone beeps again. Using my right hand, I swipe the screen to see his new text.

Tor

I never said I liked it either, Angel. I hate it.

I turn my phone over so I can't see the screen anymore. If Chloe realizes I'm getting text messages that are upsetting me, she'll start asking questions, and there's no way I can tell her about this, as much as I wish I could. I'm just not ready to admit to anyone yet how I really feel about him.

His truck is in the driveway on Friday afternoon when I get to his house, and it causes a moment of panic for me. I wasn't expecting to see him today. Usually I clean up his house, do his laundry, brush the dog, and prepare a dinner for him that's easy to heat up, and I leave.

I grab the two bags of groceries I just bought and walk down his brick walkway to the front door, hesitating, not wanting to use my key to let myself in. I still don't feel right just walking into his house when I know he's inside. Instead, I ring the doorbell and wait.

"Come in!" he bellows.

When I step inside, I'm surprised to find him lying on the couch propped up on a bunch of pillows wearing gray sweatpants and a wrinkled white T-shirt, his hair all loose and messy like he just woke up. Diogee is sleeping on the floor next to the couch, but immediately lifts his head and wags his tail when he sees me.

"Hey . . . what are you doing home?" I ask, taking the bags into the adjoining kitchen and putting them on the counter. I pull out my phone and send a quick text to my dad to let him know I'm safe and sound.

"I hurt my back again at the shop yesterday."

"Oh no, again? Did you take your pills?" He's had problems with his back ever since his truck was rear-ended while he was at a traffic light years ago.

He nods. "A bunch of them already. Why the hell do you keep knocking? You have a key." His tone is edgy from the pain as he turns to reorganize his pillows behind him.

I empty the grocery bags onto the kitchen table and start putting things away. "I feel weird just walking into your house when you're home. It feels rude and invasive."

"Kenzi, you can come in anytime. I'd never have someone over here in the middle of the day if that's what you're worried about. I have a job, remember? And I don't walk around naked. So just come in."

"Okay." I admit I'm happy to hear he doesn't have women here during the day, but then, of course, I wonder if he has anyone over at night.

"I was going to make you a beef and broccoli stir-fry for dinner. Do you feel all right to eat?"

"That sounds great, actually. All I've had to eat today is a Valium, Vicodin, and an orange juice cocktail, so real food would be good."

After I put the groceries away, I cross the room and sit on top of the coffee table in front of the couch to talk to him. His eyes are glazed from the high of the pills, making them look like glassy onyx gems.

"Tor, you can't take pills on an empty stomach like that."

"You sound like my mother." He scowls.

Diogee sits up and lays his head on my leg, peeking up at me with his big black eyes.

"Hi, puppy. Did you miss me?" I lean down and kiss the top of his head.

"He's an attention monger. He's constantly nudging my hands to get petted or laying his head on me, like he just did to you, with that face."

Laughing, I rub the dog's ears. "I think he's good company for you."

"Yeah, I guess he is. He sleeps with me every night and at least he's still here in the morning."

I try to ignore that comment that hints at more info than I care to know right now.

"Can I get you anything?" I ask. "The heating pad? Or maybe an ice pack? What helps with the pain?"

He shakes his head. "None of that shit helps."

"Okay. I'll just vacuum and do your laundry, and then straighten things up a bit."

"Skip the vacuum. The noise will make my head explode."

"All right. What else can I do to help? Maybe you should take a hot bath or shower?"

Squinting, he falls back against the pillow, grimacing in pain. "I don't fucking know. I'm sorry, Angel. I'm in a ton of pain. I can't even think straight. Just pet the dog and make dinner. You don't have to do anything else."

Seeing him in so much pain and the cranky mood it's put him in bothers me and makes me want to do something—anything—to make him feel better. When I was younger, I used to rub his back and even *walk* on his back sometimes when it was hurting him, with my mom yelling that there was no way that could be safe for a back injury, but he said it felt good. Giving him a back massage would probably be really inappropriate after what's been changing between us recently, though, so I nix that idea.

He opens his eyes and grins when he catches me looking at him.

"You still look at me the same way you did when you were a baby," he murmurs.

"How's that?"

"Like I'm the only thing you ever want to look at."

Not breaking eye contact, I smile at the truth in his words.

"Maybe you are."

His eyes close and he takes a deep breath as if he's inhaling my words and needs them to take his next breath. When he opens his eyes, he reaches out to rest his hand on the side of my neck, his thumb slowly brushing back and forth over my cheek. My heart jumps at his touch, and I freeze, not moving, not wanting to do anything to interrupt the moment.

"When you were little, you used to come running to me when I walked into the room, and you'd hug me like I was your favorite person in the world. You have no idea how that felt." He swallows hard. "To feel so unconditionally adored."

I remember that feeling of giddy excitement every time my uncle Tor came in the room, and although my excitement of seeing him hasn't diminished, it's totally different now.

"You made me feel the same way," I admit. "I still feel that way, Tor. But now I think I want to do a lot more than just hug you."

His hand grips my neck tighter.

I lick my lips nervously and say, "And I think I want you to do a lot more than just pick me up and swing me around and make me laugh."

I nearly forget how to breathe when he presses his thumb to my lips. "Don't say things like that, Kenzi," he whispers, his eyes flashing even darker. "You don't know who you're playing with."

Without even thinking, my tongue peeks out to run across

his finger, and his eyes widen, riveted to my lips as I taste him. "I'm not playing. And I know exactly who you are." I don't want to hide my feelings anymore, so I embrace this moment of new bravery.

"Oh yeah?" His voice is low and sexy, and it does indescribable things to my insides. "Who am I?"

"Did you forget?" I ask playfully, leaning a little closer to him, his hand on my neck pulling me forward, gently coaxing me even closer. "You're the man I'm going to marry someday."

"Fuck." He exhales the word and pulls my lips down to his, and our second *collision* is just as amazing as the first—slow, tantalizing, and consuming. His mouth covers mine, his tongue delving deep as his free hand grips my waist, pulling me off the coffee table and onto the couch with him. His hand slides from my hip to the back of my thigh, pulling me until my chest is flush against his, my legs straddling him. An unexpected whimper escapes me as my body settles perfectly against him and his massive hard-on presses between my thighs, causing my entire body to quiver with electric pulses. *Wow.*

Groaning, he grips the back of my neck tighter, his fingers in my hair, and kisses me deeper, his lips smoldering on mine. My body instinctively seeks his out, my thighs spreading wider over him, wanting to feel more of him. *Needing* to feel more. Ripples of longing I've never felt before tremor through my body as I slowly move against him, unsure of what I'm doing but loving the feeling of him growing even harder beneath his sweatpants. His hand moves from the back of my thigh to the small of my back, holding me firm against him, and I like how possessive it feels. A little voice inside my head tries to tell me my first experience grinding against a man's body should be with any one of the millions of single men on the planet and not with Tor, but I ignore the warning. I may be seventeen, but I can feel without a shadow of a doubt our bodies and hearts were made to be together, like scattered puzzle pieces needing to be put back together.

Suddenly he pulls away and exhales with a hiss. "Shit. *Fuck!*" he swears, causing the dog to jump up. As he pushes me off him, I fall back onto the end of the couch and he sits up, swinging his legs off the couch and planting his bare feet on the floor.

"Kenzi, I'm sorry. I'm so fucking high on pills right now," he says, running his hands through his hair. "You need to leave. *Now*."

"Wh-what? Why?" I'm still lost in the euphoria of his kiss, of feeling him so hard against me, my mind cloudy and humming, still wanting more of whatever just happened. I want a total head-on collision.

"Please. Go." He points to the door like I'm some kind of squatter who wandered into his house.

"Tor..." I touch his arm, but he yanks away from me.

"Kenzi, you have to go. I mean it. I can't be around you when I'm high as a fucking kite. I don't know what the hell you're doing to me."

I stand on wobbly legs, completely engulfed in confusion. "I'm...I'm sorry...," I stammer. "What about dinner?"

I'm in a daze as he walks with me to the kitchen, where he scoops up my keys and hands them to me. "Don't worry about dinner. And don't be sorry. This isn't your fault. It's me. I'm messed up."

He practically pushes me to the front door, where I turn to look up at him, clutching my phone and keys, tears falling down my cheeks. "What's happening to us?" I ask.

His deep chestnut eyes are filled with regret as he shakes his head. "I don't know, Angel, but I think we need some time apart."

"Time apart?" The concept of that sounds so out of place to

me. That's a term reserved for people in a relationship that's going bad and need to get away from each other to regroup and calm down, and to think about whether they want to be together or not. That's not us. I don't ever want to consider not having Tor in my life.

"When are you going to Katherine's this year?" he asks.

I'm taken aback by his question. "Why would you ask me that? I'm not sure I'm going. I planned to stay home this year."

"I think you should go for the summer. I think we need to put some space between us for a while."

His words steal my breath.

"You want me to go away?"

"I just think we need to get our heads straight. We've been spending too much time together."

"We always have, Tor. For like my entire life."

"I know, and that was obviously a mistake on my part."

My throat clenches along with my heart. "So you regret all the time you've spent with me?" My entire life flashes before my eyes, wondering if every memory of us together was nothing but annoyance for him while it meant so much to me.

"No, Angel. Not one minute. But I think now that you're older, it has to stop. You should be with friends your own age. Find guys your age to date. And I should be spending time with women my age and not with you. This is all fucking wrong." He puts his hands up and backs away from me.

"But it doesn't feel wrong," I protest weakly.

His eyes are hard as steel. "It's wrong. Trust me. We should never be touching or kissing, for any reason."

"I can't believe you want me to go away," I say in disbelief.

"I think it's for the best," he says simply, his walls building up again.

"For you, maybe."

"No, for both of us. But especially for you. You just can't see it."

"That's total bullshit. I like being with you. And being kissed by you is amazing—"

He grabs my shoulders and bends down to get at eye level with me. "Stop!" he hisses. "It's just a crush, Kenzi. It's normal for your age. It'll go away."

I scoff at him. "A crush? If that's all it is, then why do you feel the same way, Tor? You're a little old for a crush, aren't you?"

"I don't even fucking know anymore, Kenzi. I just know we need to get away from each other."

I can't even fathom wanting to get away from him. All I want is to get closer to him, not farther away.

"I don't know what to say," I say. "I'm confused."

"So am I," he says softly, releasing my shoulders. "I'm trying to be honest with you, Kenzi. But this is really hard because I also have to do the right thing. I can't let emotions get in the way of reality."

"What does that mean?" I ask.

"It means that I'm all fucked up. I have feelings for you I shouldn't have. I'm not going to lie to you about that. But I have to be the adult here and do the right thing. This can't happen. I don't know what's wrong with me."

"I'm not a baby, Tor. I'm going to be eighteen in less than two months. That's an adult."

"It's still wrong in like twenty other ways."

I look into his eyes, pleading. "I don't want to believe that."

"We shouldn't even be having conversations like this, Kenzi. I don't know what the hell is going on anymore." He crosses the room and grabs his water and bottle of pills off the coffee table and gulps down another handful of painkillers and muscle relaxers. "I really think you should go now. Please."

I reach for the doorknob, my emotions a tornado inside. Hearing him admit he has feelings for me makes me want to throw my arms around him and hug him into oblivion, but he's taking it all away and hiding it like it's some kind of dirty secret that needs to be destroyed, and he wants me to go with it.

"Please don't do this," I beg. "Don't push me away."

"Kenzi, don't make this worse for us. I'm in a ton of pain right now. I can barely think straight from that and all the pills I've taken. I'm trying to be gentle about this, but I just need you gone."

Gone. Over and done with. No more. Done. Finished. Ended. That's what he wants.

My unwanted heart cracks.

"You're a jerk," I choke out. "You want me gone? Then fine, I'm gone."

His shoulders slump in defeat. "Don't say shit like that to me."

"I've never thought of you as weak, Tor. But I guess I don't know you as well as I thought I did."

He comes back to stand in front of me at the door where I'm still standing with my hand on the knob. Diogee follows him, tail wagging, oblivious to what's going on.

"Trust me, Kenzi, there's nothing fucking weak about this at all. I hate hurting you and it's killing me inside."

"Well, that's funny since you just hurt me more than anyone else ever has."

I storm out of his house, slamming the door behind me, and jump into my Jeep.

"Never drive upset." My father's words ring through my head as I back recklessly out of the driveway. Here I am, already driving

with a broken heart, barely able to see through the tears in my eyes.

Spending the summer in Maine with Aunt Katherine is looking better and better. I've never been a crier or the type of person to slam doors, let alone call people names. Between the fight with Jason and now all this emotional confusion with Toren, I don't feel like myself. This isn't how I wanted to start my life as an adult. Maybe Tor is right; I need to get away from everyone for a while for a major reset.

CHAPTER 13

Kenzi—age fourteen

Toren—age twenty-nine

When I wake from my nap, the house is quiet. Too quiet. I'm not used to it and I don't like it. Even though my mom has always traveled a lot with her band and I'm used to her not being home much, this feels different. Her absence has left a deafening silence that seems to be screaming that she's gone and never coming back.

I get out of bed and wander down the long, dark hallway to my parents' bedroom, where the door is closed halfway. Just as I approach the door, I hear voices, and my heart skips with hope. I think somehow Mom has come back and she's home, right on the other side of the door talking to Dad, cuddled in bed laughing.

But she's not.

I peer inside the dim room and my father is sitting on the bed with his head in his hands, crying. Uncle Tor is sitting next to him with his arm around him, holding my dad as he sobs.

"I can't do this. I can't do this. I can't do this . . ." my father is saying over and over again.

"You can. You're okay."

"I don't know how to live without her."

"Ash, she's still here. Don't give up. I know it's hard, but you gotta have faith."

"I just want her back. I miss her so fucking much."

"I know you do. We all do."

"And what about Kenzi? How am I supposed to raise a daughter by myself in a rock band?"

"I'll help you. Your family will help. I promise she'll be okay. I'm not going to let anything happen to either of you." Tor presses his lips to my dad's temple and leans his head against his, his other large, inked hand holding the side of my dad's head as he talks softly to him, comforting him. While some people may think that's odd, it is so them, and I am grateful that I'm surrounded by people who love each other so deeply, so unconditionally, that they aren't afraid to express it. It's a shame that most people won't show compassion and affection to others out of fear of judgment or rumors of their sexuality. I've always loved the bond that Tor has with my parents and now with me.

I quietly back out of the doorway, unseen and unheard, and make my way back to my bedroom, quietly closing my door behind me.

Up until recently, I've never seen my father cry before. He's always been a rock, the one who helps everyone else, always smiling, always positive. Watching him fall apart scares me, and I feel like I've lost both my parents.

TOR

I've been riding for two days straight, with no destination planned other than *far the fuck away*. I don't care where I end up. Wherever the road takes me, that's where I'm going. Tesla agreed to stay at my house to take care of the dog until I get back so I wouldn't have to worry about him. I told the guys I'd be out of the shop for a few days so they'd have to pick up the slack and take care of the Devils' Wolves tasks on top of it. I hardly ever take time off, but I need it now.

And now I'm six hundred miles from home, dirty and tired,

and I still can't get away from the demons in my head, and even worse, in my heart.

Fuck yeah, I'm running away. Maybe she was right. I'm weak. A seventeen-year-old girl has completely derailed my brain and rocked me off my ass. I should be stronger than this. Even Sydni never had my head all twisted up like this and she had years of practice.

I thought a nice long ride and camping out in the woods would bring my head back around and give me some clarity. The stillness of the woods, with nothing but the sound of birds chirping in the morning, crickets at night, and the wind in the trees is therapeutic for me. But the thing is, it isn't just my head that's messed up. It's my heart.

I think I'm falling in love with her, and I'm powerless to stop it. I can feel it, like a train with no brakes, coming faster and faster, straight for me. Soon it's going to crash, and it's not going to be pretty.

My head is telling me I'm sick and fucked in the brain. Not just for having feelings for a woman so young, but for being physically attracted to her, too. But my heart is telling me this is my girl, my other half—the one I've been waiting for. And let's not even get started on my dick and what that part of my anatomy is thinking and wanting.

All of this just complicates the shit out of my life. This is entirely new territory for me, not being in control of my own feelings, and I'm not dealing with it well.

These feelings can't be normal. I have adult women who want me. I can sleep with them, I can love them—I can do anything with a handful of women I know. All I have to do is put the effort in, and they'd be mine any way I want them, without any baggage or dark clouds of doom hanging over us.

The problem is the only girl I really want is an adorable, smart, loving, almost-eighteen-year-old who I've been taking care of since she was born. Of course, she's the only girl I can't have. Karma, you are one demented bitch.

How the hell did this happen?

A year ago, I didn't feel like this. Sure, I loved and cared about her, and enjoyed her company. But that was it. We went from an uncle and niece relationship to a friendship, and that's all it ever was. There were never any other feelings involved, not even in the slightest.

So what the hell changed? How come every time I'm near her now, all I want to do is kiss her? Why do I keep losing control around her? Why can't I get her out of my head? Sure, she's beautiful, but I've never been the type of guy who can't control himself around good-looking women.

Even more screwed up is she seems to feel the same way. Kenzi isn't the flighty type and she's always been mature for her age. She's not a silly, giggly teen like my sister was, jumping from guy to guy. Kenzi's like Asher—she knows what she wants and she doesn't deviate for anything. Knowing this scares the hell out of me even more because if she says she wants me, then she knows it one thousand percent, without a doubt. That's what I've been wanting, needing, and looking for in a woman for so long. Someone who knows what they want and isn't afraid to grab it.

But not like this. Not with her.

As I pack up my small pup tent and sleeping bag and secure them onto the back of my bike, I know I'm heading back home with absolutely zero resolution to my Kenzi dilemma. Thankfully she's in Maine now and I won't see her for at least two months. Quitting each other cold turkey should break whatever this new wacked-out connection is between us for good so things can go back to normal.

I hope.

♥ ♥ ♥

After riding for about two hundred miles, I pull over to the side of the winding mountain road to drink some water and stretch my back out, which is starting to ache from all the hours on the bike and sleeping on the ground for two days. I can't wait to get home, take a hot shower and a muscle relaxer, and sleep in my own bed.

I'm just about to get back on my bike when I see something moving out of the corner of my eye in the tall weeds on the side of the road. Removing my sunglasses, I walk over and see that it's a taped-up cardboard box. And it's moving.

Something's inside it. Scratching. Trying to get out.

Oh fuck.

I glance up and down the road, but there's absolutely nothing out here. No houses or stores. It's just a road going up the mountain with nothing but woods on both sides for miles.

Kneeling, I pull my knife out of my belt clip and carefully slice along the tape, not sure what the hell I'm going to find in this box, bracing myself for the worst.

A tiny paw shoves through the small space I've cut open, and I quickly cut the rest of the tape as a small gray furry head pokes out. At first, I think it's a squirrel, but it's a kitten.

"Shit," I swear under my breath, gently taking the tiny ball of fur out of the box and cradling it in my hand. It looks to be about six weeks old and is all blue gray with a tiny white spot on its chest. As I stare at it, it begins to mew in my face at the top of its little lungs.

"Shh...I got ya, little one," I say softly, gently rubbing its head. It purrs loudly in response, rubbing its fuzzy head into my palm. I check its body over for any injuries, but it seems fine from what I can see. Other than being taped into a box and thrown onto the side of a desolate road like garbage to die a horrible death. I check the box again, but there's nothing inside and no markings on the outside. Some asshole just taped a kitten into an empty box and left it to die.

Days like this, I hate the fucking world. I could easily choke the shit out of the person who did this, leave their ass on the side of the road and feel no remorse whatsoever. In fact, I'd probably enjoy it.

I snap a few pictures of the box and the surrounding area before I carry the kitten back to my bike and pour a tiny bit of water from my thermos into my palm, which the kitten laps up quickly.

"Dude, you have no idea how lucky you are," I say to it, rubbing its itty-bitty ears, which are like tiny velvet triangles. "What are the odds someone like me would find you out here in the middle of friggin' nowhere?"

My mom has said a hundred times, sometimes God puts the right people in the right place for a reason. I'm not a religious person, but right now, I'm thinking she's right.

Unfortunately, my options for getting this kitten home safely are limited. My phone has no reception, so I can't even call one of my brothers to come meet me in a car. I sure as hell can't zip it up into one of my saddlebags because I'm pretty sure the roar of my pipes so close will give it a heart attack. I can't stick it back in that box and try to hold it for another two hundred miles.

"Fuck it. You better be cool, kitten," I say as I tuck it against my chest and zip my leather jacket up. "Don't go all Freddy Krueger on me and get us killed, deal?"

I kiss the top of its head before I zip my jacket up a few more inches. This is probably not the best plan I've ever had, but I have no idea how else I can get this poor thing home. Hopefully it won't scratch the shit out of me.

I start up the bike and get back on the road slowly, letting the fur ball cuddled up against my chest adjust to the noise and movement and hoping it doesn't freak the hell out. After a few seconds, I can feel it purring up against me, vibrating against my heart. So far, so good.

We head for home, stopping once at a gas station so I can fill up my tank. I slowly unzip my jacket a few inches to check the kitten, and it pokes its head out and rubs against the stubble on my chin, still purring.

"You think you're a biker cat now? Don't get any ideas. This is a one-time ride, kitten." I can't believe it's not scared out of its skull after enduring the rumble of my engine, but it seems pretty content just hanging out inside my jacket, which I guess is better than being taped up in a box. I tuck him back in and hop on my bike to get this last stretch of miles over with.

As I cruise down the road, I wish Kenzi was with me. She would love this kitten. I can almost see her face if she had been with me when I found it. She would have cried and ground her teeth in anger, and she'd probably have it named by now and would be begging me to talk Asher into letting her keep it.

I'm not a cat person, but maybe Diogee would like someone to hang out with while I'm at the shop all day. Looks like biker box kitten is coming home with me to stay.

"Holy shit, you're turning into Dr. Dolittle," Tesla says when I pull the kitten out of my jacket and tell her how I found it in a box.

"Well, I couldn't just leave him there." I hand the kitten over to my sister so I can take all my gear off. "Call Mom and ask her if she can come over and check it out for me and bring me whatever I need. I've never had a cat before."

"You're keeping it?" she asks in surprise.

"Why not? I thought the dog would like the company." Sitting on the couch, I take off my jacket, belt, and my boots. My entire body is aching.

Tessie lays the kitten on the couch between us as she calls our mom, and Diogee sniffs the newcomer with interest, gently nudging it with his nose, and the kitten rubs against his face.

"Nice . . . ," I say, petting Diogee's head. His tail wags as the kitten continues to rub on his nose and rolls over on his back, purring. I think they're going to be fine together.

"You sure you want a kitten, Toren? This is just a baby," Tesla says when she gets off the phone. "And this dog is clingy, too. They're both going to want a lot of attention from you."

I lay the kitten on my chest and stare into its amber eyes. "Good. I need some distractions in my life."

"Why? What's going on? Is that bitch screwing with your head again?"

Tesla isn't a fan of Sydni and has never even attempted to hide her feelings about it. Today is no exception.

"Nah, she and I are done. I just have a lot on my mind lately."

"Good. You should have kicked her to the curb years ago." She disappears down the hall and comes back with her overnight bag. "Mom said she'll be here in about an hour. I should get going. The dog was good while you were gone. I wouldn't mind watching him again for you if you need me. I went grocery shopping for you, too. You can't just live on protein powder and fruit, Toren. You have to eat real food."

"Thanks, Tess. I appreciate you coming over here at the last minute. And I do eat, I just ran out of food."

"Anytime," she says, then frowns at me with concern. "Are you okay? You seem off."

I pet the kitten with one hand and the dog with the other. "Yeah, I'm fine."

"If you want to talk, you're always welcome to stop by. I feel like I never see you. Tanner, Taran, and Tris come over all the time, and you've never even been to my new apartment. You're turning into a recluse like Ty."

My gaze switches up to my sister. Her natural hair color is blond, but today it's dark auburn and has grown out a few inches past her shoulders. She's changed and matured a lot in the past year, moving out of Mom's house to get her own place after landing a job as a hair and makeup artist. And she's right, I don't see her nearly enough because all I do lately is work, do what I have to for Devils' Wolves, and then go home. Other than the bonfires and the occasional rides with Asher, I don't really socialize.

"You're right. We'll hang out soon."

"Good luck with this zoo you're acquiring," she teases, flipping her hair over her shoulder. "Call me or stop by. I mean it."

"I will."

♥ ♥ ♥

My mom shows up an hour later armed with kitten food, a cat bed, litter box, dishes, and toys, and gives me a course in Kittens 101.

"You're filling a void," she observes as she eyes me on the couch, with the kitten on my chest and the dog lying with his head in my lap.

"What are you talking about, Ma? I'm tired. Sleep is the only void I want to fill right now."

"Taking off for a weekend to the middle of nowhere? Keeping the pets you've rescued? You've been doing this for years, honey, and you've never wanted to bring any home," she says. "Now look at you."

I shrug. "So what? I like these two. They're different."

"You're lonely, Toren."

Scoffing, I lean back against the couch and close my eyes. "I'm tired is what I am, Ma. Nothing else."

"That's probably true, since all you do is work. Latching on to these animals is your heart's way of telling you that you want to love and be loved back. You're trying to put together a little family."

Opening my eyes, I look at her like she's nuts as she's standing over me near the couch, analyzing me like moms do. "You been smokin' Tanner's weed, Ma?"

She shoots me a scolding glare. "Do you know how many people come into the shelter every day adopting an animal because they're grieving? Or depressed? Or lonely? Trust me, I know what it looks like."

I wonder if she's right. I've rescued hundreds of animals since I started helping her when I was twelve years old, and these are the first two I've ever wanted to keep.

"So maybe I'll grow into a crazy old single cat man," I joke.

"I guess there are worse things that could happen. Why don't you and Lisa come over for dinner one night this week? I'd love to get to know her better. She seems lovely."

"Lovely?"

"Yes. Nice. Polite."

"Eh..." I curl my lip. Lisa's just not doing it for me, no matter how lovely she might be.

"Then come by yourself if you want. You can hang my new ceiling fan while you're there. Bring Diogee. You need to socialize him or you're both going to be weird around people. You need to get out more."

I think I'm already weird around people. Just a few weeks ago

I told a woman my dick was on a vacation. In fact, I think I may have surpassed weird a while ago. I'm not going to admit that to my mother, though.

Letting out a sigh, I agree to stop by, but mostly because I want her to have the new ceiling fan, not because I want to practice social skills with my dog.

"We have a new volunteer at the shelter. Her name is Dani. I could invite her over, too. She's pretty, and she has two cats, a dog, and a ferret. I think you'd like her."

"Ma. No. I don't want to be set up with anyone. Especially with someone who owns a ferret. That's an instant fuck no."

"Why? What do you have against ferrets?" She walks around the living room, picking up the dog toys and putting them all in a pile by his bed. I know as soon as she's gone he's going to spread them all over the house again.

"They're evil. They're little fuzzy lunatic ninjas."

She sighs in utter frustration. "All right, then. I tried. Call me if you need any help with the kitten. And you should bring it over to the vet as soon as you can for a real checkup. Maybe have Kenzi bring him over for you. She's been helping at the shelter a lot the past few weeks and she's really good with the animals."

A burn spreads in my chest at the mention of her name. "She's gone to Maine for the summer. I'll take the kitten myself."

"Oh," she says in surprise. "She didn't even say goodbye. I hope when she gets back home she'll still volunteer. I love having her there. She has some really good ideas."

"I'm sure she will, Ma. She told me she wants to. She left sorta at the last minute. She was excited about driving her new car and going on a road trip." *Lies and excuses. The first of many.*

My mood shifts from bad to worse once my mom is gone. Kenzi didn't say goodbye to me, either. She just left without so much as a text or a phone call, which is unlike her. She always says goodbye. If Asher hadn't mentioned to me that she left before I went on my excursion in the woods, I wouldn't have known.

I can't stop thinking about that afternoon when I told her to leave. I don't know how many times in the past seventeen years I've watched her bottom lip quiver with emotion while tears welled up in her eyes and streamed down her cheeks. This time was different, though, because I've never been the one to cause her tears. I've always been the one to wipe them away and make it all better. I've always been the hero to that adorable little blond-haired girl who has morphed into a sensual woman in the blink of an eye, and now I don't know what to do with her.

It took every ounce of self-control I had to resist taking her in my arms and kissing her tears away, telling her I didn't mean what I said and everything will be okay. As always, I ached to make everything better for her. But I couldn't. That's what Uncle Tor would do, and unfortunately he went up in flames the moment we touched. That guy is gone, and she can't ever have him back. Just like I can't ever have my little blond-haired princess back.

One forbidden touch, one taboo kiss, and we destroyed who we were. I don't know who either one of us is anymore or how we got all fucking tangled up in this mess of lust and love that should never exist. But it does exist, and no matter how much I try to deny it, it keeps coming back to get in my face, refusing to be ignored.

And now she's gone, just like I asked.

I want her back. So fucking bad.

CHAPTER 14

Kenzi—age seventeen

Asher—age thirty-two

As soon as I wake up, I can feel something is wrong. There's a darkness in the air—something foreboding that makes a chill run down my spine as I climb out of bed, even though the house is not cold. I find him sitting on the couch in the living room. The television is off. There's no music playing. And that's very unlike him, because sound is his passion. He's staring at the floor and doesn't even seem to notice that I've walked into the room.

"Dad?" I say tentatively, afraid to jolt him out of the trance he appears to be in.

His head raises unnaturally slow, and he starts to tremble. This is it, I think to myself. Mom is really gone. She's no longer lingering between life and death, holding us as emotional hostages in her limbo. It's over.

I run across the hardwood floor and kneel in front of him. That's when I notice the blood. On his hands, and on his shirt. It's smeared, and not wet, but sticky. It has to be recent.

"Oh my God. Daddy...are you hurt?"

"It's not mine," he whispers.

"What happened? Whose blood is this?"

"Katie's dead."

I feel like the life got sucked out of me as my mind tries to process what he just said, hoping I must have heard him wrong. Katie is my five-year-old cousin. Five-year-olds don't die. Especially ones who are so happy and healthy like Katie.

"What? No . . ." *I shake my head as tears start to track down my face.*

"Lukas and I had to identify the body. Vandal had a car accident, and she was in the back seat. It's his blood."

"Uncle Vandal? Is he . . . ?"

He shakes his head. "He's okay. Hurt . . . but okay."

Gulping, I tug at his bloodstained shirt. I can't be near it, and he shouldn't be either. "Let's take this off, Dad," *I say softly, and he lets me pull his shirt over his head. I take the soft throw blanket off the top of the couch and gently wrap it around him. He's still shaking uncontrollably and I'm afraid he's in shock.*

"I can't get it out of my head. She was so little . . . It was awful. I feel sick." *He chokes on his tears and presses his palms against his eyes.* "I can't stop seeing her little broken body."

I put my arms around him and hug him close to me, fighting the waves of devastation rippling through my own body.

"I'm so sorry, Daddy."

I don't know what else to say, or how to comfort him. He needs his wife, not me. I have never experienced death before this, and I'm torn between falling apart myself and needing to be strong for my father. All I can offer is words I've read in books or heard in movies. "Let's try to remember her before. How cute she was. Don't think about tonight. That's not her anymore."

Maybe I should call my grandmother, or Storm, my other uncle, who's very close to my dad. They must be going through the exact same feelings of grief and disbelief right now, though, and probably won't be able to console him any more than I can.

My father clings to me, hugging me so tight I can barely breathe. "I'd die if something happened to you. I can't ever lose you, too."

I stroke the back of his head. "Nothing is ever going to happen to me, Dad. I promise."

♥ ♥ ♥

KENZI

It wasn't easy convincing my father I could make the two-and-a-half-hour drive to Maine safely by myself without crashing, getting lost, getting kidnapped, picking up a hitchhiker, or getting several speeding tickets. After much debate, I finally convinced him to let me go. He didn't understand my sudden decision to leave as soon as possible, and he stood in my room with a worried look on his face watching me pack a suitcase like a demented squirrel with way too many nuts.

"I don't understand why you're leaving in such a rush. Did something happen? Did Katherine say something?" he asks.

There's been a slight rift between my father and my aunt Katherine since my mom's accident. She wanted me to come live with her permanently, stating that I needed to be raised by a mature woman now and not by a bunch of rock stars. My father won that battle, agreeing to let me spend the summers with Katherine. But honestly, I don't think my aunt has ever really trusted that her only sister's child was being raised right. I've never met my mother's parents since they basically disowned her when she got pregnant with me, so Katherine is the only relative of my mother's that I have any contact with. Every time I visit, she begs me to stay permanently. I always leave, though, because I miss my dad, my family, and Chloe.

And Tor.

"Everything is fine, Dad. Katherine hasn't said anything other than she's excited I'm coming. I guess I just want to get away and think about what I want to do with my life now. That's all." After the fight with Tor earlier today, I just want to get away from everything.

"I get that. I just wanted more time with you myself this summer. I have a tour in the fall. And then again in January. I feel like you're running away from something."

I hate upsetting my father, and I worry about leaving him because I know he's lonely even though he refuses to admit it. He looks so young to me today, wearing ripped-up jeans and a black shirt that's unbuttoned with all his chest and ab tats visible, and a black baseball hat on his head backward, his long hair spilling out from beneath it. He doesn't look like a typical father and sometimes I forget he's as young as he is.

"I know, Dad. I'm sorry. I'll call and text you every day. And I'll come back at the end of July or early August, so we'll still have time together before you leave."

"But I'll miss your birthday. It's your eighteenth and I wanted to have a big party for you."

I inwardly cringe. "I hate parties. When I get back, I'll have a few friends over for one of your bonfire nights. That's all I want." I smile reassuringly at him. "You don't have to do anything special for me."

His brow creases with worry. "Your mom would want something special for you for your birthday. She would want me to do something memorable for you."

"You make every day of my life special, Dad," I say, and I mean it with all my heart. Not a day goes by that he doesn't tell me and show me how much he loves me.

"You could come on tour with me. It'll be fun now that you're older. Your uncles would love to have you around."

I check the clasps on Snuggles's cage to make sure they're secure before I can load her up into the back seat of my Jeep. "I might just take you up on that. Let's see how the summer goes, okay?" I'm not sure if Toren still wants me working at his shop when Gretchen leaves. I guess I'll cross that bridge later after things settle down.

"Good enough. I just want you to know I don't want you to move out. I know a lot of kids your age want to get out on their own and get their own place or live with their friends, but I like having you here with me."

He walks over to the rabbit cage and peers in, poking his finger through the bars to pet her, then turns back to face me, and the desperation in his eyes tugs at my heart. "I can work on giving you more space and not prying into your life, and I could hire a builder and section off part of the house so you have your own apartment. This place is big enough to do that; we have rooms we don't even use. Your mom thought we'd have more kids some- day..." His voice trails off, and his hand goes up to finger the tar- nished silver skeleton key that hangs around his neck on a thick strand of leather. He never takes it off because it was hers. "What- ever you want, I'll do it."

"Daddy..." I won't barter with my father's love. I refuse to demand things for myself in exchange for companionship and security for him. "You don't have to do any of that. You don't bother me. You're not even home much. Trust me, I'm not in any hurry to move out."

"Good. I don't want too much to change." He swallows and meets my eyes. "I have a good feeling...about your mom. She would want you here when she comes home. Think of all the things you can tell her—"

Counting to five, I try to level my voice. "Dad," I say sternly. "Mom isn't coming home."

We stare at each other, and I watch him fight to keep his hope alive, and damn it hurts so bad. I've stood in denial with him for years. I've refused to talk about her and what happened. I've lived in limbo with him because it seemed like the easiest way to cope with the tragedy of what happened to her. Even now, after years have passed, I still can't say the words, and neither can he. So much power hides in words, and once you speak them, you give them life, and you have to accept the truth that comes with them.

Hiding from the facts guarded my sanity for a long time, but now that I'm getting older, I know I can't run from it forever, and neither can he. It's just not right.

"I think she will," he replies, his voice soft and determined. "Having faith and love can work miracles, Kenzi. If I've taught you nothing else, please believe in that. We can't give up on her."

I chew my fingernail, swallowing back all the things I should be saying right now to bring my father back down to reality, but I can't do it to him. Who am I to smash his hopes about the love of his life? Maybe he's right, and love and faith really can defy mounting facts that point to the opposite of what we want to believe.

"I won't give up, Dad. I promise." But honestly, what I really mean is that I won't give up on my faith in him.

As he hefts up the rabbit cage in his muscular arms, a smile spreads across his face, and all I can think is that I want a man to love me someday like my dad loves my mom. That unconditional, no-matter-what, *I will fuck with anything that tries to get in my path* type of love. I hope wherever my mom is, she knows how deeply he loves her, how he refuses to give up on her or stray from their commitment for any reason. I hope that makes her fight just as hard as he is.

"Let's get you two loaded up and on your way." He winks at me as he carefully carries my rabbit out to the hallway.

I need to do a lot of serious soul searching this summer and sort out my feelings, and not just about the whirlwind of new emotions Toren has awakened in me. Obviously, I can't live with my father forever, and I'm worried that the longer I stay with him, the harder it will be to ever leave him if my mother doesn't come back like he believes she will. I'm afraid we're totally enabling each other, and not really moving on with our lives. We're going through the motions, waiting for something to happen that may never happen. How can that be good for either of us?

It takes me a little over three hours to get to Aunt Katherine's house because I felt like I had to stop at every single rest stop to use the bathroom, whether I really had to go or not. I kept worrying that if I didn't stop, I'd have to pee a few miles down the road and wouldn't be able to find another rest area. Total new driver struggles.

Driving slow with the bunny in the back seat, even though my father rigged the seat belt around her cage to keep her from sliding around back there, seemed like the best thing to do. I wasn't exactly in a rush, and listening to my favorite music while I drove, belting out lyrics in a voice that would make my father cringe in horror, puts me in a good mood. Having my own car and driving someplace entirely alone is giving me a new sense of freedom and independence. I can feel the stress leaving me with each passing mile. Maybe Tor is right; I really did need to get away to clear my head. Maybe I've clung to him in ways I shouldn't have and misread my own feelings for him. Hopefully the time apart will help us figure it out so we can go back to being normal again.

"Oh my God, look at you!" Katherine exclaims, running down the driveway as I climb out of the Jeep. She immediately pulls me into a tight hug, her lavender perfume filling my lungs. "You look so grown up!"

I welcome her embrace and return it with just as much excitement. "You look gorgeous as always." It's always a bit of a shock to my heart to see her because my mother shared her same beautiful long hair, friendly eyes, and perfect smile. Katherine's hair is brown and wavy, which was also my mom's natural color but she dyed it often depending on her mood. They're ten years apart in age, but Katherine has always looked much younger than she is.

"Let me look at you!" She steps back and fluffs my hair with her hands. "I can't believe it's been a year. You really have to come more often, Kenzi. I miss you so much. I barely recognize you."

"Well, now that I can drive, I can come whenever I want. I miss you, too." I open the back door of my Jeep, and she takes my suitcase as I unhook the rabbit cage from the seat belt and we head inside together.

The Inn is a beautiful, three-story elegant Victorian house with four private suites and my aunt's private living space on the first floor, which includes a small galley kitchen, living room, master bedroom, and guest room, where I'll be staying. Aunt Katherine likes to greet all the guests personally in the front lobby, and she also prepares the gourmet breakfasts, dinners, and midday snacks. She's an amazing chef, and that's probably where my love of cooking came from. She has two women who have worked for her for years, Tina and Bethany, who do all the housekeeping and help out in other areas if Katherine is busy. I usually help with the meal prep and serving when I stay here, but Katherine also makes sure I have time to relax and enjoy myself. Meeting the guests has always been one of my favorite parts of staying at the Inn, and I've met some very intriguing people over the years I'll never forget. Most notably was a magician who seemed to be able to guess every number or color I was thinking of without fail.

"Why don't you get settled, call your dad, and then meet me out on the porch and we'll talk before dinner?" Katherine suggests, laying my suitcase on the four-poster bed in the guest room.

"Sounds good."

After a quick talk with my dad, I get Snuggles's cage settled by the window, give her some fresh water and food, put all my clothes in the closet and dresser and my makeup and hair products in the small adjoining bathroom.

I meet up with Aunt Katherine on her private porch that overlooks the water. She has a plate of crackers, cheese, and fresh fruit waiting for me with a fluted crystal glass of water with a twist of lemon.

"Spoiling me already?" I tease with a grin, taking a seat beside her at the small bistro table. "All of my favorites."

"Of course." She smiles. "I have to tell you, it's so strange to see you driving your own car. You're growing up too fast."

"My dad says the same thing."

She nods. "I'm sure he's having a hard time with it. How has he been?"

"Good. Working on the new album. They're going on tour in the fall. He wants me to go with him."

She grimaces. "I'm not sure you should be traipsing around with all those men, Kenzi, and sleeping on a bus. Even though they're your uncles, there's going to be roadies, and fans, all sorts of strange people. You're a beautiful young lady who needs privacy."

"I'm not sure I'll go. I have to think about it."

"Is he still visiting Ember?" she asks, staring down into her cup of Earl Grey.

"Every weekend when he's not touring."

Nodding, she shakes her head in disbelief and takes a sip of tea. "Let's not talk about that," she says. "I want to have a great time and focus on you. Tell me, how was your prom? I got the picture you texted me, and you looked absolutely gorgeous."

I place a slice of cheddar onto a wheat cracker and take a bite before answering. "Do you want the truth or a happy lie?"

"The truth. What happened?"

I sigh and eat the other half of my cracker before I tell her about the disaster that was my prom and then the aftermath of getting teased by half my class for bailing on one of the hottest guys in our school and being nicknamed the slutty prude.

Aunt Katherine touches my hand. "Oh, honey. I'm so sorry. What a bunch of jerks. I really wanted you to have the best time and have good memories. What's wrong with kids these days?"

"I don't know, but it really sucked. Thank God Toren came to get me that night. Please don't tell my father; he doesn't know I had a crappy time. I told him it all went okay."

"I promise I won't tell him."

"Thanks. It will just upset him, and I can't do that to him. He has so much on his mind already."

"You can't always protect him, Kenzi. I know your intentions are in the right place, but he's the adult, not you."

"I know. But you know how he is. He's so sensitive, and he takes it hard when I'm upset, like he thinks he could have somehow prevented it from happening. Then he wants to try to make it better."

"Trust me, I know how he is. He's the most empathetic man I've ever met in my life, but someday he's got to come to grips with the fact that he can't fix things for everyone. Your dad is like this...mysterious guardian angel. He always has been."

I laugh affectionately at her description. "Yeah, he kinda is." I gaze out at the water for a few moments. "So what about you? Anything new? Are you seeing anyone?"

"Actually, yes. I've been seeing this guy named Thomas for about three months. He's been divorced for eight years and has a daughter. She's ten years old. I've only met her once because we're trying to take things slow, but she's really sweet. Very shy."

"Oh wow!" I exclaim, surprised at the news. "I'm so happy for you! Where did you meet him?" Katherine has been single for a long time. About five years ago, she went through a bad breakup after she found her fiancé cheating on her. I remember her having a very hard time getting over the pain and betrayal of that.

"Believe it or not, he stayed here for a week. It's not often I have single men staying here alone, so at first I was a bit leery of him. Then I found out he had just lost his mother to cancer, and he wanted to spread her ashes in the water, so he stayed here to kinda get his head together. We hit it off right away." She grabs her phone that's lying next to her teacup. "Here, I'll show you his picture. He's really good-looking."

She flips through her phone and then hands it to me. He reminds me of Ryan Reynolds, only with slightly graying hair at the temples. "Wow! He's hot!"

Taking the phone back, she smiles at his picture, her cheeks turning pink, and that makes me feel so happy for her that she's met someone who she's obviously very interested in.

"Thanks. I like him a lot. He's such a nice guy, too. I was hoping we could all have dinner while you're here so you could get to know him."

"I'd love to."

"I told him all about you, and he's excited to meet you. He's actually been to concerts for both of your parents' bands, so he was a little excited to hear that you're their daughter. He's not a crazy fan, though. So don't worry. He won't be hammering you with questions."

Thankfully I've never been targeted by overzealous fans of my parents' bands. Years ago, Sydni and Toren were at a bar with my parents, and a fan was obsessing over Sydni, trying to talk to her and take photos of her. Apparently he kept trying to touch her, and Tor went off on him and ended up beating the guy's ass pretty bad, which is how he ended up in jail for assault. Even though the guy had been harassing Sydni, he hired a lawyer and filed charges, also trying to sue Sydni for emotional distress. People do the craziest things.

CHAPTER 15

I thought of you today.
But then again, I think of you every day.
The only difference was today
I could think of you without pain.
Without crumbling.
Today, I thought of you, and I smiled.
And it was all worth it.
I'd do it again.
Every tear, every sleepless night, every day of missing you.
I would do it all again, just to have you.
I miss you. I want you. I love you.
I wish for you.

🤍 💜 🤍

KENZI

I love waking up at the Inn because the cool breeze blows through the bedroom windows, and I can see and hear the water if I sit up in bed. Watching the sun set and rise every day is a beautiful bonus.

My moment of tranquility on the tenth day of my visit quickly fades as my eyes lower from the view out my window to Snuggles in her cage. Usually she sits atop her little wooden house and stares out the window or sleeps peacefully up there, enjoying the fresh air, her little bunny nose twitching.

But today, she's lying on her side in the cage, up against her pile of hay. Throwing my quilt off, I race over to her cage and pull the little door open, reaching inside to stroke her.

"Snuggles?"

My tiny best friend is unmoving. Not breathing. Her little nose incredibly still.

She's gone.

"No, no, no...," I whisper, gently stroking her ears. "Please wake up."

Years and months of pent-up anguish roll over me as I lean my forehead against the metal cage. The heartache that came from losing my mother, then my little cousin, the teasing at school, and the confusion with Tor rips through me as I stroke my bunny's tiny lifeless body.

I want it all to stop. I want off this ride.

I didn't realize I was screaming and going into hysterics until Aunt Katherine came rushing into the room and had to pull me away from the cage while Tina covered it with a sheet and they both sat with me on my bed, trying to calm me down. Katherine made me chamomile tea and rocked me like a baby while I cried over my little rabbit that lived so much longer than most do but still wasn't long enough. I feel safe having my aunt comfort me like my mother used to, so I let her, instead of fighting it like I normally would. If I close my eyes and listen to her voice, it's almost like mom is here with me again, telling me everything is going to be okay, and she loves me with all the love in the world.

I cry until I have no more tears left, and then Katherine puts me on the phone with my father, who cries with me and offers to come be with me, but I tell him no. There's no sense in disrupting his schedule and making him drive all the way out here, so I assure him I feel much better after having a good cry and I'm in good hands here at the Inn.

After Katherine leaves to prepare the midday snack for her guests, I fall asleep, exhausted from crying. I dream that Toren came to me, the faint scent of his earthy cologne enveloping me in its familiarity as he gently brushes my hair from my face and presses his lips to my cheek.

"I'm so sorry, Angelcake," he whispers.

"Tor?" He's here, sitting on the edge of my bed. Blinking, I expect him to vanish back into my dream, but he's still here, big and incredibly masculine in this tiny room with its canopy bed and flowered curtains.

"You're really here?" I push myself up to lean against the headboard, eyeing him, still expecting him to disappear.

If smiles could heal broken hearts, his definitely holds that magic. "Of course I'm here. Your father called me after he talked to you."

I throw my arms around his neck and hug him tight. I love this man without end. No matter what, I know that will never, ever change. He *is* my heart.

His muscular arms circle me and he holds me until I slowly and very reluctantly pull away from the haven of his chest. "I'm so glad you came," I say, reaching for a tissue from the box on my nightstand. I don't want to cry anymore, but new bittersweet tears are already welling up behind my eyes.

"I loved her, too," he says simply. "And I have something for you." He reaches into his worn leather jacket and my mouth falls open as he pulls out Mopsy, my old, raggedy stuffed bunny that he gave me for my fifth birthday. I thought I had lost her and threw quite a tantrum, which led to him taking me to adopt Snuggles.

I slowly take the plush toy from him, confused as to how he has it after all these years. The ear is ripped, just like it was long ago, so I know this is definitely the same toy and not a similar one he found at a garage sale someplace.

"It's my Mopsy...I thought she was gone. I totally forgot about her."

"I know." He nods and a faint smile crosses his lips. "A few days after you lost it, I found her in the bushes by the front door of your house. It must have fallen out of your little backpack." His smile turns into a disappointed frown. "I feel like shit that I didn't give it to you, Kenzi. I just wanted something of yours, I think. It's been in my closet all this time. I know I'm an asshole—"

"No." I stop him, my voice wavering. "You're not. I totally understand." I reach out and hesitantly touch his cheek, making him look at me. "I wanted your things, too. I always wanted some part of you to hold on to."

"I guess I felt that about you, too."

My heart hammers as we stare at each other, his dark gaze drifting from my eyes, to my lips, then back to my eyes again, debating. Struggling. I hold my breath, waiting for him to kiss me again, feeling that intense undeniable pull, but instead, he grabs my hand from his cheek, quickly brushes his lips across my knuckles, and rests my hand on the bed, pulling his away.

"Kenzi...I can't." His stormy eyes close and he shakes his head.

I nod and hug my stuffed toy against me, biting my lip to keep my tears at bay. He scoots closer to me on the bed, his leg pressing against mine through the thin quilt that's covering me, and I want him closer. I want to know what it would feel like to mold my body up against his and fall asleep in his arms. I'm envious of childhood me, who used to climb on his lap and nap with my head nestled between his shoulder and his neck.

"If it's okay with you, I'm going to take Snuggles back to your house tonight, and I'm going to bury her next to your water fountain. When you get back home, we can plant some flowers and get a special stone for her, okay?"

"You'd do that?" This incredibly sexy man, who must have better things to do, is going to drive almost six hours round trip to bury my pet bunny for me. Just when I thought I couldn't possibly love him more, the space in my heart that is only for him doubles in size. I blink at him, teetering between bursting into tears again and wanting to kiss him madly. Is this my pseudo-uncle taking care of me, or is this a man who has feelings for me doing things that would make him the most awesome boyfriend in the world?

"That's why I came here so fast. I thought you'd want her home."

I'm unable to bring myself to look at him. I'm afraid if I do, I'm going to kiss him, whether he wants me to or not, because he's got my heart in a major chokehold right now. "I'd like that a lot," I manage to say.

"Listen, Angel. I know how much you love visiting Katherine. Don't let this ruin your stay, okay? I don't want you to attach bad memories here. You gave that rabbit an amazing life; she lived way longer than most rabbits do, and I think this was where she wanted to go—sleeping in your room close to you, with a beautiful view. Hell, if I had the choice, I'd go the same way someday."

I finally look up at him, and I can't hold back what I'm feeling any longer. "Do you have any idea how much I love you?"

His broad chest rises and falls slowly, and I now recognize this as him trying to gain control of himself. Trying to prevent another collision. As he absently touches the plush toy lying between us, he answers in a soft, somewhat melancholy tone.

"I hope as much as I love you."

Yes, I do.

He slowly stands, and I feel like he's taking pieces of my heart with him. Pieces I need to be whole. I have no doubt we've always loved each other, but now I'm not sure what kind of love this is. I used to think love was love and there was no gray area, but I'm learning it's just not that simple after all. Love is like an onion, with a lot of layers and a lot of tears before you get to the good part.

"I want you to go in the other room while I take care of her. Then I have to head out so I can get home before dark. Your dad's waiting for me. Apparently he wants to supervise and say some words."

I can't help but smile through sadness, because that is so much like my father to want to do a eulogy for a bunny.

"Okay...can you wait out in the hallway for a few minutes while I get dressed?" All I have on is the thin T-shirt and boy shorts I slept in last night and even though he's seen me barely dressed a hundred times, it suddenly feels too intimate.

I catch him glance down my body hidden beneath the blanket before he looks away, pulling my beanie down a little lower over his forehead. "Yeah...I'll come back in a few minutes."

Just as he reaches my door, I call out to him. "Hey, Tor?"

He stops and turns around with a questioning look on his face.

"When I get home, I'm giving this back to you. I want you to have it." I hold up Mopsy, and he grins and nods before he closes my bedroom door behind him.

I wait on the back porch as Tor prepares my bunny and puts her and her cage in his truck, and when he comes back to the house to say goodbye to Katherine and me, I walk back outside with him so we can be alone before he makes the drive back home.

"I can't even tell you how much this means to me, Tor."

"I already know. Just remember what I said—enjoy your summer."

"I will."

The breeze carries his cologne, and I inhale it deep into me, aching to have any part of him be mine to keep. I don't want him to leave. I want to grab his hand and walk along the water with him and make wishes. I want to watch the sunset with him and cuddle up with him against the cool breeze and talk the night away. "I've missed you since I left, Tor. I don't like not talking to you."

He looks at his feet and then slowly back up at me. "I miss you, too. But this doesn't change anything. There can't be anything between us."

I tilt my head and stare up at him, feeling shorter as I stand barefoot next to him on the quiet street. "There already *is* something between us."

"Kenzi…"

"We can try to ignore it all we want, but it's still there. I don't think you can just make it go away. Right?"

He stares off behind me now, through the trees and toward the very place on the beach I wish we were cuddled up together right now, instead of standing here in denial.

"I know I'm young, but I'm not stupid. I know what real feelings are. Can you really stand here and say that what we're feeling isn't happening?"

"No."

"Why are you so against it? Maybe we could be happy…"

His head snaps to face me. "We can't, Kenzi. You're seventeen. I'm thirty-two. You're my best friend's kid. Trust me, it would never, ever work. Not one person in our lives would accept us. Think about that. Think about how close you are to your family. Think about how close *I* am to your family. And now think about how disgusted they would be. How much they would hate me. Could you be happy with that?"

I shake my head as the truth of his words sinks into my soul like a boulder. "No. That would be awful."

My God, he's right. I can't think of one person who would be happy for us. Maybe Chloe, but she would mainly be interested in me having sex with someone older and hot and probably wouldn't be concerned with much else. Everyone else would go completely ballistic. My father and my uncles would want to kill Tor and most likely send me off to live with nuns.

"So, that's why, Kenz. Let's just be happy we have a great friendship. That's more than most people have. How's the saying go? Lovers come and go, but friends are forever? That's what I want. You, in my life forever, with nothing fucking it up."

"I want that, too. I just thought..." I lick my lips nervously as I bravely look him in the eye. "I thought I could make you happy."

His complexion pales a shade. Maybe two shades. "Kenzi, you do make me happy. I love hanging out with you. But all other facts aside, I need a grown woman to be in a relationship with." He rubs the scruff of his face and looks at me uncomfortably. "There are things I need and want that you can't give me."

I try to swallow past the lump of embarrassment, anger, and sadness that has lodged in my throat.

"Oh." *Of course.* He's talking about sex, and while he knows I'm a virgin, he probably can also figure out that I've not done much more than kiss. Men seem to have a radar for that sort of thing and I must be a big red beeping dot on the inexperience map. "But maybe you could teach—"

He interrupts me before I can go any further. "No. Hell no. We are not talking about this." He lets out a low whistle and shakes his head. "You gotta stop doing this to me, Kenz. It's not cool. I'm only human, ya know. I mean, fuck."

"I'm sorry."

He grabs my hand and holds it, and it brings me back from sinking into the depths of extreme awkwardness. "I love you," he says. "Seriously, you're my favorite person on this planet. But I want us to go back to how we were. Friends, okay?"

"Okay."

My legs get weak when he winks at me and I hold on to his hand for a moment too long as he tries to let go.

"Now I'm heading outta here to take care of your bunny. I'll text you later." He places his hands on the sides of my head and leans down to kiss my forehead. His affectionate gesture causes my heart to twirl. He's always been this way, but my body's and heart's reaction to it lately is entirely different than it's ever been before. When I was little, it made me feel adored. When I was an early teen, it felt annoying and embarrassing. But now it's a life force I can't seem to get enough of.

"I don't want you to be sad. Enjoy your vacation. Promise me?"

"I promise."

I wave to him as his truck pulls away from the curb, the hero who bought me a bunny to cheer me up when I was five years old now driving her little body back home to lay her to rest for me. I know I shouldn't be feeling so deeply for him, or wanting to feel his lips on mine and be tangled in his embrace, but I crave all of that and so much more.

If he thinks I can't be a real woman and make him happy in every way a man needs to be happy—that *he* needs to be happy—then I'm going to prove him wrong. A long time ago, my mom told me to always follow my heart, and mine is galloping toward him like a wild horse.

CHAPTER 16

Kenzi—age sixteen

Tor—age thirty-one

Every week when I clean Tor's house, I feel guilty that he pays me fifty dollars because his house is always so clean already. I wipe down his kitchen and bathrooms, do his laundry if any is lying around, clean out his refrigerator, and vacuum. Today I feel like I should try to do more to justify my fifty, so I clean all his windows and mirrors, and move as much of his furniture as I can to vacuum under it. In the corner of his bedroom is an old glass jug that's about two and a half feet high with a big handle on the side. The jug is filled with mostly quarters and dimes that reach about three inches away from the top opening of the jug. It's been in the same place for as far back as I can remember. I try to move it so I can vacuum underneath it and around it, but it weighs a ton. I can't budge it for anything. He comes into the bedroom just as I'm cleaning it with glass spray cleaner and a cloth.

"Uncle Tor, what the hell is this thing?" I ask him from where I'm sitting on the floor next to it. "I wanted to clean around it but it weighs about a hundred pounds."

He kneels next to me. "It's a special family tradition. Do you want to know what it is?"

"Well, now I'm intrigued, so yeah, you hafta tell me." I always want to know as much about Tor as possible because he's not like anyone else I've ever met before.

"*This bottle used to belong to my great-grandfather. He started putting coins in it when he was twelve years old, and when he fell in love with my great-grandmother, he dumped out all the change and that's what he used to buy her engagement ring, because he didn't have much money. Then he gave the jug to my grandfather, who did the same.*"

I smile at him, happy that he shared such a close family memory with me. "*Wow, that's pretty cool. Did your dad do the same with your mom's ring?*"

"*Yup, and then he gave it to me when I was fourteen. My brothers each have a bottle, too, but this one here was my great-grandfather's, so it means a lot to me.*"

Fascinated with the romance of the tradition, I stare at the jug, wondering how many quarters and dimes are in there. One time I guessed how many jelly beans were in a bottle for a class project and was only off by two, but this is way harder.

"*How much money do you think is in there?*" *I ask with curiosity.*

"*I'm not sure. A lot. A few thousand at least.*"

"*Damn. That's going to be a big diamond.*"

He ruffles my hair and stands up. "*I'm sure she'll be worth it. If I ever get married, that is. The bottle's almost full and I don't exactly have anyone to propose to. I hope I don't wreck the family tradition and end up with just a big bottle of money.*"

"*I seriously doubt that.*"

My heart twinges with a slight beat of jealousy over the woman who will someday get to be Mrs. Toren Grace.

💛 💙 💜

TOR

I see we haven't been properly introduced. I'm the asshole who broke the fragile heart of a seventeen-year-old girl by telling her she can't give me what I want and need.

The reality of it all is that I think she's probably the only woman on the planet who actually *can* give me everything I've ever wanted, needed, and dreamed of. Somewhere the universe fucked up big and screwed up our timing. I should have been younger. She should have been older. We should've met as strangers, bumping into each other in some random way. As I stand under the shower and let the hot water spray over me, I can see in my mind how we should have met. She'd be rushing out of a cafe, on her way to the craft store to buy parchment paper and ink the color of night for her favorite fountain pen. I'd be walking down the sidewalk, and we'd crash into each other. She'd drop her purse, and I'd bend down to help her pick up her things. There'd be a penny on the ground, and when I hand it to her, our fingers would touch. She'd look at me with those big green eyes and that shy smile of hers that fucking shatters me, and that would be the start of our forever. She'd be wearing jeans with holes in the knees, an eighties band T-shirt, little leather motorcycle boots with pink socks peeking out of the tops, and that beanie on her head with the purple heart that would eventually become mine. Her sensual cuteness would captivate me, and I'd force up the courage to ask her out, afraid of never seeing this magical little creature again. She'd write her number on my hand in writing so beautiful that I'd never want to wash it off. Instead, I'd take a picture of it so I could keep it forever and call it "the day my wife gave me her phone number."

Why couldn't the powers that be have given us that scenario?

I wonder what made little Kenzi Valentine decide I was husband material when she was just five years old. And fuck me, I think she still believes that. I can see it in her eyes in the way she looks at me like I'm the only person in the world that matters, and it literally stalls my heart. She's been committed to me in her own way for twelve years, which is twisted irony considering that no one else has been capable of that.

Stepping out of the steamy shower, I wrap a white towel around my waist and head out to the kitchen to make my morning protein shake, and there she is, standing at the window in my dining room looking out at the backyard.

"What the hell are you doing here?" I ask, and then turn to the dog, who's just sitting there acting like it's okay for anyone to waltz into our house. "And why the hell don't you bark when people come in? You suck as a dog."

He wags his tail at me and gets up to follow me to the kitchen, with the still nameless kitten right behind him like a fuzzy shadow.

"When did you get all these pets? It's like a zoo in here. My allergies are going to go crazy," she says, turning away from the window to look at me.

"I asked you a question," I repeat, taking my blender out of the cabinet.

"You've been avoiding me, so I decided to just come over."

"That's what happens when people break up, Syd. They avoid each other. Permanently."

When I turn around to get milk out of the fridge, she's leaning over the kitchen island, her cleavage spilling out of the tight black tank top she's wearing. I ignore her lame antics to get attention. That shit doesn't work with me.

"Tor, come on. We've broken up a million times, and we always get back together. Stop being a drama llama. We belong together."

Sydni isn't the one that got away; she's the one that won't go away.

I shake my head, pour milk into the blender with my protein powder and a handful of frozen fruit, and answer her with a sarcastic laugh. "No, we don't. And you can't just be coming into my house anytime you want."

"I have a key, remember?"

"Not anymore. I want it back."

"Are you serious?"

"Yeah, I am. I don't want you showing up whenever you feel like it."

She pulls her keys out of her purse and unhooks my house key, slamming it down on the countertop between us. "Here. Happy now?"

"It's a start."

"What's wrong with you? You never act like this with me."

"I know, Syd, and maybe that's been the problem. I let you have your way for too long and now I'm done." She picked the wrong day to show up and try to make amends. I have way too much on my mind already to be adding her back into the mix.

"Have my way?" she repeats. "What the hell does that mean?"

"Are we seriously going to hash this shit out again?" I press the power button and the blender starts its angry racket of mixing, drowning out her voice. She stops talking and waits until I turn it off to start up again.

"I'm going on tour soon. I'd like to work things out before I leave."

"Work what out?"

"Us." She comes around the kitchen island to stand in front of me, her long fiery red hair almost reaching to her ass now. Her makeup is flawless, as always, with thick black eyeliner lining her eyes, the color of them mocking me today. Sydni has a thing for colored contact lenses and today she chose green, making me want to pull them out of her head because they remind me of Kenzi's, only without the sparkle of the gold flecks hers have.

"There is no us anymore."

"Why not? Is there someone else?"

The thick shake goes down my throat and almost comes back up again. There's never been anyone else in the past. I focused on work, Devils' Wolves, taking care of my family, and spending time with the someone else who I never realized was a *someone else* until right at this moment. The main reason I don't want to give Sydni another chance is because I don't want her anymore. I force down another gulp of the chalky drink as I face the cold, hard truth—the moment I kissed Kenzi, she became The One. *Maybe she always was.*

"Well?" Sydni prods. "Is it Lisa?"

"No. We're just friends. I haven't even slept with her. I sleep with this dog and cat every night."

"Is that because you love me?"

"No, Syd. It's because I love myself."

She rolls her eyes at me, a gesture I despise. "You know I don't care about who you fuck, Tor. I'd only care if you had feelings for another woman. Sex isn't a threat to me, but I won't share your heart."

I stare into the fake eyes of the woman I spent years in a relationship with, wondering where we went wrong.

Downing the last of my drink, I place the cup in the sink before turning to face her again. I tighten the towel around my waist and lean back against the counter. I'd rather be having this conversation with clothes on, but I know she isn't going to give me a few minutes to go get dressed. She'll follow me to the bedroom and try to divert this conversation into other oral activities to distract me.

Pushing my wet hair out of my face, I say what I should have said years ago. "Syd, I never wanted an open relationship. Ever. It's just not my thing."

"Since when? We've been this way for ten years, Tor."

I shake my head. "No. You wanted it that way. You wanted

the freedom to screw whoever you wanted while you ran around with the band and I had to stay home."

She laughs and crosses her arms. "Come on, Tor. You got to bang anyone you wanted while I was gone. We both had fun. I think, as usual, you're jealous that I'm living my dream and you gave yours up."

"One time," I admit through clenched teeth, furious over her last stab. "One fucking time I was with another woman and it made me feel sick. But you? I don't even want to know how many guys you've been with under this free-to-fuck-anyone deal you tried to rope me into just so you could suck and fuck your way across the country."

"I'm not a slut."

"Then don't act like one. I heard you slept with Vandal Valentine a while back. He's a lunatic, Syd. His cheese has completely slid off his cracker. Ropes and chains? What the hell is wrong with you that you'd want to get in bed with that kind of crazy?"

"I wanted to try something new. I've been friends with him for years, and I trust him. It's no big deal."

"So you just had to fuck him, too? Someone I know and have to see all the time? He's Asher's fuckin' cousin. Was that your way of living out your fantasy of being with Ash? I hope you didn't sleep with all his brothers, too. Have some fucking class."

Mad tears brim in her eyes. "This isn't fair, Tor. You never said you didn't want freedom. We agreed when I was home, it was just us, but when I was on the road, we could both do what we wanted as long as feelings didn't get involved. Now you want to throw it in my face? This is so like you, to not ever talk and then just blow up and try to blame it all on me."

"You're right. I should have said something years ago and put an end to it. I was so hell-bent on trying to make you happy that

I just let you do whatever you wanted. And I guess I thought that since you supposedly loved me, you'd stop after, I dunno, the first three guys maybe?"

"I didn't love any of them. You're the only one I've ever loved. You know that."

"Whoop dee fuckin' doo, Syd. Is that supposed to make me feel better?"

"Yes. Sex doesn't matter. It was just stupid party fun."

I turn my head up toward the ceiling and laugh. "Oh, I see. Well, how about a few months ago when you said you wanted to get married, because...wait a second, let me think on the exact words you used...*Asher won't ever let go of Ember and you're tired of waiting around for him to give you a chance. So I'm just the next best thing?*"

"I didn't mean it like that."

"Riiiiggghhht. It's a good thing Ash has some morals and won't touch you with a ten-foot pole or you wouldn't even be standing here right now, would you? You'd be sleeping with him and forgetting all about me until you needed something."

She glares at me and I know what I said is true; she'd definitely choose him over me.

"I'm not going to apologize for something you agreed to, whether you took advantage of it or not. Now that you've told me how you feel, I'll stop." She steps closer and runs her hands up my bare chest, clasping them behind my neck. "We'll start over, then. With a commitment to each other. Maybe it's time we take things to the next level."

I refuse to put my hands on her. "C'mon, Sydni. Do you really think you can do that? Be gone for months and not fool around with someone?"

"I think so. You can meet up with me every few weeks. That's what the other couples do."

The thought of flying around the country to meet with her in hotels for nights of sex and rushed dinners and conversations, only to come back home alone, doesn't exactly fit into the plan I wanted for my future.

Her pink-stained lips press against my chest, her hands tightening around my neck. I close my eyes, willing myself to enjoy her touch like I used to, hoping to feel a spark. When Kenzi touches me, my heart feels like it's going to fly out of my chest. No matter where she touches me, even if it's just my hand in an innocent way, I feel it everywhere. The euphoria of her spreads from my head to my toes, electrifying every inch in between, making me want to grab on to her and never let go. Her touch reaches right into my soul and friggin' owns me.

Why, why, why am I thinking about Kenzi when I have a gorgeous woman trying to climb me like a tree right now?

Sydni's mouth moves up to my neck, gently biting me, but the feelings don't come. My dick is bored, and so am I. I'm completely numb to her. Grabbing her hands in frustration, I pull her off me.

"What's wrong?" She comes back at me, reaching for my towel this time, but I push her away. *Why are women always trying to pull my clothes off?* I probably could make bank if I become a stripper at this point.

"I can't do this right now."

"Jesus, Toren. It's been months."

Hmm. It's been months for me, but I wonder how long it's been for her.

"I don't care. I need some time to think."

"So you'll think about giving us another chance?"

"Maybe," I reply, brainwashing myself so I'll forget about Kenzi. "Let's see if you can get through the entire tour without being with someone else. And when you get back home, I want you to have a full STD panel done. Then we'll talk about maybe starting over. And that's a huge fuckin' maybe, Syd, because honestly, I just don't know if I can do this with you again."

She lets out an exasperated sigh. "Fine. If that's what it takes, I'll give it a shot."

I can't believe she needs to give not screwing other men *a shot*. Like it's going to be some kind of feat of extraordinary talent to keep her mouth and her legs closed until she can be with me, the guy she claims to love.

"Yeah, well, I won't hold my breath."

"You don't have to be a jerk, Tor. I said I'd try." She rubs at her nose. "And what about this dog and cat? If we get back together, I'll be sneezing nonstop."

I reach down to pet Diogee, who's almost always at my side. "Then I guess you'd have to take an allergy pill. Or not come over. They're not disposable. This is their home."

"We'll see about that. I have a feeling if you have to choose between pussies, you'll choose mine," she says with a smirk.

I know she's joking, but I'm not seeing the humor in it. "One thing I've learned over the past few months is I can live without it, Syd. You don't have any power over me with that. So, the pets stay, no matter what."

It's bugging me that she didn't even ask their names or want to know how I saved them. She didn't sit on the floor and pet them or show any interest in them at all. Unlike Kenzi, who treats this dog like royalty—brushing him and trimming his nails. Making him all-natural peanut butter dog treats from some recipe she found on Pinterest. She even ate one herself first, to make sure it tasted good. If that's not love, I don't know what is.

Fuckin' Kenzi, creeping back into my mind again. Always haunting me.

CHAPTER 17

Kenzi—age thirteen

Tor—age twenty-eight

I smile at the framed photo of my parents that's on the night table on my mom's side of the bed. They're about fourteen and fifteen in this picture, and they're kissing but smiling against each other's lips. They look so young but also so much the same. It's my favorite photo of them.

"Mom, how did you know Dad was the one?" My eyes linger on the photo for a moment longer before turning to her. She's lying on her stomach at the end of their bed, writing in her journal as she does every night, her long blond hair falling around the rims of her nerdy, yet trendy, red-framed glasses.

She chews on the end of her pen, her face lighting up as she's thinking about my dad. I love how much they love each other. Never fighting, always hugging and kissing, always whispering secrets to each other and pulling each other closer for kisses. It's like they existed in their own little bubble of love and forgot the rest of the world existed.

"I just knew. I'd seen him around school and thought he was incredibly cute. But the first time we actually met face-to-face, he looked into my eyes with a dreamy smile and said 'Oh shit. There goes my heart.' We stayed in the park all day that day, just holding hands and talking. We found out we had a lot in common. Music, writing, the same foods and movies, the same fears and dreams. I felt like I had met the other half

of myself. He walked me home at midnight, gave me my first kiss, and told me he could see his entire life in my eyes." She closes her journal, a big smile on her face. "Needless to say, I fell totally head over heels in love with him and we've been inseparable ever since. My parents were less than thrilled, but nothing they could say or do could have kept me away from him."

"That's awesome," I say wistfully. "I want to fall in love like that someday."

She rolls over onto her back and stares at me, upside down, her hair hanging off the edge of the bed. It's easy to see how my dad was so easily taken by her playful eyes, loving nature, and beautiful smile. She's the kind of woman you just gravitate toward and want to be close to. She makes everyone around her feel loved and beautiful, just like my dad does. Together, they are the perfect fairy-tale couple.

"You will, baby. Don't ever settle or be afraid to love. I always want you to follow your heart, no matter what."

KENZI

It's not even 8:00 a.m. yet and my phone is blowing up with text messages.

Chloe
Happy birthday to my girl! I love you!! Call me!

Rayne
18 baby! Woot! Love ya, my little chickadee!

Sailor
Happy birthday, beautiful. Hope it's the best

Uncle Storm

> I refuse to accept that you're 18. Stop it.

Uncle Talon

> Happy birthday, sweetheart. See u soon. :-)

Uncle Lukas

> Happy birthday little one. Stop by and I'll give you your first tat ;-)

Finn

> 18 spankings, Kensington. My palm is waiting.

When I meet up with Katherine for breakfast on her private porch, she comes out with homemade waffles with whipped cream and strawberries with a candle in the middle, singing "Happy Birthday." I blow out my candle and hug her, trying hard to hold back the tears I can already feel coming on again. On days like this, I miss my mother so much. In many ways, she was more like a best friend to me since we basically grew up together, and it rips my heart up that she's not here. I'm getting older now, and she's stopped, forever at twenty-nine.

"I have a surprise for you," Katherine says as we start eating breakfast. "A good friend of mine in town is a photographer, and she said she would love to come by and shoot with you and make a professional portfolio for you."

I swallow my bite of waffle, my interest piqued. "Wow, that would be amazing. I've been hoping to do some more modeling. Most of my shoots are from two years ago and I look so young."

"That's exactly what I told her. She does fashion, boudoir, and weddings mostly, and she has a really great eye. I thought as a birthday present, I'll pay for her to do some different shoots for you. I showed her your prom photo because it's the most recent I had, and she thinks you're stunning. She's really excited to work with you."

"I'm excited, too. Maybe I should go into town later today and pick up some outfits to wear? I didn't bring much with me other than jeans and shorts. I'd like to pose in something nicer, maybe even a tiny bit sexy. What do you think? Do you think that would be okay? Or a big mistake?" I'm not sure I'm good at being sexy in any way but I know if I want to do some modeling, then I have to at least make an attempt. Chloe is always telling me to work what I've got but I seriously have no idea how to do that.

"I'll have Tina cover me and I'll go with you. I could use some time out of here myself. And I think something a little sexy but classy is fine. No nudity, though, please." She laughs. "You're eighteen now. I've seen some of Anna's work and she can make you look gorgeous and alluring without looking trashy. She does hair and makeup, too. Trust me, this is going to be fabulous and I think it will definitely boost your confidence once you see how beautiful you are."

Three hours later, I'm in a small boutique in town trying on lingerie for the first time in my life when I get a text from Toren.

Tor:

> Happy birthday, my Angel. Hoping this year brings you nothing but happiness, love, and dreams come true. I've loved watching you grow up from an adorable, feisty little girl to the beautiful woman you are today. Your parents and I are so proud of you. Always remember how special you are, and no matter where life takes you, you'll always have all my love and support. xo

I can't stop reading his message, trying to decipher if these words are from the man who helped raise me or the man who kissed me like he wanted to devour me.

He's both.

Therein lies our dilemma. He'll never be one or the other. He'll always be both to me, just as I'm sure I'll always be both his best friend's little girl and the woman he suddenly has unwanted feelings for. We're always going to be twisted up, caught in the web of our past and teased by the glimpses of what we *could* have been.

A knock on the dressing room door startles me and I nearly drop my phone. "Kenzi? Are you okay?" Aunt Katherine asks, her voice full of concern.

"Yes," I say through the door. "I was just adjusting the straps. I'll be out in a second."

Taking a deep breath, I type back.

> You had a huge part in helping me be the person I am today. You've been my rock since the day I was born. I will always and forever love you the most. xo

There's so much more I want to say, but I don't let myself for fear of making him mad and uncomfortable again. I can picture him in my mind so clearly right now, sitting with his legs crossed on the floor of his shop in front of an old Harley, with his cell phone in his hand, smudged with grease, a faint crooked smile on his lips as he reads my text. He once told me those were his favorite words, and I hope he knows that over the years they have come to mean much more to me than they did when I first wrote them at seven years old.

CHAPTER 18

My love,
For all the times I pushed you away
My heart was trying to pull you closer

♥ ♥ ♥

TOR

"Grab the rope out of the truck," I yell to Tristan.

"Tor, you can't go down there with your back problems."

"No shit, that's why you're going. Get the fucking rope."

Tanner laughs as our brother takes off for the truck. "It's about time the kid gets his hands dirty," he says.

"True, bro. Let's not drop him, though. I'm not going in after him *and* the dog."

We stare down over the side of the bridge as Tris runs back to the truck. The river is raging beneath us, and a black Lab is clinging to the side of the embankment, his back legs in the water. It's a miracle he's not being swept away by the current, and the only thing I can surmise is that his collar must be snagged on something like a rock or tree branch, keeping him where he is. If whatever it is lets loose, he's going to be dragged down into the water and downstream and will most likely drown.

It's almost impossible to climb down the sides of the steep hills on either side of the river. So he either fell in or got thrown in.

This bridge is nicknamed Suicide Bridge because a few people have jumped to their death off it a few times over the past few years. The river runs over huge granite rocks that are sometimes covered by the water if we get lots of rain and flooding.

When Tristan comes back with the rope, we rig it around him and he climbs down the steep mountain with us holding on to the rope at the top of the bridge so he can't fall. When the dog sees him, it starts to get excited and digs frantically at the embankment with his front paws, whining.

Tanner and I are both pretty big guys, so we don't have much trouble holding up our one-hundred-eighty-pound little brother, but the weather is stormy today with strong gusts of winds that keep blowing him around.

"Tris is Mom's favorite, ya know. If we lose him, she's gonna kill us," Tanner teases.

"I'm Mom's favorite, asshole," I joke back. "If we lose him, I'm telling her you pushed him in."

"Grab the dog, you wuss! I got shit to do!" Tanner yells down at him.

"Don't make him nervous, man."

He gives me his evil grin. "It's good for him. Too bad Ty's not here. He'd jump right the fuck off this bridge and grab that dog in about two seconds flat. We wouldn't need this rope bullshit."

Tris reaches for the dog, tries to grab him, misses, and tries again.

"Let's lower him a little more."

A few more inches of rope give him enough slack to grab the dog, but he's struggling trying to hang on to the rope with one hand and holding the dog with the other.

"This wasn't our best plan," Tanner observes.

"Probably not."

"Grab him and haul his ass up!" Tanner yells.

"He's stuck!" Tris yells back.

"What the fuck? I should have done this myself." I lean over the bridge to see what's going on.

"Relax, man. He's trying."

Finally Tris grabs the dog's collar and yanks him up, hoisting him under his arm. The dog is soaking wet and obviously scared out of its mind, clawing at his chest.

"Pull me up before I drop his ass!" he yells up to us.

We haul him up the slippery hill and I grab the dog when he's at the top edge of the embankment, looping a slip lead around his neck. I kneel and check him over while Tanner gets Tristan untied from the rope. The dog seems fine, despite being very thin and malnourished. I'm pretty sure this is the dog we've been trying to trap for months. I can't wait to tell Kenzi since she was getting so frustrated about him not going into the traps to eat the meat we kept leaving for him.

The dog is trembling but still wagging his tail, probably feeling somewhat triumphant for eluding us for so long but now happy to be safe. My favorite part of dog rescue is how happy most of them are to finally have a person touch them gently and treat them with care. Their appreciation is evident in their eyes as they brave making eye contact with us, hoping we're someone they can trust.

"All right," I say. "I'm going to drop him off at the vet. I think he's okay but who knows if he's got internal injuries." I fist-bump my younger brother. "You did good, Tris."

"I wasn't expecting him to be so heavy. He was like dead weight."

"They usually are when they're scared like this. They just freeze up, or even worse, they try to bite us or run off."

"I'm glad he's okay."

Tanner punches him playfully on the arm. "You better start lifting some more, little bro."

Tris laughs and heads back toward the truck they came in. "Whatever, old man. Let's go."

By the time I take the river dog to the vet, get home, shower, and eat, it's after nine and I'm beat from running around all day. Diogee and the kitten join me on my king bed as I get comfortable on what has become my side and put something mindless on Netflix until my brain settles down enough for me to fall asleep.

I'm just dozing off when a melodic chime sounds from my nightstand, making my eyes snap open. It's the new tone I programmed for Kenzi's messages. I fumble for the phone and squint at it in the dark.

Kenzi

> I wanted to say hi and let you know I'm thinking about you

I'm instantly awake and smiling as I type back.

> Hey you. I was thinking about you too. I had microwave meat loaf for dinner. I have no idea what I just ate. It may have been iguana meat. I miss your dinners. ;-)

Kenzi

> I see what I mean to you now ;) You're probably buried in white fur too, huh?

> Pretty much.

Kenzi

> I'm not sure I feel bad...

> I miss everything. Not just you taking care of me.

Kenzi

I miss you, too.

My eyes latch on to those words and I'm very aware of how quickly and naturally we slip into these moments of what I can only think of as longing. *And flirting.* I attempt to U-turn the conversation with idle chatter.

I have good news. Remember the dog we've been trying to catch by the river for months? We got him today.

Kenzi

Omg finally! Is he okay?

He is now. He was actually stuck IN the river, off Suicide Bridge. Tris had to go in on a rope to get him out.

Kenzi

Holy crap! That's amazing. I'm so proud of you guys!

Thanks. He's super thin but he's going to be fine. Mom's found a foster for him already.

Kenzi

I'm so glad he's finally safe.

Me too. So, are you enjoying Maine?

Kenzi

Yes. Sailor came by a few days ago and took me for lunch. He was visiting a friend who lives out here. He's a really sweet guy, very quiet and polite. I'm designing a tattoo for him.

The mystery meat dinner turns in my stomach.

That was nice of him.

Asshole drifter.

Kenzi

Yeah. We had a nice day. So, Katherine's friend is a photographer and took some pix of me for my portfolio. She thinks maybe I could do some shoots with her and get paid, like for products, or maybe even for a magazine.

That would be great. I'm proud of you.

I'm still stuck on Sailor spending the day with her. I want to ask her if they're dating but I don't want to come off like some jealous teenager. Could he seriously have friends out there, conveniently located near Kenzi's aunt? I'm not buying it.

Kenzi

We'll see what happens. Do you want to see some of the pix she took?

Before I can answer, a photo begins to load on my phone screen. I was expecting the usual pose of her leaning against a tree or sitting by the ocean with her hair blowing. I sure as hell was not expecting to see her stretched like a cat across a white silk-covered bed, her long honey-blond hair flowing all around her, wearing a black bra that's just barely covering her full breasts with gold glitter sparkling across her perfect stomach leading down to matching black lace-edged panties. One of her legs is bent up, laying over her other thigh, the hint of her tight ass curved up. And on her feet, those little black leather boots that make my blood pressure spike every time she's got them on.

My mouth suddenly feels like it's filled with a hundred cotton balls, and my heart is jackknifing in my chest.

I swallow, near panic, as another photo loads, this one of her kneeling on the bed, her hair longer, hanging down in front of her naked chest, just barely covering her breasts. Her jeans are unbuttoned and unzipped to show off cherry-red panties. A hole is torn from just above the knee to her inner thigh, the worn and frayed denim edges revealing delicate flesh that's begging to be touched.

A war erupts in me, part of me fighting to throw my phone across the room and not ever see her this way, and the other part of me hungering for more as my cock grows harder with anticipation as another photo starts to come into view beneath the others.

Shit. I can't take any more.

This one nearly does me in when it fully loads. She's sitting in the sand at the edge of the beach with some kind of mermaid costume on, her long legs covered by the tight, sparkling scaled material, the water lapping up onto her. She's leaning back, looking up toward the sun, her breasts held by a bikini top of seashells, jutting upward in the most tantalizing way. A tiny starfish hangs from a chain around her neck, resting in the valley between her breasts. A thin gold headband wraps around her head, holding back her hair that is somehow almost three times longer than it was the last time I saw her. It's now streaked with blue and green to match her mermaid fin, flowing down her back and pooling onto the sand behind her. I'm so lost in the photos, scrolling back up to look at each one again, that I forget she's on the other side of the phone waiting for me to say something.

Sitting up, I ignore the dog's accusing stare as I type back to her with shaky fingers.

> A little warning would have been nice.

Kenzi
> I wanted to surprise you.

> You definitely did.

The pictures are slowly destroying me, demolishing my walls, burning up my self-control like an unstoppable inferno. I hate her for forcing me to see her this way and for making me want her so fucking much that my body is literally aching for her.

No. I don't hate her. I love her. I need her.

Kenzi

You don't like them?

I'm jerked back to reality as I realize I'm the first and only man to ever see her this way—as a woman and not a little girl. I know all her insecurities, and I know how hard this was for her because she doesn't see herself as sexy or attractive. She's a jeans, T-shirts, and boots kinda girl. She's effortless and clueless in her own beauty, and that just makes her even more attractive. I can only guess how vulnerable she feels, sitting there waiting for me to say something reassuring to her.

My brain spins round and round like a merry-go-round that's tilting off its axis. This moment, my response, could change everything. Do I do the right thing and reply as her lifelong friend? Say something polite? Or do I show her a piece of the man she's playing with?

I'm tired of the fight.

I'm lonely.

I want to play.

My fingers fly defiantly over the keyboard, leading me straight into the fire.

Are you kidding? I fucking love them. You look incredible. Are there more?

Kenzi

Yes.

I want to see them. Please.

I feel dizzy and intoxicated as more pictures flood my screen. I'm like a rabid junkie getting a fix, and I can't get enough. All the photos are classy and sensual, but capture her perfectly in a way I've been trying to pretend for months I haven't noticed. She's turned into a drop-dead gorgeous woman with a body that could very well turn me into an animal and make me beg for just five minutes with her.

How did your hair grow so fast?

Kenzi

It's extensions. They clip on.

Oh. The way it hides you but gives just enough of a peek is driving me crazy. It's the perfect tease.

Kenzi

I could grow my hair that long if you want.

No. I like you exactly as you are. Don't ever change for anyone. Not even me.

Kenzi

You really like them? I've never posed like this before. Do I look awkward?

Hell no. I love them. I can't stop looking at them. It's killing me they're so tiny on my screen.

Kenzi

I was really hoping you would like them. I was so nervous.

Don't be. Did you send these to Sailor?

I'll go into an all-out rage if she says yes. I'll hunt that fucker down and smash his phone and beat him until any memory of seeing her like this is gone from his brain. I can't stand sharing women anymore and there is no way in hell I could ever share her.

Kenzi

> God no. I would never do that. He's just a friend. Some of these are for my portfolio and the others are just for me to have.

I lick my lips and adjust my throbbing cock under the sheets. I swear I want to paw at my phone screen right now just to have any piece of her I can get. This is sheer torture.

> Why did you send these, Kenz?
> What are you trying to do to me?

Kenzi

> I want you to see ME. I want you to want me like I want you.

The air leaves my lungs. Is she trying to kill me? Does she have any idea what she's saying? And the effect it's having on my thumping heart and other southern regions of my anatomy?

> Make no mistake, Angel. I want you. Bad.

I've completely lost my mind. We should stop this before it goes too far into places we have no right to be in and will never be able to back ourselves out of without some major damage.

But it feels so good.

Kenzi

I want to see you. Send me a picture of you.

No. I don't do selfies.

Kenzi

Please? I love all your muscles and your tattoos. I won't show anyone. It's only for me to look at when I'm alone.

My heart feels like it's going into cardiac arrest, pounding so hard I can hear it and my head is thundering with the aftershock of her words. She wants me. She wants me to want her.

Ugh. It's all so fucking wrong. Taboo at its finest.

The devil plants his ass on my shoulder. It's just playful texting, though, right? I'm not touching her. She's hours and miles away from me. It's late and dark. We're sleepy. It's safe.

Before I can change my mind, I turn on my bedside lamp, push the covers down low around my hips and snap a picture, cropping it to make sure my hard-on isn't visible. She'll like this one because it shows my hair all messy around my shoulders, which I always catch her eyeing, plus my chest, abs, and all the ink that comes with it. I always assumed she was too young to appreciate all the work I put into my body, but apparently she's not. I hit send and wait.

Kenzi

Ohmy. Wow. Thank you xoxox

You like?

Kenzi

I love it. Your muscles are just wow. Thank you for including your hair for me. :-) And that ab V or whatever it's called...omg. **Faints**

There's a big goofy smile on my face that I'm not used to. I've never had this cute flirting stuff with anyone before. She's kidnapping me into her world, and I'm slowly surrendering, a willing hostage.

Kenzi

I have a few more of me...

Five more photos come through, and while these are thankfully less sexy, they are just as beautiful with her wearing a mint-green sundress that brings out her eyes. She's sitting on a wicker swing I recognize as being on Katherine's front porch. She's more natural in these photos, with no hair clip things and less makeup, but she looks breathtaking, older, and elegant. The last picture, however, instantly becomes my favorite. It's a moody setting, grainy black and white, taken in her bedroom at the Inn. She's standing at the window with her back to the camera, completely nude with the thin gauzy curtain blowing behind her like a veil. Her perfect round ass and the swell of her breast is visible through the curtain as the light coming from the window gives her a beautiful silhouette, accentuating all her curves. She's looking down and off to the side, her mouth slightly parted, her long ebony eyelashes lying against her cheek. It's hands-down the most sensual photo I've ever seen. I want to print it, frame it, and hang it over my bed where it can be the first thing I see every morning. My finger slides across the screen, along the curve of her waist. Wishing. Wanting.

That last one, Angel. It fucking ended me.

Kenzi

I like that one, too. I can't believe that's me.

Me either.

> I'm speechless. I think I'm going to need a cold shower.

Kenzi
LOL

> I'm dead fucking serious. The things I would do to you. You gotta stop.

Kenzi
Tell me.

> No.

Kenzi
Tor. Don't close up. I like you this way. Just let us have this for tonight. It's just fun fantasy. Make it my birthday present.

> I already have a present for you.

Kenzi
Then let me have two :-)

My chest tightens. I want to give her everything. I want to *be* her everything. I type something quick and generic but then delete it, because it's cheap and lame and she deserves better. There was a time when I penned lyrics that screamed of heartache, desire, and undying love. One thing I know I can do is make love to her with words.

> I would have loved to come up behind you in that last picture, pull your hair to the side, whisper in your ear, and ravish your neck with my mouth until you fall back against me. I'd slowly run my hands up your body and caress those perfect tits of yours until you were begging me for more.

My breathing speeds up as I type to her. This is like crazy fucking foreplay, and I'm hard as a rock for her. My phone is silent, but I can feel her waiting for more. Even miles away, our connection resonates between us.

I'm going to burn in hell.

> I'd bend you over that windowsill, spread your thighs, and slide slow and deep into you. I'd want to hear you gasp and feel your body all tight and wet around me. I'd tilt your head back and kiss you until you're delirious and can't breathe without me. I'd carry you to the bed and make love to you until you fall asleep in my arms and I'd count the minutes until I could be inside you again. I don't think I could ever get enough of you, and I'm afraid I'd love you and fuck you to the point of mental and physical exhaustion. And then I'd do it all over again until neither one of us can even consider the idea of ever not touching again.

Silence. Minutes of it.

Maybe I scared her away. Maybe she thinks I'm a pig.

I *am* a pig.

Kenzi
Toren. Do you mean all that?

I love when she says my name. And types it. And now I want to hear it on her lips when I'm buried inside her.

Have I ever lied to you?

Kenzi
No.

> Sorry you asked now?

More long moments of silence torture me as I stare at the ceiling with the biggest hard-on of my life, cursing myself while I wait for the coveted sound of her text. Just hearing that small musical chime lately turns me all inside out.

Kenzi
Not at all. That was the best present ever. I'm actually shaking.

She's ruining me. I want to run my fingers over her warm, quivering flesh and feel what I'm doing to her. I want it so bad I'm on the verge of jumping on my bike and riding nearly three hours in the middle of the night just so I can do exactly that.

But I can't. Because the truth is cruel; she's still her and I'm still me, and we were never meant to be this way with each other.

> Ok we have to stop now. Game over.

Kenzi
:(

> We both know this is wrong.

Kenzi
I wish it wasn't. :(

> Me too, Angel. But we should go now.
> I have to get up early and I'm going to
> have a hard time falling asleep after this.

Kenzi
I will, too.

> Thank you for sharing your photos with me.
> You're breathtakingly beautiful. In every way.

Kenzi

> Thank you for sending me yours. :-) Don't take this wrong, but you're beautiful, too. Like a dream.

> We'll talk again soon. I love you.

Kenzi

> I love you, too. Xo

I'm pretty sure there's now a seat in hell with my name engraved on it. Sleep is impossible for me when mere inches away from my pillow is a four-inch device that holds all my deepest desires, fantasies, and sins. It's way too tempting. I've tried to be strong. I've tried to keep her away and yet still hold on to our special bond, but it's all crumbling around me.

Exiling her from my life isn't an option. Not talking to her? Not seeing her? Giving up our little us-isms? No fucking way. It would be like cutting off one of my own limbs.

In the discreet darkness of my bedroom, I transfer her photos to my laptop, where I can analyze every detail of her forbidden curves. Every little birthmark. Some I've actually kissed, at a time when it was simply cute and innocent between us. The playful lift of her smile and her enticing mossy-green eyes seduce me from the fifteen-inch screen. She's given me the gift of being able to ravish her with my eyes here in the privacy of my house and the chance to play out my fantasies with the help of my right hand.

Hello, Satan. I know you've been waiting patiently for me since the demise of the good and noble Uncle Tor. I have a feeling I'll be staying here awhile.

CHAPTER 19

Tor—age fifteen

Ember—age fourteen

Asher—age fifteen

Being shy sucks. It took me weeks of smiling at the new girl in our class, Ember, to work up the balls to ask her if I could walk her home after school. She's shy, too, though, and now we're walking in awkward silence. I want to hold her hand, but I can't tell if she wants me to. I've got my guitar with me, slung over my back in its case since I'm playing in a school project, so I ask her if she wants to stop at the park and listen to me play. I lose myself in the music when I play, and it always calms me down, stripping me of my insecurities. One thing I know I do well is create music and write lyrics.

"Sure," she says. "I do some singing. I'm not great, but I love to do it anyway. If it makes your ears hurt, I promise I'll stop."

It turns out she does, in fact, have an amazing voice, and my shyness starts to fade as we sit at a picnic table and I play some of her favorite hit songs and she sings along. I try not to stare at her, but it's hard not to. She's one of the prettiest girls I've ever seen, and the fact that we both have a passion for music is a surprise bonus I wasn't expecting.

"I thought I heard you twanging over here, man." Asher's raspy voice breaks into my daydream of asking Ember out to a movie this weekend.

"Hey," I say as he approaches us. "Do you know Ember? She just moved

here last month. Ember, this is Asher Valentine." Asher is way more outgoing than I am, so maybe he can help us break the conversation ice.

"Actually, we haven't met yet," he says, giving her his full attention. "Wow, you've got some gorgeous eyes." He grabs his chest. "Shit. There goes my heart."

"Nice to meet you." She giggles and gives her dazzling smile over to him. "Are you guys brothers?" she asks.

Asher laughs. "Nah. Everyone thinks that, but we're just friends."

"You guys look a lot alike. I actually thought you were the same person when I first saw you in the halls. It took me a few days to realize you weren't."

"It's definitely not on purpose," I say. "Just a weird coincidence. Ash has a younger brother who looks like him, too. And I guess, a lot like me."

Asher flashes a grin. "God thought I was so perfect he wanted to make some backups of me." He winks at Ember. "Just in case."

She giggles again, and I can feel myself slipping into the background. "You're that perfect?" she asks.

"Yup."

Her head tilts and she can't seem to take her eyes off him, and he's staring right back at her like I wish I had the courage to before he showed up. Suddenly, it's like I'm not even here, and my daydreams wither away.

Defeated, I put my guitar back in its case and snap it shut. "I should get going."

"Oh...," Ember says, looking from me to Asher, like she's torn between us.

"I'm going to hang out here for a while and then go over to the diner for a burger," Asher says, still holding her attention. "You want to stay and talk for a while? I'll buy you dinner and walk you home."

"I'd love to." She turns to me. "You don't mind, do you, Toren?"

I shake my head and force a smile. "No, not at all."

But the truth is, I did mind. I minded a lot.

💜 💜 💜

KENZI

Tor's texts have me *aflutter*. That's the only word I can think of to describe this new feeling. I think my gram would be impressed with that word. My insides are shaking, rattling, and rolling all about, and I can't get my heart to settle back down into normal, calm beats. I've been lying in bed for an hour since we said good night, but I'm too *afluttered* to sleep.

I quietly slip into the hallway and pad down to Aunt Katherine's small kitchen to make myself a cup of tea. It's odd how at home I only drink coffee, but when I'm here I drink all sorts of assorted teas and don't go near coffee at all. I'm not sure why this is fascinating to me at 1:00 a.m., but it is. With the steaming ceramic cup in my hand, I go back to my room and close the door behind me with a soft *click*.

Before I made my tea, I spent a half hour rereading the entire text conversation. Tor's reactions to my photos and then his detailed description of what he wanted to do to me was definitely a surprising eye-opener.

Tor has an erotic side.

And that just ramped up his yum factor even more.

If his words are true—and I have zero reason to doubt him—he wants to show me that side of him, even though he's struggling with it because of all the alleged wrongs involved.

I stare out the window at the moon and its neighboring stars casting a shimmering reflection on the water, contemplating as I sip my tea. Is it really wrong for us to feel this way? If we care about each other, love each other, and want each other...is that wrong? And if it is, then why? Because of our ages? Because he's my dad's best friend? Because he's taken care of me?

Do those things make it wrong...or do they actually make it more right? Why is it acceptable to get involved with a total stranger, who could do any number of things to hurt you or betray you, but not get involved with someone who has cared about you since the day you were born?

Is it all a matter of social perspective?

Is it possible that falling in love doesn't always start when we think it might, and sometimes, it starts way before we're ready, and grows slowly over time, allowing two people to truly fall in love with every aspect of each other? Rather than the more typical way of meeting a stranger, being attracted to them first, dating them, having feelings for them, and then hoping they'll like you, too, and not rip your heart out?

I wish I had someone to talk to about all these confusing feelings, but I'm not ready to even attempt to go down that road yet.

Grabbing my phone, I perch on the edge of my bed and read over the text conversation again, frowning at my own words. My replies to his photo and to his sensual admissions are disappointing. I should have come back with an equally honest admission of what I want and felt. He crept over the wall tonight, took a peek at me, and let me see a peek of him. Maybe it was wrong of me to send him the pictures to lure him out, but I wanted him to see me in a new light. As a new adult. And I was hoping to see more of him.

From the dresser, I pull out the decorated box of notepaper and the fountain pen that I brought with me with the intention of mailing Chloe and my grandmother notes while I was here. Instead, I sit on the floor and handwrite a note to Tor. He's the one who introduced me to calligraphy and he's always loved the handwritten notes I've given him. With the evolution of the cell phone, I've used that as my main tool of correspondence with him, but for something special like this, I know he'll appreciate it in my own writing.

Dear Tor,

Tonight your words were what I have been hoping to hear. You took my breath away and gave it back to me again. I have not been able to fathom never touching again since the first time you kissed me, so don't be afraid of loving and fucking (your word) me into exhaustion. I want you to show me what that feels like someday. Just thinking about it is making me breathless all over again.

I want you to be my first. I want you to be my last. I want you to be all the in-betweens. I want you. Just you. Only you.

And I want to be all yours, in every way.

I know you're scared, but I also know how strong you are. We can be scared together, and we can be strong together. Trust that I know what I want. Haven't I always?

I'm here, waiting, anytime you want to climb over the wall again. And if you have to run back to the other side again, that's okay. I'll still be here.

I love you the most,
Kenzi
xo

I take a picture of the note with my phone camera and send it to him. Mailing would be much more authentic but would take too long. I want him to have this when he wakes up.

Five minutes after I get back into bed, a text comes through and I know it has to be from him.

Tor

Why aren't you sleeping?

Why aren't you? ;-)

Tor

I've been busy treating myself like a playground since you had to tease me with your pictures.

OMG

Tor

Sorry. I have no filter when I'm exhausted and deprived.

I'm not complaining :-)

Tor

You wrote me a letter. I miss seeing your writing.

I'll do it more.

Tor

Only you could make the word fucking look beautiful ;-)

LOL thanks

Tor

I don't think I've ever heard you say fuck before.

I didn't say it, I wrote it. And I was quoting you.

Tor

Someday I'm going to get you to say it :-)

Someday works for me ;)

Tor

Kenz...I'm too tired to fight my feelings tonight.

Good. I've declared tonight as being all rules off.

Tor

Oh really?

Yes. Tomorrow we can go back to living in denial.

He's quiet for a few moments and I wonder if he fell asleep with the phone in his hand.

Tor

Don't hate me tomorrow when I'm back to normal.

> I'll love you more tomorrow.

Tor

You're really killing me tonight. It's not fair.

> I like honesty, Tor. If this is the only way you can do that with me, I'll take it.

Tor

This would be easier if you would just push me away, ya know.

> Sorry. No can do. :-)

Tor

I'm going to type one more thing, then we're going to bed. I can hear birds chirping.

> Ok...

Tor

I've always loved how unconditionally you love me.

Ah. The power that words can hold is nothing short of amazing. They can hurt you, and they can heal you. Or they can completely gut you. And sometimes, like now, they can make everything right in your world.

> I always will. Now go to sleep.

Tor

You too, Angel. Maybe if we fall asleep at the same time, we'll see each other in our dreams.

Wow, Tor...I never knew you were a romantic.

Tor

There's a lot about me you don't know ;-)

After eighteen years, I seriously thought I knew everything about Tor. But cracks spidered through the wall between us tonight, and glimpses of him have seeped out through his words. He's sensual. He's lonely. He's possessive. He's playful. He's romantic. And he's afraid of getting hurt.

I pull the thin cover up over me and hug my pillow, eager to fall asleep now with the hope of meeting up with him in our dreams.

CHAPTER 20

Kenzi—age thirteen

Tor—age twenty-eight

I glance at the clock again above the fireplace. It's only five minutes later than it was the last time I looked at it, but it feels like an hour has passed. I've been sitting in this chair in Asher's living room all night, listening to the tick of that clock with one ear and the sound of the door with the other. But there hasn't been a sound at the door, and with each passing minute I'm getting more worried.

I call her phone again and it goes straight to voice mail. I don't bother leaving a message.

"Fuck," I mutter, grabbing my car keys off the coffee table. I pull on my sweatshirt as I head for the back door just as she's coming in.

"Where the hell have you been?" Anger and relief flood through me. "Why didn't you answer your phone?"

Her big green eyes widen as she peeks up at me from behind her bangs. I grab her chin and lift her face up into the light.

"Are you wearing lipstick? And eyeliner?"

She pushes my hand away. "Maybe. A little. My phone battery died." She skirts by me and opens the refrigerator, taking out a pitcher of iced tea.

"Where have you been, Kenzi? It's eleven o'clock. I've been calling you for three hours. You didn't even tell me you were going out. You just disappeared."

She pours herself a glass and puts the pitcher back, shrugging nonchalantly at me. "Chloe's cousin picked me up and took us and some other friends to the movies. Chill out."

"I'm not going to chill out, Kenzi. You're supposed to let me know where you are and who you're with."

Glaring at me, she tries to push past me to leave the kitchen but I grab her arm.

"Don't walk away from me."

"You're being a jerk. You're not my father, ya know. And I'm not a baby. I'm allowed to go out with my friends. I don't have to sit here with you on a Friday night."

I cross my arms in front of me and stare her down. "Fine. Next time your parents go on tour, they can find someone else to watch you. You think I want to waste my time sitting here while you run around and act like a brat? I have a life."

"I'm not a brat."

"You're acting like one."

"Then just go home. I don't need you here. You were ignoring me anyway."

"Fine. I'm outta here." I storm out through the back door and cross the yard to my truck parked in the driveway. Fuck this shit. If I wanted to deal with this, I'd have a kid of my own. I throw my truck in reverse and turn to see her running down the walkway toward me.

"Uncle Tor . . ."

Sonofabitch.

I stop the truck and roll down the window. "Get back in the house, Kenzi. It's late."

She clasps her hands on my car door, tears running down her face, smearing her eyeliner. She hasn't figured out yet that waterproof makeup is best for getting through life.

"Please don't leave."

"*You told me to leave. So I'm going. I'll call one of your uncles to come stay with you and they can figure it out with your parents.*"

"*They all treat me like a baby. I didn't mean it, Tor. Please don't go.*"

"*I can take you to your grandparents, then. You can stay with them till your dad is back.*"

She reaches into the truck and grabs my shoulder. "*Please don't do that. I want to stay here with you.*"

I know she hates having to stay with her grandparents because they smother her with too much attention and try to give her tons of gifts. Kenzi's never liked to be spoiled or lavished with expensive gifts by her wealthy family.

"*You can't just leave and not let me know where you are, Kenz. And you have to be home by your curfew. The rules don't change just because your parents are away.*"

She nods, swiping at her tears with her fingertips. "*Okay. I promise. Just don't leave me. I didn't even want to go to the movie but you were on the phone with Sydni for hours. So when Chloe asked me to go . . . I left.*"

The phone marathon with Sydni started earlier today. I'd hung up on her three times but she kept calling back, trying to justify the photos of her I saw on the internet. With two guys. One of them a drummer from another band who left a status on social media about his sticks being played with recently in a sexual way by a female rocker and he's auctioning them off to donate to charity. I've felt sick to my stomach all day with that vision stuck in my head.

Sydni's explanation that it was something fun that would benefit something good wasn't making me feel any better. And now I have a jealous thirteen-year-old to pacify.

"*Is that what this is about? You're upset because I was on the phone with her and not paying attention to you?*"

She lowers her eyes and fidgets with my door lock. "*Kinda. I thought we were going to watch a movie together and make sundaes. Then she called and that was it. You forgot about me."*

I turn the truck off and climb out, slamming the door behind me. *"Look, I'm not a mind reader. If you're upset about something, you have to tell me. You can't run off. I've been a mental case worrying about you."*

"I'm sorry."

"C'mon. We can still watch a movie and make some wicked sundaes. I'm starving."

"Can we pile pillows and blankets all over the floor and camp out in front of the TV like my dad used to do with me when I was little? I don't even want to watch the movie in the theater room. I want to hang out in the living room by the fireplace."

I'm sure my back will be screaming in the morning if I lie on the floor all night, but I'm willing to risk it.

"Yeah. Actually, that sounds perfect, Angel."

She grabs my hand as we walk back into the house together. "Good. I just want to be five again for a while."

I don't blame her. I want to be a little kid again, too, and forget about all the shit that's happening in my life.

TOR

After sexting with Kenzi, I feel like I've developed multiple personality disorder. One of me feels sick and ashamed of myself for being so weak and the other me can't get her off my mind and is itching to recapture that exhilarating feeling with her again. Last night made me feel more alive than I have in a long time and now that I've had a taste of her, I want more.

So much more.

As I work on the engine of a beautiful old Indian motorcycle in the shop, my brain keeps rewinding back to the pictures she sent me. And her handwritten note. And the fact that she hasn't texted me yet today.

Is she waiting for me to text her first?

Or is she mortified about the things we said to each other?

Does she regret sending me the photos?

My suck level is high when it comes to all things relationships.

When lunchtime rolls around, I lock myself in my office and give her a call. Texts are fun but I need to hear her voice.

"I was hoping you'd call me," she says when she picks up, and I can hear the smile in her voice.

"Were you?"

"Yes."

"It's a good thing I called, then. I wouldn't want to disappoint you."

"I don't think that's possible," she replies. "So, how's your day? You must be tired."

"It's the usual Monday. And yeah I'm beat, but you're worth it."

"Well, thank you."

"What are you doing today?"

"Not much. I'm having dinner with Aunt Katherine and her new boyfriend tonight."

"Very nice. I'm happy for her, she deserves to be happy after what that asshole did to her."

"Yeah, she really does. She seems pretty crazy about this new guy, so I hope it works out."

I glance at my door to make sure no one's around but lower my voice anyway.

"Kenzi, about last night—"

"Tor," she interrupts. "You don't have to say anything."

"I feel like I should."

"Sometimes saying nothing says more."

I laugh into the phone. "You sound like your dad."

"I do, don't I?"

"Yeah." I clear my throat. "I should probably go. I just wanted to hear your voice."

"I really love you, Tor."

She says it like she's declaring the sky is blue. Without one tiny shred of doubt in her mind. Like she knows it's what my heart needs to hear.

"I love you, too, Angel."

"I'm eighteen now."

I grip the phone tighter in my hand.

"Trust me, I know."

"I'll be coming back home soon."

Like I haven't been counting down the minutes.

"I know."

"I'm coming after you, Mr. Grace. You can run, but you can't hide." Her words are teasing and playful but the raw truth behind them is undeniable.

Fuck. Stick a fork in me. I'm done.

That night I have a tattoo appointment with my good friend and artist, Lukas Valentine, who also happens to be Asher's cousin.

When he gets me situated in the leather chair in his work area, I hand him the faded piece of paper with the image I want him to do tonight. He looks at it for a few minutes, his black shaggy hair falling over his eyes, then chews his lip ring as he lays the image on his worktable.

His silence makes me think I made a mistake having him do this one and I should've gone to someone that I don't know to have a picture tattooed on my chest that was drawn by a little girl. Especially when that little girl happens to be the tattoo artist's niece.

I'm so fucking stupid.

"So, how ya been, man?" he finally asks, leaning over me in the chair. The familiar buzz and burn of the gun starts on my left pec.

"Good. Work's been busy so that's always good."

He nods. "Same here. Business is going great."

"Asher's been raving about your violin intro on the new CD."

"Yeah?" His eyes immediately light up at the mention of his playing, like a true musician who's passionate about their craft. Lukas is one of those multitalented people who can play every instrument under the sun, without ever having had any lessons. His favorite is the violin, and he can go from playing classical to metal on it seamlessly like he was born with the thing in his hand.

"Yeah. He said you fuckin' killed it."

"Good to know." He hums along to the music playing from his MP3 player. "Do you want to talk about this?" He nods at the needle dragging into my skin as he shades in a replica of the heart Kenzi drew for me when she was seven. I like how it hurts to have something she gave me embedded into my skin forever.

I shift uneasily in the chair. "I don't think I can."

Shit. I shouldn't have come here. What the hell was I thinking?

"Understood. I'll do the talking, then."

I trust Lukas. We talk a lot when I come in here to get inked and he's sort of like a goth pseudotherapist. I know he's not going to crucify me, but I also know he's about to throw it down and tell me like it is.

He pulls back to look me in the eye. "You're treading into a minefield, Tor. I'm not gonna lie. But you know that already, don't you?"

"I do."

"I guess I don't have to ask if you love her. The fact that you're getting a heart and the words 'i love you the most' permanently inked into your chest says it all, doesn't it?"

I wonder if I can admit my feelings for Kenzi out loud to someone. Especially to someone who also loves and cares about her.

I take a deep breath and I let the words out into the air, knowing there's no turning back now.

"Yeah, I love her. More than anything. Nothing's happened, though. I kissed her and that's it." I said it. I just admitted I'm in love with an eighteen-year-old girl. To her uncle. *Her real uncle.*

He lets out a low, dramatic whistle. "I'm going to assume Asher doesn't know."

"No. Things between her and me changed a few weeks ago. It happened kind of suddenly. My mind is completely fucked over it."

"I'm sure it is," he agrees. "And nothing like that happens suddenly, man. I think it's been happening for a long time."

The fact that it's true makes me wonder if there really is something wrong with me. If I've been falling in love with Kenzi for years; what the hell kind of person does that make me?

"Asher's like a brother to me, Lukas. I love him like he's my own blood. I'd never do anything to disrespect him."

"But... you love her, too."

"I don't want to hurt or lose either of them. But I can't wrap my head around this ever having a happy ending."

He leans back in his stool and lays his gun on the table. "Ivy's twelve years older than me. A lot of people have a hard time with that. Hell, she had a hard time with it at first. I had to chase her around to make her see me for *me* and not as an age."

I glance down at the design on my chest that's half finished. My plan is to show her when she comes back home from Maine. A long time ago I told her I would keep her drawing and her words forever. I'm sure neither one of us ever thought I'd have it marked on my body for the rest of my life, but I want this in a bad way.

"Kenzi is fine with my age. It's harder for me. I used to babysit her. I feel like I should have my balls chopped off or get my head examined."

He lets out a laugh. "Nah. Don't be so hard on yourself. Everyone who knows you knows you're a good guy. The heart wants what the heart wants, man. We don't get to pick who we connect with."

I shake my head with doubt. "Most days I think it's best if I just walk away."

"She'll haunt you for the rest of your life, Tor. I gotta think that's going to be way worse than facing the truth."

"I really don't know."

"Want my advice? Work this out in your head. If *you* can't accept your feelings, no one else is going to either." He picks up his gun and goes to work on my chest again. "Talk to her. Figure out if this is something you guys are both willing to fight for. And if it is? Don't let go. Asher will come around. He's not going to let his little girl and his best friend out of his life, trust me. Asher's all about love and family."

That might be true but I don't think Asher is going to be on board with me sleeping with his daughter, no matter how long we've been friends. He'll rip my head off and beat me to death with it.

"Thanks, man. I hope you're right. If I come up missing, my body is probably in pieces somewhere in the woods behind his house."

"That's not going to happen. If you need to talk, I'm here. I don't judge. And to be honest? I think you and Kenzi are good for each other. She's a sweet girl and she's kinda way beyond her years in a lot of ways. I don't think she'd do well with a guy her age at all. Just my two cents."

An hour later, I'm riding home with a piece of plastic taped over the evidence declaring that I'm clearly and stupidly in love with Kenzi Valentine. Lukas's words definitely hit home. If I can't accept my feelings for her, no one else will. Especially her.

I'm done being screwed with and treated like a yo-yo. I need someone who's going to commit to me one hundred percent and spend the rest of my life with me. I want to start a family and put all crazy shit behind me. Can I really get that from an eighteen-year-old girl?

CHAPTER 21

Tor—age seventeen

Asher—age seventeen

Asher and I are in his father's private home studio jamming when Ash drops this huge bomb on me.

"We're getting married two weeks after we graduate."

My hand freezes on my guitar and I stare at him sitting on a stool in front of the mic with a big grin on his face.

"Married?" I repeat.

"Yeah. We don't want to wait. We're going to get a small apartment in town; I already put a deposit down on it. We don't want to live with my parents anymore."

I blink at him like he's insane. I can't imagine why anyone wouldn't want to live here for their entire life. His parents' house is monstrous, with an indoor and an outdoor pool, sauna, freakin' music studio, and bathroom for every day of the week. Not to mention a refrigerator that's always stocked with food.

"Ash, you guys are living in a small mansion here. You have your own suite of rooms. You don't even pay rent. Why would you want to move out?"

"Because my parents are always hovering."

"They're hardly ever here."

"We still want our own place. It's not fair for Ember to have to live here with my parents and my brothers and my sister. She needs her own *place so she feels like we have our own home. I want you to be my best man, too."*

"Well, fuck yeah."

"And we want you to live with us."

Whoa. He's throwing way too much at me and making my head spin.

"Um, come again?"

"Live. With us."

"Are you bent? Why would you want me to live with you?"

"Don't you want to get out of your parents' house?"

"Yeah, but aren't you getting your own place so you can be alone? Me being there kind of defeats the purpose."

"We want you to live with us. We can write more songs and practice more if we're all together. And we'll need some help with the baby. Kenzi loves you. You're the only one who can get her to stop crying."

I knew there had to be a catch.

"So you want me to be like a live-in babysitter?"

He laughs. "I guess. Like a manny. You can pay the cable bill and buy groceries and I'll pay for everything else. C'mon, it'll be fun."

I make a few hundred dollars a month working for my father at his bike shop. The plan is for me to work there full-time after I graduate, at least until the band takes off and we're living on the road. I can feel it in my gut—we're going to make it big soon.

Asher does landscaping after school and on weekends, plus he gets an allowance from his parents just for existing. I think it's ridiculous, but I don't know what it's like to come from a wealthy family, so I keep my mouth shut about it. So I guess we could afford an apartment. My mom will probably have a shit fit that her oldest baby is moving out, but she'll still have my brothers and sister living there so she won't be dealing with empty nest syndrome yet.

"Do I get my own room?" I ask. "Because I'm not sleeping on the couch every night. I don't want my face where your ass has been sitting."

"*Of course you get a room. I'll take you over there tomorrow so you can see it. There's actually a loft upstairs, so you'll be on your own floor with lots of privacy. You know, in case you ever actually date someone,*" he hints, punching my arm.

"*Worry about your own dick. Mine is fine.*"

That's a bunch of crap, though. My best friend is getting married and has a baby who is almost two years old and I haven't even gotten laid yet. Even though meeting Ember totally accelerated Asher's life plan, from where I'm sitting, he's got everything.

♥ ♥ ♥

KENZI

Being back home is bittersweet. I feel this way every time I come home from visiting Maine. When I'm there, I miss everyone here, but then when I come back home, I miss Aunt Katherine and the peacefulness of the Inn. Before I left, she had a long talk with me and asked me to come live with her and work at the Inn. The thought is very tempting. I just don't know if I'm ready to leave my father or be that far away from Tor.

My bedroom feels empty without Snuggles in her spot by the window that she spent twelve years inhabiting. I'm grateful my father cleaned her cage and put it in the basement so I wouldn't have to see it, so barren without her, as soon as I got home.

There was a tiny black organza bag on my nightstand when I got home yesterday, and inside it was a small tuft of her fur.

Underneath it I found a handwritten note:

I thought you might want to have this to remember her.
Love forever & longer,

Tor

Today I read the note again, my heart bursting with even more love for him over the incredibly thoughtful and sweet things he always does for me. I don't even think that Tor *tries* to be this way; it just comes naturally for him.

I can't help but wonder if he did things like this for Sydni. Or Lisa. Or are these gestures and sentiments only for me due to our long history? As selfish as it seems, I want this side of him to be only for me. Reserved for me alone and no one else.

I didn't text Tor last night when I got home because I spent hours sitting with my father on the patio talking about everything we missed in each other's lives over the past two months. At one point, he went inside to get a cold drink and came back with three gift-wrapped boxes for me, all in pink paper with silver bows.

"Dad, you didn't have to get me gifts."

"Don't be crazy." He leans down and kisses the top of my head before taking his seat across from me. "I can't believe you're eighteen. That blows my mind, baby. It feels like just yesterday we brought you home and had no idea what to do with you."

I smile at him as I open the largest box. "You did great, Dad. I made it to eighteen without ever smoking pot, getting drunk, getting a ticket, or losing a limb. And I'm pretty sure I've never told you to go screw yourself. So, job well done."

"When you put it that way, I feel like the best father on the planet."

"To me you are."

Pushing the white tissue paper aside, I pull out a charcoal sketch of Snuggles on canvas. My hand flies to my mouth as I choke back tears.

"Daddy...oh my God. It's my Snuggles. This means so much to me." In the lower right corner is the signature of my uncle

Lukas, and that just makes this even more special. Lukas is an amazing artist.

"I didn't have any pictures of her so Lukas had to draw her from his memory. I hope it's okay. He said he can fix anything that you'd like changed, or he can start over with a new one."

"No," I reply quickly, taking in all the details of the incredibly realistic drawing. Lukas captured her exactly and I wouldn't change a thing. "It's absolutely perfect. I'm going to have to call him and thank him."

"Actually, he'll be here tomorrow night for your bonfire birthday get-together, so you can thank him in person."

"Even better."

Smiling, I pick up the next box and unwrap it as he takes a few pictures of me.

"I want your mom to see these someday," he says, and I must make an involuntary face because he quickly puts his phone back down on the table and holds his hands up like he's surrendering. "Okay, I won't take any more and we won't talk about that. Just open your presents."

This box is filled with different types of stationery, a new leather planner, monogrammed note cards, and matching envelopes.

"Aw, Dad. You're feeding my new planner addiction. I love it."

"Chloe told me you wanted that one to go with the ten others you have," he teases.

"I did. I'm going to actually use this one, though." I have no idea what I'll be planning, but I feel like it will motivate me to do something every day if I have to write it down.

My dad slides the last, and smallest, box across the table to me.

"I've been waiting to give you this one."

I put my hand on it and study his face. "Uh-oh. That means it's going to be extra special. Is it going to make me cry?"

"It might."

I open the box slowly, and inside is a smaller, red velvet oval box. It has a tiny gold clasp that I lift with my fingernail, and inside is a white gold and diamond watch that belonged to my mother, gifted down to her on her eighteenth birthday from her grandmother. My mom absolutely loved this watch and only wore it on very special occasions like Christmas and her and Dad's wedding anniversary.

I carefully lift the watch from its white satin pillow and turn it in my hand, the light catching the sparkling diamonds. The glittering gems always fascinated me when I was younger; I used to call them tiny stars.

"Dad...are you sure?" I ask with uncertainty. I'm not sure I should accept this when Mom isn't here to give it to me herself. I can't bear the thought of doing anything that would upset her or taking something that meant so much to her.

He nods, his eyes dark pools of emotion. Love. Sadness. Pride.

"I'm positive, Kenzi. She always planned to give it to you on your eighteenth birthday. She wanted you to have it."

"Will you put it on for me?" I ask, handing it to him. My eyes are misty as he takes it from me and gingerly clasps it around my wrist. It's delicate and beautiful and a hundred memories of my mom wearing it flip through my mind.

"I promise I'll take care of it just like Mom did," I say, wiping at my eyes with my napkin.

"I know you will, baby. She knew that, too."

I try to reimagine this night if my mom were still here and not trapped in a wakeless sleep. Her hair would be long and loose, and she'd have on a flowy blouse and cutoff jean shorts, one of her favorite casual go-to outfits. She'd sit close to Dad and they'd hold hands and smile while they watched me opening my presents. I'd feel their love radiating from them like I always could, and I'd get that happy warm fuzzy feeling inside just being part of their little bubble. My mom would jump up in excitement after I opened the watch, and she'd put it on my wrist and kiss my cheeks and go on and on about all the things she had planned for us to do together. Mom was always so excited about me growing up and being her best friend.

"I heard you had lunch with Sailor while you were out in Maine," Dad suddenly says with a hint of rare displeasure.

"Yeah, he has family nearby. Kind of a small world. We had lunch and then drove around talking. I'm designing a quote tattoo for him."

He pushes his hair off his face and fixes a thoughtful expression at me. My father has shifted into thinking mode, which may or may not go well for me.

"Are you two dating, then?"

"I saw him once, Dad. Geez."

"Once is a start."

I quirk my eyebrows up at him. "We're not dating. It was purely on a friendship level. He's really sweet, though, and he was very polite. He didn't even kiss me or ogle at me or do any sort of thing that would make you want to kick his ass. Okay?"

"Good," my father says.

"I'm eighteen now, Dad. You can't get nervous every time a guy pays attention to me."

"I can't help it. I like Sailor; he's a good kid. But I think he's too old for you. He's traveled, he's in a new band, probably has lots of experience..."

My stomach contracts with nerves as my father continues to go on about the perils of dating a young musician, and I can barely pay attention to what he's saying. Sailor is in his early twenties. A far cry from Toren's thirty-two years. If my dad thinks Sailor is too old for me to be dating, he'll go totally loco if he finds out I have feelings for Tor that go way beyond friendship.

After the texting with Tor a few weeks ago, my dreamer mind had fabricated a scenario where Tor and I are happily dating and my father, all our friends, and our families accepted us as a couple. This conversation is a major bitch-slap back into the reality that the chances of that ever happening are nearly impossible, no matter how much we might be wishing for it.

"Hot damn," Chloe says. "I'd love to be the cheese in that sandwich." Rayne and I follow her gaze across my backyard to where Tor is talking with Sailor and Finn. We're sitting in chairs by the pool, catching up since I just got back from Maine. There's more people at the bonfire tonight since my father announced it was also to celebrate my birthday, which I really didn't want, as I don't like being any sort of nucleus of attention.

"Seriously," Rayne agrees. "I don't know who's hotter. But it's basically a club sandwich since there are three of them. Let's do marry/fuck/kiss and figure it out."

"Ooh I love that!" Chloe squeals. "I'll go first." She narrows her eyes at the guys as her brain works them over. "I'd marry Sailor, fuck the hell out of Tor, and kiss Finn. And if Tanner were here, he'd be my alternate fuck. I can't get enough of him."

I almost choke on my soda at her words about Tor. He's *mine*. I fight the urge to jump out of my chair and claw her eyes out.

Rayne sits up straighter as she takes her turn analyzing the trio of men. "I'm going to have to marry Tor, fuck Finn, and kiss Sailor. And since we're adding alternates, I'd totally marry Tristan. That boy is so sexy and adorable. I could just eat him up." They turn to me. "Okay, Kenz. Your turn."

Of course now that it's my turn, Tor is walking toward us with his sexy swagger, drink in hand, his muscular chest stretching his thin white T-shirt.

"Why do you ladies look like you're up to no good?" he asks with a grin when he reaches us.

Chloe bats her eyelashes at him. "We're doing marry/fuck/ kiss with you, Sailor, and Finn with your brothers as alternates."

Tor lets out a chuckle. "Is that right?"

"Yeah, but Kenzi hasn't picked yet," Chloe adds. "You should know, I didn't pick you to kiss or marry, Tor. So you do the math. But Rayne picked you to marry."

Tor does a mock bow to Rayne. "Thank you, Rayne, for not treating me like a piece of meat. And, Chloe, I don't think you could handle this." He winks at her and takes a sip of his soda.

"I'm up for the challenge," Chloe teases back, and I can feel myself burning up with jealousy over her blatant flirting. I don't want her or anyone else handling him.

"Well?" Chloe urges, poking my arm. "You didn't pick, Kenzi. You're the birthday girl, so you can have two alternates."

"I think I'll pass," I answer, glancing up at Tor. "I'm going to go get something to eat."

Rising, I walk across the yard to the deck to make myself a salad. I know Chloe is just playing around but it really struck a little green nerve in me. The mere thought of Toren having sex with another woman or marrying someone makes my heart hurt.

My phone vibrates in my pocket, so I pull it out while I'm standing next to the table of assorted salads.

Tor

I want to know your answers

I look up and do a quick scan of the yard to find him sitting by himself next to a tiki torch, his eyes on me. My heartbeats skip under his gaze.

> You're my pick for everything.

Tor
> You would be mine, too.

> I think Chloe has a thing for you :/

Tor
> Who's Chloe?

I smile at my phone and then sneak a peek back at him. He flashes me a devious smile and waves.

Shaking my head, I take my plate over to the gazebo, where my dad is singing and Sailor is playing guitar. My dad's younger brother, Mikah, is playing percussion on small conga drums behind them, which I love the sound of. I sit in a nearby lawn chair and eat my salad as I listen to their unplugged version of an old love song.

"I used to be a musician, too. If that's what you're into," he suddenly whispers in my ear, dragging the nearest empty chair over next to mine.

"Once a musician, always a musician," I retort. "It's in your blood. And I'm not *into* musicians. I'm into someone who can make me feel."

He plucks a cucumber slice out of my salad and chews it slowly. "Feel what, exactly?"

I shrug. "Everything. I want to experience everything and feel everything."

"Everything is a dangerous path, Angel."

"Not if it's with the right person."

He holds my eyes for a few moments before breaking contact. "You actually look older to me now. I'm not sure if it's because I haven't seen you in two months or if you changed while you were gone. But you look older."

"Maybe it's because you allowed yourself to think about what you would *do to me*, as you put it."

"Jesus, Kenzi," he whispers. "Don't bring that up here. We're surrounded by your family."

"No one can hear us over the music. There's not even anyone near us."

"I don't care. Just don't talk about it here."

Sighing, I turn my full attention to the band, my father's voice like smooth velvet even sitting here in his backyard with no mic. I let my eyes shift over to Sailor, who smiles at me when he catches my eye.

Tor sees it, too.

He leans closer to me, almost knocking his lawn chair over onto me. "What's up with you and him?"

"Nothing, why?"

"He just smiled his little pretty-boy smile at you."

I laugh. "Really, Tor? You're all growly over a smile? I just had to witness Chloe practically getting on her knees in front of you. How do you think that felt for me?"

"As you saw, I didn't encourage her."

"Thank you. That would have gutted me."

"Where would Sailor fall in your marry/screw/kiss list?"

"That depends."

"On what?"

"On if you're one of the options."

"You're so naughty, Kenzi." He shakes his head and leans away. "I refuse to consider Sailor in any way. Even for a game. You have my heart, and you know it. We can sit here and make a list of all the wrongs but it still won't change how I feel, Tor."

"Trust me, I know the feeling."

The song ends and Tor stands up. "I'm going to do something special, just for you," he says, and I watch with curiosity as he goes up to my dad, says a few words, then takes the guitar from Sailor, shooing him out of the gazebo like he's a puppy.

My father is all smiles as Tor drags a stool closer to him and then begins to play one of their oldest songs that my parents and Tor wrote together when they were teens.

To the best of my knowledge, Tor hasn't played in front of people since he left the band years ago. I'm pretty sure he doesn't play alone because the guitar case in his closet never looks like it's been moved. But the way he's playing the guitar so fluidly and perfectly right now is like he never stopped.

Sailor has taken the chair beside me that Tor just vacated, which I'm sure is only going to further agitate Tor's suspicion that Sailor might be interested in being more than friends, but I can't ask him not to sit with me.

"Whoa," Sailor says. "No one's heard Toren Grace play in years."

"I know," I say, not taking my eyes off the man who owns my heart and is now recapturing a dream he gave up, just to give me a glimpse of himself that I never got to see.

"He was one of my inspirations when I was younger," Sailor continues. "Storm is great, too; they just have very different playing styles."

My dad's brother Storm took Tor's place in the band after he had to leave when his father passed away, and Sailor is right—Storm is super talented and the fans love him. He slipped into the band with ease without causing a disruption to their songs. I'm still a little perplexed and slightly disappointed that everyone in my family has amazing musical talents except me.

The next song they play is the song that put them on the map and launched the band's popularity. It's a ballad about losing your first love, and while I'm sure I've heard it at least a thousand times, this slimmed down acoustic version is raw and intimate, sending chills down my spine. I've always known Tor wrote this song, but before today I never wondered if there's personal inspiration behind it. Now it's got me thinking. Other than Sydni, who has broken his heart? He didn't start dating Sydni until my mother introduced them, which was after this song was written. Was there someone else along the way he's never talked about? Or is it simply just a well-written, emotional song?

They play two more songs, and I'm practically hypnotized watching Tor play. I grew up watching musicians, quite a few were friends of my dad or other bands they toured with, but there is something erotic about watching a man you're attracted to play the guitar. The sensual words he typed in our text messages are on repeat in my mind as I watch his fingers move over the strings, wondering how they would feel touching me. That day he kissed me on the couch was the first and only time he ever put his hands on my body in any kind of sexual way, but the memory of the possessive way he pulled me onto him and the burn of his hand on the flesh of my lower back makes my insides quiver.

Later, my father and my grandmother bring out a huge cake blazing with candles and my dad sings a rocked-out version of "Happy Birthday" to me like he does every year. A few people have left cards and gifts for me, but thankfully my father doesn't make me open them all in front of everyone like I'm five. I'd rather open them in private and then send handwritten thank-you cards to everyone.

As it gets late, our guests start to filter out, most of them coming to hug me and wish me happy birthday before they leave. I've been so caught up talking to everyone that I didn't get a chance to thank Toren for playing guitar for me. I walk around the backyard trying to find him, and finally walk around to the front to see if his truck or bike is still here, and my heart takes a nosedive when I see him standing by his truck with Sydni. I try to look away, but I can't. They're standing closer than friends would be, and her hands are on his chest, but not pushing him away. His arm is resting on the truck next to her head, as if he's going to lean down to kiss her. I so wish I could read lips because I can't hear what they're saying from where I stand hidden among the manicured bushes at the side of the house.

I jump when he suddenly slams his fist against the truck, and she pulls her hands away from him.

They're fighting.

I turn to walk away and trip over part of the stone landscape. When I look back, he's looking right at me. Our eyes lock and flash for a brief moment before I tear mine away.

Crap.

I beeline into the house, embarrassed at being caught spying on him. Could I be any more immature? Trying to avoid the guests in our kitchen, I go down the other hallway and run right into Tor, who must have come in through the front door. Grabbing my arm, he quickly and discreetly steers me into the laundry room and closes the door behind us.

I stare up at him, trying to catch my breath from walking too fast. Or maybe from being so close to him in this small space.

"What were you doing out there?" he asks. "Eavesdropping? That's not like you, Kenz."

I shake my head and try to find my voice. "No. I was looking for you so I could say good night and thank you for playing the songs for me. I haven't seen you play since I was a little girl. I guess I just wasn't expecting to see you with Sydni. I'm sorry."

"Don't apologize."

Backing up a few inches, he glances down at my legs. "You skinned your knee." He grabs a paper towel from a shelf next to the washing machine, runs some cold water on it from the sink, and kneels in front of me.

He gently dabs at my knee with the paper towel, then tosses it into the trash. I wait for him to stand, but he remains kneeling in front of me, his hand on the spot behind my knee. Tor has fixed many boo-boos for me over the years, and maybe he's thinking of all those times, like I am right now. We've reached that odd moment again where the lines of who we are to each other have been blurred.

More like obliterated.

I reach out and move my fingers through his long hair, my nails grazing along his scalp, and he places a soft kiss right above my skinned knee before he finally stands, grabbing my waist and lifting me effortlessly on top of the clothes dryer, moving to stand between my thighs. Without breaking eye contact, he reaches behind him and locks the door.

"Nothing is going on with Sydni. She just likes to push my buttons and piss me off." His hands are on my waist as he talks, and I have no idea what to do with my own. Right now they're white-knuckling the edge of the dryer.

"You don't have to explain, Tor."

"Yeah, I do. I don't want you thinking she and I are back together. Things are just getting really complicated."

"Does *she* think you're getting back together?"

"I don't know what goes on in her crazy brain, but we are definitely not together. A few weeks ago we talked and she asked for another chance."

"What would that be, then, the hundredth chance?" I ask, unable to hide my sarcasm, which is attempting to cover up my fear of her getting him back.

"Something like that. But that was before you and I...talked," he says nervously, his eyes shifting down between us and then back up to my face.

"So you're not going to give her another chance?"

"No." He shakes his head. "I can't even consider that when all I can think about is you, now, can I?"

Finally, he's saying the words I've been waiting so long to hear.

"I can't stop thinking about you either," I say, my voice shaking in tune with my trembling insides.

"I want to show you something. That's why I pulled you in here. It's kinda your birthday present."

I'm confused as he slowly lifts his shirt up, until my eyes land on his chest, right above his heart, where there's a new tattoo of the scribbled heart drawing I made for him when I was a little girl, with the words *i love you the most* beneath it in my writing. My breath catches as I stare at it.

"When did you get that?"

"A few weeks ago."

He moves even closer and my heart tries to break free from my chest to jump into his as he leans in to whisper in my ear.

"Do you still mean it?"

"Yes. I always will," I say breathlessly.

He leans back to look into my eyes as he pulls his shirt back down. "Good. Because it's there forever now."

"I'll mean it forever. I promise."

On impulse, I lean forward and touch my lips to his for a stolen kiss, and he inhales sharply in surprise.

"That's what I want. So fuckin' bad," he whispers with a raspy voice as he leans his forehead against mine. "Kiss me again. Then I have to get out of here."

His hands tighten around my waist in encouragement as he waits for me, and my insecurity kicks in, knowing he's waiting for it, wanting it, and not pushing me away. I don't want to disappoint him by kissing like an eighteen-year-old virgin.

Even though I am.

Reaching up, I grasp his wide shoulders and pull him closer, wrapping my legs around his waist before tilting my head up to meet his lips that still have a slight taste of my birthday cake. He lets me drive the kiss, not pressing further or taking control, which I wish he would do. I want him to pull me closer and kiss me deeper like he did the other times we kissed, but he's not. He's completely still, breathing against my mouth, waiting for me.

I open my eyes to find his dark and fiery, staring into mine. Our mouths linger against each other, while my heart is fluttering in my chest like a hummingbird. He's all man between my legs and under my touch—wide, rock hard, and powerful. He smells of rain and woods and grease, and it's provocative in this tiny space of detergent and bleach. I want to pull his shirt off and run my hands over his smooth muscles, kiss him in places I've only dreamed about.

His nose nudges against mine, his lips brushing across my cheek. "You can do whatever you want," he whispers, as if he can feel all the things I'm thinking.

I *want* to do everything.

But there's some kind of disconnect between my brain, my heart, my hands, and my lips. In my mind, I pulled him closer, ran my hands under his shirt and over his chest and abs as my lips trailed down his neck, chasing after my hands, tasting him, kissing the words on his chest.

Instead, I plant a quick kiss on his mouth and pull away, untangling my legs from around him as he lets out a deep sigh.

"All right," he says, his voice thick with...disappointment?

Yes. He's disappointed. In me.

My heart and stomach sink together as I jump off the clothes dryer and he moves away from me.

"You get out of here first and then I'll leave. I don't want anyone to see us coming out of here together."

"Okay," I say awkwardly, reaching for the doorknob. "Thank you for playing the songs for me, Tor. It was amazing to finally see you and hear you play."

He nods and runs his hand through his hair before meeting my eyes again. The fire is gone from them now, replaced with their usual shroud of melancholy.

"Happy birthday, Angel."

I unlock the door and peer outside to make sure no one is milling around in the hallway before I leave the room and go directly upstairs to my own, closing my door behind me before I burst into tears.

I let him down. He gave me a chance to show him how I feel and what I want, and I let my nerves and inexperience get in the way and destroyed the moment.

Once again, that bitch called *reality* is knocking on my door, here to remind me that regardless of how we feel, I'm still a teenager, and he's still a grown man. No matter how close we might be sometimes, we are still worlds apart in so many ways.

CHAPTER 22

Kenzi—age five

Tor—age twenty

After strapping the pink helmet onto her head, I hold the handlebars of the small bicycle I bought her for her birthday, waiting for her to get on.

"My wheels are gone," she says skeptically, touching the seat and blinking up at me.

"You don't need the training wheels anymore. You can ride it without them now, like we practiced on your old bike."

Her teeth chew her bottom lip. "Are you sure, Uncle Tor? I don't want to fall and ruin my new bike."

I lift her up and gently place her on the seat. "I'm going to run right next to you. I won't let you fall, Angel, I promise. Do you trust me?"

She smiles at me, the gold flecks in her jade eyes sparkling under the bright summer sun.

"I trust you."

I wink at her and place my hand on the back of her seat. "Okay, then. Start pedaling."

She grasps the handlebars with as serious a face as a five-year-old can make and starts to pedal slowly, wobbling a bit. Grasping her seat, I jog next to her as she picks up momentum, and soon she's pedaling perfectly on two wheels.

"You're doing it!" I yell as I slow down and let her go ahead of me on her own so I can watch her.

She turns her head to look for me, turning the front tire sharply, and she goes down right in front of the neighbor's house, arms and legs sprawling on the pavement.

"Shit," I mutter under my breath, running to her. "Are you okay?" I ask, helping her stand up.

"You made me fall," she says tearfully. "I was looking for you and I fell. You promised to stay with me."

"You're right. I just wanted to see you do it all by yourself. And you did it. You don't need me to hold you up, right?" I pick up the bike, glad to see it's not broken, but her knee is bleeding and her palm is all scraped up. Ember's going to kill me.

She glares at me and shakes her head, the helmet twisting crookedly on her head.

"It's better when you hold me up."

I take her small hand in mine. "Maybe for now you're right. Let's go back to the house and fix up your knee, okay?"

"Okay. I won't tell Mommy you let me fall."

I don't know why, but those little innocent words slice through my heart. I've never let her get hurt before. No matter what, I'm never going to let it happen again.

♥ ♥ ♥

TOR

Tristan is standing over me in my work area as I'm kneeling in front of this old Indian bike that I feel like I'm never going to finish. Finding parts for this bike has been nearly impossible and has put me way behind with my schedule.

"Speak or go away. I'm busy," I say, grabbing a wrench.

"I need a week off."

"Need or want?"

"Does it matter? What's up your ass lately?"

I stand, grab a rag to wipe my hands off with, and turn to face my brother. Even though he's twenty-four, he'll always be my little brother in my eyes.

"A week off is a long time. I'll have to rearrange some work since you're the only one who does what you do. When do you need it?"

"In about two weeks."

Two weeks doesn't give me much time to move things around for the custom paint jobs we have booked, but Tris hardly ever asks for time off, so I really can't complain.

Sighing, I nod. "Okay, then. We'll work it out. Can I ask where you're going?"

He shoves his hands into the front pockets of his faded jeans and looks down, his dirty-blond hair falling down into his face.

"I'm meeting with a local service dog rep to go through the screening process for a therapy dog."

My attitude instantly diminishes. Mom and I have been after him for years to look into a therapy dog to help him with the seizures he suffers.

"Tris, that's great. Why didn't you tell me?"

"I don't know." He shrugs. "It's just taken me a while to accept it, I guess."

"It's nothing to be embarrassed about."

He's always tried to hide the fact that he has seizures, like he thinks there's something wrong with him. It's kept him from making friends and he's never really dated anyone, at least as far as I know. He and Tyler have both become like hermits and that worries me a lot. I don't want my brothers spending the rest of their lives alone. *Like me.*

"Anyway, so now I have to meet with them in person; then

they do a home check, I meet with a few of the trainers, and then I get put on a waiting list for the right dog."

"Take all the time you need, then." I lightly squeeze his shoulder. "This is worth it, trust me. Do you need any money?"

"Nah, they work on donations and I already made one."

"We'll organize a ride to raise some money to donate to them, too. Does Mom know?"

"Yeah, she's the one who pushed me into it. A few of their service dogs are rescues, so Mom has worked with them before."

"Good deal," I say, glad that he's going through with this decision. "This is a good thing, Tris. If it can make your life a little safer, that's all that matters. Right?"

He nods but still has that uncertain look in his gray eyes. "I hope so."

"Be positive. And, hey, I wouldn't admit this normally but since I brought home that big white fluff monster, I'm not as lonely. It's nice to have him and that cat waiting for me when I get home after a long day."

Laughing, he shakes his head, turns, and walks away. "I'm starting to worry about us, man," he jokes, turning his head. "We need to find us some chicks."

Speaking of chicks, it's been almost a week since I saw Kenzi at the bonfire, and my emotions are still all over the place from that night. The way her eyes were glued to me, glowing with a mix of love and lust as I played the guitar did way more than just turn me on like mad. It made me itch to start playing again. Every night since then I've dragged my guitar out of the closet and sat in my backyard brushing up on my old favorite songs and toying around with some new ones.

I miss my dreams.

I can still feel her lips on mine, in that daring moment when she kissed me all on her own and almost made me tear her clothes off in Asher's laundry room while he was probably twenty feet away eating her birthday cake.

I feel sick.

I feel tortured.

I feel unhinged with want for her.

I feel a deep ache in my heart that only she can soothe.

I feel like I'm stabbing a dagger straight through my best friend's back.

The scales are tipping, though, and it's scaring the shit out of me.

I pull my phone out of my back pocket and type out a quick text, my stomach immediately knotting up.

> I'm taking tomorrow off and going for a ride.

Kenzi

> Um ok? Thanks for the update? Shall I expect further notice?

I laugh at the screen, loving her little snarky attitude.

> Be outside at 8am. Jeans, boots, and your helmet.

Kenzi

> I'm going too?! :-)

> If you want to...

Kenzi

> Of course I do!

> Good.

Kenzi

> Woot! I haven't been on your bike in years!

> Because that seat on my bike has been reserved.

Kenzi
For who? :-(

The woman of my dreams ;-)

Kenzi
Eep

Wtf is that?

Kenzi
It means like wow

Speak English. I'm old, remember?

Kenzi
You are not. You're so cute

Please don't call me cute

Kenzi
But you so are!

I'll see you in the morning, Angel.

Kenzi
I can't wait! <3

No one's ever sent me a heart in a text message before. I touch it lightly with my finger, the knot in my stomach fraying and unraveling with threads of hope. Her love and excitement are contagious, and I honestly don't want a cure. I want to die of this sickness, if I can. Nothing and no one has ever made me feel as happy and content as she does. Not even playing or riding has been able to reach far enough into me to pull me out of the bitter state of mind that I've been dwelling in for years.

But she has. Without even trying.

The moment I try to relax into this new feeling of content-ment, the ugly monster of the situation rears its head again, sinks its claws into my heart, trying to tear it away from her, laughing at me for being naïve enough to think spending a day with her would be okay.

She comes out of the house when she hears my bike pull into the driveway looking all sorts of cute and sexy in jeans, a black long-sleeved shirt with a big yellow smiley face on the front, her hair in a long braid with a little skull clip at the end. And those damn black leather boots that for some crazy reason always seem to turn me on. I'm starting to think maybe I have a foot or shoe fetish I never realized before. I quickly shove the thought to the back of my mind to be dealt with later. I want today to just be a day for us to spend time together alone, to see how it feels to just spend a day with her with no labels on us. I don't want to think about our past or the future or Ash or anything else except just us.

She approaches me with a big smile and kisses my cheek.

"You're on time. I'm impressed," she says, pulling her helmet over her head. I don't wear a helmet but there's no way I'm letting her go without one.

"Hop on." I nod to the small seat behind me and she grabs on to my shoulder as she climbs on and sets her feet on the pegs.

"A few rules," I say, turning toward her. "I don't want you falling off, so keep your hands on me."

"That won't be a problem," she replies with a playful tone, wrapping her arms around my waist.

I stifle a laugh. "Behave yourself. Being on the bike is serious. This isn't a big two-wheeled vibrator. Pay attention and move your body with mine, okay?"

Her arms tighten around my waist. "Seriously, Tor, you just said vibrator and told me to move my body with yours while I've got my legs and arms wrapped all up around your amazing bod. I'll do my best to behave given all those circumstances."

I lean back against her and lay my hand on hers clasped over my stomach. Having her so close, with her perfume enveloping me and feeling the warmth of her thighs pressed against my legs, is making my blood rush through my veins like liquid fire. I thought a ride in the mountains would be safe territory but now it's turned into a subtle act of foreplay.

Am I complaining? Hell no.

"Well, when you put it like that, Angel, enjoy the ride," I tease back, starting up the bike before she can throw more fuel onto the flames. I'm not used to riding with a woman or feeling anything but the rush of air in my face. It figures she would be the first to turn this all around for me.

And again, I'm not complaining one bit.

I've ridden these roads for almost my entire life. First, on the back of my old man's bike when I was a little kid, and then on my own when I was old enough to ride alone. Today I take it slower than I normally do, and Kenzi keeps her arms around me, loosening up her embrace just a little as she starts to feel more comfortable. I'm not sure when the last time she was on the back of Asher's bike, but I'm guessing it's probably been over two years.

When we get farther up the mountains, I pull over onto a small area for parking and kill the engine, motioning for her to hop off before I put the kickstand down. She gives me a squeeze before she gets off and takes her helmet off while I take a bottle of water out of my saddlebag.

"You having fun?" I ask her, taking the helmet from her hand and resting it on the back of my bike.

She nods, her eyes dancing with the same happiness I'm feeling. "I really am. It's beautiful up here."

"It is." I reach for her hand and she immediately slides hers into mine like we've been together forever.

And maybe we have.

We walk a ways into the woods, following the beaten trail to where there are groups of small waterfalls running down the mountain. The air is cooler up here than it was down in our town, and it makes me want to pull her closer to me and put my arm around her. As if reading my mind, she looks up at me and leans her head against my arm.

"I'm glad you asked me to come," she says softly.

"Me too. I've been wanting to do this for a while."

When we reach the first waterfall that pours over the cliff, we sit next to each other on a huge rock nestled into the side of the mountain with large tree roots twisting around it. I'm glad no one else is here today. Most times when I come up here there's other riders or couples here, and sometimes kids running around making a lot of noise.

"You glad to be back home?" I ask.

"Yeah, I always get a little homesick, even though I love being with Aunt Katherine. She asked me to come back and stay there. Like permanently... to live there and work with her."

A flash of hot pain sears through my gut and up into my chest. "Is that what you want to do?" I ask, trying to keep my voice even.

She runs her finger along a soft patch of moss on the rock. "It's tempting. I like being there and meeting the new guests is always pretty cool. And she would teach me how to cook more meals so I can be more helpful." She raises her eyes to mine. "But I also was looking forward to working with you at the shop like we talked about and volunteering with your mom at the shelter and helping you with the rescues."

"I'm sure there's an animal shelter near Katherine's where you could volunteer."

"Yeah...that's true but you and your mom are like family, so it means more to me. Before I left for Maine, your mom and I were talking about things we could do to raise more awareness about the shelter and rescue, and how we can help people more who have lost their pets like printing lost posters for them. If we had a high-speed laser printer, we could print off a few hundred lost notices in just a few minutes and start hanging them around town right away. For most people, it takes them days to print those things and they only print like twenty. I wanted to buy the printer and donate it." Her thin shoulders shrug shyly. "I don't know, I was just thinking of ways to help. It makes me feel good."

I try to speak but I can't because I'm too busy fighting the urge to kiss her again. She's so damn perfect for me. And maybe I made her that way by spending too much time with her over the years. I meshed her into every part of my life, and now she's grown into someone who cares as much about the things that are important to me as I do. Sydni never invested herself into the pet rescue with me and often rolled her eyes when I talked about it. She definitely wouldn't be caught dead at my mom's shelter bathing dogs or walking around town hanging posters of lost pets. It always bothered me to not have someone who would be involved in that part of my life with me. Especially after growing up with two parents who were so dedicated to their mission that they built their entire lives around it.

Kenzi continues to talk, completely clueless to the fact that she's crawling even deeper into my heart and making me want to run home, dump my jar of change onto the floor and stick a monstrous ring on her finger. I start to feel dizzy and I gulp my

water, hoping it will wash away the tangled-up thoughts and feelings I'm having.

"I was thinking it would be nice to maybe have some sort of
grief counseling available for the people who have a missing pet
that we find out has passed away while it was missing. Like that
poor lady whose dog got run over. Remember how devastated
she was?" She blinks back a tear. "When Snuggles died, it took
me days to stop crying. I can't imagine what those people feel like
who lose their pets so suddenly and tragically, ya know?"

I nod and drink more water.

I will not think about proposing to an eighteen-year-old girl.

"What? Is it all stupid?" she asks.

"No, not at all."

"Then why aren't you saying anything?"

"You just sorta amaze me sometimes, that's all. I love how your
mind works." I put my water bottle on the rock next to me again.

"So you like my ideas?"

"No, I *love* your ideas. So will my mom."

She beams. "Really? I was going to talk to her next week."

"Seriously, she'll love all of it, Kenz. I'll even split the cost of
the printer with you. How's that sound? It's a wicked cool idea
for us to do that to help people. The faster the posters go up, the
better chance they have of finding the dog."

She nods with excitement. "I like being able to do something
that makes a difference. It makes me feel important and like I'm
doing something that actually matters. I don't want to be the rich
rock star's kid who does nothing. I want to help."

"Yeah. It's kind of an addicting feeling."

"It really is. What about me working at the shop? Do you still
want me to when Gretchen leaves?"

Yes, I want you with me every moment of every day of every year.

"I do but I have to admit, I think working at the Inn is way more glamorous and will give you more of a future. Why would you want to work in a dirty bike shop answering phones and doing mundane shit all day?"

"Because then I can be close to you. It's your family's business. It's not just a random job to me. It means just as much to me as the Inn."

I nod slowly and listen to the rush of the water that's barely drowning out the screams in my own head. She's doing every-thing she can to be part of my life, and I can either let her or I can put a stop to it. I can end this all now and watch her go back to Maine. I know she'll be okay. She'll forget about me eventually and will meet someone her own age, and I'll move on and find someone who isn't her and we'll both be fine. Things will go back to how they were before.

Right. Keep telling yourself that and maybe you'll believe it.

"Let's think about it," I finally say. "I want you to do what's best for you, and not do things just so you can be near me. No matter what you choose, we'll still see each other. Maine is a nice, easy ride. I can visit you whenever we want to spend time together. You don't have to get involved in all my stuff just to see me."

"I know that, but I *want* to be involved in your 'stuff.' And not just to see you. It's more than that. I wouldn't get involved with the shelter and work at your shop just to stalk you, Tor. I'm not that crazy."

Chuckling at her stalker comment, I grab her hand and thread our fingers together. "I know you're not. I just want what's best for you. That's all."

"I want what's best for you, too. I want you to be happy."

That statement throws me. "You don't think I'm happy?"

She tilts her head and quirks the corner of her mouth as she thinks about that. "Honestly? Not really. I don't think you are. I watch you a lot at the bonfires, and I hardly ever see you smile. You've always kinda had this dark broodiness about you."

"Dark broodiness?" I repeat, slightly offended. "Get outta here. You've been reading too many of your grandmother's romance books."

She smacks my shoulder playfully. "Don't make fun of me. I'm being serious."

"Then don't call me dark and broody. Fuck. At least give me some better words."

"Hmmm..." She studies my face, seriously trying to come up with words to describe me. "Okay, I'm gonna go with tortured and romantic," she says triumphantly.

"Wow..." I look away from her, not really wanting her to see that she's so right that it hurts.

"What? You don't like those words either?"

"I think you're pretty spot-on. As usual." I keep my eyes on a butterfly fluttering around by the waterfall. It reminds me of her, so beautiful and free, innocently playing so close to something that could suck her right into its depths and consume her.

"How would you describe me?" Shyness laces her voice, which is not something I hear in her often.

Taking a deep breath, I turn to face her. "There are a million words I could use to describe you, Angel. We could be here for days. Weeks, even."

She giggles. "Just pick two like I did."

Damn. If I pick the wrong words, I could hurt her feelings and I don't want to ruin the good day we're having. She watches my face with hopeful anticipation as I search my brain for exactly the right words.

"Okay. I have three."

"I get a bonus word?" she asks.

"Yes, because you're that special. So, I'm gonna go with enchanting, adorable, and loving."

She breaks out into a huge smile. "Enchanting! I love that! I sound like a magical fairy!"

"Something like that."

Leaning closer to me, she kisses my shoulder, her mouth so close that I can smell the strawberry gloss on her lips and I want to taste it so bad my mouth is practically watering. She wore the same stuff the day I kissed her on the couch. The taste stayed on my lips for hours afterward, tantalizing me long after she stormed out and slammed the door in my face. I ache to push her down on this rock and kiss her again right now, but I'm fighting that…*hard*. I wanted today to be a day of us spending time together alone and just enjoying each other without any sexual or emotional turmoil.

I was stupid to think that could happen, though, because I can't be within twenty feet of her now without wanting to kiss every inch of what I glimpsed in her pictures. Or wanting to just stare into her eyes for hours on end and tell her how much I love her.

Now she's looking out at the river in front of us with a faraway look in her eye. A few strands of her golden hair have come out of her braid from the ride and are blowing lightly across her cheek. She looks beautiful.

"It's so pretty and peaceful here," she says dreamily. "Don't you wish we could live here, up in the mountains in a little log cabin with the sound of the water around us?"

"Yeah. I do."

"It might even be better than the little house with the porch and the picket fence," she adds.

"They both sound great, Angel. I have no doubt you'll have one or the other. Or maybe even both someday."

She turns to me. "It would only be great if you lived in them with me."

I try not to fall off the ledge we're sitting on. I hate that she has the ability to completely rock me with just words.

"You're only eighteen, Kenz. You've got lots of time to think about where you want to live and who you think you want to live with, trust me."

She lets out a short huff. "You're never going to think of me as an adult, are you?" she accuses, trying to pull her hand out of mine. I hold on to her, not letting her go.

"That's not true, Kenzi. I *do* see you as a beautiful, mature, sensual woman. But I also see the little girl I watched grow up, and sometimes it's hard for me to *not* see her when I look at you. It's hard for me to let her go. You have to cut me a little slack and try to understand that."

She nods and chews her lip. "I'm sorry. I know this is harder for you than it is for me in a lot of ways. I guess I'm a little bit of a brat; I just want to be with you and forget everything else. So that probably *is* my immaturity showing."

"I wouldn't say it's immaturity. I mean, how can you help yourself when I'm so insanely irresistible, right?" I joke, trying to lighten up the mood.

Her mouth falls open and she starts to laugh. "Look at you, all in love with yourself," she teases. "It's true, though. There's definitely something about you, Tor. Every girl I know drools over you."

I lift our hands up and press my lips against her knuckles, holding her hand there. "I really only care what you think. They don't see me like this. Only you do."

Her hand starts to tremble with nervousness in mine, and I wonder if things ever went further with us if she would be a shaking bundle of nerves. I have to admit, a part of me likes that I make her so shaky. It makes me want to make love to her until she explodes and then calms in my arms. I want to watch and feel that transition something fierce.

"Can I ask you something personal?" she asks.

"Sure." I kiss her hand again and wait for the shaking. *One... two... shaking starts.* My cock hardens like a rock in my jeans wondering where else she's quivering.

"You're not like this with anyone else? This sweet?"

"No. Never like I am with you. Not even close."

"I'm glad," she says. "I know I'm being a brat again, but I want that part of you all to myself."

"Well, you got it."

Her eyes settle on my mouth as it rests against her hand, and she licks her lips, wanting me to kiss her. I can feel it emanating from her like white heat.

I fight the temptation. "Just so you know... I'm not seeing anyone else. And I haven't been physical with anyone in a long time. I don't want you feeling like some side toy for me."

Her gaze shifts up to lock with mine as she absorbs my words, and I watch the way the color of them changes in the sunlight from light green to a deep forest green.

"Are we seeing each other?" she asks, her voice wavering.

"I think we're way beyond seeing each other in a lot of ways, Kenzi."

"What are we, then?" I can barely hear her over the sound of the water, and I almost wish I hadn't. I don't know the answer to that question, and that's what's been shredding up my insides for months.

"I'm trying to figure that out, love," I answer quietly.

That seems to satisfy her for now as she nods slowly and then looks back out at the water, but I feel like I have to say more.

"The thing is...I'm afraid of how much I want you. And need you. I want a lot, Kenzi. With you, I think it's going to be way beyond anything I've ever felt before."

"Is that bad?"

"I honestly don't know. But I do know I'm looking for my last relationship, and you haven't even had a first yet."

"I already told you I want you to be my first and last everything, Tor," she says softly. "I meant it."

"I know that, and I want to believe it. You have no idea how much I want to."

She sighs, the tiny vein in her temple throbbing in frustration over my doubts, but I can't lie to her. I'm not at a stage in my life where I want to go through a fling or deal with indecision several months down the road.

"Did you bring our pennies?" she questions.

I grin and let go of her hand reluctantly to dig into my front pocket, taking out the two coins I brought with me.

"Of course I did."

"Can we do something different this time?"

"Okay..."

She takes one of the pennies from me. "Let's wish for the same thing at the same time. Then hopefully it will come true." Her eyes glimmer with hope just like they did when she was a little girl and would talk about exciting things that she couldn't wait to see or do. One of the things I've always loved most about her is her never-ending hope and positive outlook that she inherited from her father.

"I like that idea. What are we going to wish for?"

"To live happily ever after. Together."

A hard lump forms in my throat at the realization that there isn't anything in this universe—wishes or otherwise—that's going to allow that dream to come true. I'm most likely going to be the first guy to break her precious heart, even though that's the last thing I ever want to do. Maybe this was my role all along... to be the one to make her feel everything for the first time, both good and bad. Maybe I'm supposed to guide her through life and do my best to lessen all the blows for her. Maybe I'm her safety net.

"We're not a fairy tale, Kenzi."

Her hand clenches around the penny defiantly. "We *can* be, Tor. You just have to believe in it enough."

"Real life doesn't work that way. I wish it did, believe me. I want that more than I've ever fuckin' wanted anything."

"Then just do it," she begs. "For me?"

Of course. I'd do anything for her. So I agree.

We toss our two tarnished pennies into the water while we stand on the edge of the river, holding on to each other's hands for dear life and wishing *(make that begging)* to live happily ever after. Together.

I didn't realize when we first sat down that this is the exact place where her own parents' fairy tale ended, or I never would've brought their daughter here.

CHAPTER 23

Kenzi—age fourteen

Tor—age twenty-nine

"Kenzi Valentine?"

I look up from the test I'm taking at the woman standing at the door of my classroom saying my name. I recognize her as working in the principal's office.

"Can you come with me?" she asks when we make eye contact.

"Um . . . okay."

The other kids in my class watch me as I shove my book in my backpack and grab my bag, some of them whispering as I make my way through the desks to the door. My teacher takes my test from me as I near her desk.

"Don't worry about the test, Kenzi. You can make it up."

"Is something wrong?" I ask the woman as soon as I get out into the hall. "Did I do something?"

"No, nothing like that. Your aunt and uncle are here."

My aunt and uncle?

As we walk down the empty hall toward the office, Uncle Toren and Aunt Sydni come into view, waiting for me in the front lobby. I can tell immediately by their somber faces that something is very wrong.

"Kenzi . . ." Aunt Sydni says, taking a few steps forward. "There's been an accident. Your grandmother asked us to come get you."

My breath hitches in my throat and my blood goes cold as my mind flips through the Rolodex of everyone I love . . . Mommy, Daddy, Gram,

Great-Gram, Pop, Chloe, Talon, Storm, Rayne, Lukas, Mikah, Katherine, Vandal.

"Wh-what do you mean?" I ask, searching both of their faces.

Uncle Tor pulls me into his arms and hugs me tight, his breathing ragged. He's got grease on his clothes and hands, and a smudge on his face, meaning he came right from work without any time to change or wash. Aunt Sydni's wearing sweatpants and no makeup like she just got out of bed. It's clear they came here to get me in a rush.

"What happened?" I ask, my face still buried in Tor's chest. "Who is it?"

"It's your mom." He pulls me away to look into my eyes, his hands moving to my shoulders, squeezing them gently. "I'm sorry, Angel. It's not good. We're going to take you to the hospital. Everyone is there."

His eyes are bloodshot and puffy, and so are Aunt Sydni's, meaning they were both crying before they got here. Now they're wearing fake, weak smiles, trying not to worry me, but I can tell something awful has happened.

As Aunt Sydni signs the form to take me out of school, I cling to Uncle Tor, my body shaking uncontrollably. I want to ask what happened but I can't get my mouth to work.

"Is she dead?" I finally force in a hoarse whisper.

"No, sweetheart. But I can't lie to you ... it's bad." His strong arms go around me again. "I promise I'll stay with you. We'll get through this together. Everything will be okay."

TOR

During the ride back home, her hand slips under the front of my shirt and rests against the skin right above the waistband of my jeans, every so often feathering up toward my chest or across my rib cage, slowly exploring me. I should tell her no groping when we're riding but I'm enjoying her touch way too much to make her stop. On the easy, straight roads I reach back and run my hand down the outside of her leg. She squeezes her thighs tighter around me as she presses her body closer to mine.

We pull over at an ice cream stand so she can use the restroom, and then sit at a picnic table to enjoy ice cream cones in the shade. We watch a couple with triplets who look to be about five years old attempt to eat theirs but end up mostly wearing them. We can't stop ourselves from laughing and the mother laughs with us. "Wait till you two have your own," she says jokingly.

Yikes. They think we're a couple. Maybe the age difference between us isn't as visibly obvious as I thought it was.

"Do you still want kids, Tor?" Kenzi asks. When I turn away from the messy little kids to answer her, her tongue is swirling around the vanilla ice cream, her lips all creamy, and my brain short-circuits watching her. I'd do anything to have her lips and her tongue on my cock just like that. Or anywhere on my body.

"Earth to Tor?" she says, giggling and nudging my leg with her boot.

"Huh?" I drag my eyes away from her mouth. "Kids?"

"Yeah."

"Someday, yeah."

"You'd make a great dad."

"Think so?"

"Definitely. Look how good you were with me all the time when I was little."

No. I can't think about that. Thinking about that makes me feel sick and twisted. I can't think about shoving my cock into her mouth one minute and then remember rocking her to sleep when she was a baby the next. I stand and throw the rest of my cone in a garbage can buzzing with flies. What the fuck am I doing with her? Why am I playing with fire and tempting us both with something we can't have? I wonder if I should see a therapist about this mess I've gotten myself into, to help me figure out if what I'm doing is completely fucked up or if it's actually acceptable if we both want it. *And* we're both consenting adults now. *And* we love each other.

But she's still my best friend's daughter. Regardless of all those other things, that fact will never, ever change.

She wants to see the dog and the kitten, so I bring her back to my place instead of straight to her house after our ride. I didn't tell her about the kitten when I first found her; I surprised her by letting her come over to clean when she got back from Maine, and the kitten was sleeping on the couch when she got there. She called me at the shop all crazy excited after she saw her and I told her about how I found the kitten in a box on the side of the road. Originally, I thought the kitten was a boy, but it's actually a girl. Needless to say, Kenzi fell immediately in love with the kitten just like she did with the dog.

"Did you name this poor kitten yet?" she asks me now, sitting on the floor with both the dog and the kitten crawling up in her lap for love. Kenzi is like a pet whisperer. They all love her.

I sit on the couch and pull off my boots, thinking we'll relax and have a bite to eat before I take her home.

"Yeah. Kitten. It goes with Diogee."

She smirks at me. "That's lazy, but it fits her." She picks the kitten up and cradles her against her chest. "She's so adorable, Tor. I want to kidnap her and take her home with me."

"Your father will have a shit fit. You can come over here and hang out with them anytime. I keep telling you that."

She pouts. "It's not the same. I miss having my own pet."

"We could get you another bunny," I offer. I considered surprising her with one but wasn't sure if it would just make her grief worse. I didn't want her to think I was trying to replace Snuggles. After talking to Mom about it, we decided it was best to wait.

Putting the kitten down, she watches her walk off to chase Diogee's tail and then pulls the clip out of her hair, unbraiding it and letting it all fall around her shoulders in soft waves.

"I've been thinking about that, and I think I do want another one. I love the Lionheads."

"What the heck is that?"

"It's a breed of bunny with a really fuzzy face and head. They're adorable; they almost look like little toys."

"Find one and I'll take you to get it," I say without hesitation.

I move into the kitchen and open the refrigerator, rummaging around to see what we could have for dinner that's quick and easy.

"You want hamburgers?" I ask, my head still in the fridge when I feel her warm hands slide up my back. I turn around and shut the door behind me, surprised at her touch. She's being way more daring today than she ever has before.

"I'm not hungry," she says, gently resting her palm on the center of my chest and peeking up at me, eyes burning with love and desire.

Her touch has pushed my last button. The last of my self-control crumbles, replaced with a mix of raging frustration and desire I can't even begin to extinguish. I push her hand off my chest and steer her back against the wall, crushing my lips to hers, my hands gripping her waist. Her gasp against my lips should have been one of fear, or maybe shock, but one glance at her darkening eyes tells me neither one of those is what she's feeling. *Not even close.*

"Is this what you want, Kenzi?" I whisper against her lips. "Is this what you've been begging for all day, touching me?"

"Yes," she replies breathlessly. "I want you."

I slowly back away from her, torn between throwing her out and dragging her down the hall to my bedroom. "You don't even know what that means."

Her green eyes lock onto mine and I can see I'm wrong. "Wanna bet?"

Holding her gaze, I yank off my worn T-shirt and toss it to the floor, watching how her eyes take in my bare chest and then drift hungrily to my abs. I want her to run. *I want her to stay.*

"Well, here I am. Show me."

I know every single one of Kenzi's expressions for every feeling she has ever felt. But I've never seen this look of sheer smoldering desire on her face before. Her eyes stay on mine as she steps toward me with zero hesitation, zero doubt. She completely owns her determination to do exactly what I asked—show me.

The space between us disappears quickly, and she backs me up against the adjacent wall, her hands coming up to hold my face as she goes up on her toes to kiss my lips.

"You," she says softly. "*You* are what I've always wanted. And yes—way before I even knew what that meant. But I know what it means now."

She lowers her head and kisses my bare chest, right above the tattoo of her words. Her lips are soft, wet, and warm. Tantalizing.

"I want all of you," she continues as her lips move across my flesh. "Your love, your body. Your past, your present, your future. Everything."

I can barely breathe as her mouth and hands trail down my chest to my stomach, and I lean back against the wall with my heart drumming loud and fast. My little Kenzi is fading away into the background. This woman in front of me has stepped into her place, saying all the words I need and want to hear, touching me in all the right ways, turning me on, making me fall harder. Blinking, I almost believe she'll disappear and this will turn out to be just a fucked-up hallucination, but she's still here, now kneeling in front of me with her hands on my thighs.

When her lips press against the front of my jeans, directly over my cock, I suck in a breath and my hand drifts to her head, gripping her hair.

"Kenzi...," I whisper raggedly, staring down at her. I don't know what she's done to me, but I'm powerless to do anything but just let her do whatever she wants. She plants small, quick kisses along the length of my cock, and almost makes me explode when she gently bites the head, her teeth grazing over the material of my jeans.

Yanking her up by her hair, I cover her mouth with mine, my chest heaving against hers as my hands slide down her back to cup her ass cheeks, grinding my cock against her.

"You're playing with fire," I rasp out.

"I don't care."

"Make me stop, Kenz. Please...," I beg, knowing I'll never let her go if she doesn't stop this. She's got me too far gone to turn back and her new level of sensual confidence is throwing up way too many green lights.

"No," she says simply, wrapping her arms around me, kissing me just as hungrily as I'm kissing her.

"Push me away."

"Never," she whispers, pulling me even closer.

"What's gotten into you today?" I demand, moving my lips down to suck her neck.

"I don't know...," she breathes, tilting her head back, letting me suck the delicate flesh of her throat. "Being so close to you all day...touching you...it feels so right. I don't want to stop."

"Then we're not stopping till we've had every fuckin' inch of each other." I move my lips back up to hers and stare down into her eyes. "Once we start this, we can't go back, Kenzi."

She gulps, a hint of nervousness finally showing, and then she nods.

"I know, Tor. This is what I want." Taking a small step backward, she pulls off her shirt and drops it onto the floor, mimicking my dare.

"I want you to touch me," she says, and suddenly it's Christmas in August as I'm staring down at cleavage for days surrounded by thin, teasing black lace that I want to chew through to get to her. The power keeps shifting between us and now it's my turn to be knocked back into shyness. I feel like I'm fifteen again, awestruck by how beautiful and perfect she is, afraid to touch her or speak for fear of scaring her away.

I don't let that shy kid in me resurface for long, though. He's got no right to be here anymore and I'm not letting him ruin this moment for me.

"Oh, I'm going to touch you," I reply, palming her full breasts and rubbing my thumbs over her nipples peeking through the lace. Her lips part in an excited, sultry sigh.

Bending down, I kiss her and walk her down the hallway to my bedroom, not breaking the kiss or taking my hands off her for a second. After kicking the door closed behind me, I push her onto the bed and crawl on top of her, hovering over her, reading her face. I need to know she's ready for this or I'll never be able to live with myself.

Reaching up, she pulls the hair tie out of the back of my hair and smiles when my hair falls down into her face.

"You like that?" I ask softly, stroking her cheek with the back of my hand.

"I've dreamed about you on top of me like this, with your hair in my face."

I suck in a quick breath. "You never told me you dream about me."

Her hands skim up my chest, over my shoulders, and clasp behind my neck as she stares up at me. "I was afraid it would make you pull further away from me."

"I don't think I can pull away anymore. It's a battle I can't win."

She pulls me down to her lips. "I don't want you to." Her voice is as sweet and soft as her kiss. "Ever." She kisses me again, pressing her body up against mine. "Please." Her lips touch mine again, soft and tinged with a dash of strawberry. *Irresistible.* "This feels right."

It *does* feel right. So right that any thoughts of this ever being wrong are being sucked out of me like a vacuum by her lips on mine and her hands slowly roaming over my back, the lace of her bra chafing against my chest, stoking my desire for her until I can't hold back anymore. Crushing my lips down on hers, I kiss her long and deep, using my leg to move hers apart to sink between her thighs, and we both moan and exhale, as if we've been holding our breath forever waiting for that first moment of full-body contact.

I move my lips to the pulse at her neck, kissing and biting her as I move my way down to her chest, kissing the soft swell of her breasts and sliding my tongue deep into her cleavage. I unclip the front clasp of her bra and push the dark fabric away, revealing the most perfect set of tits I've ever seen in my life. Round, firm, creamy pale mounds with tantalizing pink tips begging to be touched. I cup her left breast in my hand before lowering my head to lick a slow circle around her waiting nipple before sucking it into my mouth. Her sudden gasp and the hardening of her tip against my tongue makes my blood pump harder as I drag my tongue across her chest to her other breast, ravishing it with my mouth while I continue to tease the other with my hand, playing the damp pebbled bud with my calloused thumb as I wildly flick my tongue over her. She arches up to me, clutching handfuls of my hair, mewing like a kitten, losing control.

Standing, I reach down and grab her foot, quickly yanking one sexy little boot off, then the other before going for the button and zipper of her jeans, my eyes on hers the entire time. Her breathing is heavy as she watches me with wide, lustful eyes. Her fingers grip the comforter as I undress her. When she's naked on my bed, my heart races as I give myself a moment to take in her flawless skin and hourglass curves, wanting her more with each inch my gaze devours.

I kick off my own boots and unzip my jeans, entranced by her eyes and the way her breasts move up and down with each breath she takes. When her pink tongue darts out to lick her lips as I step out of my jeans and boxers, I'm completely unhinged for her mentally and physically.

Her body is engulfed by mine as I climb back on top of her. She trembles beneath me, either from fear or excitement or probably a mashup of both. My mouth is on hers, our tongues dancing and teasing as I move my body over her. The feeling of flesh on flesh has my cock like a rock between us, pressing against her, seeking her heat. Reaching down between us, I slide my hand between her thighs to gently stroke her pink lips. She's so wet already that it obliterates any ideas of patience and gentleness I may have had. I want in, and I want it now.

Her nails dig into my spine, and she gyrates against my hand as I finger her, our mouths meeting breathlessly. We're caught up in a frenzy of kissing and groping, fighting to get closer and crawl inside each other, and that's exactly what I'm going to do.

"Are you still on the pill?" I ask against her lips, my fingers expertly strumming over her clit.

She nods and moves her hands down to my ass, trying to pull me between her legs. "Yes...," she says breathlessly. "For you."

"Good," I growl, moving between her thighs. She doesn't waver at all when I grab my cock and rub the head up and down between her wet lips and over her clit, coaxing her into that crazy place of wanting nothing but sweet release. *Of wanting nothing but me.* She writhes and wiggles beneath me, her eyes fluttering closed as she starts to shake and arch up, moaning my name as she climaxes. I give her a few moments before sliding inside her with one deep, smooth thrust. She's incredibly wet and tight, moving her body perfectly with mine, curving her leg around my waist and pulling me deeper into her, letting out a small cry when I'm met with a brief moment of resistance followed by a flood of wet warmth that vaults me into a new realm of carnal desire.

She's mine.

I kiss her through the pain and whisper love to her as I drive into her harder and faster. She clings to me, arching up to meet my thrusts, echoing my whispers. I try to force myself to slow down but I can't take it anymore and finally let myself go, gripping her outer thigh to pull her tight against me as I explode inside her.

"I love you...," I murmur with my lips against her ear. "Forever and longer."

Time stands still as we rock against each other, our bodies slippery with sweat, her lips pressed against my chest, kissing that spot over my heart that's forever marked with her words.

And now, her kiss. Her touch. Her love.

After today, I can never deny the truth again. *She completely owns me.*

CHAPTER 24

Kenzi—age eighteen months

Tor—age sixteen

I stroll into Asher's parents' kitchen and set my guitar off to the side before I join Ash, Ember, and the baby at the table where they're eating lunch.

"Tor!" Kenzi shrieks from her high chair, pointing at me with an excited smile.

"Holy shit, did she just say your name?" Asher asks.

Ember shakes her head and wipes the baby's face. "No," she says. "Your name is not going to be my daughter's first word. She said door."

"Pretty sure she said Tor," I say, grabbing Kenzi's little chubby hand that's reaching out for me.

"Tor!" she yells again, kicking her legs and giggling.

Asher leans back in his chair and shakes his head. "She's definitely saying Tor, hon."

Ember lifts the baby out of her chair and sits her on her lap. "Great," she says, glaring at me, but with a playful smile on her face. "That's because you spoil her, Toren. And your name is easy for her to say."

Kenzi's green eyes lock onto mine and I wink at her. Anyone who can make me smile like she does deserves to be spoiled. I can't lie, knowing her very first word is my name is the coolest thing that's ever happened to me.

💛 💜 🤍

KENZI

His kisses are so soft and tender as our breathing slows back to normal that it almost makes me fall apart from emotional overload. He leans up on his arms to stare down at me, gently pushing my hair away from my face. His eyes are darker than I've ever seen them, scanning mine like I'm ancient hieroglyphics he's trying to decipher.

"Are you okay?" he asks after a few long moments.

"Yes." I'm really not sure if I'm okay or not. I feel lightheaded and my body is humming and quivering beneath his. He's still inside me, my insides contracting involuntarily around him. Everything happened so fast. I spent the entire night last night mentally coaching myself to get my shit together and act like a woman with him today. To be sexually assertive and confident. But all the erotica books I've read and the short soft porn movies I was able to view on the internet hadn't prepared me for how it would all actually feel to have him on top of me, so huge and muscular, or how long and hard he would feel thrusting inside me, spreading and tearing me open to take him. I didn't know an orgasm could feel so amazing, or that feeling him shudder and come would make me feel like the entire world just stopped and only we existed, as one continuously joined, unbreakable heart.

But nothing could have prepared me for the torrid expression and emotion I'm seeing in his eyes right now.

"I love you."

There's a faint vulnerability in his voice, unlike any other time he's said those words to me. This is no longer friend or you're-almost-family-to-me love. No. This is heart-pounding, you-have-the-power-to-gut-me, I-can't-get-enough-of-you romantic love. I feel it, too.

Reaching up, I push a lock of his hair behind his ear and touch his cheek.

"I love you, too. So, so much."

He slowly eases out of me, causing a tiny bit of pain, and moves to sit on the end of the bed with his back to me, running his hands through his long hair. I feel wet and sticky and unsure of what comes next, so I sit up and crawl closer to him, lightly touching his back.

"Tor?"

He nods and turns slightly toward me. "I just need a minute, Angel." His voice is low. The anguish radiating off of him is palpable.

"Okay . . . ," I reply. I want to hug him and tell him everything is perfect. That I've never been happier. That this was meant to be. That I'm so in love with him that I can't even put it into words. But I know that won't fix whatever he's feeling right now, and guilt eats at me. I led him down this path today. I hadn't expected it to end up here in his bed, though. I thought we'd kiss and make out on the couch, maybe take our shirts off and touch each other. I didn't know I'd unleash a sexual animal in him that wouldn't stop until it had its fill. I don't regret that we made love, but I do regret that what we just did could be tearing him up inside. I want him to be happy, not tormented.

"Can I take a shower?" I ask, respecting his need for a little space. "I feel kind of sweaty and sticky."

"Of course. You can use my shower. I'll wait here for you." He reaches for my hand and gives it a squeeze, then picks my clothes up off the floor where he threw them, his hands shaking as he holds them out to me. "I think your shirt is in the kitchen." He stands and walks over to his dresser and comes back with one of his T-shirts for me to wear. I try not to stare at his body as he stands there completely naked, but it's hard not to look when he's all muscles and ink and so damn beautiful.

"Thank you," I say softly. "I won't be long."

"Take as long as you need. I'm not going anywhere." He pulls me to him and kisses my lips before I disappear into his private bathroom, which I've actually never used before today. I've always used the bathroom and shower in the main hallway of the house. It feels intimate being alone in his bathroom, using his soap and shampoo, but I like it because it all smells like him. The warm shower feels soothing, and I briefly wonder if I'm supposed to somehow clean my insides since he came inside me or if it just comes out on its own or stays there or what. I feel completely clueless and stupid. Why doesn't anyone ever talk about things like this? Did I space out in sex ed and miss the parts that covered all this? I know I can ask Tor anything but that seems like plastering a big I HAVE ZERO EXPERIENCE across my forehead. And even though he knows I'm a virgin (or was until a few minutes ago), I don't feel like I should make it even more obvious. I'm going to have to talk to Chloe or Rayne about this sex stuff. I can just tell them I'm curious or dating someone they don't know, and hope they don't grill me for too many details.

Oh God. I'm going to have to keep a huge part of my life a secret from my friends and family. For how long?

I rinse the conditioner out of my hair and turn the water off. I can't think about all of that right now and let my mind start racing out of control with questions and worries. My mom always told me to take things day by day and step-by-step and not worry about things until it was the right time to worry about it.

But when is the right time? How will I know?

That familiar stab slices through my chest at memories of my mom. I wish she were here so badly. I know I could tell her the truth about Tor and she would understand without judging us or making us feel like we were partaking in some evil act. She'd answer all my questions, calm my fears, and give me hope that it would all be okay. She'd talk to my dad and get him to accept us as a couple. She'd work her magic and make it better for all of us.

After I towel off and dress, I open the bathroom door to see Tor still sitting on the bed, only now he's wearing jeans rather than sitting there completely naked. He's made the bed and put our shoes neatly next to the door. He still appears to be deep in thought and I'm worried he's going to tell me we have to forget this ever happened between us, like he did the first time we kissed.

"Come here, beautiful," he says, patting the spot next to him, and when I do, he turns to me, holds my face in his hands, and gives me a long, deep kiss that shakes me right down to my toes.

"I wasn't planning on this today, Kenz," he says when he pulls away. "I'm sorry."

"Sorry? Why?"

"It's just not how I wanted it to happen. I would have been slower, more gentle. Made it more special for you with candles and rose petals or something."

"Tor...every moment was perfect. I wouldn't change anything."

"I would. Your first time should have been special, and probably not with me."

Tears immediately spring to my eyes, something that seems to be becoming a habit for me. "Don't say that. I only want it to ever be you," I say, sniffling. "I don't care about slow and gentle. I care about you just being you and not holding back or hiding your feelings. You made me feel loved and wanted."

"You are. More than you know."

"Was it disappointing for you?" I hate when my mouth takes

on a life of its own and asks questions that I really don't want to hear the answer to.

"What? Are you crazy? I nearly lost my mind. You put me in a friggin' frenzy. It's taking every bit of self-control I have to not throw you back down on the bed right now and never take you back home. I knew I wouldn't be able to get enough of you."

Despite being newly raw and torn, my insides respond to his words by quivering, and my pulse picks up speed. I want him to touch me again. I want to feel him everywhere and get lost in that indescribable euphoria of him again. I lay my hand on his leg, my fingers reaching for his muscular thigh. "You can do that."

He breaks out into a wide grin that makes my heart swoon. "Don't tempt me, please. You're going to be sore."

"I don't care if it hurts."

"I do."

"So...we're going to do it again? Someday?" I ask shyly.

He lets out a long sigh. "Kenzi...we need to think for a few days, okay? If we do this—try to be together—it's not going to be easy. It'll be messy as fuck."

"I know. But if we both want it, we'll find a way to make it work, right? Isn't that what people do?"

"Yes...but there's just a lot involved we have to think about. No matter what, Kenzi...I don't want you to get hurt or start your life in the middle of a secret affair. You know I want better than that for you."

"*You're* what's best for me.

He chuckles sarcastically. "You're the only one that will think that."

"Isn't that all that matters?" I shoot back at him.

He covers my hand on his leg with his. "I wish. But your father is my best friend, Kenzi. I love him just as much as I love you. I've known your entire family since I was seven years old. They matter to me. *You* matter to them. What my own family will think matters to me. How people might treat you matters to me." Any trace of a smile fades from his face, replaced with overwhelming worry. "My head is fucking spinning."

"So what do we do?" It all sounds so grim when he lists it out like that.

He touches my chin and tilts my face up to his, kissing my lips softly. "First, I tell you I'm fucking crazy in love with everything about you." He kisses the tip of my nose. "Second, we both need to put some serious thought into this before we take any more steps. I hate to do this to you, but I need you to not tell anyone about this until we have our heads straight about what we're going to do. If and when Asher finds out about us, it has to come from us and no one else."

"I won't tell anyone, Tor. I promise. I don't ever want to hurt you or my father. That would kill me."

"That's what I'm afraid of, Kenz. Of you getting hurt in the cross fire of this and being torn between me and your father."

I cling to him and he puts his arms around me as the weight of that sinks into me. Choosing between Tor and my father would devastate me. I love them both with every bit of my heart and soul and hurting either of them is unthinkable.

"Please, Tor. We can't let that happen."

"Shh..." He cradles the back of my head and tightens his embrace around me. "I know, baby. Just let me think and I'll find a way to make it work." His lips brush across my cheek. "For months I've wanted to have you in my arms like this...Let's just focus on us for tonight."

"I would love that," I whisper.

He props all his pillows up against the headboard and leans

back against them, pulling me on top of him so I'm lying between his legs, with my back against his chest, my head resting on his shoulder. He wraps his big arms around me and holds me against him, clasping my hands in his.

"This is heaven," he says with his lips against my ear.

"It is. I want to stay just like this with you and never leave."

His breathing changes, going from steady to deeper. "You have no fuckin' idea what it does to me when you say things like that."

"Tell me." I tighten my hold on his hands, running my thumb along the black artwork on the back of his hand.

"It makes me think I can have everything with you. It makes me think you'll never break my heart."

My own breath catches as a wave of emotion surges through me. This man, with his arms wrapped so tightly around me and his heart pounding against my spine, isn't the man I grew up knowing. This is someone who's been hiding in the shadows; deep, dark, and hopelessly romantic. There's a mix of fear and hope in his words, all tangled up together in a cocktail of turmoil.

I twist my head toward him. "I'll never hurt you, Tor. Ever. Haven't I been promising my undying love to you since I was five? It hasn't changed."

"Just don't make promises you aren't sure of. Please."

"I hope you don't, either."

He cups the side of my neck and turns my face toward his, his lips landing on mine.

"I don't want any broken promises between us," he says in a low voice, pulling me up onto him and turning me so I'm sitting on top of him, straddling his body. I respond by kissing him with as much passion as I know how to do with my limited experience, hoping actions are louder than words. Our kisses start soft and slow but soon turn deeper, his tongue delving into my mouth. I grip his broad shoulders, remembering how badly I want to touch him when we danced in his living room the night of my prom. He moves his hands slowly under my shirt to cup my breasts through my bra. It's not long before he's pulling my shirt off and I unclasp my bra and throw it off to the side of the bed, shocked at how easy and natural everything flows with him. Maybe because I've fantasized about being with him for so long, now that it's happening it feels familiar to me. Or maybe it's just chemistry between us.

"Fuck, you're so beautiful," he groans, kneading my breasts and burying his face between them, moving his lips from one to the other, sucking my nipples until I'm grinding against his erection, lost in his touch. I had no idea anything could make me feel so electrified. His hands move to undo my jeans while his mouth never stops ravishing my breasts, and I kneel up to wiggle out of my panties and jeans as he pushes his own pants down and kicks them off.

"I don't want to hurt you so we're going to do something different," he says, his voice gravelly with lust. "But it'll still feel good, I promise."

"Everything you do feels good," I whisper.

He flashes me a wicked sexy grin that makes my stomach go into spasms.

"It's only going to get better, love." He presses two fingers against my lips, gently pushing them into my mouth. "Suck on my fingers, baby."

I'm surprised by his words but I do as he asks, sucking his fingers into my mouth and swirling my tongue around them, and his eyes go wide as he watches me. His cock twitches between us and I ache to feel him buried inside me again, spreading and stretching my body just for him. The pain and pleasure of it earlier made me feel erotically delirious, causing me to spread my legs wider and dig my nails into him, wanting him harder and deeper.

When he pulls his fingers out of my mouth, he reaches between us and rubs his wet fingers between my legs, smearing my saliva all over my lips. No one's ever touched me there before, and my body instantly reacts, quivering and flushing with warmth. Spreading my folds with his fingers, he gently pushes me down until I'm flush against him with his cock wedged between my lips.

"Keep your legs spread and slide yourself back and forth over me," he coaxes, grabbing my hips and moving me so my sex glides from the base of him all the way up to the head, and then back again. And he's right, even though he's not inside me, rubbing along his hard length feels incredible.

Leaning back against the pillows, his gaze drifts up my body, not stopping until he reaches my eyes.

"That feels so good...," he groans softly, cupping my breasts in his hands again. "Don't stop, just let yourself go and get off on me. I want to watch you come."

"Tor..."

Nervousness creeps up on me. Surely he's not used to having to do things like this just to be with a woman. I'm afraid my age and inexperience are more glaring by the minute. He tears his eyes from where our bodies are joined and glances up at me again, his expression going from hungry with desire to sheer concern.

Grabbing the back of my neck, he gently pulls my head down and kisses my lips. "You're perfect, Kenzi. Every single inch of you, inside and out. You're turning me on like fuckin' crazy." He kisses me again, always knowing exactly what I need to hear and feel, and I continue to ride along his shaft, arching my back to press my clit against him.

"There ya go," he whispers, his fingers grazing over my nipple, sending more sparks throughout my body and down into my core. "Feel how hard I am for you? For months I've been hiding that from you but now I want you to feel every inch of what you do to me."

God. All his walls are down and his voice is like black velvet; soft, smooth, dark, and seductive. It lulls me and fades my insecurities as I rub myself against him. His mouth and hands are everywhere with mind-blurring skill. Gripping my hips, caressing my breasts, his lips on my mouth one moment, and then licking the curve of my breast the next—he's got every part of me craving him and I can't get enough. Finally I can look at him without hiding the fact that I'm doing it, and now my eyes are glued to his muscular chest and defined abs as I move against the hardest part of him, mesmerized. His dark tousled hair falls to his shoulders and I can't resist clutching it in my fingers. He's truly every woman's dream. I can barely grasp the fact this incredibly sexy grown man with rippling hard muscles, and covered in tattoos that I've watched women literally drool over, and who also has a heart made of pure solid gold...wants *me*. Loves *me*. He could have anyone, and he waited for *me*.

He growls against my lips when I let the tip of his cock press against my wet entrance and I get my first taste of real sensual power. He wants me. Maybe even needs me.

Angling my hips just the right way, I lower myself onto him and he inhales sharply, gripping my waist, his cock plunging deep. A small cry sounds in my throat, but again, the sensation of pain and desire is intoxicating for me, intensifying when he whispers my name and shudders, losing himself in me completely just as I am with him.

I really *can* give him everything.

That's all I've ever wanted and wished for.

CHAPTER 25

My love,
We promised each other forever.
If you think I've let you go, you're wrong.
You're mine. I'm yours.
Forever.

♥ ♥ ♥

TOR

Nothing can fuck your shit up faster than the girl you've got your cock buried in getting a text message from her father telling her she should come home because it's after midnight.

I wanted to keep her with me in my bed all night and ask her to not go home. I wanted her to tell her father that she was spending the night at Chloe's house and she'd be home tomorrow.

Then I remembered that once I was the guy who enforced her curfew. Told her to never lie to her father about anything. I almost laughed at the insane irony of it, only it wasn't funny. It was terrifyingly confusing.

Fuck me.

Day one of having Kenzi was nothing short of a dream and I'm not going to let these bumps in the road ruin our happiness. We knew it would be hard. We knew it would be difficult. We knew there would be lies.

Is she worth it? Yes.

So I drove her home in my truck and when she went inside, she told Asher that she had been at my place playing with the dog and then we watched a movie and lost track of the time. When she sent me a text an hour later, when I was back home alone in my bed that still smelled of her perfume and I was missing her like crazy, she told me her father told her she could have stayed here. Because she was with me.

Safe.

Was she safe? Of course. But Asher wouldn't think so if he knew I had just spent hours dragging my tongue over every curve of her delicious body, pummeling away her virginity with nine inches of his best friend and fingering her into orgasmic bliss while telling her I'm going to love her for eternity.

Now it's the next day and I'm standing outside my sister's apartment door, wondering if I'm at the wrong address. This is an upscale mill apartment in Manchester, probably getting at least twelve hundred per month in rent. How is my little sister affording something like this? I have no idea how much a hair and makeup artist can make, but apparently it's a lot.

Shrugging, I ring the bell, hoping she's awake, and home. After a few seconds her door opens, and she's standing there, with her hair up in a messy ponytail, wearing a short, black silk robe.

"Toren!" she says with obvious surprise. "I didn't know you were coming over. Come in."

I saunter into her apartment and gaze around at the stark white walls, chic modern decor and furnishings like glass tabletops and funky vases. Everything is white, black, and red. I feel like I just walked into an abstract painting.

"You live here?" I ask, not hiding my disbelief. I was expecting a cute little studio with cheap throw rugs, colorful throw pillows, hand-me-down furniture, and clothes thrown around like when she lived at Mom's house.

"Um, yes, why?"

"Alone? Or do you have a roommate?"

"Alone. You know I hate people."

"Hmm. It's just so...neat. And expensive. Is this couch real leather?" I run my hand across the soft black cushion. Yes. It's leather.

She curls her lip at me and turns to walk into the small kitchen with granite countertops and stainless-steel appliances. "You want some coffee? I literally just crawled out of bed."

I follow her and sit at her kitchen table, grabbing a thick white envelope lying in the middle of the table next to a vase of red silk flowers. It's stuffed with cash. A *lot* of cash.

"You rob a bank?" I query, thumbing through all the bills.

"No," she replies from the noisy latte maker, not turning around.

I frown at the envelope. "Dealing drugs? Stripping, maybe?"

She turns and snatches the envelope from me and shoves it in a drawer before she goes back to making our coffees. "No, Tor. It's just tips from work."

"Nice. Maybe I need to switch jobs."

"Ha ha," she jokes, handing me a cup and sitting gracefully in the chair across from me. "So what brings you here?"

"I wanted to check in on my little sister, but it looks like you're doing just fine." My gut tells me something is very off here. I doubt I could afford to live in this place, so how is she swinging this?

She nods over the rim of her mug. "I am."

"I kinda need someone to talk to," I say, shifting my attention to why I'm here and forgetting about her rent and furniture, which is really none of my business. "A woman's point of view would be appreciated, I guess."

She smiles and leans forward on the table, pushing her long dark hair behind her diamond-studded ear. "Ooh, now this sounds good. Ask away."

"How would you feel about being with a guy older than you?"

"How much older? Like eighty?"

I shake my head at her in frustration. Eighty! "No, like early thirties."

"Do you mean to just fuck, or to actually date?"

"Jesus, Tess. To date." The thought that my little sister would even consider just fucking and not dating makes my stomach turn.

"Is he hot?" she asks next.

I shrug and sip my coffee. "Yeah."

"Rich?"

Shit. "Does that matter?"

"Well, yeah. To some. Nobody wants to date some loser with no ambition and no money."

Kenzi wouldn't care. She has her own money anyway.

I lean back in the chair and meet her blue eyes. "Let's say he's not rich but he's comfortable."

She rests her chin on her palm and muddles this all around in her mind. "Yeah, I would. Older guys are better."

"Why is that?"

"They're more mature, usually. More experienced. Probably out of the playing-video-games-all-day phase, which is really annoying. Older men give younger women a sense of security, I think. Like they can take care of us in every way. Physically, emotionally, financially. I think all women secretly want to be treated like spoiled, adored little girls."

I nod and stare down into my mug, wondering if Kenzi thinks of me that way. It wouldn't be bad, because I want to take care of her, but I also want her to have fun with me and be able to enjoy her youth. I don't want to force her to grow up.

"Why all the questions, Toren?"

"I'm curious. I met someone younger..."

Her ice-blue eyes home in on me like two bright beacons cutting through fog.

"Holy shit," she breathes out slowly. "It finally happened."

"What?"

"You and Kenzi Valentine. I knew it!" She smacks her palm down on the table triumphantly. "I always knew something was there between you two."

"Tessie, don't be crazy," I scoff at her, but fear snakes through me. I didn't think she would figure me out so quickly. I thought I could just nonchalantly pick her brain to see if I could get some insight on how a younger girl would feel about dating an older guy. Now she's got me cornered.

She tilts her head at me. "Seriously, Tor? Come on. Stop the bullshit. Obviously you need to talk, so let's just drop the charade, okay?"

It's hard to admit, but she hit the nail right on the head. I *do* need someone to talk to before I lose my mind from keeping this all bottled up inside me. I know I can talk to Lukas, but the fact that he's related to Kenzi and Asher still makes me nervous. I need to talk to someone who's not personally invested in Kenzi.

"You have to promise that this stays between us, Tess."

"Of course it will. You look like you're about to have a mental breakdown. Your eyebrow is twitching. I knew something was up when you took off a few weeks ago. Were you with her? Is that why you went away for the weekend?"

"No, I was alone. But things were starting to happen and I needed to get away to think. Usually I talk to Asher about everything, ya know? But I can't tell him I'm freakin' in love with his kid."

Her mouth falls open. "Wow. I never thought I'd actually hear you admit it."

"What's the point in lying to you? I love her. I want to marry her."

"Whoa." She puts her hand up. "Let's back it up, cowboy. She's eighteen."

"I know. I don't mean tomorrow, Tess. But someday, when she's ready to make that commitment. That's what I want."

Her eyes are wide and glassy as she reaches across the table and grabs my hand. "My God, Tor. I knew you had a thing for each other, but marriage? That's a huge step for her to even think about at her age. Asher will flip his fucking lid."

"Why do you think I'm so fucked up?"

"And what about her? How does she feel?"

"She loves me, too. She wants the same things I want."

"Yeah, today, maybe. But she's eight-fucking-teen. Look how much I've changed in the past two years, Tor. Am I the same person I was when I was eighteen?" She raises her eyebrows at me.

"In some ways yes and others no."

"Exactly."

"So you don't think it can last? You think she'll just change? Want someone else?" I try to picture Kenzi with another man and I can't. I can't even force that scenario in my head. My mind goes blank. I can only see Kenzi with me, and I can only see myself with her.

"I don't know. But I think it's a very big possibility."

I pull my hand away from hers. "This isn't helping me," I grumble.

"I'm trying to be honest, and you have to hear it. But on the other hand, Tor...you guys have obviously had some kind of deep connection for years that hasn't gone away, right? So maybe it can last. I know this is hard, but only time will tell."

"I guess you're right." I nod. "But let's just say she and I date. Do you think we look weird together? Does she look too young? Do I look old? I don't want people staring at us."

"I know you have mirrors in your house, Tor. You're not fat and bald for God's sake. You look great. Your body is like a damn Greek god. And you've still got that rock star look going on with the hair and tattoos. So no, you don't look old." She pauses to sip her coffee. "Don't even get me started on Kenzi. That girl is gorgeous. And she doesn't even have to try. It's so unfair. She doesn't look or act eighteen, so I think once again, you're okay if you're worried about visual appearances."

"That makes me feel better."

"What about conversation? Do you have things to talk about? Things in common? She hasn't turned into a babbling idiot, right?"

I laugh. "Definitely not. That's not a problem for us at all. We've always had great conversations."

"How about sex? Have you slept with her?"

Memories of Kenzi on top of me last night and holding her in my arms for hours afterward float through my mind. "Yesterday was the first time we ever slept together. It was amazing."

She sighs. "I'm glad to hear you waited till she was eighteen."

"I'm not an asshole, Tesla. I do have some morals left."

"Were you her first?"

"Yes."

She gapes at me again. "Wow. Talk about setting the bar. My first guy was a scrawny sixteen-year-old who barely knew where to stick it. She's going to compare every guy in her life to you. That's going to be a tough act to follow."

"Don't even say that."

"If you guys *do* somehow make this work, it's wicked romantic. For you to be her first and only for her entire life? That's just crazy awesome. And the fact that you'd wait for her to grow up to marry her? It's like an epic fairy tale." She stares off across the room with a giddy smile on her face. "It's like every little girl's dream. To find the prince."

"I'm not sure I'm much of a prince."

Smiling, she says, "In her eyes, you are."

"So if we were together, you'd be okay with it?"

"Why wouldn't I be? I want you to be happy, and I like Kenzi. I hate that bitch Sydni and Lisa is just stuck up."

"She's not stuck up. You just have to get to know her."

"I'll pass. Are you still dating her, too?"

"Hell no. I'm not seeing anyone else at all. I haven't even slept with anyone for over six months. The minute I started having feelings for Kenzi, I just couldn't do it."

"Impressive."

"No, it's love. I only want her. That's it."

"Mom will be ecstatic. She totally thinks you're gay."

I sputter into my coffee. "What? Are you fucking kidding?"

Laughing, she nods. "Yup. She's been really worried about you lately and thought you were hiding in the closet. I think she'll be glad to find out you're in love, even if it is Kenzi. Mom loves her; she's all into the animal stuff. She fits right in."

I wonder if that rumor has been floating around town and for how long.

"I can't believe this shit," I say. "But yeah, she does fit into my life. That's important to me. I'm never going to give up Devils' Wolves."

"So let's talk about your biggest hurdle, because it's not

anything between you and Kenzi. You two seem to be fine. It's Asher, right?"

"Yup."

"Does he have any idea? Have either of you dropped any hints?"

"No."

"Maybe you should start. Ease him into it slowly. He probably already has some kind of inkling, Tor. Even *I* knew and I really don't pay much attention to anyone around me."

That's true. Tessie has always been stuck in her own head and a bit on the unsocial side.

"I've run a million different imaginary conversations with him in my head. And I can't see any of them coming out okay. I can't see him accepting her with me. He'll think I betrayed him and took advantage of her. He'll think I'm a child molester. He'll fucking hate me."

She tilts her head. "I'm not sure about that. He *knows* you, Tor. He knows you're not the kind of guy to do something like that. You've taken care of her for her entire life. He knows how much you love her."

"See *that's* what I'm worried about. What you just said. You don't think it's sick that I can feel this way for her when I took care of her when she was a baby? What does that say about me?"

"I don't think it's that black and white. It's a unique situation. You're not related to her. Even though you babysat her, and she called you Uncle, you were still *just a friend*, Tor. That's what you have to focus on. You're a friend who helped your friends take care of their kid because they were only fifteen years old when they had her. You were just a kid yourself. You pretty much grew up with her. None of this is a normal situation, so how could there have been a normal result?"

I lean my elbows on the table and put my pounding head in my hands. "I don't know. I just want us to be able to be together and be happy, but I feel like people will crucify me."

"Stop beating yourself up, Toren. You haven't done anything wrong. You fell in love. Look at the world we live in. Falling in love with your best friend's daughter who's fifteen years younger than you is nothing in the grand scheme of things, trust me. She's a legal adult now and she can make her own decisions. 'Nuff said."

"We're afraid of throwing Asher over the edge. He's all fucked up over Ember still. I don't think he can take another blow."

"I understand that, and it's great that you both care about him, but you and Kenzi deserve to have your happiness. The world didn't stop just because of what happened to his wife. I know it sucks and it's devastating and heartbreaking and I hate to be harsh, but that's the facts, Tor. You can't tiptoe around him forever."

She stands, comes around the table, and puts her arms around me. "You're a good guy. You took care of all of us when Daddy died, and you took care of Kenzi and Asher when they needed you. You deserve to be happy. And if Asher can't see that you're the best guy in the world for his daughter? Then he's insane. No one will love her like you do."

"Thanks, kiddo." I squeeze her arm. "I just have to get my head straight."

"You will." She lets me go and crosses her arms to study me. "You're just going to have to be patient with her, Tor. As mature as she might be, she's still young, just like me. We want to have fun, be a little stupid sometimes, sow some oats."

"I know."

"So if she acts crazy sometimes, you're going to have to let her. Have fun with her, don't be too serious. You're the boyfriend now, not the uncle. You can't control her and assert authority over her or she'll resent you."

I hadn't really thought about all that yet. I wonder if when Kenzi turns twenty-one she'll want to go to clubs and stay out all night partying. I already went through that. I can't picture her doing that based on how she is now, but Tesla's right—who knows what the future will bring?

"Great," I mutter.

"Tor...," she warns. "Just take it one day at a time."

I nod at her, still feeling overwhelmed. "I'll try."

"And smile," she adds.

"I'm smiling on the inside," I tease, grinning.

"Not good enough."

"I'll work on it." My cell phone vibrates in my pocket and I pull it out to see a text from Kenzi on my screen.

Kenzi

> I got maybe two seconds of sleep last night. I can't stop thinking about you.

"See? Now that's a smile," Tesla says, eyeing me. "Lemme guess. A text from Kenzi?"

"Yeah."

> I know the feeling. ;-) Get some sleep, Angel. I'm going to see you soon. At Tesla's now then going to the shop. I'll call you when I get there. I love you. Xo

Kenzi

> Tell her I said hi. I love you, too. Sooooo much.

"Okay, Tor. I said smile, not look like the joker," my sister teases.

I put my phone away and grin at her. "This is what she does to me. She says hi, by the way."

"Tell her I said hi back when you talk to her."

"I will. I should get going. I'm supposed to be at work." I stand and push my chair under the table. "Thanks for the talk, Tess."

"I'm glad you came to me. I love you a lot, in case you forgot."

"I love you, too."

"You and Kenzi can come here together anytime. I won't tell anyone. If you just want to hang out with another person someplace safe...you're both welcome here. Or if she needs someone to talk to, she can come to me. I haven't talked to her in a while, but I still think of her as a friend."

"Thanks. That might be good for her. Her friend Chloe is kind of unpredictable, so neither of us really trusts her to not accidentally slip up if she knew." She walks with me to her door. "And don't leave that much cash lying around in the open anymore," I advise, still worried about that pile of money she's got. I've seen people get stabbed for less money than that.

"Don't worry, I'm taking it to the bank later."

"Good. I'll talk to you soon."

CHAPTER 26

Kenzi—age two

Tor—age seventeen

Kenzi loves the park. Sometimes on the weekends when Ash and Ember want to get some alone time, I grab one of the dogs from my mom's shelter and I take them both to the park to get some air and exercise.

The autumn air is crisp as we walk through the park. Kenzi and the dog are both enjoying kicking up the leaves and hearing them crunch under their feet. A pretty girl around my age with short blond hair is walking toward us with a small dog along the path that winds around the lake. As we approach each other, her dog starts to get all excited and runs to us, dragging the girl with her on a long leash.

Laughing, I kneel down to pet the tan wiggling dog.

"I'm sorry," she says breathlessly. "She gets excited to see people and other dogs."

"That's okay, at least she's friendly."

"Your dog is much calmer. I think mine might need to go back to puppy class."

"He's not mine. He's a rescue from the shelter, and he's about ten years old. I volunteer there, so I take one out every weekend to get some exercise."

She smiles at me. "That's really sweet of you to do. I just moved nearby, so I'll be here a lot on the weekends, too. Maybe I'll see you again sometime."

Kenzi giggles as the little dog moves to her next and starts licking her face.

"She's adorable," the blond girl says. "Is she yours?"

Standing, I take Kenzi's hand. "Yeah, she is."

💜 💜 💜

KENZI

I've lost five pounds since Friday. Today is Monday. I don't weigh myself often, but Friday morning the digital scale in my bathroom was beeping, so I weighed myself just to make sure it was working after I put new batteries in it. This morning I stepped on it again because I haven't been able to eat and was just curious. I wasn't expecting to see five pounds gone.

Ever since Tor and I slept together, I've been frazzled. Almost manic. My stomach feels like I'm stuck in an elevator that keeps going up and down randomly throughout the day and night. My heart suddenly palpitates and a wave of dizziness follows. Yesterday I sat at my desk to work on a request I received from a local poet who wants all her poems written in calligraphy to be framed for her office, and all I could do was draw pretty, ornate hearts of various sizes. And Tor's name.

Thankfully, the poet isn't in a rush. And thankfully, I have a lot of paper and ink since I wasted a lot with my daydream-induced swoony scribbling.

Sleeping is now reduced to two-hour increments, where I wake with a jolt several times throughout the night, covered in sweat, heart racing, my sex quivering and damp, and I'll reach for my cell phone and reread all the text messages he's sent me recently.

I am hopelessly in love with Toren Grace.

Now that we've stepped over the line, I'm consumed with

thinking about him, and us, and the past, and the present, and the future, and *everything*. So much everything. My emotions go from being excited and happy to nervous and scared with almost no in-between.

He said we should *think*, and that's all I've been doing. Thinking, thinking, and even more thinking. And worrying. What if he decides that this can't happen? That *we* can't happen? What if he decides it's too much stress? Or that I'm just too young? What if he can't face my father with the truth? What if my father has a major meltdown?

I realized this morning that I've worried so much about what his decision will be, and the mental torment that he's going through, that I haven't really thought much about myself. This isn't just about Tor dating a younger woman, and him dealing with the possible wrath of his best friend. This is also about me dating a much older man and causing anguish to my father and to my family.

Can I endure that?

With Tor's love and support...yes. I believe I can.

Blue reusable grocery bags are all over Toren's kitchen, and Kitten has taken up residency in an empty one that has fallen onto the floor. I may have bought too much food. I'm not sure why I feel like baking a yummy apple pie and broiling up a filet mignon for him, but I do. I'm on a mission. Perhaps sex and love changes what you want to give a person. Or at least put in their mouths.

In more ways than one.

I didn't get to see Tor over the weekend because he had to work on Saturday, and I promised his mother I'd help at the shelter bathing a few of the dogs. Yesterday he went riding with my father, which is something they do almost every Sunday when my dad is home. I stayed upstairs in my room even though I knew Tor was outside in our garage because I didn't think I could see him without throwing my arms around him or making some kind of lust-filled face at him that my father might notice. I watched them ride off together from the window seat in my bedroom, and seeing his long hair flying in the wind behind him and the tautness of the muscles in his arms as he gripped the handlebars brought back the delicious memories of those same arms enveloping me in his bed.

The dog and the kitten follow me around the house as I straighten things up, start his laundry, and run the vacuum over all the carpeted rooms, which will have tufts of white fur scattered about again in less than an hour. All the while, my mind bounces like a Ping-Pong ball with questions. Does he want to see me again? Does he regret sleeping with me now that he's had a few days to think about it? Was I painfully awkward and inexperienced?

Just as I'm about to start on the apple pie, my phone beeps.

Tor
How's my Angel?

That plunging elevator feeling overwhelms me once again just reading those three little words, typed by him. To me. And that one tiny word in the middle makes my heart soar like a wild bird.
My.
I'm his.

Missing you xo

Tor
Are you at my house?

Yes.

Tor

I'm on my way there. Taking my lunch break to come kiss you.

OMG Really?! :-)

Five minutes later, I hear his bike roaring into the driveway. I wait at the front door for him with a pounding heart, holding myself back from running to him just in case a neighbor might see me. His long jean-clad legs carry him up the walkway quickly. He shuts the door behind him, his eyes locking onto mine with the biggest smile I've ever seen on him as he immediately reaches for me, cupping his hand on the side of my throat and bending down to cover my mouth with his, slow and deep. *Possessive.* I wind my arms around his neck and hang on to him as my legs turn to jelly, threatening to let me melt into a puddle at his feet.

This is the best hello of my life.

His tongue sweeps against mine and a small growl sounds in his throat before he pulls away slightly. "I've been waiting three fuckin' days to kiss you again," he says with a soft, raspy voice. "I couldn't stand it for another minute." He rubs his thumb along my jawline and kisses me again, gently sucking my lower lip into his mouth.

"Ditto," I say when we part for air again. "I thought you wanted to think..."

"I have been. Nonstop. I've been thinking so much my brain hurts."

Moving my hands up from the back of his neck to cradle his head, I pull him down and plant a kiss on the center of his forehead. "There," I whisper. "I kissed it better for you."

"Yeah," he agrees huskily. "You did." His lips meet mine again and his hand grips my waist, pulling me closer to him. "You make everything better."

I swallow the lump of happy emotion in my throat as he takes my hand and leads me to the kitchen, where he inspects all the baking ingredients and supplies I've got laid out on the counter with keen interest.

"You're making me something special, aren't you?" he finally asks with a crooked grin.

I nod excitedly. "Yes. Filet mignon with mashed potatoes, sautéed fresh green beans with garlic and parmesan, and an apple pie."

His eyes go wide. "You're spoiling me. Please tell me you're staying for dinner. I'm not eating all that without you."

"If you want me to."

"Of course I want you to. I want to see you as much as I can."

I play nervously with the small canister of cinnamon on the counter, wondering if he'll make love to me again or if we'll just eat together and then I'll leave. The truth is I want to be in his bed again, with him on top of me all hard and sexy with our bodies connected while he whispers words that people don't say aloud. Words I can't wait to hear him say again.

"Then I'll still be here when you get home," I reply, turning back to him.

His eyes stay on mine for a few moments, his gaze filled with a longing that makes a warm tingle flow down my spine.

"I wish I didn't have to go back to work." He pulls me against his chest, where I fit perfectly. Different from how I used to, but perfect now. "I'm having a hard time focusing there knowing you're here in my house."

"I'm sorry. I don't want to distract you from your work."

He lifts my chin up. "Kenzi...it's a good distraction. I usually don't have anything to look forward to at the end of the day other than coming home to these two lazy fur monsters. Knowing you're going to be here, all sweet and sexy, with a kick-ass dinner and homemade apple pie you made for me is like hitting the lottery."

The sparkle of light in his eyes makes me hug him even tighter. I love hearing the playful, teasing, hopeful tone in his voice. He's got it all wrong, though. I'm the one who hit the lottery.

♥ ♥ ♥

Later that day, I'm still so jittery and nervous that I'm not even sure I can eat any of the dinner I've made for tonight, no matter how good it smells in the broiler. I only thought of him when I planned it and had no idea he'd ask me to stay.

Is this a date?

I have no idea, but I definitely want it to be.

He said he's been thinking, but he didn't tell me if he reached any sort of conclusion about what he thinks of us being together and what we do next. As for me, I've been thinking about him and us and still have only come up with one unwavering constant: All I want is for us to be together. Somehow, someway, I want us to be able to be together as a real couple and just be happy. I want our loved ones to be happy for us.

Diogee and Kitten run to wait by the front door together when they hear Tor's bike pull into the driveway for the second time today, and I get the feeling this is a nightly ritual for them and his earlier midafternoon visit was just as much a surprise to them as it was to me. As I stand next to them and wait for him to come inside, I'm struck by how cute it is that they seem so excited that he's home, but it also makes my heart hurt a little with the realization that Toren's been coming home to a dark, empty house for a very long time, with no one at the door waiting for him.

Maybe it's too soon for me to be thinking thoughts like this, but I want to be waiting for him at the door every day next to his dog and cat.

Breathe, Kenzi. Slow down.

When he walks through the door, he tweaks my heart when he hands me three red roses, then bends down to give the dog a cookie and the kitten a crinkle ball toy.

I'm speechless, standing there holding my first roses, watching him play with the kitten on the floor, seemingly oblivious to how freakin' perfect he is.

"What?" he finally asks, standing. My beanie is on his head, only it's faded now from the sun beating down on him when he rides. Tufts of dark hair stick out from the sides of the hat, and he has a small smudge of grease right above his left eyebrow that I want to reach out and rub off. He looks a bit disheveled and tired but he wears it well and it adds to his rugged charm.

"Why are you looking at me like that?" he asks.

"I just didn't know you'd be like this," I answer softly. "Roses..."

He moves closer to me and leans down to kiss my cheek. "Because now I'm your lover. Not your friend. Not your godfather. Not your dad's best friend. Big difference."

I blink at him, swaying, my heart racing. The word *lover* feels so...intimate. Powerful. Adult. *Sexy.*

He's still close to me, our bodies almost touching but not, his lips just inches away, when he brushes my hair away from my face.

"I love you, Angel. But I won't baby you when you're in my house, and in my bed. If we do this, the little girl and the uncle are left at the door." He kisses the spot behind my ear and brushes his lips across to my cheek. "Can you do that?"

I nod. "Yes."

"You know that a little rough isn't meant to hurt you, right? I would never hurt you."

I turn my face into his, my lips barely touching his. "I liked it a little rough." My words are just above a whisper, but I know he hears them from the way his breathing changes.

I've read an embarrassing number of romance and erotica books over the past few months in what I can only describe as a quest for personal research, and I can't lie—the rougher, harder, alpha scenes definitely got to me, and made me turn those pages faster. I secretly hoped he would be that way, and I even dreamed of him that way.

He hums and lets out a deep, sensual laugh. "I kinda knew you would. You like to drive me wild, like you did with those pictures. Don't you?"

Guilty.

"Yes," I whisper as his fingers slowly trail down my arm, from my shoulder to my wrist. I shiver from the featherlight touch.

"You can tease me as much as you want, Kenzi. I love it. Just be sure you're okay with me taking it."

"I am."

This unfamiliar side of him is deeply appealing to me, stirring desires in me that I've never felt before. Usually, I pretty much know exactly what Tor will say, and how he'll act. I know him like I know myself, and it's comforting and familiar. While that part of him is still here as a safety net of sorts, this darker, sensual side is pulling me in like a magnet. The tinge of unknown lurking in him is exhilarating.

He leans against the wall next to the front door and tugs on my hand, pulling me to him. He's watching my eyes and my breathing, gauging my reaction to him, probably expecting me to be nervous but hoping my desire for him overrides my anxiety.

It does.

"I'm not sure what smells better...your perfume or dinner,"

he murmurs, leaning down to kiss my neck. I wonder if we're ever going to move past the front door or if we're going to stay right here. He seems content here and in no rush to go anywhere else, and I'm okay with that, too.

I laugh lightly. "I think it's definitely dinner. Are you hungry?"

His mouth closes against the hollow of my throat, sucking lightly. My fingers curl around the fabric of his shirt. My eyes flutter closed.

"I'm starving." He nips at my collarbone. "I'm just not sure what I want to eat first."

Wetness pools between my thighs as I clutch the roses in one hand and his shirt in the other, swaying into him, seeking out his mouth with mine, craving more. He delivers, his kisses rough and demanding, teasing me to kiss him back with just as much fervor.

"Tor..." I pull away from him after a few heated minutes and try to catch my breath. "I don't want your dinner to be ruined."

He lets out a groan but smiles. "You're right. It smells awesome. Just don't forget where we were."

As if.

"That would be impossible."

After he quickly washes up, he puts the roses in a vase and sets the table while I arrange the food on serving dishes like Aunt Katherine taught me, and I think she would be very proud of my presentation of meat and vegetables.

We slip into comfortable conversation while we eat and chat about our weekend. We laugh at Diogee and Kitten, who have perched themselves right next to the table, their big eyes pleading for food, and Tor tells them there is no way in hell he's letting them have any of the best meal he's ever eaten because he's eating every single crumb himself.

And he did.

I half expected him to lick his plate when he was done; he made such a fuss over how perfect the filet was cooked and the flavor of the green beans from the subtle spices I simmered them in. Of course I'm hanging on every compliment, beaming inside. It's his smile that really does me in, though, because Tor doesn't often share a smile that lights up his face and reaches his eyes, turning the blackish brown to a light hazelnut. He grins a lot. He smirks a lot. But a real smile that erupts from his soul is a gift, and he's given me many tonight.

We take Diogee for a walk in the woods behind his house after dinner, holding hands as we walk along the dirt path, working off some of the meal we just ate to make room for dessert.

"Let's talk," he says when we return to the house, and he leads me to the couch after he takes the dog's leash off. I follow him with nervous anticipation and sit next to him, turning my body to face him. He rests his hand on my leg and stares at the floor for a moment before looking back at me.

"Today was nice," he says. "Like, beyond nice."

"I think so, too."

I can see him biting the inside of his cheek, something he does when he's nervous or mad, to stop himself from speaking before he's ready to.

"I don't know what to say," he finally admits quietly.

"Oh." I meant to just *think* the word, but it seeped out of my mouth with its tonal mix of part disappointment, part surprise, and part sadness.

"I'm usually good with words, Kenz. But you make me a fuckin' mess."

"I'm sorry."

"Don't be sorry." He recedes back into his quiet mode, staring at the floor.

"Maybe I should go," I say softly.

He grabs my hand. "No, don't go."

"We don't have to talk, Tor. You don't owe me any kind of answer or explanation. I'm just as confused as you are."

"No . . . we *do* have to talk. We can't go into this just blind. You know how I feel about relationships and sex. It's not a game."

"It isn't for me either. I hope you know that?"

"I do, but I also want to make sure you're with me because you really want to be, not just to go along with what I want. I can't stand the thought of you or anyone else thinking I used the fact that I'm older than you to coerce you or something."

My eyes bug out at him. "Are you serious right now?"

"Fuck yeah, I am."

"I'm my own person, Tor. You didn't coerce me. I'm not even sure I know what that means in this context, to be honest."

"It means to force, or intimidate."

"No. Actually, I think I pursued you more than you pursued me."

He lets out a big sigh. "Let's not even talk about that part."

I cross my arms across my chest. "There was no coercion. Or games. Or hypnosis. Or voodoo dolls," I say. "There was just me falling for you all on my own and making wishes on a shit ton of pennies."

That gets him to smile again. "You're so fuckin' adorable."

"So are you."

I think he actually blushes. "You're the only person I'd ever let get away with calling me cute and adorable, ya know."

"Nobody else better be thinking of you that way," I tease back. "I don't want to have to get all beast mode on someone."

"Trust me, no one else is. You in beast mode sounds sexy, so let's just change the subject before I forget what I wanted to say."

The kitten jumps up on his lap and squishes into the small space between us, purring and making herself comfortable for a nap, and Diogee has settled at his feet, with his head resting on top of Tor's foot. I love how they love him because I feel it, too. Just like them, I want to curl up against him and be as close to him as possible.

"It's been a long time since I've felt really passionate about anything, Kenzi. When I was younger, it was my music. I lived and breathed it. It was my world. I was so fuckin' close to getting that dream." Dark regret shrouds his eyes and steals his smile away.

My heart sinks for him and his grief over his dreams. "I know how hard that was for you, Tor. My parents talked about it a lot."

"Giving that up sucked. It hurt to see your parents move on because we were a team. It was always supposed to be the three of us making it big together. Watching from the sidelines wrecked me in so many ways. So I thrust myself into riding, and my work with Devils' Wolves, and you." He glances away from me and stares across the room. "Every time I saw you, it was like a sense of peace just came over me. I can't describe it. Being around you took away all the anger and regret I felt about losing my father and having to quit the band and take care of the business and my family. You were like my little oasis that I could escape to." He turns back to me. "I guess that sounds like a pretty fucked-up thing to say about a little kid, huh?"

I swallow over the emotion welling in my throat. "No, Tor. Not at all. Weren't you the only one who could get me to stop crying? To get me to go to sleep at night? I love my parents to death, and I have an amazing family, but you've always been the one I gravitated to. Whether you want to admit it or not, we've always had a connection, or a chemistry, call it what you want, and it's changed and evolved as we've gotten older. And ya know what? I don't think it's bad in any way at all. I think it's something beautiful and special and incredibly rare. How many people can say that they have loved the same person their entire life, in so many different ways?"

"Probably not many."

"Exactly. When I look at you, I don't see my father's friend, or my uncle, or my godfather, or an older man. All I see is the person I've always loved and who has always made me safe and happy. That's it. I just see *you*."

His head falls back against the couch and he closes his eyes. "You say that so beautifully."

"Because it's true." I lean toward him and kiss him softly on the lips, waiting for his eyes to open. "Our wishes are coming true."

He lets out a deep breath and smiles. "I hope you're right. I've been racking my brain, trying to figure out what's the best thing for us to do. What's the *right* thing for us to do. And I can't come up with a fuckin' clue. All I know is I want to be with you." He links his fingers with mine. "I can't fight the rights or the wrongs anymore. I don't care how old I am or how young you are or anything in between. All that matters is *you* are my forever. You always have been. You always will be."

I literally cannot even breathe as I try to memorize what he just said to me. I have a feeling there is not much more that he or anyone else could ever say to me that could possibly hold more love and meaning.

"I *am* your forever, Tor. And you're mine."

"So what do we do?"

I take a deep breath. What *can* we do?

"I think we should give ourselves some time together before we tell anyone. To make sure we're ready. Then we can tell my dad and everyone else and hope for the best. If for some reason we realize we're just not good as a couple, then we end it and no one has to know it ever happened." He frowns at me and I know he hates the idea of seeing me behind my father's back. "Tor, I think it's the best way."

"I don't like either one of us deceiving your father. Or anyone else. I hate lies and deception."

"I do, too. I just think we need to be sure before we create a bunch of stress for everyone. Including ourselves."

His brow creases with worry and his fingers squeeze mine tighter. "Do you have doubts? About us?"

"Not at all. But as you said before, this is a new level for us. To be together in this way."

"I don't think I'm going to have any doubts, Kenzi. Ever. You're what I want. I love you."

If he were to say those words a million times, I will never get tired of hearing them. Every time he says them, they sound different on his lips, and they sound different to my ears, like a melody that has a different note each time it's played. The same but never predictable. They're not just words that he repeats like a parrot. With Tor, every word comes from his heart. That's what I want for my forever. Words that I can believe to be true no matter what.

I drag myself back into the conversation, even though I only want to sit here and listen to his voice and feel the warmth of his hand on my leg and enjoy how being close to him makes my skin tingle.

"Tor, I feel the same way. Our biggest hurdle is going to be my father. I'm worried about hurting him. I'm afraid it will ruin your relationship with him, and that will kill me to see you both hurt, because of me. And on top of all that, I don't want him to be disappointed in me, or feel betrayed in any way."

"All my thoughts exactly." He blows out a breath and I can tell he's worried about all the things I pointed out just as much as I am. "I wish this was easier," he says. "But it's not. It might not ever be."

"I know. Let's just give ourselves until he's back from the tour, okay? We can't turn his whole world upside down when he's been working so hard."

"You're right. But it can't go on for months like that, Kenzi. We're not going to sneak around and lie to the people we love for months on end. I don't want you to be that type of person."

"All right," I agree. "When he gets back, we'll talk to him."

He gently picks up the kitten and lays her on the floor next to the dog, then stands and reaches for my hand to pull me to my feet and directly into his arms.

"So . . . are we together now? A couple?" I ask nervously.

"I think we've always been together." He bends down and kisses my lips. "But yeah, we became an official couple the moment I took you into my bedroom."

I want to jump up and down and freak out with happiness but I force myself to remain calm.

For about two seconds.

"So you're my boyfriend now?" I ask excitedly, bouncing on my toes.

An adorable grin spreads across his face. "That's how it works. I'm yours. You're mine."

I circle my arms around his waist and stare up at him as waves of happiness ripple through me. My brain is frozen, stuck on his words.

"Wow," I squeak.

"Wow?" he repeats.

"I'm so happy. This feels so right with you . . . I don't even have the words to describe it."

"Then don't talk...show me." Tor can pop his internal clutch and switch gears from nice and sweet to dark and sensual with lightning speed. My mind and body follow him into the fast lane, and I'm instantly quivering and wet.

I pull his head down to kiss him and reach for the hem of his shirt, pulling it up. We part just long enough for me to pull the shirt over his head and then our mouths crash together again. I wrap my arms around him and revel in the size of him and the feel of his hard muscles under my hands. I could touch him for hours and be completely content. Grabbing my hair, he gently pulls my head away from his lips and guides my face down to the center of his chest.

"I want to feel your lips on me." His whisper pierces the silence and my stomach does a triple flip-flop. I like when he tells me what to do and the rush it makes me feel. With my hands on his shoulders, I move my lips across the plane of his chest, kissing and lightly licking him as I move from one pec to the other, trailing my tongue over his tattoos. His fingers tighten in my hair and he exhales.

"Tell me what you like," I ask softly, wondering how and where men like to be kissed.

His answer comes fast. "Everything. Everywhere. Touch me...kiss me...whatever you want to do to me, I'll love it. Trust me." I feel his lips press against the top of my head. "There is absolutely nothing on this earth you can do wrong with me. Just follow what your heart and body want to do."

Easier said than done when you've never touched a boy before, let alone a grown man with a body that commands attention from the entire female race and has hard, hot confidence stamped all over it. I don't know where my courage came from on Friday when we slept together, but I'm trying to channel that inner gutsy girl now.

I let my feelings and desires come to the surface, pushing past any insecurities, and allow my lips and hands to explore his body while his hands slowly move over mine, caressing me in all the right places. When I reach to unzip his jeans, he grabs my hands and pulls me up.

"Let's wait on that." He kisses my lips. "I have a better idea for tonight."

"What's that?" I ask.

"Me licking you until you're delirious followed by some of that apple pie you baked; then I'm going to force myself to let you go home."

Before I can say anything, he picks me up and carries me to the bedroom, putting me down to stand at the foot of his bed. He slowly begins to undress me, starting with my shirt and bra, his eyes burning as he kneels in front of me and pulls off my shoes and socks and then goes for the button of my jeans.

With his teeth.

I gasp and my hands fly to his shoulders to keep myself steady as he somehow unbuttons my pants with only his teeth and then tugs down the zipper. His hands grasp the waistband and work my jeans and panties down to my ankles where he waits for me to step out of them. When I do, he slowly runs his hands up the backs of my legs to cup my ass and presses his face against my stomach. Sliding his hands down to the back of my thighs, he gently pulls them apart.

"Spread your legs for me, baby." Raw, raspy words that make my heart pound even harder and put me in a spellbound state. I almost faint when his mouth touches my most private parts and his tongue slides tantalizingly between my lips.

Holy shit. I had no idea something could feel so freakin' amazing.

His large hands move back to squeeze my ass as he works his

tongue slowly back and forth, in and out. My legs begin to tremble from the millions of little nerve endings in my body that he's got all electrified.

"Lie down." His voice sounds far away, on the outskirts of the tunnel of ecstasy I'm falling into.

I practically fall onto the bed, my limbs like wet noodles, and he pushes my legs farther apart as he climbs between them, licking his lips, his eyes languidly traveling from the apex of my thighs, up to my face. He reaches out and touches his fingertip to my lips, and I instinctively kiss it before he glides it down over my chin, to my throat, between my breasts, and over my stomach, leaving a trail of goose bumps in its wake. With his eyes still locked on mine, he slides his finger farther down to rub my clit in slow, teasing circles, before he grabs my hips and pulls me down to the edge of the bed in one fast, effortless yank. Kneeling, he guides my legs to rest on his shoulders and delves his mouth between my legs, making me cry out from the sudden incredible sensation of his wet tongue and mouth covering me.

My back arches up and I press my hips to him when he pushes a finger inside me, slowly fucking me with it while he flicks his tongue wildly over me one moment and then sucks me into his mouth the next, building me into a total frenzy of wanting more, more, more. I grip his comforter, and my thighs tighten shamelessly around his head as I lose myself against his mouth, letting him take me to a place of euphoria that I never could have imagined in my wildest fantasies.

As I lie panting on his bed in a daze of bliss, he comes up and stretches out next to me, pulling me so we're both on our sides facing each other. I lift my face to his and kiss his wet lips, and another small surge of wetness pools between my thighs when his tongue pushes deep into my mouth and I can taste myself all over him.

"I could lick you all night," he says when we pull away.

"I don't think I could take anymore," I admit. "That was the most amazing feeling ever."

He lets out a laugh. "I guess the boys don't know what they're doing, huh?" he teases.

"I have no idea. All I know is that was just like, wow."

He grabs my chin and tilts my face back up to his. "Wait a sec...Have you ever done that before?"

Heat rises to my cheeks. Did he really not know that I haven't done anything sexually? Other than just kissing and a little groping?

"Kenzi?" he urges.

"No. Nothing like that. I've only kissed a few boys and then Jason groped me a little...but we never went any further."

He immediately leans up and looks down at me, his face all serious. "Fuck, Kenzi. Why didn't you tell me?"

"T-tell you what, exactly?" I stammer. "You knew I was a virgin."

He shoves his hand through his hair. "Yeah, but I thought you'd done *some* stuff. I'd be going a lot slower with you if I had known that."

"Tor, you just said earlier you didn't want to baby me."

"There's a difference between babying you and slowly easing you into new sexual experiences."

"I don't want you to go slow. I want you to do what you would do with any other woman you're with."

He shakes his head. "Kenzi, I can't do that. I want you to have good experiences for all your first times and I feel like I've totally bulldozed you. The way you responded to me made me think you've done some of this before."

Now I sit up. "You haven't bulldozed me. And I responded to you because it feels right and just seems to be coming naturally. I wanted you to be my first everything."

He lays his hand across my bare stomach. "I still would have been. I just would have moved a lot slower, been gentler, and not come on so strong. This is what I meant by coercing."

I shake my head vehemently. "You haven't pushed me or *coerced* me. I don't want you holding back. Like you said to me earlier, I want us both to just follow our feelings."

He sighs and softens his voice. "I do, too. I'm wicked fuckin' attracted to you, though. I've never felt like this before and I don't want to be an animal around you if you're not ready for it. That's not fair for you."

"I feel ready, Tor. You turn me on like crazy, too, and all I can think about is that I want more and more of you."

I feel humiliated by this conversation. I want him to see me as a woman and not like a kid or someone who has to be treated delicately. I can tell that he has a ton of pent-up passion in him, and I don't want him to have to stop himself or force himself to slow down. Even though I know he would be doing it out of respect for me, it's not what I want.

I pull my legs up and hug my knees. The last thing I want is him deciding that I'm just too young for him after all, or feeling guilty or uncomfortable about having sex with me. That will never work.

He strokes my hair. "Kenzi, don't get upset."

"I don't want you to decide you need an older woman because I'm too much work."

He scoffs. "That's crazy talk. Loving you isn't work. I'm not that shallow and you know it. I don't want to hear you saying things like that."

"I don't want to feel inadequate. I've met your girlfriends, Tor. I've seen you with them—"

"Stop." He interrupts me before I can say any more. "Don't you dare compare yourself to them."

"It's hard not to. Sydni is gorgeous..."

"Kenzi, I can make a list of about a hundred things that make Sydni very *ungorgeous*. You're beautiful and sexy and I love who you are as a person. You're the whole package for me. Nobody else has ever come close."

I turn my head to peek at him over my shoulder. "Really?"

"Really."

Oh God. Someday Sydni will know we're together. I can't even imagine what she'll say to me. Or to Tor. She'll lose her shit completely. My stomach plummets just thinking about the crazy she'll unleash on us.

"Tor...have you thought about how Sydni will react if and when she finds out about us?"

"I'll handle her." His tone is clipped, his current distaste for her clear.

He nuzzles his face into my neck. "Let's not worry. Today has been such a great day. I don't want it to end with you upset."

"Me either."

"Then let's just be happy we're together and go wolf down that apple pie you made."

We ended up eating the entire pie in bed, with a can of whipped cream, sharing a fork.

CHAPTER 27

Tor,

There's so much I want to say, yet I can't find the right words.
So, I will say the only thing that I can say with utter truth.
The only words that honestly
say everything that needs to be said. And heard.

I love you the most.
Always.

💜 💜 💜

TOR

It's possible I've lost my mind, but I don't care. I'm too happy to care. If I've gone insane, then that's okay. I'll own that shit. I'll wear it like a badge. I'll be Captain Crazy.

I'll do anything. I'll be anything. As long as it means I get to spend my life with her.

I want to throw myself on the Asher gauntlet. I want to get the poison out in the open and give the wound air to breathe. And hopefully heal.

I want to move forward. I'm already tired of hiding and walking on the thin ice of the situation, waiting for a huge fucking crack to form and suck us into the lake of deceit.

Every night for the past few weeks I've sat on the floor with Diogee and Kitten, and I've dumped out the change from the glass bottle to roll up in those little paper rolls. Most of these old glass jugs are five gallons, but this one is bigger, probably around eight gallons if I had to guess, and I wish my father or grandfather were still alive so I could ask them what it was originally used for.

The hours that it takes every night to count and roll the coins doesn't bother me. With every quarter I place in the paper roll, with every minute that ticks by, I reflect on the past. I think about the present. I hope for the future and what I can have. A wife. A family. A love that transcends time, age, titles, and social expectations.

I don't add up a final total until I'm completely finished and have a fairly large pile of rolled-up coins in front of me that Kitten decides is a mountain that she must climb.

Six thousand twenty-five dollars and one cent.

Yup. There was one lone penny in that entire jar and it was at the very bottom, so I put it back in, because I feel like it's good luck now.

When the time is right, God willing, I'm going to ask my best friend for his daughter's hand. Yeah, that sounds fuckin' crazy. I get it. But I want his blessing. *We* need his blessing. I'm going to make him see how much I love her, and how serious I am about committing to her one thousand percent. I have no idea when or how that's going to happen, but in the meantime, I'm going to find the perfect ring so I can propose when the time is right.

It's Friday night and while I wish I could take my girl out to a nice restaurant for dinner, we had a great night being us. She met me at my house after work, and then we drove around for about an hour hanging up two hundred lost dog posters she had printed earlier using the laser printer we purchased. Then we set up a new trap for an older lost dog that's been sighted a few times in a field a few miles away. On our way back home, we stopped at a drive-through and ate cheeseburgers in the parking lot while listening to our favorite music.

By the time we get back to my place, it's still relatively early, so we decide to start watching season one of *Vikings*. Just as we get comfortable on the couch all tangled up together, there's a knock on the door.

"Shit," I curse as Kenzi moves away so I can get up. I swear it better not be Sydni here to try to resurrect things.

When I open my front door, I'm surprised to see Asher standing there.

"Ash. Come on in." I try to sound casual as I close the door behind him.

"I saw your Jeep in the driveway. I'm glad you're both here," he says to Kenzi, and I see the flash of fear in her eyes as she looks across the room at me.

Kenzi sits up. "Yeah, I helped Tor hang some flyers and we were just going to watch some TV before I went home."

"You want a beer? Iced tea?" I ask him, trying to act normal. He knows Kenzi hangs out here all the time, so it's not new or sketchy. It doesn't scream WE'RE HAVING AN AFFAIR.

I hope.

"Nah, I'm good, man." He takes a seat in the chair in front of the window and I go back to the couch but position myself at least two feet away from Kenzi. "I've been at the facility all day. She's been squeezing my hand." He flexes the fingers of his right hand as he talks.

"Daddy . . . the doctor said those are muscle spasms."

"Kenzi...let him finish," I say softly. Asher's excited tonight, and even more hopeful than he usually is, and I don't think we should push him down. Hope is all that keeps him going when it comes to Ember.

"I know," he says. "That's what they've said in the past, but it's a little different now. She seems to be responding to my voice. The doctors are discussing the possibility of some experimental drugs."

"Ash, that's great news. Do they think the drugs wil—"

"No," Kenzi pipes up. "You can't let Mom be some kind of guinea pig."

Asher looks at Kenzi like she just slapped him. "Of course I would never allow that. But if they think it might bring her back, how can I not let them try? I can't live with myself unless I know I've done everything possible to help her."

"Dad, you have. There's nothing you can do. She's brain-de—"

"Kenzi, stop," I say, shaking my head. "There have been cases where patients have woken up. I've read about them."

"Exactly," Asher says. "It's rare, but it does happen. It could happen with her. She's young, and healthy, and she has a lot to live for. She *wants* to live. I know she does."

Kenzi shakes her head. "I just don't want you to get hurt, Dad. You know I want Mom back just as much as you do. But all this stuff scares me. Experimental drugs? I don't want anything bad to happen to either one of you. At least now...she's peaceful. She's sleeping." Her voice cracks with emotion and I reach across the couch and grab her hand without even thinking if it will raise a red flag.

Asher thinks nothing of it and that makes me feel like shit just as much as it gives me hope. I should probably let go of her hand, but I can't. Not when she's near tears and squeezing mine so tightly. And this—*this*—is what Asher is feeling. The love of his life squeezing his hand.

"I know...but if she woke up and could talk, and move again...I could bring her home. We could hire a live-in nurse while she recovers."

Now his hope is starting to climb to unrealistic levels and that's not fair to him or Kenzi. *Or Ember.* So I try to gently step in. There was a time for a few years when we did this dance several times a week and none of us can live like that again.

"Ash, she may not come back like that," I say quietly. I hate to kill his buzz in any way, but Ember suffered a severe brain injury. The chances of her ever being able to talk and make full sense are slim. "I think you need to really think about this long and hard and grill the shit out of the doctors about the experimental drugs and any case studies they have."

"I plan to. I'm just excited about *any* hope at this point. I know she hears me. I can feel it. She knows I'm there."

"I'm sure she does," I agree, because I honestly do believe that wherever Ember's brain has gone, her heart knows that he's there with her.

I have an entirely new respect and understanding for the intense love that Asher feels for Ember now, because that's how I feel about Kenzi. I would do anything for her and I'd never be able to give up on her.

"Kenzi, why don't you come with me next week? I know it makes you uncomfortable, but maybe if she hears your voice, too, it will help."

I already know she'll say no, and he does, too. Kenzi can't handle seeing her mother like that and I don't blame her at all. It's not easy in any way to see someone you love hovering somewhere between life and death. After the accident, Kenzi would sit next to Ember's bed for hours and just cry and beg her to wake up. After having a few meltdowns that required the staff to give her sedatives, her grandmother and her aunt insisted she stop going.

"I can't," she says tearfully. "Please, Dad..."

Fuck. I hate that I can't put my arms around her and comfort her like I should be doing if this situation weren't so screwed up. This is sheer torture.

"Tor, tell him please, I can't," she begs, and it's not unusual for her to put me in the middle. She's done it her entire life when she's scared or upset. It just feels way worse right now.

"Okay, let's all just calm down," I say. "You know how uncomfortable she feels there, Ash. Why don't you wait until after you talk to the doctors more, get some more info, and then we can decide if Kenzi should go. I'll go, too," I suggest. "Maybe hearing all of our voices together will help. Maybe she'll remember the old times."

Asher nods. "That's a good idea. I'll definitely be getting more information and meeting with the specialists. Kenzi, you know I don't want to upset you. I would never make you do anything you don't want to do."

Kenzi stands and crosses the room to give him a big hug. "I know, Dad. I'm sorry. I love you and I just miss Mom so much."

"I do, too. That's why I want to do whatever I can."

I excuse myself and go into the bathroom to give them a few minutes alone. Once there, I stare at myself in the mirror and splash some cold water on my face. I want Ember to recover, and I know we all have to hope and think positive, but I don't want to see Asher and Kenzi get their hopes up only to have them shot to hell all over again. I could never voice this to them, but what if Ember did wake up but was absolutely nothing like herself? What if she can't speak, but instead moans and cries? What if she thrashes around and twists her body, instead of lying peacefully as she is now? They'll never be able to cope with seeing her that way.

I leave the hall bathroom and check my bedroom real quick. It feels weird having Asher in my house even though he's been here more times than I can count. I'm worried something personal of Kenzi's could be lying around in a place it never should be in. Like her panties tangled up in my bedsheets. Not that Asher would be in my bedroom, but still.

When I join them, I'm glad to see they're playing with the dog and the kitten and the mood is lighter and happier. Seeing them together in my living room playing with my pets only reminds me of how much I love them both and how I can't even consider losing either one of them. I wish I could pull Kenzi into my arms and snuggle on the couch with her and have Asher join us for a movie and just be a happy family. We've done it a hundred times and now suddenly it's all taboo and wrong.

When Asher tells us he's going to head home, Kenzi tells him she's going to stay for a while to finish watching our show and he hugs us both goodbye before he leaves, oblivious.

Betrayed.

I *feel* sick. Kenzi *looks* sick.

Somewhere in hell, Satan has just pulled out a bag of marshmallows and is roasting them in my honor.

Kenzi looks at me with guilt, chewing her bottom lip after she closes my front door behind her father. "I'm sorry, Tor."

"We're going to have to tell him, Kenzi."

"I know...after his mini tour, though, please? He's worked so hard on all the new songs. It's not a long tour, a month, maybe? When he gets back from that, we'll sit down with him together and tell him. Or I'll tell him alone, if that's better."

"No," I insist. "We do it together."

"Okay." She fingers her necklace nervously. "I can't even think about what he's saying about my mom. Do you really think she'll ever be better?"

Her green eyes look pleadingly at me, and I wish I could say yes. I want her to have both her parents back and have a normal, happy life. It's all I've ever tried to give her—some normalcy and security.

"I honestly don't know, Angel. Your mom's accident, the trauma to her head, and the brain activity afterward was unusual. The body and the brain are a fuckin' mystery; no matter how much doctors and scientists study it, there are always things that stump them. Unfortunately, there are times that no matter what, they can't make someone better. Like your dad said, all anyone can do is try. But miracles do happen."

"He thinks he can love her back to life, Tor. That's what he believes."

"Ya know what, Kenz? I wouldn't be at all surprised if he could."

She launches herself into my arms and kisses me like I've never been kissed before. It nearly knocks me over, and it has nothing to do with her throwing herself at me and everything to do with the depth of the love I can feel pouring out of her every breath.

I want to push her down on the floor and kiss her lips until they bruise and bleed. I want to punish her for wanting me when she shouldn't, and thank her for wanting and loving me with so much of herself when I need it.

Young love . . . first love is so innocent. So pure and trusting. So all-encompassing. I shouldn't be on the receiving end of that love from her at my age, but in all honesty, she's my first love, too.

CHAPTER 28

Tor—age twenty-four

Asher—age twenty-four

I'm sitting in the old creaky chair in my office at the shop, trying to make some sense out of all the financial spreadsheets the accountant threw at me.

I don't understand numbers. Or profit and loss.

Neither did Pop, apparently.

I mean, I know what it is, but I don't know how to fix it so I have more profit and less loss.

I haven't taken a paycheck for myself in three months just so I could pay my brothers. I'm hungry and exhausted and worried.

I hear footsteps at the door and turn to see Asher standing there.

"It's midnight, Tor," he says.

"I know."

He comes in and throws a small brown paper bag and a white envelope onto my desk.

Looking up from my mess of papers, I ask him what it is.

"Open them."

Inside the paper bag is a steak and cheese sandwich, extra cheese, salt and pepper, with grilled peppers. It's my favorite and my mouth is watering just from looking at it.

"You didn't have to do this, Ash."

"Oh yeah? Did you eat today?"

*I bite into the sandwich and almost groan from how good it tastes.
"No."*

"Then yeah, I did have to do it. Open the envelope."

*Swallowing, I slice the envelope open with a knife and inside I find a
check for fifty thousand dollars, made out to me. I stare at it, the zeros
blurring in front of me. I've never seen a check for this much money in
my entire life.*

"What is this?"

"A check." He leans back against the wall.

"I can see that. For what?"

"For you. To fix this mess you're in."

*Shaking my head, I shove the check across my desk toward him. "I
can't take your money, Ash. I appreciate it, but I can't."*

*I take another bite from the sandwich, which I will accept. But not
money.*

*"You need the money, Tor. Don't be stupid. It's a loan from my inheri-
tance. I don't need it. My family wants to help you."*

*Fifty thousand dollars would fix so much. I could get this place back
in order, get out of debt, finally have a little money for myself again to
eat and be normal.*

"Asher, I can't."

*"You can, and you will. You wrote the first songs that are making me
money, Tor. You think I forgot that shit?" he asks. "No, I fuckin' didn't."*

"I get royalties. That's enough."

*"It's not. Your father left you a business that was in a hole, man. He
didn't have any life insurance. For four years you've been working your
ass off trying to take care of everyone and keep this business going. This
shop can be great but you have to get out of the hole first or else you're
just spinning your wheels. I can't watch you kill yourself anymore. Especially when I have the means to help you."*

"Ash—"

"Shut up and take the money. My dad has a friend who's a business and marketing consultant. He's coming on Friday to help you get a business plan together."

I finger the edge of the check. I've never taken money from anyone before. But he's right—I'm sinking like the Titanic.

"I don't know when I'll be able to pay you back."

He shrugs. *"I don't care if you ever do. I just want to help. You're my best friend. I don't expect or want anything back."*

💛 💜 💜

KENZI

Tor and I see each other whenever we have the chance. On the days I'm at his house, he comes home for his lunch break and we eat lunch together. Sometimes I stay until he comes home after work and we have dinner, talk, play with the pets, and make love.

I've been getting quite a few orders for handwritten wedding invitations, and hand-lettered tattoo designs, all by word of mouth. I've also been volunteering at the shelter as much as I can, and the veterinarian who takes care of the sick pets there hired me to do something that is very close to my heart. When her practice has a patient that passes away, they make an imprint of the pet's paw in ink on notepaper, and she has me write a small, inspirational poem about eternal love on the bottom of the card, and I add the pet's name and dates. Then it's sent to the owner for them to keep. I personally think it's very sweet.

Today is Sunday, and Tor's out riding and having lunch with my father. We haven't seen each other for three days due to just work and life stuff getting in the way, and I'm missing him a lot. To keep my mind busy, I've taken on the project of organizing all my pens, papers, and ink when I get a text message.

Tor

I miss you.

I miss you more ;-)

Tor

Can you meet me at my place tonight? Around six?

Yes.

Tor

Can't wait. I love you.

I love you, too.

💜 💜 💜

"Perfect timing. I just got here," he says when I let myself into his house, which is something he insists on. He hates when I knock.

We kiss hello. A sweet, soft kiss on the lips and we're both smiling as we do so. I still get butterflies when I see him, even though it's been a few weeks since we officially started seeing each other as a couple.

"I have to take the great white furry one for his walk. You want to come?"

"Of course."

Diogee starts to prance as soon as he sees Tor get his leash, and then he waits by the French doors that lead to the backyard for Tor to snap his leash onto his collar. We walk through the yard and out the gate leading to the woods. In just the past short few weeks, we've started to develop even more rituals, like walking the dog together.

"How was the ride?" I ask.

"Good. Humid, though. We rode down Hampton Beach, and it reminded me of your prom night."

"Ugh, don't remind me of that."

"It seems like so long ago, doesn't it?"

I nod as we pause for Diogee to sniff around in the dirt and old leaves. "It really does."

"I think that was the night everything changed between us. I don't even know why. I've thought about it a lot, and I don't know what the fuck happened. It's like something just switched."

Nodding, I lean against him and kiss his shoulder. "I know what you mean. I felt it, too. When we danced together. The way you touched my cheek." I smile and squint up at him. "The look in your eyes. I was petrified."

He lets out a laugh. "Why were *you* scared? You're the one who was talking about putting me in a box," he teases.

My face heats up at the memory. "Oh my God, I did. I'm surprised you didn't run and hide."

"No way, baby. I wanted you to put me in that box and keep me."

"I'm definitely keeping you, but I'm keeping you out of the box for good behavior."

He winks at me. "Good to know."

As we make our way down the path and circle around back to his house, it starts to drizzle. Locking the gate behind us when we get into his yard, he lets Diogee off leash to run the yard and then pulls me into his arms.

"Dance with me," he whispers.

My heart swells and I rest my head against his chest. "There's no music," I say, even though it doesn't matter. Our bodies are already swaying together.

"There's always music. Listen to the sound of the raindrops and our heartbeats." He holds me tighter and presses his lips to my forehead as our bodies move together in the rain.

I used to hate the rain, thinking it was gloomy, depressing, and the ultimate hair-wrecker, but now he's changed that for me forever by turning it into something incredibly romantic. I'll never be able to see or hear rain again without remembering this moment with him.

"How do you make me love you more and more?" I murmur, sliding my hands up the back of his shirt, always wanting to be touching his skin. I hate any kind of barrier between us. Like clothes. Clothes on him are a sin.

"So my evil plan is working?" he asks playfully.

"To make me love you even more? Then yes, it's working."

"Good." He squeezes me tighter, our clothes sticking to our bodies. "We're getting pretty wet. I'm going to take you inside now and make you even wetter."

Yes.

My heart speeds up as he takes my hand and leads me back into the house with Diogee at our heels. I have no idea what he's got in mind and that just adds to the anticipation and excitement of being with him. I've learned that Tor loves my inexperience rather than resents it, as I first worried he might. I think being the only man who has ever really touched me turns him on, and I don't mind that at all. I can understand the possessiveness he feels.

He takes me into his bathroom, closing the door behind us, with a flash of that sexy grin I can't get enough of, before he slowly takes off my damp clothes. His focus is one hundred percent on undressing me, his eyes riveted either on mine or slowly gazing over the parts of my body he's revealing. He doesn't distract either of us by kissing me like we see in the movies, and that's something very intense about him that I've grown to appreciate. He likes to watch his hands move over me, glancing up to catch my breathing and the expression on my face.

"Turn the shower on," he says softly, pulling his own clothes off as I do so. He checks the water temperature with his hand before putting his arm around my waist and pulling me under the water with him. His body towers over mine in the small shower, and when he bends down to kiss me, the warm water sprays over his head and then cascades down over us.

He backs up slightly and moves his hands down to my waist. "Turn around," he says, his voice growing huskier, and when I do, he grabs my hands and places my palms against the tile in front of me. The familiar scintillating hum courses through my body, spreading that feeling of excitement, longing, and a tinge of nervousness from the unknown. His lips come down on my shoulder while his hands slowly slide down my arms, brushing across my breasts, and over the curve of my waist, stopping to fill his hands with my ass cheeks, squeezing as he presses his hard cock against the small of my back.

"You have the most perfect ass," he whispers as the steam from the hot water drifts around us. His hand moves down between us and slides between my wet thighs, his fingers reaching forward to rub my clit, the water mixing with my own wetness.

"Do you want me?" His teeth graze the back of my neck as his finger slowly pushes into me, a small moan escapes my lips.

"Always."

"Tell me." His lips curve against my neck, and he pushes his palm up against my sex, his middle finger pressing perfectly against my sweet spot. "I want to hear your sweet voice say something dirty."

Without hesitating, I say exactly what I'm thinking. "I want to feel every inch of your cock rammed in me right now."

"Fuck yeah," he hisses. He backs away from me and lets the water spray down my back, then grabs the bottle of lavender body wash I keep here, squeezing some into his hands. I stay where he put me, still facing the tile with my hands flat against it, and he begins to rub the lather all over my back. My nipples harden against his palms when he reaches around to cup them, gently pinching my nipples before moving his slippery hands down to soap up my thighs, running his hand between my cheeks on the way, his fingers lingering and pressing into places that make my breath catch.

His hand tangles in my wet hair and pulls my head back to him, his lips capturing mine, licking the drops of water that have dripped down to my mouth. I twist my head back to kiss him deeper when he grips my waist, guiding my lower body to meet with his and pushing us so the stream of water flows between our bodies. His hand moves between us, fisting his cock and pushing the slick head into me. Grabbing my hips, he thrusts up into me long and deep, making me go up on my toes from the force of him filling me.

"If you ask for every inch, I'm going to give you every inch," he rasps against my ear, his voice so sexy it makes me sigh and arch my back, craving even more of him. His hands slide up and cover my breasts, cupping them for leverage as he continues to plunge in and out of me, his forehead leaning against the back of my head. As his breathing becomes more ragged, he reaches up to grab the showerhead above us, detaches it, and flicks the controls with his thumb. I'm vaguely confused but too focused on his cock to care—until he holds it between my legs and the pulsing water sends my throbbing nerve endings into total overdrive, launching me into an instant orgasm. My legs almost buckle beneath me but he wraps his arm around my waist to hold me as he pulls his shaft all the way out, then sinks back into me, his balls slapping against me with every thrust.

"Tor..." Orgasmic delirium has me liquifying under his touch, as if my bones are melting. Dropping the showerhead, he spins me around and grabs my ass, lifting me up and pushing me back against the tile wall, his stiff cock finding home again as I wrap my legs around his waist. He kisses me with wild hunger, pumping into me while the dangling showerhead spins around, spraying water everywhere. He moans against my mouth and stills, buried deep inside me, his kisses halting to slow, deep, and soft, and I feel him surge and pulse as he comes. I move my pelvis in slow circles against him, milking and caressing him with my tightening walls. Exhaling deeply, he stares into my eyes and loosens his grip on me.

"Damn...I love you," he says, his voice filled with raw emotion.

"I love you back," I say breathlessly, raining kisses over his face and smoothing his wet hair back.

He lowers me to my feet and we take a lightning-fast real shower together, as the water has gone mostly cold. When we step out, I realize water has sprayed onto the floor from the showerhead flinging around. I kneel down and wipe up the water with an extra towel. "That was pretty amazing," I say, the ecstasy still quaking through my body.

He grins down at me and my eyes are drawn to that incredibly sexy V as he wraps his towel around his narrow waist. "You're not allowed to touch that by yourself. I hold the keys to the magic shower stimulator."

"Oh, really?" I tease.

"Really."

I stand and kiss his cheek. "I wouldn't want to do anything without you anyway. That would be cheating."

A frown replaces the smile he had a few seconds ago and his eyes turn a shade the color of molten chocolate. "You actually mean that, don't you?"

I squeeze the excess water from my hair with the towel and look at him quizzically. "Mean what?"

"That you wouldn't cheat on me."

My stomach pitches just thinking about that. "Of course I mean it. Are you crazy? Why would I ever cheat on you?" I poke his abs playfully. "You're the perfect man. Sexy, sweet, caring, you love pets, you beat up bad guys, you kiss bunny noses...Should I go on?"

He leans back against the sink and watches me as I dry myself off. "I never told you about this but Sydni cheated all the time. Of course she didn't think of it as cheating because we were in a so-called open relationship, but she was the only one with the opening. I wasn't into it."

I look at him in confusion. "Open relationship? What's that?"

"It means you date and sleep with other people but still have an ongoing relationship with someone else. It's like mutual permission to cheat."

"Oh!" I say in surprise. I had no idea. "Ew."

"Yeah, ew."

"Did you...?" I don't want to know that he's been having sex with half our town.

"Once. A long time ago. I was young and thought it would be fun to be able to have a free pass to sleep with anyone I wanted. But it sucked. I felt guilty and dirty. Back then I cared about Syd a lot, but over the years with all that going on, it destroyed us. Especially her obsession with your father."

"Were my parents like that, too?" I ask, starting to feel sick. If my parents were in a relationship like that, it would ruin everything I believed about them.

He wraps a thick white towel around me and pulls me to him. "Hell no. Your parents were completely committed to each other. Asher hasn't touched a woman in years even though Sydni has done everything but beg on her knees to blow him."

I breathe a sigh of relief but I'm still nauseous thinking about how Sydni has been chasing my father—her best friend's husband, on top of sleeping with other men when she could've had Tor. She's worse than I thought.

"I'm sorry, Kenz. I shouldn't be talking like this. Sometimes I forget that he's not just my friend, but he's also your dad."

"It's okay. You can talk to me about anything. I just don't understand why Sydni would do that when she had you."

"Variety, fun, excitement, riding different dicks. Who the hell knows." He shrugs but it's obvious her behavior has hurt him.

"You don't ever have to worry about that with me, Tor. I don't care if I'm eighteen or fifty. I'll never want anyone but you."

He swoops me up into his arms, kissing me as he carries me to his bed. My head falls to the side and my gaze lands across the room as his lips tickle my neck. It takes me a moment to register what's different about his room today, and then it comes into clear view. The glass jug, the one that's been filled with coins for as far back as my memory goes, is now empty.

The engagement ring family tradition.

It seems like a lifetime ago when he told me about the tradition, but in fact, it's only been two years. I distinctly remember the unexpected feelings of jealousy that crept over me at the time, picturing him with some lucky woman who would become his wife someday, and secretly wishing it could be me.

My arms tighten around him, his body still hot from the shower, as his lips move over my bare skin.

Could it really be me? Or am I living a temporary dream on borrowed time?

CHAPTER 29

Tor—age twenty-two

Ember—age twenty-two

"Did you tell him yet?" I ask her softly. Her breathing is soft and even in the dim room next to me, but I know she's awake.

"Not yet."

I turn on my side and prop my head up on my arm.

"You have to tell him, Em."

"I know... I just don't want to hurt him. I don't think he'll understand."

I reach across the bed and touch her hand. "He loves you. He'll understand. Trust me, he just wants you to be happy."

"I know... but I'm afraid he'll think it's like I'm leaving him in a way." She lets out a shaky sigh. "And I'm not. I just want to do my own thing. I'm always going to be Asher's wife in Ashes & Embers. They think of me as a backup singer. People don't see me as anything else. In my own band, I'll be me." She turns her head toward me. "Does that make sense?"

"It does. You have to do what's good for you, Ember. You can't just be Asher's wife and Kenzi's mom. You have to be you, too. You're an amazing singer, and I think your own band will do awesome. An all-girl rock band is fuckin' kick-ass. I think he'll be proud of you."

"I hope so."

Sitting up, I squint at the digital clock next to their bed. It's almost 5:00 p.m.

"Do you feel any better?" I ask. Earlier today she got sick to her stomach, became dizzy, and then fell in the kitchen. She's sure it's just the flu, but she asked me to stay with her while she rested in bed in case she felt sick again. Asher's away for the weekend with his dad, but when I wanted to call him to let him know she was sick, she made me promise not to so he wouldn't rush home.

"A little bit. Just tired."

"You keep resting. I'll make Kenzi some grilled cheese and keep her busy until bedtime. I'll check on you in a little while. Okay?"

"I know I say this a hundred times a week, but I don't know what we'd do without you. You're always so good to us. Our other husband." She smiles at the joke and rolls over onto her side to sleep.

We have this joke where Ash and Ember call me their other husband. Usually it's funny.

Sometimes it's not.

♥ ♥ ♥

TOR

Her skin is soft and dewy from the shower, inviting caresses and kisses over every curve, and I can't get enough of her. She sighs and writhes like a sultry snake beneath me, digging her nails into my back as she arches up to press her body against mine. Her lust and love for me equals mine for her, and that has made chemistry explosive between us.

Rolling over onto my back, I pull her on top of me and she's already a step ahead of me, knowing exactly what I want and need. Her body moves tantalizingly slow on top of me, like she's savoring every inch, every breath, every touch. She takes my cock into her with a long, smooth descent, then lifts herself up even slower till she reaches my tip before lowering down onto me

---

again, over and over again. There's no rush, no crazy bouncing up and down, no slamming of bodies. Her body dances effortlessly with mine, like we were made to be one since the beginning of time. There's no rush to reach an end because there *is no end*. Her eyes fall closed, her pouty lips parting with the ecstasy of my body filling hers as she makes love to me like we have forever.

And she makes me believe that we do have forever.

I'm lovestruck, enraptured with the sensual way her body takes ownership of mine. I can't move. I don't *want* to move. No woman has ever taken me before. Not like this—not so completely, so honestly, with such raw and uninhibited desire and passion. No woman has ever wanted me this way or made me feel so utterly and completely adored. And within that she has given herself to me just as completely. She holds back nothing and gives everything.

This is what I have been wanting and waiting for, for so long. This indescribable connection.

My hands tighten around her waist, more to remind myself that she's real than any other reason. Everything else begins to fade away. The doubts. The black cloud hanging over us.

No way in fucking hell am I ever letting this go. I'm never letting *her* go.

Her soft moans drag my gaze up her body to rest on her beautiful face, her eyes fluttering open at that same moment to meet mine, and her lips curve into the smile that changed my life so many years ago.

She leans down to kiss me, her breasts swaying, nipples brushing against my chest. She's the sexiest, most loving creature I've ever met in my life. Everything about this girl defies her age and her time on this planet.

A week ago she whispered in my ear that she was born to be mine, and I believe it.

♥ ♥ ♥

The beeping of her phone alarm wakes us both. It's a harsh reminder that she has to go home. She stirs and I hug her tighter to me under the light blanket. Her naked body is warm and soft, snuggled perfectly against me. Diogee and Kitten have wandered in and are sleeping on the foot of the bed with us.

This is my family now, and I don't like the other half of me leaving every night.

"I have to go, hon," she whispers, kissing my chest.

I groan and loosen my arm from her so she can climb out of bed to find her clothes. The all too familiar knot grows in my chest as I watch her.

"I hate this, Kenzi." I swing my legs over the edge of the bed and pull on my sweatpants.

"I don't like it, either."

"I want you sleeping with me all night and waking up with me. You leaving my bed feels like a booty call."

She pulls on her shirt and makes a face at me. "It's not a booty call, Tor."

"I can't do this forever."

"What are you saying?" Her voice wavers with the first onset of fear. "You want to break up?"

"Absolutely not. I'm saying I want you to live with me so you don't have to leave in the middle of the night."

She stares at me, one leg in her jeans and the other out. "Live with you?"

"Would you want to? If we can get through the wrath of Asher?"

She steps into the other leg of her jeans. "I'd move in tomorrow if I could. Why do you think I'm here so much now?"

"To play with the pets?" I tease.

"Well, they *are* cute," she replies playfully. "But you're much cuter."

"I'm gonna ignore that. I'm serious, Kenz. As soon as it's possible, I want you to move in with me. Will you think about it?"

She steps into her shoes. "I don't have to think about it. I already know that's what I want."

"I want you to think about it anyway. It's a big decision. And we still have a lot to get through. I just wanted you to know that's what I want."

I walk her to her car and watch her drive down the dark street, then go back to bed to wait for her to send me a text letting me know that she's home. This is definitely a part of our relationship that's driving me crazy because I don't like her having to leave every night. I want us to be able to fall asleep together and stay together in the same bed until morning.

When it comes to her and what I want, my patience is getting thin. Now that we're together, I want the freedom to be able to move the relationship forward as we want it to, and it's getting harder and harder to have to wait and hide from everyone.

CHAPTER 30

Kenzi—age eighteen

Tor—age thirty-two

"Wait here." He steps out of the truck and shuts the door before I can say anything. He saunters across the dirt parking lot to an old warehouse and bangs on a dented silver door with peeling paint. I'm not quite sure what we're doing here, but I have a bad feeling.

Soon a man opens the door and they begin to talk. Tor is doing a lot of pointing to the other side of the warehouse, and he looks pissed.

Furious, actually.

The man is also getting visibly agitated, shaking his head and yelling. I can't hear what they're saying from where I'm parked, but it definitely doesn't look friendly.

I sit in shocked silence when Tor grabs the man by the throat and literally drags him away from the door to around the side of the building, out of sight.

Shit.

My hand clutches the door handle till my knuckles hurt. I want to run out there and see what's going on, but he told me to stay here in his most serious voice. It's the voice he's always used when he expects me to listen, no questions asked.

A few minutes go by and I breathe a sigh of relief when Tor appears from around the corner of the warehouse and is walking toward the truck holding something in his hands that looks like a burlap bag with a chain hanging off it. My blood chills as he gets closer and I realize he's holding a small dog that isn't supposed to be small. It's severely malnourished.

I jump out of the truck as he nears and run over to him.

"What happened?" I ask.

"Get the door for me."

I run to open the back door of his truck and quickly spread a blanket over the seat, and as he gently lays the dog on it, I notice the chain is deeply embedded into the dog's neck, the flesh raw and ugly, oozing blood and yellow pus.

Bile rises in my throat and I cover my mouth. "Oh my God . . ."

"Fucking douchebag has had this dog chained to the back of his warehouse, with no food or water for who knows how the fuck long. The chain's been wrapped around his neck for months slowly strangling him."

"I think I'm going to be sick."

He pulls me into his shoulder. "I'm sorry, Angel. I should have warned you about this one. Let's go. We have to get him to the vet."

We climb into the front seat and I can't help but peer in the back seat as we pull out of the parking lot. The dog is so weak he can barely move, and his eyes are lifeless, glazed and defeated. Tears roll down my cheeks as I say a silent prayer for him. This is the worst abuse I've ever seen.

"I think he'll be okay," Tor says reassuringly, putting his hand on my leg. "I know it looks nasty as hell, but once they get the chain out and clean it up, get him on some antibiotics, and get some food and water into him, he'll start to slowly recover."

"You really think so? He looks bad, Tor. Really bad."

"I know. But I think he'll pull through. That fucking asshole was warned a year ago when he had another dog chained up back there that another rescue pulled."

"What did you do to him?" I ask. He dragged the guy away by his throat and I didn't see him come back.

His eyes shift up to check the rearview mirror, his jaw clenching. "You don't want to know."

"Tell me."

"I cut the chain to free the dog and then wrapped that end around his fucking neck and left him there, chained to the ground like he had this poor dog."

My heart almost seizes at the ferocity of his voice and actions. Tor can be the sweetest guy in the world, but he's got a ferocious streak when it comes to abuse of an innocent animal. He wants vengeance.

"Don't worry," he says to my gasp. "He won't die. His buddies will find him. I just want to teach that fucker a lesson. He'll never hurt another animal again."

💜 💜 💜

KENZI

> Hey you, how is your morning? I love you xoxox

I switch from my message app to a browser app, then back to my text message app to see if it will refresh, but there's still no reply from Tor, and it's showing as not read. I sent the text almost four hours ago, at 8:00 a.m. We always text each other first thing in the morning, and Tor always replies within an hour.

Always.

Even before we were dating, he would always quickly reply to my messages.

I wander through the mall, trying to remember where all the stores I like are, in what seems more like a maze than a group of stores. I don't shop often, and when I do, Chloe is usually with me and she steers us around the mall like she was born here. I finally find the lingerie store and pick out some new sexy bra and panty sets that I think will make Tor smile. The price tags practically scare me into next week but the fabric is so rich and soft and accentuates my curves much nicer than anything else I own, so I can't resist buying them.

Next, I find the craft store and load up on paper, ink, and little embellishments like lace, glitter, and gems that I've started to add to the paper of my hand-lettered work.

I glance down at my phone again as I wait in line to pay, but there's still no text from Tor.

When I get to the parking lot, I call his cell phone and leave him a voice mail:

"Hey, honey, where are you? I'm getting a little worried. Call me when you can. I love you."

I send another text, hoping I'm not being annoying as hell, but I'm worried.

> Are you okay? I just bought some lingerie I think you'll like. ;-) I love you bunches and I can't wait to see you. xo

I start up my Jeep and my phone rings on the passenger seat next to me just as I'm about to reverse out of the parking spot.

Finally!

I grab the phone with a big smile on my face.

"Hey, hon, I've been missing you all morning."

"Kenzi?"

I almost drop the phone. "Dad?"

Crap.

"Who did you think I was?"

Shit.

"Chloe."

"Oh. Where are you?"

"In the mall parking lot. I needed a few things."

He's silent for a beat. "I don't want you to panic, okay?"

My pulse instantly starts to race. "Now I *am* panicking. What's wrong? Is it Mom?"

"No, it's Tor."

My heart flies into my throat, and my stomach plummets as I try to deny away the words I just heard.

"Are you there?" he asks.

"Yes…" I swallow over the lump in my throat choking my airway. "Is he okay?"

"He was hit by a car early this morning on his bike."

I close my eyes tight against the horrible visuals running through my mind. "No…"

"He's going to be okay. I just don't know exactly what's hurt yet. I'm at the hospital now with Tanner, waiting for the doctors. They just moved him into his own room. His mom is on her way, too."

"I'll be there as soon as I can."

"You don't have to come, Kenzi. I know how much you hate hospitals. I just thought you could take care of his pets until he gets home since you spend a lot of time over there doing things for him already."

"Of course I will. I'm still coming, though."

"All right. Drive slow. I can hear you're upset, and I don't want anything happening to you, too. He's in good hands, so don't worry."

"I'll go slow. I promise."

I end the call and stare out the windshield, frozen, trying to force my breathing to relax. My brain won't stop chanting. *He's hurt. He's hurt. He's hurt. He's hurt.*

When I feel like I'm no longer on the verge of hyperventilation,

I fight the traffic for an hour to get to the hospital. Grabbing the first empty parking spot I find, I sprint to the main lobby and text my father:

> I'm downstairs. What room/floor?

Dad

> 3rd floor, room 312. Take a left off the elevator. I'm in the waiting area.

I learned when my mom was in the hospital that you have to know how to navigate around to get to where you want to go without having a visitor pass or else they don't let you get to the room of the person you're trying to see. If anyone tries to stop me from seeing Tor, I'm going to have an epic meltdown.

The key is to look determined, and in a hurry, and not make eye contact with anyone. That's what I do as I make a beeline for the elevator and poke at the glowing button with the faded 3 on it, wait for the doors to close, and then endure that dreaded lurch that almost makes me vomit as it begins its ascent.

When the doors open, I go to the left and find room 312. My heart is shattered to bits at the scene I walk into.

I stand rooted in the doorway of his room. I wasn't expecting to see Sydni sitting on the edge of his bed, her hand clutching his. She kisses his cheek as she cries over his battered body that's got tubes and beeping things attached to him. Several large bandages are wrapped around his arms and hands.

My blood boils. That should be *me* comforting him, whispering love to him, begging him to open his eyes. But of course she came back for him, because it always takes a tragedy to make someone wake up and see what they lost, or could have lost. I force myself to turn away, but I'm too late. His eyes have already fluttered open and are looking into hers. He doesn't even know I'm here. I turn quickly to leave and run straight into my father's chest.

He holds on to my shoulders and leans down to look into my eyes. "He's going to be okay, sweetheart. He's just a little banged up. He'll be fine."

I wrench myself away from him, needing to put distance between myself and what I just saw in that room before I lose control and it becomes obvious that something is going on between us. My dad follows me to where I've stopped to lean back against the wall in the hallway. The sterile smell of the hospital is nauseating and forces down my throat unwanted memories of when my mother was here.

He tries to put his arms around me again. "Kenzi, he's all right, I promise you. It's not like Mom."

"Why is she here?"

"Who?"

"Sydni." I gulp for air, and my brain screams at me to shut up, but I can't. "They're not even together. Why is she here?"

His brow creases. "Because they have a history, Kenzi. You're too young to understand. Sometimes things are complicated." He pulls me into his arms. "You have to calm down."

I stifle a scream as my body trembles and shakes, trying not to cry but I can't hold it in. Tears track down my cheeks as I gulp and cling to him. Seeing Tor hurt, not knowing if he's really going to be okay, and then witnessing another woman with him is all too much. None of this should be happening. We had plans tonight. We're going to make dinner and walk Diogee and watch Kitten chase the laser light. Then he'll kiss me until I can't breathe and we'll make love and dream of when we can be together all the time.

"It's okay." My father strokes my hair. "I know how much he means to you and how scary it all looks, but he's going to be fine. I wouldn't lie to you."

No. You wouldn't. But I'm lying to you.

"What happened, Dad? How bad is he hurt?"

He walks me down the hall to the small waiting area where we can be alone, and hands me a handful of tissues from a box on the table. I dab at my eyes and blow my nose while I wait impatiently for him to answer.

"He's lucky, it could have been a lot worse. He has a bad concussion, a few broken ribs, a sprained wrist, and a lot of road rash. I'm sure his neck and back are going to be hurting him pretty bad, too. But in the grand scheme of things, he's very lucky. He'll just need to rest for a while, his whole body is going to be sore."

"Concussion?" I repeat, my voice almost shrieking. "He hit his head?"

"Kenzi, it's not like what happened to Mom. It's different."

"How do you know for sure?"

"Because I do. Trust me."

My mom hit her head, too. And she never woke up again.

He flips his keys around in his hand. "Let's just go home. I don't want you this upset. His family is here. Sydni is here. He won't be alone. He's resting now and too many people can't be piling up in his room."

No. No, no, no. I can't leave him here without seeing him, and I want to get freakin' Sydni away from him. She's not family. She has no right to be kissing him, especially when he's not even awake.

"How did Sydni find out?" I ask. "Who called her?"

"I guess Tanner did. Why are you obsessing over Sydni?"

"I don't know. They're not together, so it seems odd. She should leave."

He shakes his head. "I have no idea what's going on between them. That's none of our business. She hasn't left his side."

My jaw grinds. This just isn't right. *I'm* his girlfriend. He loves *me*. Not her.

"I want to stay for a little while," I finally say, forcing my voice to sound as natural as I can. "I'm not going to freak out or faint."

"Are you sure?" He narrows his eyes at me. "You look pale and you're not acting like yourself at all."

I give him a weak, unconvincing smile. "I'm positive. I'll stay for a little while; then I'll go to his place to check on the pets. Maybe I should stay there until he gets home?" I know if Tor were awake right now, he would ask me to stay with them.

My father runs his hand through his hair. "That might be a good idea. Sydni is allergic, so she probably won't want to be there. Check with Tesla to be sure, but it might be easiest for you to stay there for a few days until he's home. It'll be one less thing for everyone to worry about. You'll be okay there alone?"

I nod. "Yes. The pets know me, and I know their routine."

"All right. Call me in a little while and let me know how he is and what you're doing. You'll have to come home to get clothes, so I'll see you there."

I don't tell him that I already have extra clothes at Tor's house, in my own drawer in his dresser and hanging next to his in his closet. There's also my makeup. My body wash. All my favorite foods.

We hug goodbye and I watch the nurses stare at him as he walks by the nurse's station on his way to the elevator. I glare at them until they feel my eyes on them. What kind of thirsty bitches stare at a man in a hospital? Since he grew up here, most people in town don't go crazy over him being famous, but occasionally there are people who approach him for an autograph, follow him around, or stare at him. But a hospital isn't the place to do that.

I decide I'm going to wait in the waiting room until Sydni leaves, and then I'll go in to see Tor. I'll hide in here until after hours if I have to, and hopefully the nurses won't find me and throw me out. I'm prepared to beg if I have to.

I'm immersed in a gossip magazine when suddenly Tesla comes flying into the waiting room, her black high heels clicking on the floor.

"There you are," she whispers loudly. "You're lucky I got ahold of this before someone else did, Kenzi." She holds up Tor's cell phone and waves it in front of me.

Damn!

"I don't know what you're talking about," I reply, my nerves rattling at what she may have read on there.

"You don't have to play dumb, Kenzi. He told me a few weeks ago what's going on. I know everything."

Surprise wafts over me. He didn't tell me he had talked about us with his sister. I don't mind at all that he did, but I'm shocked because he's been so worried someone will find out.

I blink at her. "He told you about us?"

"Yes. He needed to talk to someone he could trust. He's all torn up over this."

"Tesla, please don't tell anyone."

"I won't, but you better stop sending him text messages. You're lucky the Queen of Rock 'n' Roll in there didn't get ahold of his phone before I did, or your ass would be grass right now."

"I know that. What is she doing here anyway? They're not even together."

"Seriously, Kenzi, wake up. She thinks she owns him. My

mom's about to throw her out because she's trying to take control already."

I stand up and pace the room. "This is awful. How is he? Is he awake? Is he in a lot of pain? I'm going nuts not being able to be with him."

She falls into one of the chairs and crosses her legs. "He's not really awake. He opens his eyes for a few seconds but that's it. The doctor said he probably won't be coherent until tomorrow. He must be in pain; the road rash alone looks like pizza. They've got him on IV pain meds."

My chest aches with worry. "Oh my God. I hate this."

"You two are really in a mess, Kenzi. You have to lie low or someone is going to catch on. My brother has enough to deal with now. If anyone finds out he's screwing you, it's going to cause a ruckus, and that's not going to be good for him."

I shoot her an angry look. "He's not *screwing* me, Tesla. We love each other."

She shakes her head at me, her silver hoop earrings swinging. "I just hope you two know what you're doing. I'm only two years older than you, and I can't wrap my head around the thought of loving someone and planning a future with them at this stage in my life. I can't even fathom being that kind of tied down."

"You and I are very different, Tessie. I love your brother, and I can honestly say the only thing I want is to spend my life with him. I don't think of it as being tied down at all."

"I hope you feel that way in five, ten years and beyond. Because if you do a U-turn at some point and leave him, it will break his heart. He's not nineteen years old. He wants to settle down."

"Trust me, I know that, and I would never do that to him. You don't think I worry that he'll want to be with someone his own age and will leave me? We're both vulnerable."

She runs her hand through her long hair and shakes her head. "I think you're both playing with fire. Your father is going to freak when he finds out. Even though Tor is a great guy and will probably treat you like a queen, Asher isn't going to be able to see past the fact that his best friend is boning his daughter."

"You don't have to remind me, Tess. I know all of this. It's all I think about."

She pulls a pack of mints out of her purse and offers me one before putting a few into her mouth. I shake my head. I have no appetite for anything, even a tiny mint.

"Look, Kenzi... I'm not trying to be a bitch. I love my brother, and I like you. I think you guys can be happy together. I'm just a little pissed off right now because my brother is lying in a hospital bed because some fucking asshole was probably texting while they were driving. I'm not trying to make you feel bad. I know you're upset."

"It's okay," I say weakly. "I understand."

"Taran and Tris put his bike on a flatbed and took it to the shop. He's going to be so pissed when he finds out his bike is wrecked."

"How bad is it? Can it be fixed?" Tor has put so much time and money into rebuilding that motorcycle over the years, he'll be heartbroken to find out it's messed up.

"Taran thinks so, but Tor likes to do the work on his bike himself, so they're not going to do much to it."

I nod in agreement. "I thought I'd stay with the pets at his house until he's able to come home, unless you want to?"

"That would be great, actually. I work a lot of really late nights."

"Then I'm more than happy to stay."

I glance at my watch and realize it's late afternoon already. My heart feels sick with worry about Tor. Not being able to see him, hold him close, and tell him I'm here is killing me inside. Is he wondering if I'm here? Is he upset that I'm not in there?

Tesla stands. "You want to take a walk to his room with me and see how he's doing?" she asks softly. "Hopefully Sydni will be gone."

I nod and wipe at my eyes with my fingers. "Yes."

When we get to his room, I'm relieved to see that Sydni has left. His mom and Tristan are there, and I hug both of them hello, trying to not fall apart as my eyes rivet on Tor sleeping in the bed. He looks smaller and younger in just the hospital gown and a thin white blanket thrown over his legs. The dark, dried blood on his forehead and the side of his face causes my chest to constrict. I want to get a soft, warm cloth and wipe it away.

But I can't. Because right now, I'm not Tor's girlfriend. I'm just his best friend's kid.

"What did the doctor say?" Tesla asks as I move closer to the bed, taking an inventory of all the scrapes and bruises I'm going to kiss better as soon as we're alone together.

"He was in a little while ago and checked him over," Mrs. Grace replies. "They want to keep him for a day or two for observation, just as a precaution. He'll be sore and will need time to recover. His ribs and the road rash will probably cause him the most pain, and he could have some headaches for a few days since he hit his head. They've got him on painkillers and antibiotics right now."

"We're going to sue the asshole that hit him," Tristan says. "They could have fucking killed him. Not to mention wrecking a restored vintage motorcycle. That idiot is going to pay for this."

I sit gingerly on the edge of the bed and take his bandaged hand gently in mine, not caring that his family will see. They know we're close, so it shouldn't raise any questions that I would hold his hand. It's a perfectly normal thing to do with someone you're friends with.

Tesla keeps talking to her mom and brother in the background, asking a hundred questions. I'm pretty sure she's doing it on purpose to distract them from noticing me sitting on the bed with Tor, fighting back tears. I rub my thumb gently over his and watch his chest move as he sleeps. The heart rate monitor and the intravenous lines he's hooked up to make my anxiety spike but I try to remind myself that this isn't like what happened to my mother. He's just sleeping from all the medication, and he's going to wake up.

His mom is saying that we all should leave so he can rest, and I can't bring myself to just stand nonchalantly and leave the room. Not caring anymore, I lean down and kiss his cheek.

"I love you the most," I whisper to him. "I'll be back tomorrow."

CHAPTER 31

My love,
Come back to me.
My heart misses you.
My soul aches for you.
My body needs you.
My mind craves you.
You. Are. My. Forever

🤍 💜 🤍

TOR

Three days ago, I woke up in a hospital bed with the worst head-ache of my life and feeling like someone put me through a high-speed blender. And that may as well have happened, because parts of my flesh appear to be pureed. I don't remember getting hit at all, which is probably for the best because I'm feeling a rage toward the person who did this to me. When I first woke up, my mind felt empty. Blank. I couldn't think backward, and it scared the shit out of me. I sat in the creaky bed in silence, waiting for my head to clear and for the incessant throbbing and nothing-ness to subside. Sydni was there, spouting her love for me, talking about coming home with me and our future together. My head swam with confusion and pain as my brain tried to fight through the curtain it was shrouded in.

I nodded dully at her as she went on and on about getting married and having a family. It's what I wanted. It sounded good.

But it felt wrong, and I couldn't put my finger on why. The more I thought about it and tried to reverse back into my memory, the more pain shot through my head, and the nurses gave me more meds. And then the curtain would fall over my thoughts again.

On day two, I saw Kenzi hovering somberly in the doorway, her green eyes capturing mine from across the room, and it all came back in a monstrous wave.

She's my love. The one I'm going to spend my life with. Not Sydni, who has managed to position herself back in my life while I lay here beaten and in a fog.

I have a vague memory of my sister kissing me goodbye and whispering in my ear "I have your phone and all your things. That bitch went through the stuff you had on you when you got brought in here, but I took it all. She didn't get to your phone, thankfully. Kenzi is staying at your house until you get home. She said to tell you she loves you."

Pain pierces through my head again as I realize what has sparked Sydni to suddenly try to become girlfriend of the year.

When we pull into my driveway, Kenzi's Jeep is there. *Thank God.* I can't wait to see her and have her in my arms. I could feel the worry and sadness coming off her the few times she visited in the hospital. I wanted to scream at everyone to get the hell out of my room and give us a minute alone, but doing that would have made everyone suspicious of why I'd want to be alone in my hospital room with an eighteen-year-old girl.

Sure I could have called her from the phone in my room after visiting hours. If I knew her number. I've called her mobile phone and house hundreds of times over the past years, but always from speed dial on my phone. I have no freakin' idea what those numbers are, and Asher's number is unlisted.

Technology, you are a sick fuck, thinking you're making our lives easier with your one-touch buttons. Fuck you.

Sydni insisted on driving me home after I was discharged. I didn't want to cause a scene, so I agreed, just to get out of there. But now I'm putting an end to this charade.

I grab Sydni's arm as she reaches to open her car door. I'm not letting her walk with me into my house. This is going to end right here in the driveway.

"What's wrong?" she asks. "Do you need help getting out of the car?"

"No. We need to talk."

"Okay, let's go inside and talk, then. You can send Kenzi home now; she's just been pet sitting."

"No."

She turns in the seat with a confused look. "No what?"

"We're not together, Syd. Nothing has changed. I appreciate you coming to the hospital and driving me home, but now I want you to leave."

She frowns at me like I'm an unruly child. "What are you talking about? You said you wanted to give us another chance, Tor."

"I said I would *think* about it after your tour if you didn't sleep with anyone. But a lot has changed since then."

Her eyes flash with irritation. "I don't understand. I've been here for you. What could have changed?"

"A lot, actually, and I'm sorry, but we're not getting back together. Ever."

She shakes her head, her mouth twisting in confusion. "I saw the ring with your stuff at the hospital, Tor. It was in the bag with your clothes."

I cringe and brace myself. Of course I would get hit by a car after picking up an engagement ring and I hope it's not some kind of bad omen.

"The ring isn't for you," I say quietly. It's ridiculous she would assume it was for her. I'm pissed at her for even touching something she had no right to be anywhere near, getting her bad mojo all over it. Now I'm going to have to burn sage next to it.

"What?" she says.

I turn to face her and my ribs scream in pain. "It's not for you. I'm sorry, Sydni."

"Then who the hell is it for?" The rise of her voice pierces through my brain.

"That's none of your business."

"What the fuck, Tor? Are you insane? Did you just meet someone recently and decide to get married? Just like that?"

I shake my head slowly. "No. It's someone I've had feelings for, for a long time."

She stares at me, dumbfounded. "Are you serious?"

"Yes."

"Is it Lisa?"

"No."

"Then who?"

"I'm not discussing this with you."

"Why the hell not? Don't I have a right to know?"

I let out a sick laugh. "No, you really fucking don't."

"We've been in a relationship forever, Tor. You don't think I deserve to know how you just suddenly fell in love and are going to propose to them? That's supposed to be me!"

"A long time ago, I thought it could've been you. But I was

never enough for you, and you were never right for me. You always wanted or needed someone else. Several someone elses. Face it, Sydni; you don't want to be married. You just want to know I'm yours. You want a safety net." I look toward the house, my heart pulling me to go inside and see the woman who *does* love and want me. Unconditionally. "And I'm not going to be that for you."

Of course I care a little that Sydni is upset after she jumped to a crazy conclusion because she went through my personal things. Nothing will change that we have a history together, but it's over for us.

"Fine. Good luck, Tor. I hope she's everything you want," she says bitterly.

She is.

"I still care about you, Syd. And I hope you find what *you're* looking for."

"Just get out." She pushes my arm, right over the raw, torn-up section that's covered in bandages, and I see stars from the pain.

Fuckin' bitch.

Silently, I climb out of the car, my body still stiff from pain, and walk to the front door as Sydni backs out of my driveway and peels out down the street. Kenzi opens the door for me, then closes it when I get inside. Diogee and Kitten are waiting with her, the dog wagging his tail and howling at me while the kitten rubs all over my legs. This is how I want to come home every day, only without being beat to hell.

Kenzi stares up at me, her eyes shimmering with tears. "Can I hug you?" she asks tearfully. "Or will it hurt?"

I snake my arm around her and pull her against me. "You better hug me, Angel," I whisper, burying my face in her hair and breathing her in. "I don't care if you crack another rib. Just don't let me go."

"I was so worried about you." She gently wraps her arms around me and rests her head against my chest. "I couldn't get near you with Sydni there, and Tesla had your phone. I didn't know she knew about us."

"Yeah, I told her. I'm sorry about Sydni, Kenzi. I didn't know how to get rid of her without causing a scene."

Sniffling, she shakes her head. "It's okay. I'm just so glad you're okay and you're home now."

"You have no idea how much I missed you."

She peeks up at me. "Yeah, I might have a good idea."

I lean down to kiss her but she pulls back from me and looks down at the floor.

"What's wrong?" I ask as worry settles in my gut. She's never backed away from me before. "Why are you pulling away from me?"

"I saw Sydni kissing you, Tor. I know you were hurt and not even really awake, but I wasn't there much. Sydni was." She swallows hard. "I need to know if that kept happening."

My chest tightens. "Absolutely not. I couldn't stop her from coming every day. My head was fucked at first from the concussion but I definitely did not kiss her. I could barely move, Kenz. I just told her in the car two seconds ago that I appreciate her visiting and driving me but that we are completely over and I'm in love with someone else." I wish I could tell her about the ring and how Sydni assumed that it was for her, but I refuse to wreck anything to do with my proposal to her just because Sydni is an idiot. I have no idea when I'll be proposing. It could be two months or two years, but I wanted to have the ring in case I decide to be spontaneous. I don't care if we're engaged for years, I want her and the rest of the world to know I'm serious about spending my life with her.

"I believe you. I'm sorry I even asked. It was just beyond

upsetting to see her touching you and I wasn't able to even talk to you."

"I wanted to call you from my room but I didn't have your number memorized. I just sat there staring at the phone like an idiot."

"Oh! Why didn't I think to call your room after visiting hours? I totally forgot there was a phone there. I'm so stupid!"

I laugh and kiss the top of her head. "No, you're not. We were both stressed. I just want to put this crap behind us." I take her hand and lead her over to the couch so I can sit and rest. My back is already starting to hurt again. "Thanks for taking care of these guys for me."

"Don't thank me. I love them."

"We love you, too. More than you know."

She smiles at me and I wish I could push her back on the couch, kiss her everywhere, and make love to her for hours, but with my wrist and my ribs being all messed up, I can't. Lying in the hospital all banged up sucked, but it sucked even worse not being able to be close to her.

I lean back against the couch and let out a sigh. "It's so good to be home. I'm going to be home for at least a week before I go back to work. Maybe two."

She kneels on the floor in front of me and takes my boots off for me, and it's a mix of sweet and sexy as hell watching her do it.

"You need to rest," she says. "Your brothers all said they would take care of the shop for you."

"Good. Do you know what I want?"

She puts her hands on my legs and looks up at me, melting me with her big green eyes. "Tell me."

"I want you here with me every day while I'm resting."

"Ooh. Can I play nurse?" Her playful, sensual voice wakes up my cock, which thankfully escaped getting road rash.

I touch her cheek affectionately. "I was hoping you would."

"I can kiss all your boo-boos better."

"I have a lot."

"That's okay."

I cup my hand behind her neck and pull her up to my lips. "I really want to spend as much time with you as possible. I missed you like fuckin' crazy."

"Then I'll be here every day. I can't stay overnight, though, even though I want to more than anything. Sleeping here without you was like torture. Now that my dad knows you're home, I can't."

"I know." I sigh. "And I'll deal with it. I'll take what I can get."

CHAPTER 32

Kenzi—age ten

Tor—age twenty-five

"Uncle Tor?" She's standing next to the couch, gently pulling on the sleeve of my shirt.

"Yes, love?"

"Can you read to me?"

I lower the volume on the movie I'm watching and turn to face her. She's wearing her pajamas and holding on to an old book I used to read to her when she was little.

"You know how to read, Kenzi. You don't need me to read to you anymore."

"But I like to hear your voice when I fall asleep."

That puts an instant smile on my face, and now I want nothing more than to read to her. Smiling, I take the old worn book from her hands, which I have memorized from reading it to her so many times.

"I can't argue with that, now, can I?" I reply, winking at her.

She shakes her head and smiles. "Nope."

♥ ♥ ♥

KENZI

Tor's been going a bit stir-crazy in the house, so today I drove him to the beach so we could walk around and get some fresh air and sun. We hold hands and walk along the edge of the water with our shoes off and watch the seagulls.

"I love having you at my house every day," he says, squeezing my hand. "Now I don't want it to stop."

My heart soars. I can't even put into words how much I've enjoyed being with him every day. "I don't want it to stop, either. I never want to leave."

"Someday you won't have to. That's the goal, right? To live together?" He glances down at me.

"That's definitely my goal. Can I start working at the shop when you go back?"

"Of course. Are you sure that's what you want to do?"

"I'm positive."

"Then you can. Gretchen can spend a few days training you before she leaves."

"That would be great."

Something catches my eye along the water, and I let go of his hand to step forward to grab it. It's an old glass bottle.

"Damn, I thought it was a message in a bottle," I say, frowning.

"Nope. Just some asshole's garbage."

There are no trash barrels around, so I have to put the bottle back down in the sand.

"I'm bummed. I've always wanted to find a message in a bottle."

"Isn't it only worth it if it's written for you?" he asks, reaching for my hand again.

"That's so true. Even if I found one, I'm not sure I could open it and read it. It's so invasive. But how fascinating would it be to just see one? I'm curious how the paper and ink would look. I wonder how the ink and paper would hold up after years of floating in the ocean, tossed around by storms, and then warmed by the sun over and over again."

"Only you would think of that, Angel. But...here's some food for thought—how will you know if it's for you or not, unless you open it?" he teases, bumping my shoulder.

I gape at him in mock irritation. "Now that's just mean and torturous."

He gestures toward an ice cream stand in the distance. "Let me buy you some ice cream, and then I want to take you home and torture you in ways that are much more fun."

My pulse speeds up as I go up on my toes to kiss his cheek and whisper in his ear, "Ice cream sounds yummy, but I really want to lick *you*."

He groans and puts his arms around my waist, pulling me into him. "You naughty thing. I may not make the drive home if you keep talking like that."

♥ ♥ ♥

As soon as we get inside his house, he backs me up against the wall. His lips cover mine hungrily, and his hands move slowly up my arms to rest on either side of my neck, holding my face to his as his tongue twists with mine.

"My body's not that sore anymore, baby," he says, his voice raspy from the kiss. "And it wants you in a bad fuckin' way."

"I'm all yours," I whisper against his mouth, and slide my hand down his chiseled body to grope his cock through his jeans, squeezing gently. Any shyness I had about touching him has slowly faded over the past few weeks after taking care of him while he was recovering. Bathing and showering with him was the perfect opportunity for us to reach an even deeper level of intimacy, and I took advantage of it to be able to explore every inch of him.

He sucks in a breath and watches with dark, lust-filled eyes as I slowly slide myself down the wall until I'm kneeling in front of him, holding his gaze as I slowly unzip his jeans and pull them down along with his boxers. His hard cock thrusts out, and I eagerly wrap my lips around the head and slide my mouth down his shaft, filling my mouth and throat with him. He leans one arm on the wall above me and his other hand cups the back of my neck, his thumb slowly rubbing over my cheek as I move my lips up and down the hot length of him.

"I love when you suck me." The deep, breathiness of his voice sends tingles up and down my spine as he thrusts his salty crown against the back of my throat. I wrap my hand around him and grip his hot, velvety flesh in unison with my mouth, sucking him harder as I pull my mouth to the tip and then plunge back down on him, quickening the pace as I feel him growing harder and throbbing against my tongue. He fists my hair and pulls my head back, forcing me to look up at him as he drives into my mouth and then stops with a deep moan. Hot liquid spurts down my throat and I swallow, staring up at him. He looks completely content and sated with his hair hanging down over his face, eyes closed, as he catches his breath, his hand caressing my cheek.

"You just wrecked me," he finally says.

"I hope that's good?" I slowly stand and lean back against the wall where he originally had me, and he leans down for a long, slow kiss that takes my breath away. His hands sink to my hips as he settles his body between my legs.

"It's beyond good." He sucks my bottom lip between his and gently bites. "Now I need more."

We move to the bedroom, where he makes love to me to the

point of total exhaustion. After a nap, he sits up in bed shirtless and plays his acoustic guitar while I lay with my head on his thigh and listen in woozy bliss. He's been playing a lot since the accident, and I love that it seems to be therapeutic for him now rather than a bitter pill he was forced to swallow years ago.

He plays the ballad he played at the bonfire, and while he doesn't sing, I know the lyrics by heart.

I wanted your smile to be for me
I watched you from afar for so long
And finally when I had you in my reach
You got stolen away, right in front of me
Never good enough, always cast aside

"You wrote that song, right?" I ask.

He nods. "I did. In high school. Asher tweaked it a little, of course."

"Is it about someone?" Curiosity about the song has been on my mind for a while, and I want to hear the story behind it if there is one.

He chews the inside of his cheek and then looks down at me lying on his lap. "It sorta is. Or was at the time, I should say. It was more about how people made me feel."

"Can you tell me who? It's kinda sad."

"Do you really want to know, Kenz?"

A twitch of fear burns in my stomach, but I nod anyway. "Yes."

His dark eyes settle on mine and he lets out a small sigh. "It was about your mother. At least that's what sparked the initial idea."

I pick my head up off his leg and stare at him. "My mother?" I repeat. "I don't understand. Did you write it for my dad?"

He lays the guitar on the floor next to the bed. "No. I wrote it for me."

My mind starts to spin around with the rest of the lyrics of the song, about regrets, betrayal, and a love that never came to be.

I give my head a little shake. "I'm confused. You were with my mom?" My voice has taken on a waver that I don't like. I've just stepped into territory I had no idea I was walking into and now I wish I hadn't.

He shakes his head. "No. Never. But I liked her first. She was new to town and it took me a long time to get up the guts to talk to her. At the time, I thought she was the most beautiful girl I'd ever seen. I know it's hard to believe now but I was really shy when I was young."

Swallowing hard, I touch his arm. "I never knew that."

"Yeah, I had asked her if I could walk her home, and we stopped at the park to get to know each other a little more, and I was just about to ask her out on a date when your dad showed up. The rest, as they say, is history."

"What do you mean?"

"He just swooped in and I was instantly forgotten about. And that's it. I went home and left them there, and they've been together ever since."

A strange, sick feeling washes over me. I feel like I stepped in something wet and squishy while barefoot and have no idea what it is, and I'm afraid to look.

"So you had, what? A crush on my mother?"

He lets out a little laugh. "I guess so, yeah."

"How come you never told me this?"

"What's there to tell?"

"A lot, Tor. It's my mother for God's sake."

He sits up and frowns at me. "Why are you getting upset?"

"Because it's my mother. I feel weird. I had no idea you had a thing for her."

"Kenzi, I was only fifteen years old. We were just kids."

"The lyrics are pretty deep. It seems like you liked her a lot."

"I did. She was pretty, and sweet, and she could sing. I had a hard time meeting girls I connected with. But I was no match for your dad. Even though we look alike, it stops there. I don't have his irresistible charm."

"That's not true. You're just different."

"Trust me, I know," he says, his voice laced with bitterness.

I sit up and reach for my clothes, feeling very displaced suddenly. "So what about all the years you lived with us? You were with her all the time. Didn't it bother you?"

"A little at first, I guess, but I was happy for them. They were both my best friends. I loved them both and wanted them to be happy."

I stare at him as more memories flood my mind. "I remember when I was little there were times you would sleep on the bed with her. What about that?" I never saw them touch, but it does seem odd to me now that they would lie on a bed together.

"She used to get really bad migraines from being on the pill. If your dad wasn't home, she'd ask me to lie on the bed next to her when she felt sick because she used to pass out. She hated to be alone. Your dad knew about it. Shit, I've slept in the same bed with him, too, Kenzi. You know how close we all were. We did everything together."

"Did anything ever...happen?" I can barely even get the words out.

"No." He shakes his head and reaches for my hand. "Never. I would never do that. I loved them both."

"But you were jealous that he got her?"

"In the beginning, yeah. It bothered me a little. He could have had anyone and he took away the one girl I liked, like it was nothing."

I pull my hand away from his and rub my arms. "This is making me feel sick."

His mouth falls into a worried frown. "Why? Kenzi, nothing ever happened. We were just kids. I spent maybe an hour with Ember before Asher showed up. We all became best friends. And then you came along and everything kinda just fell into place." The look of anguish on his face is tearing my heart apart, but I feel betrayed that he's never told me about this. We've talked about everything over the years, but never this.

"What do you mean, fell into place?"

"I don't know. The moment I looked into your eyes, everything felt different to me. I felt like I finally had a purpose. To take care of you. You changed my entire life, Kenzi, and you've continued to do so. Being around you always made me feel at peace. I don't know how else to explain it." He lays his hand on my leg as he struggles with trying to explain himself, his brow creasing. "But it's always been there. It's just gotten stronger as the years have gone by. Maybe I'm fucked up but I've kinda started to think of it as fate that brought us together, that it all happened for a reason and we ended up exactly where we're supposed to be."

Yes. That's exactly how it's always felt.

I smile in agreement. "I've always felt that way, too. Like you were mine. I just feel a little betrayed that you never told me you had had feelings for my mom. Why would you never tell me about that?"

"I just didn't think it was important. We were fifteen. All we ever did was talk," he repeats.

"Am I like some kind of replacement for her? In your mind?"

His face contorts as if I've slapped him. "Fuck no. How can you even say that to me? What the hell, Kenzi. Do you not know me at all?"

Tears form in my eyes and I'm not even sure why this has hit me so hard. I feel jealous and somewhat shocked. I reach for my jeans on the floor and pull them on, zipping them up.

"What about the hospital after her accident?" I ask. "You were there a lot. I saw you holding her hand all the time."

"Jesus, Kenzi. She was one of my best friends. We didn't know if she was going to live. Why are you acting like this? Are you jealous?"

"Yes. Okay? I do feel jealous and I don't understand why you never told me about this. I'm worried maybe you've had feelings for her this entire time or something."

"That's insane. I never told you because it happened a million years ago. Nothing ever happened. I never even kissed her."

"It's more the feelings you had for her that bother me. The song, the lyrics—"

He puts his hand up. "That's a *song*, Kenzi. With elaborations to make it better. Your father changed a lot of the lyrics. I haven't been pining for Ember for years if that's what you're thinking."

"I don't know what to think. First Sydni is on your bed kissing you, and now I find this out. It's a lot, to me. Like ghosts are all around us."

"This is what I mean. I'm an adult, Kenzi. I have a past, and yes, that past includes a few women. I'm sorry that you don't have a past with other people, but if you did, you'd understand what I'm talking about. That shit is over and done. You know damn well Sydni has crept back over the years, but I ended things with her permanently."

I pull my pink T-shirt over my head and reach for my shoes. I suddenly just want to be alone. I'm not used to feeling jealousy at all, and I hate that I am. I know in my heart that he would never lie to me, but I still can't make the jealous stabs to my heart stop.

"Now you're going to throw my age in my face?" I say, mostly to deflect my own feelings.

"No, I didn't mean it like that, and you know it. I'm just pointing out that you don't have any past relationships, and I do, and we can't change that. But it doesn't change my feelings for you." He pushes the sheets off the lower half of his body. "Why are you getting dressed? Are you leaving? We have another hour we could spend together."

My heart tugs to crawl back in bed with him, but I'm afraid I'll keep asking him questions to appease my sudden insecurities. "Yes," I reply reluctantly. "I just want to be alone for a little while."

His eyes search mine. "Why? We had a great day and you're going to let this wreck it? Something that happened when I was fifteen? That's stupid."

"Well, thanks, Tor."

He stands and comes around to where I'm sitting on the edge of the bed putting my shoes on. "Angel, I'm sorry. I don't know why you're so upset. You know I love you with every fiber of my being, and only want you. All that crap is in the past and it's silly for you to even think about it."

I turn to face him. "How did my mom feel about you over the years? Did you guys ever talk about feelings for each other?"

He pulls back as if my question has slapped him in the face. "Never. We were strictly friends. Nothing more. We talked a lot, but never about anything inappropriate."

I sigh and rub my forehead. "I'm sorry, Tor. I don't know why this has me so upset—honestly, I don't. I guess it was just unexpected, and finding out you wrote a song about it just sorta adds to it. Every time I hear that song now, I'm going to think about this."

"I can't change that. The song is special to me because it's one of the first I wrote—when I was just a kid—and it became a huge hit. That's the only reason. Why can't you look at it as a good thing? If I hadn't been with Ember that day, who knows if your parents would have hooked up and had you? Then we wouldn't be together now."

My shoulders drop. "It makes me feel weird thinking about you crushing on my mother. It feels twisted to me." I know I shouldn't be this upset, but I think it might be because of the last thing I heard my mother say, the morning of her accident. I overheard her and my dad in the kitchen, and she said, *"Tor understands, why can't you?"* And my father replied, *"Oh, here we go again with Tor."* I have no idea what they were talking about, but now it's got me wondering all sorts of things, like maybe she had feelings for him? Could that be possible? They weren't fighting, because my parents never fought. They talked everything out. But she was definitely upset about something that morning.

Tor puts his hands on my shoulders and forces me to look at him. "It's not twisted. It was a stupid little crush that never amounted to a damn thing other than me walking her to a park. Everything feels like major drama at that age. At the time, I was jealous and pissed at Asher, sure. But that's it. You are *not* any kind of replacement. I love *you*."

I blink back tears. I know his words are true. "I love you, too. I think I just want to be alone for the rest of the night to sort out my head. It's late anyway. You know I have to go home."

He runs his hand through his rumpled bed hair, his eyes darting from me to the bed like he can't understand how a little while ago we were making love, and now we are here.

"I can't believe this is our first fight and it's about something that happened when I was fifteen. Really, Kenzi?"

"It has nothing to do with age, Tor. It's that it was my mother."

He throws his arms up in exasperation and then rubs the back of his neck. "I can't believe this."

"I just don't understand why you've never told me. You tell me everything. You always have. Why wouldn't you tell me this? It's like you were hiding it."

He pins me with dark, serious eyes. "I wasn't hiding anything. I have no reason to."

Going to him, I wrap my arms gently around his waist. "I'm sorry, Tor. Just let me go home and cool off. We'll be fine in the morning, I promise. I just need to work it out in my head. I think it just surprised me."

His arms encircle me tightly, and I know it must be hurting his ribs for him to be hugging me so hard. "There was never anything between us, Angel. I've been totally honest with you, like I always have." He lifts my chin with his finger and kisses me softly. "I would never lie to you, especially about your mom. I couldn't disrespect her, or you, that way."

"I know," I whisper. "I'll call you in the morning."

Reluctantly, he loosens his hold on me. "Text me when you get home so I know you're okay."

"I will."

I'm acting like an idiot. This I know, but I still can't seem to stop myself. Is it jealousy? Or just worry about what my parents were talking about that last morning? Or maybe it's like it's always been—anything related to thinking about my mother tends to turn my head all around into a twisted mess because she's not here to talk to. There is no closure. No answers. Just questions. It's a bizarre feeling to have your parent here, but not. Maybe Aunt Katherine was right, and I should have been in therapy to deal with my confusion about my mother.

As I'm lost in my thoughts driving home in the dark, suddenly my Jeep starts to sputter, jerking me back into focusing on driving. A small light I've never seen before has suddenly lit up on my dashboard. Squinting at it, I realize it's the gas light.

Shit.

I pull over to the side of the dark, woodsy road and the car dies. It just stops, and won't start again.

This can't be happening.

Driving to the beach and back today must have sucked up a lot of gas, and I didn't notice when I was driving us home earlier that the light was on or that the gauge had gotten so low. My father has told me a hundred times to always make sure I have a full tank of gas, and somehow I still forgot.

Grabbing my phone from the passenger seat, my heart sinks when I see that I have no service out here on this mountain road that I need to take to get home. There are a few houses on this road, but they are all set way back off the road, and I'm not about to go traipsing down someone's dark driveway right to their house not knowing what kind of person could be living there. Realizing I'm going to have to walk until I reach the small town a few miles up the road to get reception, I dig the tiny flashlight out of the center console that my father had put there, and jump out of the car.

Okay, Kenzi. You know this road. There's a full moon, so it's not that dark. Just walk. And keep walking. And walk. Fast.

I'm doing okay as I chant this over and over in my head while I walk until a motorcycle roars up the road behind me and pulls to a stop a few feet ahead of me. A chill runs down my spine as I realize it's not Tor, as I fleetingly hoped. I know the sound of his engine, the shape of his body, and the man in front of me isn't him. And, besides all that, Tor's bike is still in the shop.

I freeze, rooted to the side of the dark road, contemplating running back the other way. I never should have left Tor's house in the middle of the night over a stupid fight. The rider turns sideways to me, a lit cigarette hanging from his lips, his long shaggy hair parted on the side and hiding half his scarred face. The night glasses are covering his eyes, but I know behind them are eyes the color of turquoise. Eyes that once belonged to the golden boy of this town. Captain of the football team. Star of the lacrosse team. Voted prom king and most likely to become a star. But not anymore. Tyler Grace is a psychotic enigma with a terrible, violent past. His gravelly voice breaks the night silence as we stare at each other.

"If you run, I'll chase you. And I *will* catch you. Get on the fucking bike." His voice is raspy, as if his throat is coated with sandpaper.

In the distance to my right, I can see a porch light on at a house through the woods, and I choose to bolt down their driveway rather than stand here on a dark road with someone that I have absolutely no idea if I can trust. The fact that he's Tor's brother doesn't change what he's done, what he could do, or that he's been completely unhinged for years.

As I run down the dark dirt driveway, I hear him coming up behind me, his feet pounding on the dirt behind me.

Oh my God. He really is chasing me.

He tackles me from behind and we go down, with him snaking one arm around the front of me and using his other arm to break our fall. We land on the dirt driveway with him lying on top of me. I gasp for air, both from fear and getting the wind knocked out of me, and I'm petrified when he covers my mouth with his hand.

"Don't scream. Just breathe," he says against my ear, and eases up some of his weight off my back. His growly voice makes my skin crawl.

Slowly, he moves his rough hand across to my cheek.

"Why did you run?"

"Please don't hurt me," I beg, gasping for breath as tears start streaming down my cheeks.

"Of course that's the first thing out of your mouth."

"Tyler...please."

His finger continues to stroke across my cheek and it sends shivers of terror down my spine. "I like when you beg."

"Just let me go." I push back against him and kick my legs up, trying to throw him off me but he's too big and muscular for me to even budge him.

"No. You might want to stop squirming, though, 'cuz I haven't had a woman under me in a long time."

"Please..." My heart pounds in fear but I try to reel myself in so I can attempt to get some control over the situation. I already know he's mentally damaged. But I also know that this is Tor's brother, and somewhere in him must be the happy-go-lucky, caring, talented person that we once knew.

"You know who I am, right, Ty?" I ask, trying to keep my voice calm.

"Yup. Little Kenzi Valentine all grown up." He rolls his hips against my ass and I suck in a shuddering breath, praying he doesn't touch me anymore and hoping he's just trying to scare me in some sick demented way.

"Tor's going to be mad if he finds out about this."

He lets out a maniacal laugh. "I'm not afraid of Tor."

"What do you want?"

"You leave gifts for me. Why?"

I gulp air. "I don't know...to be nice. I thought it would make you smile."

Another crazy hyena laugh erupts from him. "You think I need to smile?"

"Yes," I reply simply, because I believe it.

"You feel fuckin' sorry for me?"

I shake my head, my cheek pressing into the dirt. "No. I don't. I just think everyone deserves to have someone treat them nice."

"Even a monster like me?"

"Even you," I whisper.

"I didn't take that girl," he says, his voice softening just a little. "And I didn't hurt her."

"I know that." And I did know that. When Tyler was found with a local girl who had been kidnapped years ago, everyone in this small town assumed he was the one who had held her captive for all those years. He was found standing over the body of a man dressed in an oxford shirt, with dark slacks and loafers who appeared to be a nice, normal man, while the girl stood by and wept, not saying a word. And there was Tyler, with wild, long dirty-blond hair, tattoos covering most of his body, which were actually hiding scars from years before, wearing old dirty motorcycle boots, ripped-up jeans, and a faded T-shirt stretched over muscles that had just been used as a weapon to take the life of someone. But in fact, Ty was the hero who saved her. He killed her real captor with his bare hands after he attacked Ty for accidentally stumbling upon the kidnapped girl hidden in a hole deep in the woods. Sadly, the press had already had their field day with the story before they knew the facts, and Tyler was crucified, pushing him even further into seclusion.

Leaning down close to my face, he pushes my hair to the side and presses his lips against the spot just behind my ear and whispers in a seductive tone.

"It *does* make me smile."

When I say nothing, he lifts himself off my back and pulls me up so we're both sitting in the dirt driveway.

"You hurt?" he asks.

I brush my clothes off and shake my head. "No, I'm fine."

"You shouldn't have run. You shouldn't be out here in the fuckin' dark, either. You got any brains in that pretty head of yours?"

"My car died and my phone doesn't work. I didn't know what to do."

"Evil lurks in the dark, waiting for girls like you. Don't you watch the news? I could do anything I want to you right now."

I blink at him, frozen with fear.

"You should've stayed in your car."

"You're right." I peek over at him in the dark, grateful the moon is bright enough to throw off enough light for me to see him and attempt to gauge his actions. "I thought you didn't talk anymore."

He turns to face me and I catch a hint of his blue eyes under the moonlight and the jagged scars that run down the side of his face. "I don't."

"Then why are you talking to me?"

"I guess I'm feelin' fuckin' chatty."

He stands and tugs me up with him, pulling my arm so hard I'm afraid it will snap. "Now you're going to get on the back of my bike, and we're going to get a container of gas. You think you can hold it without falling the hell off?"

I nod. "Yeah."

"Or if you really want to put a smile on my face, you could come home with me for a few hours," he suggests, his eyes roving over me in a way that makes me feel extremely vulnerable.

"Ty...I'm in love with your brother."

He nods and makes a clicking noise with his tongue. "Good answer." He starts to walk back toward his bike. "Move your ass, sugar," he throws over his shoulder. "Consider this repayment for all the fuckin' smiles."

I finally get home at 1:00 a.m. and breathe a massive sigh of relief when I get into the sanctity and safety of my own bedroom. This has been the strangest night of my life. While I'm glad Tyler came along to help me get gas, the altercation with him was bizarre and frightening. I feel like I should tell Tor about it, even though Tyler asked me (*more like told me*) not to.

After changing out of my clothes and into yoga pants, I walk down the hallway to my father's room. I'm glad to see he's not home as I slip inside and go straight to my mother's night table, which I'm sure hasn't been touched since the accident.

Opening the wooden door at the front, I grab the journal on the top of the stack of about ten handmade journals my father made for my mom over the years that she religiously wrote in.

The leather journal has a lock and I'm pretty sure the key is around my dad's neck, so I take it over to her jewelry armoire and use an earring hook to pick the tiny lock. I'm hoping there will be some clues in here as to what they were talking about the morning of the accident, and if she had feelings for Tor that went beyond friendship. If she did, I have no idea how I'm going to deal with that, but it's definitely going to make me feel odd in a lot of ways.

"What are you doing?" His deep voice exploding into the silence makes me jump and I drop the journal. He crosses the room swiftly and picks it up before I have a chance to react. "You picked the lock? What the hell, Kenzi." He gently closes the journal and puts it back where it was in the night table, then turns to stare at me in disbelief.

"I just wanted to read some of it," I say.

"Those are private. I don't even read those. You don't think I want to? You don't think maybe it would help me feel closer to her in so many ways? But I can't, because it's wrong. These aren't our words to read, Kenzi. They're hers."

I stare up at my father, filled with guilt because I know what he's saying is true. "I don't know how you do it, Dad. How do you keep your sanity with all of this?"

"With lots of love and faith. That's how. What are you hoping to find in these journals, Kenzi? Talk to me if something is on your mind."

I shrug helplessly. "I don't know. Lots of things, I guess. I miss her, and I feel like I should have had more time to get to know her better. But if you really want to know, I was wondering about the conversation you two were having the morning of the accident."

His forehead creases. "What conversation?"

"Mom said that 'Tor understands and why can't you?' What did that mean?"

He sits on the bed with a distant look on his face, like he's trying to rewind back to that day. I sit next to him and wait.

"Mom wanted out of the band life," he finally says. "She wanted me out, too. She was tired of both of us traveling all the time, never having privacy or enough time with you, and she wanted to have another baby. I guess she and Tor had talked about it and he was supportive of it. And I get that. There's been a lot of times when I wanted out of the band, too, but it's hard to give up. It's been my entire life. All my blood, sweat, and tears. I love the rush of the audience, of writing and singing new songs. You and your mom have always been more important to me, but leaving the band...it's just such a hard thing to even think about. It would affect my brothers, and my cousins, too, since they're in the band. I have to think about everyone involved, ya know? It's not easy."

I nod, absorbing all that. "I understand, Dad."

"That morning we were talking about it again. Sometimes your mom would mention that Tor was always so understanding, and he is. That's just who he is and what we all love about him. But sometimes I got sick of hearing it. Nobody wants to hear that another guy understands his wife better than he does sometimes. That's all it was."

He grabs my mother's pillow and holds it against his chest. "I'm sorry I yelled at you about the journal. It's just private and I try to respect her personal things."

I feel ashamed of myself for prying into her journal. "I'm sorry I tried to read them. I've just been moody and confused lately."

"I can take you to see her, Kenzi. Maybe if you just sit and talk to her, you'll feel better. That's what I do. There's a good chance she can hear us; the doctor said so."

My heart does the lurch and freeze like it does every time we talk about my mother. I don't know if I can sit by her bed, hold her lifeless hand, and chatter on about my day while she lies in a bed, trapped in sleep. A few times I've tried but it doesn't feel like she's there, and it seems cruel to talk to her when she can't respond.

What if she can hear us, and she *wants* to respond and she feels trapped and scared? What if she is really petrified, wherever she may be mentally? Or is there just nothing there anymore? These are the things that drive me insane and make me sick with worry. All I know for sure is I miss her smile and her amazing eyes that once held so much life and happiness.

"I'll think about it," I finally say.

"Kenzi...what's going on with you? You've been acting so off lately. You were totally preoccupied with Sydni being at the hospital with Tor, and you've been distant and distracted for weeks. Even the trip to Katherine's was sudden. You never just do things like that; you always plan. You're not flighty."

I struggle for the right words. "I don't know. I guess just basic life confusion after graduation," I offer weakly.

He shakes his head and turns his body to face mine. "I'm so good at reading everyone else in this family. I can *feel* what's going on with all of them, like a deep intuition, if that makes any sense. It's always been there. But with you...it's so hard." He sighs and hugs the pillow tighter. "I know this will sound crazy, but since the accident, I dream about your mom, and she shows me things. Like things that are going on with people we love. Like the day Uncle Talon got married. I dreamed that your mom showed me his wife all alone, with no one to walk her down the aisle. That's why I walked her." His eyes close and he leans his chin on the pillow. "I sound like a head case."

My heart melts for him. "No, Dad. You really don't," I reply softly. "You sound like someone who has an amazing connection with their wife and the people they love."

He studies my face some more. "Where were you tonight? It's late. Actually, you've been coming home late almost every night.

Chloe's in New York, so where are you every night? Who are you with? I feel like I have no idea what you do anymore or who you spend time with, and I don't like it. I don't want to lose you, Kenzi."

Swallowing hard, I refuse to lie right to his face. *I can't.* "I was at Tor's. Watching movies."

His stare deepens and his expression changes to one I've never seen before. He reaches into his back pocket and pulls out his phone.

"That's funny. I sent a text to Tor earlier asking if he wanted to grab a drink and he wrote back that he was spending the night with a chick. Did his plans change?"

My heart goes into ballistic overdrive. "Oh. Maybe. I'm not sure." I stand up and my legs wobble with shaky nervousness. "I'm going to go to bed. It's late."

"Is something going on?" he asks with a touch of suspicion in his voice.

"No, Daddy. I'm just tired."

He follows me down the hall to my bedroom and my panic escalates with each step. His radar is tuned directly at me and that is definitely not a good sign.

"Why are you hovering?" I ask him. "I just want to go to sleep." My phone beeps from where it's lying on my bed, and his eyes immediately go to it. I reach for it but he grabs it from my hand.

My heart stops. "Dad—"

His jaw clenches and his eyes go wide as he stares at the screen.

"What. The. Fuck," he says with agonizing slowness, his gaze shifting to mine. "Is something going on with you and *Tor?*" he asks in disbelief.

I snatch the phone away from him and quickly read the screen.

Tor

> I love you, Angel. I can't stand the way you left tonight.
> Please call me. Anytime tonight, I don't care. I just want
> to hear your voice. xo

My mind races for words. "Dad...he always says he loves me."
I try to brush it off casually and roll my eyes for added effort but
his expression takes on a fiery anger that tells me he's not going
to let this go.

"No," he says, shaking his head. "This is different. What the
hell is going on? Why is he texting you at almost two in the morning, asking you to call him so he can hear your voice?"

"We had an argument."

"About what?"

I stare at him, frozen, unable to think fast enough. I'm not a
liar. I don't know how to do this. I don't *want* to do this. My lips
quiver and tears brim in my eyes as I watch the truth settle in his,
making him take a deep breath. His hand goes to the center of
his chest, as if he's in immense pain, and his eyes shut for a long
moment before opening again, revealing tears.

"Dad...," I whisper. "I'm so sorry."

He doesn't move. He just stands there, taking deep breaths,
clutching at his chest. Fear grips me like a vise at the thought of
him having a heart attack from the shock and stress of what he's
just pieced together.

I gently touch his arm. "Dad...are you okay?" I ask softly.

"No. I'm not okay," he replies, rubbing his chest. "Did he *touch*
you?"

I shake my head. "It's not like that."

"What does that mean?"

I don't know what to say, or how to say it. How do I explain to my dad what Tor and I have? I was never supposed to go through this alone. Tor and I were going to tell him together and try to explain what happened in a way that he would understand.

I just have no idea how we thought we were going to do that.

"Kenzi?" he urges. "Answer me. What the hell does that mean?"

"We love each other." My voice shakes with a myriad of emotions. It seemed like the best, most honest answer. I thought it would cover everything that needed to be said.

"*What?*" The word rips out of him in a tormented roar that shakes the walls.

Wincing, I say, "Daddy...let me call Tor and have him come over so we can all talk together." Hopefully my dad will agree, and Tor will be able to calm him down, and then everything will be okay. Maybe even better than okay.

"I'll kill that motherfucker," my father seethes. "This is why you were so upset about Sydni at the hospital. Isn't it?"

I cringe away from him, wishing I hadn't had such a meltdown that day in the hospital. This is all my fault. I should have been more careful.

"Isn't it?" he bellows.

"Yes," I answer. "Please stop yelling. *Please.*"

A crazy grin crosses his lips, so foreign compared to his normal handsome, charming smile. "Stop yelling? You want me to stop yelling?" he asks, his voice only rising with each word.

"Yes. Please let me explain."

He steps closer to me. "Did he touch you?" The words come out of him like he's choking on them.

"Please don't do this, Dad. Please calm down and just let me try to explain."

"*Did he touch you?*" he demands again, so loud it makes me want to cover my ears.

"Yes!" I cry. "It's not like you're thinking! He loves me. I don't know how it happened, but it did. We fell in love. It's not bad, Dad. Please listen," I beg as he starts to rove around my bedroom, like he expects some clues are going to pop up from the corners. "He makes me happy. He's never hurt me or pushed me, ever."

"Did he fuck you?"

"Daddy!" Tears burst from my eyes at the vileness in his tone. He's never spoken to me this way. "Stop it."

"Did he?"

I shake my head and wipe at my eyes. "You're being horrible! Stop asking me things and let me explain, *please*. We love each other. We care about each other. He's my best friend. You know that. He would never, ever hurt me."

"You're too young to know what love is, Kenzi. He took advantage of you because I fucked up and left you alone too much thinking I could trust him, and now I'm going to rip his fuckin' heart out and shove it down his throat."

Never have I heard my father speak so venomously or with such hatred. He's a peacemaker. A lover. Always helping people work out their problems. Always caring and understanding.

Never like this.

And it's all my fault. I did this.

"I'm not too young. You and Mom were younger than me when you fell in love and look how long you lasted. So don't you dare say that to me. I'm not a little girl, and I'm not stupid. I know exactly what and who I want."

He grimaces and rubs the center of his chest again. "I'm going to be sick. He's got your head all fuckin' twisted up."

"No, he doesn't. I love him. You know he's a good man, Dad. Calm down and think, please. He's your best friend. You know what kind of man he is. He would never hurt me, and this has been tearing him apart. He didn't want it to happen. You have to believe me."

"Then it never should have fuckin' happened!" he shouts. "He's an adult. He knows better. He should have some fuckin' self-control." He glares at the standing framed photo of Tor and me on my dresser, taken when we were younger, and slams it down onto its glass face. "I trusted him with you, Kenzi," he says, coming back to stand in front of me, his eyes wild and his jaw clenched. "I trusted him with my baby girl and *this* is what he does?"

"He never wanted to hurt you."

"Hurt me?" he spits out. "He's fucking *destroyed* me, Kenzi. And so have you."

I swallow back more tears as my heart cracks. "Please don't say that, Daddy. I love you. Tor loves you. We never meant for this to happen."

"When?" he asks, snapping his head to look at me. "When did this happen?"

It's always been happening. I take a deep breath and try to think back.

"A few months ago. A few weeks before I graduated, I think." My God, it seems like so long ago when it all started.

"He touched you when you were under eighteen?" he asks, his voice oddly leveled.

"He kissed me but that was it. Nothing else happened until I was eighteen. The age of consent is sixteen. He didn't do anything wrong. We waited until I was eighteen." I know none of what I'm saying changes anything at all. It will always be wrong to everyone around us.

His eyes close and his head hangs down. "I'm going to fucking kill him."

"Please stop saying that. *Please.*"

"He betrayed me, Kenzi. You don't screw with your best friend's daughter who's a teenager and has been through the trauma of losing her mother when you're supposed to be looking after her. It's wrong no matter how you want to slice and dice it in your own head."

I suck in a deep breath. "He's the one who was there for me the most, Dad. Everyone else was all wrapped up in their own grief or life. Including you," I remind him. "Tor was with me *all the time*. He's been taking care of me forever, so don't stand there and act like he's some kind of pig because you know damn well he's not. You turned him into a live-in nanny for God's sake! He took care of all of us when we needed him." My voice rises with each word and my body starts to tremble with a mix of anger, fear, and devastation. I take another deep breath and lower my voice before I continue. "Maybe you need to remember all that." I swipe the tears from my face as I attempt to defend the man who somehow became the glue in my life.

He slams his fist down on the top of my dresser. "That's right, Kenzi. He was supposed to be taking care of you, not turning you into his own little fuck toy behind my back."

Before I can stop myself, I've slapped him hard across the face. He touches his cheek and looks at me like he has no idea who I am.

That makes two of us. I don't know who I am right now, either.

"I'm sorry," I whisper shakily. "But I am *not* a fuck toy. I know you're mad and upset, but I won't let you disrespect me. Or him. Or what we have."

As my words sink in, he nods slowly and softly says, "I just love you so much, Kenzi. This is killing me."

"I know that, and I'm sorry. But that's no excuse for you to say nasty things."

He sits on my bed and puts his head in his hands. His body shakes with silent sobs. My heart slowly dies watching him in emotional agony, knowing this is my fault.

"You're right." He lifts his head. "I didn't mean what I said, sweetheart. My mind is just completely wacked right now."

Seeing him so gutted is terrible. I just want this all to stop before it gets worse. "I think we should just go to bed and talk about this in the morning, Dad. When we're calmer."

"I can't do that. He's going to tell me to my face what he's done. Tonight."

My breath catches. "You're going over there? Now?" I ask, worry washing over me in a tidal wave.

"Yes. He and I are going to have a nice long talk," he answers sarcastically.

I hang on to his arm and try to stop him from heading toward the door. "Dad, please. He's still recovering from the accident. Please don't touch him," I beg, sobbing uncontrollably. "If you hurt him, I'll never forgive you. I swear to you, I won't." I plead with my eyes and cling to the sleeve of his shirt.

"Kenzi, this is between me and him. Don't call him, don't text him, and don't show up over there, either. You need to let me deal with this."

"It's the middle of the night. Please leave him alone and just go tomorrow when you've calmed down. We'll go together," I offer, trying to sound hopeful. "That's how we had planned to tell you. We just wanted to wait until after your tour."

He wrenches his arm out of my grip. "This isn't going to wait. I need to talk to him alone. Go to bed. We'll talk more about your part in this in the morning. And don't plan on ever seeing him again."

I open my mouth to protest but he cuts me off. "I'm still your father, Kenzi, and I'd like you to listen to me." Sadness fills his voice and infiltrates the air between us. "We've never fought before this, Kenzi. Ever."

"I know," I answer tearfully. "I hate it. I can't stand seeing you this way, so angry and upset."

"Then do as I ask, please, and let me handle this with him. I want you to go wash your face and lie down. We'll talk in the morning."

I sit on my bed and cross my arms, hugging myself. "I'll never stop seeing him, Dad. I love him and need him too much. Just like how you feel about Mom. I'll never let him go," I say as he heads for my bedroom door again.

He halts with his hand on the doorknob and turns slightly toward me. "We'll see about that."

I fall apart the moment he leaves, crying into my comforter like a child having a tantrum, but I just can't stop. Feeling helpless and terrified, I'm consumed with the guilt of the damage I've created between two best friends that will probably never be able to be repaired. I've never seen my father so angry before and I'm afraid of what he'll do to Tor. We never should have let this go on without telling my father, and now I blame myself for wanting to wait. Everything just spiraled out of control. I don't know how we can possibly ever make this right again.

CHAPTER 33

Tor—age seven

Asher—age seven

"Mrs. Johnson thinks we're brothers. 'Cuz we look alike." He's followed me over to the rock I'm sitting on at the corner of the fenced-in school-yard. I always sit here alone during recess and either draw or write in my sketchbook.

I nod at him. We both have hair the same color and length, touching our shoulders. Unlike the other boys in class with their short, spiked hair. I refuse to let my mom cut my hair because I want to tie it back like my dad does when he rides. I've never talked to this kid Asher before, but I know about him. His parents are famous. His father is a musician, and I love music. I know all his songs and I play them on my old guitar. Asher is lucky.

"You don't talk much, do ya?" he says, sitting next to me.

"Not really."

"So we're gonna be friends. I like how quiet you are."

"And what if someday I'm not quiet?"

"We'll still be friends. Best friends are forever."

💛 💜 💜

TOR

"Finally," I say into the phone. "I've been a wreck waiting for you to call."

"Tor...," she gasps. "My dad is on his way there. He knows about us."

I bolt up in bed, instantly wide awake. "What? What happened?"

"It's my fault, I'm so sorry," she cries. "I tried to read my mom's journal and he caught me. I was acting weird and he could tell something was wrong. You know how he is...Then he took my phone and he saw your text."

"Oh, shit." I climb out of bed and pull my sweatpants on, cradling the phone against my shoulder.

Her breathing is erratic and she's sniffling and coughing as she tries to talk. It's making me want to crawl through the phone just to hold her. "He went insane, Tor. It was awful. I've never seen him like this. I'm scared..."

"Angel, calm down, baby, okay? Please don't cry. I'll take care of it."

"I'm afraid he's going to hurt you."

"He's not going to hurt me," I reply, even though I'm sure he will. And I deserve it if he does. I stepped over a huge line of trust between us, and I know him well enough to know that this is not something we're going to talk out. This isn't a disagreement about how a song should end or whose bike is fastest or what beer is the best. This is about his best friend putting his hands all over his little girl. That's all he's seeing and hearing right now, and I'll take the punishment for it because I know I would feel the same way if the situation were reversed.

"Tor, please don't fight with him," she begs. "I know you could hurt him but please don't."

"Don't worry, Kenzi. We'll figure this all out. Everything will be okay." Car headlights shine across my windows. "He's here, so I'm going to go talk to him. I want you to just calm down, okay? I love you."

"I love you, too."

I don't wait for Asher to knock. I just go to the front door and open it, and his fist immediately crashes into my face. I stumble back as blood spurts from my nose and splatters across the wall. He slams the door shut behind him.

Steadying myself, we stand eye-to-eye, glaring at each other. We are equal in height and build. Equal in strength. Our love and protectiveness for Kenzi just as equal. I know neither one of us will back down.

"You motherfuckin' pig," he growls. "You touched my daughter? You're her *uncle*."

"Ash—"

He punches my face again, and as I shake it off, he sucker punches me in the ribs, and I feel a harrowing snap.

"I trusted you," he states, looking me in the eye, forcing me to see the pain, betrayal, and devastation seeping from his soul. Making me feel it with him. "How the fuck could you do this to me?" He shoves me hard in the chest and I stumble backward again.

"You gotta know I fought this. I fought it with every part of myself. I tried to put distance between us, to try to forget the feelings I had for her, and change the feelings she had for me—all of it. But everything just kept coming back stronger. I just couldn't fight it anymore," I admit. "I love her more than anything. I think I always have, as fucked up as I know that sounds. We have a connection. She makes me happier than I've ever been, and I know she feels the same way about me."

He shakes his head as if he almost pities me for believing my own words. "She's only eighteen, Toren. She has no idea what she feels."

"That's not true."

"Whatever the hell you think is going on, it ends today." He shoves his finger into my chest. "I've given you everything, Tor. I've saved your ass a thousand times. You can't have my daughter."

My jaw clenches. "I'm not letting her go. With or without your blessing, I'm spending my life with her."

His head tilts up to stare at the ceiling before he looks back at me. "Listen to yourself. What the *fuck* is wrong with you? She thought of you as her *uncle*. You babysat her for years! How sick are you?" He shoves me again, hard, and my ribs scream in pain.

"You're right. It did make me feel sick."

"So you just kept doing it? What the fuck, Tor? I can't wrap my head around this." He grips his head with his hands, glaring at me. "Who *are* you?"

I shake my head as blood drips from my face onto my carpet. "I don't know. I couldn't stop. I know it was wrong, Ash. And I'm so fucking sorry. You have no idea how much this has been killing me inside."

"Killing *you*?" he bellows. "No. This is killing *me*. When did you start touching my little girl, you sick fuck?"

The accusation I've dreaded hearing has finally been spoken, and it sounds worse than I ever could have imagined.

"I never touched her. I swear. This only happened a few months ago. I never once thought of her other than as my niece and a friend before that. I swear. I have never touched her or thought about her inappropriately. I could never do that."

"You're fucking sick," he states, hatred heavy in his voice as he points at me. "You were my best friend. I was supposed to be able to trust you." He punches me again. This time, I fall backward onto the floor and he takes the opportunity to kick me hard in the ribs with his steel-toed boots.

Clutching my side in blinding pain, I stare up at him. "You *can* trust me. I love her, Ash. I'd never hurt her."

"Shut the fuck up!" His boot rams into the other side of my rib cage, and I see stars from the pain.

I try to sit up, and pain sears through me. "You practically handed her to me, Asher. You can hate me all you fuckin' want but don't act like I'm some kind of predator. I've cared about her since the day you put her into my arms and then left me to take care of her while you and Ember ran around with the band."

"Mother-fuck-you, Tor. This is about Ember, isn't it? You wanted her and you've hated me ever since I got her. You think I didn't know that? Do you think you can just take my daughter as some kind of consolation prize?"

I slowly stand up, my vision blurry. "This has nothing to do with Ember. That was kid stuff."

"That's bullshit. You're pissed because I got Ember and I got to keep the band while you lost everything. So now what? Screwing my kid is payback?"

I scoff at him. "*You* lost everything, Asher. Not me. Your wife's in a coma because you let her fall off a fucking cliff." I lean in close to his face, and then glance down at his wrist, where beneath the ink and the leather bracelets are deep scars from where her fingernails dug in and ripped out his flesh as she clung to him before she fell. "I *never* would have let her fall. And now you've lost your daughter *and* your best friend. Congratulations."

His eyes go dark with contempt. I just delivered the lowest blow, but I'm beyond caring. "Don't talk to me about Ember," he says. "I want you to stay the fuck away from my daughter."

I shake my head, refusing to back down. "That'll never happen. I'll never let her go, Ash. I love you like a brother, man, and I want to fix this shit with us. But I'll never give her up. I love her too much."

"Fix this?" he repeats. "Fix this? You think you can fix the fact that you betrayed me? Lied to me? Put your hands on my little girl? I have no idea who you even are. She's a kid, Tor."

"She's not. Open your fucking eyes, Ash. She's just like you. She knows exactly what she wants. She always has. She's not some giddy, stupid-ass teen."

He's not hearing any of it. "No. You've messed with her head. Why, Tor? Sydni wasn't good enough? Or Lisa? Or any other girl in this town? You had to seduce an innocent girl who looked up to you, adored you, and trusted you? How the hell do you even sleep at night? You're a fucking psycho just like your sicko of a brother. At least he has the decency to hide."

His words snap my brain and I can't control myself anymore as I ram my fist into the side of his face. "Don't talk about my family, Ash. I'll fuckin' bury you." I grab his throat and push him up against the wall, effortlessly lifting him off his feet and choking him. "I love you, man. I let you get your punches in, but I'll choke the shit out of you right now if you push me."

His hands close around mine and I watch his eyes start to bulge and redden before I let him go. He staggers away, gasping and glaring at me with even more repulsion.

"I love her," I say. "She loves me. I'm going to marry her someday when she's ready. I know you're pissed. I would be, too. And I'm really fuckin' sorry. But maybe try to think about the fact that *you* picked me to care for her and love her, and I did just that. Our feelings grew with us and nothing and no one can change that. Not even you. I will never, ever hurt her." I take a deep breath, pain tearing through my chest and ribs, and I soften my tone, hoping he'll hear my words and believe them. I need him to accept us or it's going to break Kenzi's heart. And mine. "I know you can't see it now, man. But your daughter has someone in her life who loves her and cares about her just as much as you do. I'll never cheat on her or treat her bad. I'll support anything and every-thing she wants to do. She's safe with me. *Always*. Maybe someday you'll be glad your best friend has someone to love him, too."

His expression stays hard. "You're out of your fucking mind. I'll never forgive you for this. After everything I've done for you, you stabbed me right in the back and in my heart." He spits a mouthful of blood onto my carpet. "You're fucking dead to me, Tor. I don't ever want to see your lying, deceitful face again. And you can bet your ass I'm going to do whatever I can in my power to keep Kenzi away from you and try to undo the damage you've done to her head. Do yourself a favor; stay the fuck away from her. Let her be a kid and grow up and date and have fun."

"She doesn't want that."

"*You* don't want that. Don't be a selfish prick. Let her grow up and make adult choices."

"Like you did with Ember?" I throw back. "She was fourteen when she got pregnant. You going to stand there and tell me either one of you ever regretted being together and having Kenzi?"

"No, we didn't. But we were both kids and we were dumb and in love. You're a fucking adult. You've had your chance to have fun and sleep with all sorts of women and make mistakes and fig-ure out what and who you want in life. Kenzi's lived in a bubble. I don't want her strapped down to you."

"Like I'm so fucking bad?"

"Well, you couldn't keep Sydni happy, could ya?" he reminds me with a smirk.

I don't even let that comment bother me. "Sydni thinks she's a bag of potato chips that needs to be passed around. That's got nothing to do with me, man. Kenzi is in an entirely different league than Sydni."

His nostrils flare in anger as he moves toward my front door.

"Stay away from my kid. If you really do love her? Let her go and give her a chance to grow up."

I open the door and shove him hard through it. "Get the hell out of my house."

He takes two steps out and then turns to me with an evil grin. "Oh, you just reminded me I hold the mortgage to this house. That makes it *my* house. You've got two weeks to pay what's owed or get your ass out of it." He waves at me as he walks toward his car. "Good luck, douchebag."

Fuck.

I punch the wall and fall to the floor in emotional and physical agony.

I just lost my best friend. And now I'm going to lose my home because I'm pretty sure I don't have seventy-five thousand dollars lying around.

Next will be Kenzi.

I can feel it deep in my gut. He's going to do whatever he can to keep her away from me, and he'll succeed, because Asher just has that kind of natural persuasive power over people.

As I lie in pain with the dog and the kitten on my lap, falling in and out of a sense of consciousness, I wonder if what he said is right.

Maybe I'm supposed to let her go.

CHAPTER 34

Kenzi—age one month

Tor—age fifteen

Ember—age fifteen

"There you are," Ember whispers, coming into the nursery.

She peeks into the baby's crib, and then looks me over, sitting in the rocking chair two feet away.

"Thank you for putting her to sleep. I'm sorry I got stuck on the phone with my sister."

"It's okay. She went right to sleep. No crying."

"She always does for you," she says with a smile. "You don't have to stay in here. You can go hang out with Ash. He's home now."

I stand and walk over to the crib. Leaning down, I gently rub my finger over the baby's tiny hand curled up into a tiny fist next to her face. "I like watching her sleep. She's so peaceful," I say.

That's true, but I don't tell Ember that I saw a show about SIDS and now I'm petrified of Kenzi never waking up. I lie awake at night worrying about it, and always end up watching her sleep if I'm hanging out at Asher's place.

"She is. I didn't know I could love her so much."

I didn't know I could, either.

♥ ♥ ♥

KENZI

Of course I don't go to bed like my father told me to. I sit in the dim living room with a small Tiffany lamp giving off the only light and stare at my parents' wedding picture hanging over the fireplace. I wait almost two hours, never expecting him to come home with a bloody nose and swollen eye.

"Oh my God," I gasp. "He hit you?"

"I hit him first," he answers, wiping at his face with a dish towel he must have taken from the kitchen on his way in here. Like it matters who hit who first. My heart is pounding with fear and anger that they would actually resort to hitting each other. Stupidly, I had hoped they would just talk like adults.

"Dad!" I burst into tears. "I don't want you guys to hurt each other. Why can't you just talk?"

He falls onto the couch next to me. "This goes beyond talking. I'm furious with him and I want to hurt him."

"I don't like you this way," I sob. "This isn't you at all. Mom would hate to see you this way. Both of you."

He puts his arm around me, pulling me until my cheek is resting on his chest. He gently rubs the back of my head.

"I know, Kenz," he answers softly. "I hate this, too. It's killing every part of me."

"How bad did you hurt him? Is he okay?" I ask, crying against his chest. I can't bear the thought of Tor being in any more pain. I want to get in my car right now and drive over to his house and never leave him again.

His chest heaves beneath me. "Don't worry about him. He's a big boy."

"I want to go see him. I have to make sure he's all right. He just got out of the hospital—" I try to sit up, but he holds me against him.

"No," he answers firmly.

"Please, Dad. Don't be like this."

His hand continues to slowly rub the back of my head. "I want you to stay away from him, Kenzi." His voice is low and gravelly from yelling and I pray it doesn't affect his upcoming tour. "It's for the best, trust me. I know you don't believe me, but you're too young to be in a serious relationship with an older man. Especially one who practically raised you. He's got your head all messed up."

"He doesn't. Not at all," I protest.

"I want you to grow up and find yourself, Kenzi. Have fun. Date guys your age. Find something you want to do. Come on tour with me if you want. Just give yourself time to live before you make such huge commitments. You'll thank me someday."

"Do you regret me and Mom?" I demand quietly, wondering if he regrets getting married and having a family so young. Maybe he was never as happy as he appeared to be. "Is that why you're being this way?"

His lips touch the top of my head before he replies. "I don't regret one moment. You and Mom are everything to me."

"Then why can't you believe that me and Tor can have the same?"

His heartbeat hammers against my cheek. "Because it's wrong. He's too old for you. You called him your uncle for almost your entire life. He babysat you. It's perverted, Kenzi. I feel sick just thinking about it." He pauses and his hand stills on the back of my head. "Did he ever touch you when you were younger? Make you do things? Maybe play odd games?"

I lift my head up and stare at him, horrified at the mere idea of any of that. "Never. How can you even think that? He's your best friend, Dad. I know he took care of me but our relationship changed. We became more like friends as I got older. And then that slowly turned into more. It happened over the course of eighteen years. It grew and changed and evolved. None of those feelings were there when I was five, or ten, or fifteen. I know deep down you know that. You or Mom would have known. And I would tell you if I had any memories at all that were creepy. There aren't any. Not one. You have to believe that."

"I'm trying to."

"He was terrified when things started to change. He pushed me away, he yelled at me. He made me go to Aunt Katherine's to put space between us. You have no idea how much he fought it, Dad," I say. "And honestly? I pulled him. I *wanted* to be in a relationship with him and I knew he felt the same way. I kept pulling him out of his denial. So be mad at *me*."

Shaking his head, he swipes his other hand across his face with the towel he's holding. "I can't be mad at you. But I'm disappointed that you would lie to me and do things behind my back. I thought we were close enough where you could tell me anything."

My stomach burns with emotion. He's right, I could always tell him and my mom anything and everything. "We are. But I knew you would never understand this and I was right."

"You knew I wouldn't understand it because it's wrong."

"No," I say firmly. "I knew you wouldn't understand because it doesn't fit into what *you* think is right."

He's silent, staring off across the room as he idly rubs circles on my back.

"Dad...I love you, but you have to let me make my own choices. I'm an adult, whether you like it or not."

"I totally understand that. But there is no way in hell I can look at you with him, or be in the same room with him knowing he's had his hands on you. I'll go crazy." He pauses for a moment. "I can't lose you, too, Kenzi. I can't have Mom being the way she is, and you out there living your life and not being a part of mine."

"Then just accept us. Don't make me choose. At least *try*," I beg.

"I can't," he replies with tortured regret thick in his voice.

Despair floods through me, seeping into every crevice of my heart and soul. I'm trapped and torn between the two men I love most in the world. I can't imagine hurting either one of them or walking away from either one of them. Choosing one would only hurt the other, and that would devastate me for the rest of my life.

I love them both. I need them both. I want them both in my life.

After I convince my dad to shower and go to bed, I quietly go back to my room and send Tor a text, my fingers shaking over the tiny keyboard.

> Are you okay? I've been so worried.

Tor

I'm only worried about the pain this is causing you.

> Did he hurt you? He said he hit you and I know you hit him.

Tor

I didn't want to hit him but he said some really nasty things and I snapped. I'm sorry. Is he ok?

> He's fine. He just fell asleep. Please tell me if you're ok.

Tor

> He fucked up my ribs pretty bad. I'm pretty sure he rebroke a
> few. He may have broken my nose, too. Tris is coming over in
> about an hour to take me to the ER.

I burst into uncontrollable tears as more anger and sorrow over
this situation swell up in me.

> I can't believe he hurt you like that.
> I'm so sorry, Tor. This is my fault.

Tor

> It's not, Angel. I should have talked to him when this first
> started. Or just never let this happen at all. I knew all along
> there wouldn't be a happy ending.

My heart clenches like a fist has grabbed hold of it, and my
stomach sinks at his words. If he retreats back into the mindset
that we shouldn't be together, my heart will shatter into a million
pieces.

> What are you saying? Are you giving up on us?

Tor

> I'll never give up on us. I just don't know what to do. I can't come
> between you and your father. That will eat me alive and you'll
> eventually resent me.

> I could never resent you. I love you.

Tor

> I love you, too. I just need to think. And so do you.

> That's all I've been doing. I want to see you.

Tor

> I want to see you too but let's wait until later today. Let me
> get cleaned up and clear my head. There's something else
> I have to tell you.

Okay...

Tor

> Asher loaned me the money for this house. It was a cheap
> fixer-upper when I bought it. He wants all the money owed
> or he wants me out in two weeks. I'm going to have to move.

What?! He's taking your house away? I can't
believe he would do that. I'll talk to him.

My God. How could my father turn so cruel? Can he really
hate Tor just like that? After being best friends their entire lives?
I can't even fathom that.

Tor

> Please don't. I'd rather not be owing him anything anymore.

I'm devastated about this. I'm so disappointed in him.

Tor

> Don't be. He loves you. Trust me, I expected all this and worse.
> I have to go shower and change before Tris gets here. I'll call
> you as soon as I get home. Please don't worry, Angel. I love you.
> We'll figure something out.

I crumble again after our texting. I finally give in and call
Chloe, spilling out the entire story in between hysterical crying
spurts. She listens patiently while I ramble in mostly jumbled and
incoherent sentences.

"Wow," she says when I'm done. "I wish you had talked to me sooner, Kenzi, rather than going through this alone. What do you think friends are for?"

"I'm sorry...I was afraid to tell anyone."

"I understand now. I probably would have done the same. But damn, you slept with the walking orgasm? I need to just let my imagination run with that for a few minutes."

I let out a little laugh, which I know is the response she was aiming for. "Still focusing on sex?" I try to tease back.

"Sadly, yes. Is he as good as I imagine he must be? I mean that body...that voice...that hair...those eyes. All that ink..."

"Chloe. Stop."

"Come on, give me something here and then we can get off the subject of his hotness."

Sighing, I can't keep the grin off my face as memories of making love with him cycle through my mind. "Fine. He's amazing, Chloe. Not that I have anything to compare him to other than books and movies, but yeah. He's incredibly romantic and sensual, and he pretty much turns me to mush in every way possible. Happy now?"

"Damn. I hate you right now."

"Thanks?"

"I mean that in the most loving way possible. I'm very jealous. But also happy for you. You deserve someone like him. And seriously, Kenz, I saw this coming for miles. You two have been attached at the hip for your entire life. His eyes literally dazzle when he looks at you and you look like you're going to melt when you look at him. It was clearly obvious."

"Really? It was that noticeable?"

"I definitely caught the vibe."

I wonder how many other people could tell something was

going on between us? How did my parents not notice if everyone else did? Or could they just not even fathom that anything could be growing between us?

"I'm so confused, Chloe. I don't know what to do. My dad is so pissed and heartbroken over this. I've never seen him this angry. He beat the shit out of Tor. You know my father—he can't stand fighting or violence in any way."

"Yeah, but you're his little girl. That changes everything."

"I guess you're right. I had no idea that he loaned Tor the money for his house."

"It sounds like over the years your dad really did everything he could for Toren. Paying for his lawyers, helping his business, making sure he got all the royalties he's owed, helping him get a house. Him finding out that Tor was sexually involved with his daughter must seem like a massive betrayal for him. How could it not?"

"But it's not just sexual, Chloe. We love each other and want to spend our lives together. It's not a fling. This is real."

"I understand that, but men don't really think that way. I think all your dad is seeing is his best friend, who's his age, crawling all over his daughter. It's a typical father reaction, I think."

I sink down onto the floor and rub my pulsing forehead. I've had a massive headache since this all started last night and it's not letting up.

"I don't know what to do, Chloe. I'm so confused and heartbroken."

"Do you want my honest advice? I don't know if it's the right advice, but it's my best advice based on how well I know you and your situation and how you grew up."

I brace myself. "Okay. Let's hear it."

"I think you need to get away from both of them for a while."

Her words make my heart lurch. "Chloe..."

"Just listen. You've spent your entire life encapsulated in this little world with your parents, and the band, and Tor. I think your family is great; I love your dad and I think Tor is a rare gem, but I think you need to cut the cord from both of them for a while and just be *you*. You and your father are way too attached to each other. He has to learn how to let you go, and you have to stop trying to take care of him."

I let her words filter in and take hold. Deep down, I know what she's saying is true. I just don't know *how* to let go. And I don't think my dad and Tor do, either. We're all mangled up in each other.

"I don't know..."

"Kenzi, you have to do some soul searching and stand on your own for a while without your father on one side of you and Tor on the other. Your father needs to accept the fact that he created this monster he now hates. You can't shove two people together practically twenty-four seven and expect that nothing may grow from it. And I think in some ways, your dad is holding on to you because of what happened to your mother. You're not her," she says softly. "He needs to stand on his own, too, and so does Tor. I mean, seriously, the guy has spent almost his entire life with you. He took that role of guardian and freakin' ran with it. I'm not saying he's not really in love with you, because I think he is, but I think you guys all need some major separation to get your shit together. After you all do some thinking and settling down, *then* figure out where you want to go from there." She pauses, giving me time to absorb. "I know you won't come here to New York, so why don't you go to Katherine's for a few months? You love it there and she doesn't suffocate you."

"I'm afraid to leave them," I admit. "I'm afraid they'll kill each other. I'm afraid I'll lose them both. I'm afraid of missing them."

"I know you are. But I think you have to, for all of you. Give them time to work this out between them. Maybe they will, maybe they won't. Give Tor time to think, and give yourself some time to get out from under them and then follow your heart. I think in the end, it will be what's best for all of you."

"What you're saying all makes so much sense. I'm just scared. I don't want to hurt them. I'm afraid if I leave Tor, I might lose him forever."

"If that happens, Kenzi, then it just wasn't meant to be. But I honestly think the guy will wait a hundred years for you."

I lean back against my bed, mulling this all over in my mind. Everything Chloe said rings true. I haven't been able to think of any other solutions.

As frightening as it feels, it seems like Chloe's advice might be what needs to be done for all of us to find our way to the other side of this.

💜 💜 💜

I stand in the doorway for a few moments before I cross the room with slow, light steps, and lower myself into the blue vinyl chair next to the bed.

Taking her hand in mine, I'm comforted by how warm it is. I run my finger over her wedding band. Never taken off.

There is life here. There is hope here. There is so much love here.

"Mom...I'm so sorry I haven't been here."

Her eyes are closed. Her breathing is soft and even. Her blond hair cascades around her on the white pillow like a golden halo, and she looks as beautiful to me as she did the day this happened to her. She still looks so young and vibrant.

"I miss you so much. I'm eighteen now and so much has happened. I wish we could talk. I know you could help me and would have the right words to say. I'm in love with Toren, Mom. I know you would understand. I want what you wanted. I want to get married and have a baby and just have a nice, simple, happy life with Tor. He wants that, too. Daddy is so mad. He can't see that what we have is so special and so right. I don't want to lose either one of them, but they're tearing each other apart and I'm stuck in the middle."

I swallow hard.

"I'm going to go stay with Aunt Katherine for a while. I'm going to have to leave Dad alone, Mom, and I'm sorry. I've tried to take care of him for you. He misses you and loves you so much. He's still committed to you in every single way. But we need you. Especially Dad, he's so lost without you. You always had a way to calm us all down and make everything better. So if you're in there somewhere and you can hear me, try to come back. We're all here for you and we love you."

My heart jumps when her fingers move ever so slightly in mine.

She moved. Dad was right.

"Mom…" My voice wavers as a tear tracks down my cheek. "Can you hear me? If you can, just move your finger again. Please…"

I wait, unmoving, barely breathing until her ring finger moves a teeny bit, giving me goose bumps.

"I felt that," I say softly. "You have to try to wake up, Mom. I know it's hard and maybe it hurts. But we'll take care of you. No matter what. You're okay. You're still beautiful. Are you afraid that you're hurt? You're not. You're perfect. You just hit your head and you drowned for a few minutes. I don't really know what happened, but I know that you're okay other than you can't wake up. You're breathing by yourself." I can't help but wonder if maybe she thinks she's broken, or disfigured, or other horrible things like that. Maybe it's scaring her into staying suspended where she is. "You can understand me. I know you can. I think you're just tired and weak. That's all. But we can fix that." More tears stream down my cheeks.

"Are you okay, Miss Valentine?" An older, gray-haired nurse places her hand gently on my shoulder. "What a nice surprise to see you here today."

I blink back my tears and look up at her. "She moved her hand. I felt it. Then I asked her to do it again and she did."

She nods and smiles, the corners of her eyes creasing. "Yes, I'm sure she hears you, honey."

"Then she should wake up, right?"

The nurse shifts her eyes over to my mom, then back to me. "She will when her mind and body are ready."

"But what if that never happens?" I ask desperately.

She squeezes my shoulder. "You just have to have faith, Miss Valentine. It's all in God's hands. But I think your mother is very happy you came here today. Sometimes all we need is a little time to get things right in our heads. I hope you come back."

As she walks away, I turn back to my mom.

"I have faith in you, Mom. I love you. I'm going to try to fix this mess so we can all be happy. I promise I'll come back soon."

CHAPTER 35

Kenzi—age eighteen

Tor—age thirty-two

A tiny package came in the mail for me today, and I've been afraid to open it. Even though it has no return address, I recognize his handwriting on the address label. I put it off to the side to open when I'm alone.

Later that night as I'm sitting in bed at the Inn, I tear open the padded envelope, and inside is a small black velvet pouch. Taking a deep breath, I reach inside and pull out two tufts of fur, which I immediately recognize as Diogee fur and Kitten fur.

There's a tiny note inside:

"I know how much you must miss their fur, so here's a tiny bit for you. Be impressed—I vacuum every day. :) They miss you. I know you love my hair, too, but sending you that seemed creepy. Don't forget me, Angel. I'm still here. Always. I love you forever and longer."

💛 💜 💙

TOR

"Oh my God." She covers her mouth with her hand and starts to cry as soon as she sees me. "I can't believe he did this to you."

I pull her into my arms, ignoring the pain in my ribs and chest. All I care about right now is being close to her. "It's okay. I'm okay."

"It's not okay, Tor. This is awful. He broke your ribs." Her voice cracks as she holds on to me.

"They'll heal. I'm way more worried about what this is doing to you." I swipe my thumbs across her damp cheeks. "You're so beautiful, Angel. Please don't cry."

"I can't help it. I hate what's happening to all of us."

"I do, too." We cross the room to sit on the couch together. "He's too mad to talk to, Kenzi. Maybe in a few days I can try again to explain how I feel about you, and make him see that I never hurt you, or did anything perverted with you."

"I told him you didn't. It makes me sick that he could even think that about you."

"He just needs time."

She chews her bottom lip and grabs both of my hands in hers, squeezing them tightly as she peeks up at me from beneath her long bangs.

"Tor...I've been doing a lot of thinking. I even went to see my mother this morning."

I'm shocked, but in a good way. Kenzi hasn't seen her mother in over a year. "Wow. I would have gone with you, so you wouldn't have to go through that alone."

She shakes her head. "No. I *needed* to do it alone. That's kind of what I want to talk to you about."

I wouldn't be surprised if a black cloud just settled over my house, because I can feel it, like a dark shadow, stealing away all my light.

Stealing away her.

She swallows hard. "I think we all need some time apart. I need some time away from you and my father. And I think you need some time away from me and him, and him away from you and me."

I knew this was coming.

"Kenzi..." I want to get on my knees and beg. Or propose. Anything to make her stay, because I know she's leaving. I can't stop her, and I may never get her back.

Her hands squeeze mine even tighter like she's afraid to let go, and I don't want her to.

"I don't want to lose you, Tor," she says tearfully. "I love you so much and I still want everything we talked about. But I think we all need some time to really be apart and just *think*. I'm going to move in with Aunt Katherine for a while."

A lone tear slides down her pink cheek as her eyes search mine frantically, the same green eyes that have looked to me for help, love, and guidance for eighteen years. The same eyes I fell in love with and want to be looking into for the rest of my life.

She promised me forever.

She made me believe I could have it.

I'll never let her go ... but I have to set her free.

Please come back to me, I beg silently.

Please always love me the most.

I force myself to nod and agree. It's one of the hardest things I've ever had to do. "Maybe you're right." I cough into my hand and swallow back the pain shredding my heart. How am I supposed to live without her now that I've had a glimpse of what life with her could be like? How am I supposed to come home to just Diogee and Kitten at the door without her standing there waiting to throw her arms around me? "I want you to have time to think, and really know what, and who, you want. I'll be here." I grab the back of her neck and pull her to my lips for a long, slow kiss, then lean my forehead against hers and stare into her eyes. "I'll always be here."

She chokes on her tears. "I love you so much," she whispers. "I don't want to hurt you. Or him."

"You haven't. And you won't. We'll work through this. We've all got a strong bond, Kenzi. It'll pull us through. I know it will. We're all going to get our happy ending. But maybe you're right; we just need some space to get there." I don't need space to get anywhere. What I need is her in my life, planning our future, and for Asher to just accept the fact that we love each other and to stop driving a wedge between us.

"I hope so," she replies, clinging to me even tighter. "I love you both so much."

Don't let go, I beg. *Please don't let go.*

The sadness in her voice completely guts me, and I want to take it all away. I'm torn again, between the little girl I loved and the woman I'm in love with. I'd fix everything for the little girl if I could, like I always have. But I have to let the woman fix herself and stand by her side as she does.

Her hands slide up to my shoulders, squeezing them tightly and urgently as she kisses me softly on the lips, her emotions pouring into each kiss. Silently, she undresses me, then herself, before carefully climbing on top of me and making love to me, so slowly and full of passion that I feel like she's soldering our souls together.

It doesn't feel like goodbye.

It feels like a request.

It feels like a promise.

And that's what I'll hold on to until we're together again.

CHAPTER 36

Tor,

I miss you already. Give me a few days to settle and I will write more.

I promise.

Kiss the babies for me.

I love you the most,
Kenzi

💜 💜 💜

KENZI

Six months later

"How about a tiramisu tonight for dessert? The guests will love that. Last time you made it they couldn't get enough of it," Aunt Katherine asks cheerily over breakfast.

"That sounds great."

Tiramisu is my favorite. When I first moved in with Aunt Katherine, I enrolled in a local cooking class to keep myself busy. I've learned so much, especially that making desserts is my favorite. A few weeks ago, I started baking large round sugar cookies with a white icing and then writing short inspirational quotes in colored icing on top. At first, it was really hard to write calligraphy but then I found some food pens and thin food paintbrushes. After a while I got the hang of it, and now they look really pretty and professional. The guests love them so much that my aunt is now letting me box them up for the guests to purchase and take home with them.

My dad has driven here to visit a few times, and it's been nice. He's calmer. Not as worried. He's stopped looking at me like he's waiting for me to spontaneously combust. We walk the grounds and Aunt Katherine makes us tea and we have a lot of long talks. Some turn into debates of frustration, and others actually seem to lead us into what I like to think of as progress and hope for the future.

My grandmother calls me often. She knows the truth now. Being a romance author, she's much more accepting of Tor and me being together, and actually seems fascinated with our story. I wouldn't be surprised if she ends up writing a book inspired by us. She tells me to give my father time to calm down and get used to the idea of Tor and me as a couple. She seems to think he'll come around.

I'm not so sure, but I hold on to the glimmer of hope.

Months of not seeing Tor has been hard. Actually, *hard* is not even close to describing what it feels like. It's torturous and I cry myself to sleep almost every night as I sleep in one of his T-shirts because it smells like him. He's always the first person I want to talk to when something happens in my life, whether it's good or bad, or just silly. The little compass inside me always points to him, and that's something I needed to find out on my own.

We don't ever text or call, but we do write to each other. It's what we decided to do. I use my fancy fountain pens and parchment paper, while he sticks to mostly notebook paper and ballpoint pens, and we send them through the mail. It's romantic. It's helped build patience. It's helped us choose our words with care and truth, because writing in ink does that. There is no backspace. There are no abbreviations. We pour our hearts out to each other more than we ever have. We share our fears and dreams with each other on paper in even more depth than we did in person. There is a safety in writing, in putting the words out there and giving the recipient time to absorb, ponder, and reply.

He writes me poetry.

We fall deeper in love.

The space didn't create distance; it only brought us closer.

At the beginning of my third month at the Inn, a limo pulled up in front of the Inn, and a chauffeur came out carrying a small rabbit cage. Inside was an adorable little black and white Lionhead bunny with a mop of fur on its head and markings that make him look like he has a mustache. He came with a note taped to the side of his cage:

> *This little guy came into the shelter. Apparently, he was a gift for a five-year-old boy but they didn't realize how much work was involved. I knew he had to be yours. I've been calling him Wyatt.*
>
> *Love you, my Angel*
> *Tor*

I fell in love with Tor all over again for gifting me with another adorable bunny.

I knew from our letters that Tor wasn't dating. He made it clear he had no interest in doing so, and never would.

As for me, I had a few friendly conversations with the land-scaper, who was good-looking, nice, and very tan. He lacked the tattoos and shaggy hair that I now lusted for, though. I agreed to have lunch with him at Aunt Katherine's nonstop insisting, mostly to see what it would feel like to spend time with another guy. Would there be butterflies? Would I want to see him again?

Katherine urged me to find out.

Those answers were no. No butterflies came to visit.

I knew they wouldn't.

I tried again with a twentysomething guest named Adam who stayed for two weeks while he worked on a journalism article. Adam was tall, well built, very polite, and had a nice sense of humor. I liked him more than the landscaper dude, and Adam loved my calligraphy enough to ask me to write his name out for him on a piece of canvas. And my cookies. I think he ate about fifty of my cookies. He invited me to join him for dinner twice, and the conversation flowed freely and comfortably, but it stayed platonic.

"Do you want to go for a walk on the beach?" he asked me one night after dinner.

"Sure," I replied a bit nervously. It was dusk, and somehow being in the sun felt safer and less intimate than being anywhere near any degree of the darkness of nighttime.

As we walked, he held my hand, and it felt nice, but his hands were very soft. Almost too soft.

I felt nothing. No sparks. No butterflies.

At some point, he stopped walking and turned to me. "I really like you, Kenzi," he said quietly, and then leaned in to kiss me. At the last minute, I turned and his lips landed on my cheek.

I didn't mean to be rude, but I didn't want any other man kiss-ing me. I awkwardly apologized. But it was enough to disappoint him and make him check out the next day. I found the small canvas with his name written on it in the trash can in his room.

It all just solidified the fact that I didn't want anyone else. Ever. No matter how nice or cute or smart they were. None of it mattered.

My heart belonged to Tor.

While in Maine, I learned there are so many degrees of silence. It can be comforting. It can be deafening. It can be foreboding. It can be empty. It can be the space between two sounds.

Or between two people.

Tor and my father haven't spoken at all, and that worries me. I was hoping they would hash the situation out by now. Verbally and not physically. I want them to repair their friendship. I *need* my father to forgive Tor so we can all move forward with a new slate.

I don't want to think about where it's going to leave the three of us if he doesn't. Our lives are so intertwined. I can't see a future with us untangled from each other.

For my nineteenth birthday, a small box came, and I recognized the writing on the address label immediately.

I took it to my room to open it alone, and Aunt Katherine smiled knowingly as I left her after dinner to go spend time with this box. I haven't received a letter from Tor in a month, and with each day that passed, I grew more and more nervous that he had finally just given up or that my father had said or done something to push him further away.

I open the box slowly, and inside is an old bottle, with a rolled-up piece of paper inside. A small gasp of happiness escapes me, remembering our conversation that day on the beach about messages in a bottle.

Pulling the cork out, I tip the bottle over and the paper falls out, along with a single penny. The note is tied with thin red twine that I slide off, and I gently unroll the parchment paper.

Tears spring to my eyes when I see he has also written with a fountain pen.

Tor... you do everything so right.

Taking a breath, I read his words:

> *My love,*
> *Walk in the rain with me. Kiss me in the misty fog.*
> *Let me hold you all night under the hush of the wind.*
> *I'm waiting for you. Throwing pennies... making wishes.*
> *I'm wishing only for you. Always for you.*
> *Come back to me.*
> *I'll fight for you. I'll fight for us.*
> *Wish for me, too... and I'll make it come true.*
> *I love you forever and longer.*
>
> *~ Tor*
> *P.S. My huge bottle had $6,025 in it and this single penny. Make a wish. Or several. :-)*
> *P.P.S. I'm sorry it took me so long to write, I hurt my hand at the shop.*

The frayed parchment paper is soft in my fingers, perfectly worn and aged, and I'm very aware that he chose this texture of paper, this color of ink, with careful consideration. Because he knows how much it means to me. Because he knows *me*. Like no one else ever has or ever could.

I read his words over and over again, long after I have them memorized and they're burned into my heart and soul, yet I still hold the handwritten note and stare at the words until they blur. I can hear his voice saying them, deep, yet soft and sensual. *Raw.*

I like touching the paper that I know he held in his hands. The hands that had once held me, caressed me, ignited passion and desire in me so deep that I still can't forget. And I don't ever want to.

The faint scent of his cologne drifts from the paper. Or maybe I've just wished for it so much that I've imagined it. Either way, it's comforting and stirs memories.

So many memories…

As I read his words, all the feelings rush back like acid on a wound that won't heal. He's my other half—the one who makes my heart beat. The man who makes me feel every feeling that could possibly be felt—and then some. The man who held me and loved me through almost every moment of my life. I have no past without him and no future without him. Quite simply, he is my world. There is no way I will ever move on from a love like ours. We belong to each other. I've always known it, and I am utterly exhausted from fighting it, denying it, keeping myself from it, and hiding it—as I'm sure he must be, too.

I tried. I gave us space. But now it's time for me to go back home to my love and to my heart. Time is precious, and I don't want to give any more up.

I take the penny and walk down the beach to the edge of the water, and I toss it in.

I wished for Tor.

I wished for us.

I wished for my father to accept us.

I wished for everyone to accept us.

I wished for my mom.

I wished for happiness.

CHAPTER 37

We all let go.
We followed our hearts.
We loved unconditionally.
And we all ended up together again.

🖤 🖤 🖤

TOR

I'm sitting on a bench in my garage polishing some of the chrome on my bike when a motorcycle pulls down my street and into my driveway. I know the sound of that bike as well as I know my own, and I'm wondering what he's doing here.

Two weeks after Kenzi moved to Maine, I got a simple text message:

Asher
Keep the house. It's yours.

It was a small olive branch of sorts, but I took it. That was almost a year ago, and I haven't seen or heard from him since. Until now.

"Am I due to get my ribs broken again?" I ask, not looking up at him.

"Very funny." He tosses a book onto the floor next to me.

Glancing at him first, I put down my polishing rag and pick the book up, realizing it's a photo album. Actually, it's Ember's photo album. She's one of the few people who took real photos and put them in an album.

Or, she used to.

"What's this for?" I ask.

He saunters closer to me and leans against my workbench. "Something I've spent a lot of time lookin' at, bro. At first, it pissed me right the fuck off. Then I kept looking, and I couldn't deny what was right in front of me."

My eyes narrow. "And that is?"

He pushes his long wavy hair back off his face. "Take a look. Tell me what you see."

I have no idea what trip Asher is trying to take me on, but I lay the book on my legs and start to flip through the pages of photos, which start when Kenzi was born. At first, it's bittersweet to see the photos of Ember holding Kenzi, so beautiful, carefree, and happy, and I'm sure it was really hard for Asher to look at this and see all these pictures of Ember. There's photos of Kenzi's birthdays, Christmas, first day of school, playing, her first tooth, the bunny, their wedding, and family parties. My throat tightens seeing all the pictures because I miss Kenzi so damn much.

I continue to flip the pages, and I have to chuckle at how young we all look. But then I see what Asher saw, and it hits me like a brick wall. I'm in almost every single photo with Kenzi. I'm either holding her or sitting on the floor playing with her. In many she's asleep on my chest with her arms around my neck. In others, I'm holding her hand or she's leaning against me. There's a picture of us lying on the floor with Snuggles. There's me teaching her to tie her shoe. There's me pushing her on a swing. There's her handing me presents on Christmas. There's her sitting on my lap while I play guitar. There's one where she's crying and I'm kneeling in front of her, talking to her, wiping her cheek with my thumb.

We were *always* together. Almost always touching in some little innocent, but caring, way. Constantly drawn to each other without even realizing it. Even though I always felt it, actually seeing it captured in photos is something entirely different.

It's undeniable.

I close the book and hand it back to him, unsure of what to say. I swallow over the tightness in my throat. "None of that was intentional, Ash."

"You don't think I can see that? I hate it, but it's clear as day when I look at these pictures. You were right. You two had some kind of special bond right from the start, and as much as I want to throat punch you, I can't deny that whatever it is, it's real and I have no right to fuck with it. It's taken me months to get my head around it and try to accept it."

"What are you saying?" Hope starts to grow in my chest as I listen to him. Is he actually forgiving me?

"I'm saying I get it. I don't like it. It freaks me out something fierce. But I get it." He picks up a screwdriver off my bench and twirls it around in his hand. I hope he doesn't stab me with it. "I want my daughter back in my life, Tor, and I want my best friend back. That's still you, in case you're wondering. And the only way that's going to happen is if I get over this, and hard as that's going to be, we need to bury this fight. She won't come back if we hate each other."

I'm almost thrown speechless by his unexpected admission. "Are you saying you're okay with us being together?"

He crosses his arms and looks up at the ceiling, then back down at me. "I don't think I'm ever going to be exactly okay with it, but I'm willing to deal with it if it'll bring her back and fix this mess."

I stand and wipe my hands on my jeans, in a state of shock. "I'm not sure what to say. I want my best friend back, too. And I want the love of my life back. Living like this is torture."

Even though I know in my heart that Kenzi and I are still very much together, I want her physically in my life where she belongs. I've had enough space and I'm sure she has, too.

Sadness crosses his face and I regret how my words just accidentally came out.

"Yeah, I know what that feels like, man." He blows out a deep breath. "I'm calling Kenzi tonight to let her know we're good now, and it's time for her to come home. I'll stand by whatever decision she makes." He tilts his head. "Are we good?"

I nod. "We're always good, Ash."

One Month Later

I'm walking down the sidewalk toward Lukas's tattoo parlor, texting Tanner about a few new missing dogs that we're going to set some traps for and, *bam*, I crash right into someone, knocking her phone, keys, and purse out of her hands and onto the sidewalk.

"Shit," I mutter. "I'm sorry. Totally my bad, I wasn't paying attention," I say, kneeling down to help her pick up all the stuff she just dropped.

"Neither was I."

Hearing her voice again slices through me like a hot knife through butter, but that's nothing compared to the feeling that flashes through me when we both look up at the same time and our eyes meet. It's like getting struck by lightning.

"Kenzi..." I swallow hard, feeling lightheaded. She looks the same but so different. Older. More mature. Her hair has a darker brown shade mixed in with her blond, and it really brings out her eyes, which I'm trying hard not to stare into like a lovesick puppy.

Those eyes. Holy shit, I miss those eyes.

"Tor..." She takes a deep breath as she stares at me, her eyes growing wide as if she's trying to take in the sight of every inch of me all at once.

I stand and offer her my hand to help her up. "I had no idea you were in town already," I say. I can't take my eyes off her. She looks amazing in a tight black V-neck sweater, jeans that fit like a second skin, and those damn little black motorcycle boots. The memory of the time I made love to her with nothing else on but those boots surfaces, and I quickly try to put those images out of my head. *Some things never change.*

She falters, losing herself under my intense gaze. "I moved back here about a month ago. I'm living with Rayne. That's why I'm here." She gestures over toward Lukas's shop. "She works here and I had to drop something off for her."

"I was just heading there for my tattoo appointment." A month. She's been here for a month and I didn't even know. Why didn't she tell me? Why didn't Asher tell me? Is life going to fuck me over and take her away from me when we finally have things fixed?

The corners of her mouth tilt up and her smile lights up her face. "You're still getting ink? I'm surprised you have any open skin left."

"We're working on my legs now," I reply. "How have you been?"

She pulls the strap of her bag up higher on her shoulder. "I'm doing well. My calligraphy business is going great. I'm actually designing a lot of those hand-lettered tattoos for people, especially Lukas's clients, and I'm selling a lot of the cookies I told you about."

"The cookies with the writing?"

"Yeah. A lot of brides have been buying them. And I just started making some for dogs that have cute words on them."

"Wow, that's really cool. I'm proud of you, Angel." The nickname slips out past my lips before I can stop it.

A hint of pink touches her cheeks. "Thank you," she says. "I was going to call you once I got settled."

I chew the inside of my cheek. "Why didn't you tell me you were coming home?" I ask, because I can't stand here not knowing why. "Why were you waiting to call me? What if I hadn't run into you just now?"

"Because I wanted us to reconnect with me being on my own. Not living in my father's house. Even though he's doing his best to accept it, I couldn't see having you come over to see me in *his* house, or make him watch me leave his house to go to yours and then come back again later that night. That's the place where you were my uncle and I was your niece, and I think we need to stay away from those memories for a little while, at least in front of him."

I nod slowly. "Okay. That makes sense, and I can accept that."

"I was definitely going to call you, Tor," she assures me. "Please don't think I wasn't. I just wanted us to start off right, and I wanted some time with my father, too. To make sure he's really okay. I just wanted to do everything right."

Right. That's what I want, too. Everything to be right. And normal. Without lies, and betrayal, and worry.

"Can I take you to dinner?" A year ago, we couldn't go out to dinner for fear of someone seeing us. But now I don't care. Asher already knows, so there's nothing to hide. Now I can take her on a real date.

She beams. "I'd love to. When?"

"Is tonight too soon?" I ask with a grin. No point in trying to hide my impatience, right?

She laughs and I want to kiss her so bad I can practically taste her on my lips. I wonder if she still wears that strawberry lip gloss I loved so much.

"Tonight is perfect."

"Can I pick you up?"

"Sure," she replies. "Let me write down my address for you. Me and Rayne are renting a studio apartment in a converted barn in Amherst." I wait as she digs through her purse and finds something to write on, then copies the address from her phone onto the scrap of paper.

"I know this is awful, but I keep forgetting the address," she says as she hands it to me. "I've only been there two weeks. I stayed at my dad's for a few weeks before I moved in with Rayne."

I take the paper from her and shove it into my front pocket.

"Tor," she begins, stopping to take a breath. "The message in the bottle was amazing. It really made me see everything so clearly. I loved it. Every night before I go to sleep, I read it."

"I was hoping you would."

"And I did make a wish that night. With the penny you sent."

My heart starts to pound as she moves closer to me and slips her hand into mine.

"You want to share it with me?" I lace my fingers through hers, not planning on letting her go. Ever again.

"I wished for you. And us. And happiness."

Stepping closer, I lift her chin to look into her eyes. "I can make that happen." I kiss her long and soft, my mouth lingering against hers, breathing her into me, wanting to devour her right here on the street. Her free hand clings to my arm like she's afraid she's going to fall over.

"I still love you the most," she whispers between kisses. "I never stopped."

"Neither did I, Angel. I never will."

I lean down and cover her lips with mine, and yes, she still tastes of strawberries, and of yesterday, and of tomorrow.

EPILOGUE

Kenzi—age twenty-two

Tor—age thirty-seven

KENZI

I reach for him in a drowsy haze, but he's not on his side of the bed. Smiling, I climb out of bed and walk across the hall, wearing nothing but his huge white T-shirt, to the nursery to find him sitting exactly where I knew he would be—in the rocking chair with the baby asleep in his arms. Diogee and Kitten are napping at his feet. I have to stop in the doorway for a moment because the sight of him holding our baby, with his shirt off, all covered in ink, and his long hair flowing down his shoulders takes my breath away. Every time.

Sometimes I feel like I'm living in a dream. A year ago, we had a small private ceremony at Aunt Katherine's inn. My father walked me down the aisle and gave my hand to Tor with a smile, making me cry tears of happiness. We spent two weeks there making love and walking along the beach at sunrise and sunset, kissing and talking for hours on end. It was a magical way to start our life together and we decided we'd make a ritual to go back there every year for our anniversary.

"Tor," I whisper, "why didn't you wake me? I would have come to rock her back to sleep." He's always getting up in the middle of the night to take care of the baby and I worry about him being tired during the day. I'm home all day so I can take naps when the baby does, but he has to stay awake at the shop.

"I want you to get some rest, Angel. I know how excited you are about your parents coming for dinner tomorrow. Or later, whatever time it is now." He grins sleepily. "I don't want you to be tired and stressed."

Slowly standing, he gently lays Tia down on her back in the crib and covers her with the pink fleece blanket before kneeling down to kiss her cheek. Tor is an amazing father with endless patience and love for his little girl, but I had no doubt he would be that way.

I stand next to him and stare down at our beautiful sleeping baby and rub my hand down his muscular back. "I'm fine," I answer. "Just excited that they're coming. And a little nervous." It's the first time my mother will be coming over to our house and I want everything to be just right.

Turning, he puts his arms around me. "Don't be nervous. Just act natural like the doctor said, and if she veers off, just smile and turn the conversation back to the present. And try to remember to not call her Mom."

I nod, but still feel a bit of nervousness inside. Last time she saw Tia, she thought she was hers and it was horrible taking the baby away while she sobbed in confusion. *Baby steps,* the doctor advised, as it's only been a short time since she came out of the coma. And lots of patience. That's all we can do while her brain attempts to recover and remember her life. *And us.* My father is convinced she'll get there, and his faith hasn't steered him wrong yet, so I believe it, too.

"I'm going to make those cookies she likes with the smiley faces on them."

He kisses my nose. "I like those, too." His hands slide down to cup my naked ass, and he pulls me against him, leaning in to nuzzle my neck. "Do I have time to make love to my beautiful wife?" he whispers.

"You're the boss. You're allowed to be late," I whisper back, and my hands are already diving under his sweatpants to stroke him.

"In that case," he says, picking me up and carrying me toward our bedroom, "I think I'm going to give myself the day off and spend it with my girls."

Smiling from ear to ear, I wrap my arms around his neck and kiss his cheek. "I love you. So much." He lays me down on our bed and I pull him down on top of me, wrapping my arms and legs around him in a full-body hug, immediately taking him deep inside me, never feeling like I can possibly get close enough to him. "You made all my wishes come true."

His smile nearly stops my heart with the amount of love and happiness that reaches his eyes, which always have flecks of golden light in them now, the shadows of sadness long gone and forgotten.

"*We* made all our wishes come true, Angel. Me and you."

BONUS CHAPTER

KENZI

My upper arm stings and throbs as I leave the tattoo shop, but the pain was *so* worth it. Lukas did an amazing job—the design came out even better than I'd envisioned. For the past four hours, I sat as still as I could, babbling his ear off in an attempt to distract myself from the burn of the needle while he worked his magic. Lukas—my dad's youngest cousin—is known as much for his kindness and patience as he is for his brilliant, ultra-realistic tattoo work. Now I understand why.

Lukas refused to let me pay him, even though I've been saving up for months. "Consider it a belated birthday gift," he'd said with a smile before he disappeared behind the black velvet curtain that screened his work area.

"Don't worry about it. He never charges family," Rayne assured me from her post at the reception desk, where she's effortlessly braiding a thin purple scarf into her long dark hair. She's my dad's sister, which also makes her my aunt. She's twenty-one years old, a little more than a year older than me.

Welcome to my strange, but very blessed, life.

I head toward the parking lot with my keys in one hand and my phone in the other, scanning the text messages I missed while getting my tattoo. My best friend, Chloe, has sent me a photo of her new bob cut—which looks adorable—and my dad has sent two messages asking how my tattoo appointment went.

I tap out a reply to my father and then *BAM*—I run straight into something solid in the middle of the sidewalk.

Or some*one*, to be more accurate.

My keys and phone hit the ground. I bend down to pick them up and my purse falls off my shoulder, spilling its contents because I never snap it closed. Three pens scatter. A rabbit-head Pez dispenser bounces to the side and coughs up a pink rectangle candy. A tube of glittery lip gloss rolls across the sidewalk until the tip of a large black leather boot stops it. The owner of said boot kneels in front of me and gathers up my belongings.

"Shit," he mutters. "I'm sorry. Totally my bad. I wasn't paying attention."

His deep voice penetrates through flesh and bone and settles around my heart like a cat cozying up to a fire. A rush of warmth spreads through my chest. I peek through the curtain of my blond hair, and my breath catches in the hollow of my throat.

"Neither was I," I whisper.

He visibly swallows. "Kenzi..."

"Tor." His name rides the breath I'd been holding. Much to my parents' dismay, it was my first word as a baby. I wonder how many times I've said his name since then. It must be thousands. Possibly millions. It's still my favorite word, my favorite name, my favorite everything.

He is my favorite everything.

Our eyes lock, exchanging telepathic messages in a way we've been able to do for the past nineteen years. *I missed you so much. I love you. Am I dreaming? Don't ever leave me again.*

He stands and holds his hand out, pulling me up to my feet. With a racing heart, I shove my things into my purse and comb my hand through my hair as I take him in. How is it possible that he keeps getting more attractive with age? He looks absolutely, deliciously sinful. His black T-shirt is tight across his arms and chest. The thin material does nothing to hide the fact that he's been working out hardcore again. His dark hair is shorter than it was the last time I saw him, but it still reaches the top of his broad shoulders.

"I had no idea you were in town already," he says. My body hums to life under the gaze of his soulful, hooded eyes that are now dark, serious, and slightly troubled. Butterflies awaken and stir in my stomach.

How can he be as familiar to me as my own reflection, but at the same time feel so breathtakingly new and exciting?

"I moved back here about a month ago. I'm living with Rayne." I point back to the tattoo shop. "That's why I'm here. She works here and I had to drop something off for her." Lying isn't a habit of mine, but I don't want him to know about my tattoo yet.

He nods, still holding my gaze. "I was just heading there for my tattoo appointment."

I smile at the memories of trailing my lips and fingertips over all his tattoos while making love under the veil of his soft bedsheets. Tingles buzz in my thighs and shoot up my spine.

"You're still getting ink? I'm surprised you have any open skin left," I tease.

"We're working on my legs now." He pauses and I catch the slight tick of movement above his cheek. It would go unnoticed by a stranger, but I know his jaw is clenching involuntarily with stress or worry—something that started when his father passed away many years ago. "How have you been?" he asks.

I can read Tor like a well-loved book. He's wondering why I didn't call him the moment I was back in town. I wanted to. It's been nothing short of torture to be just a few miles away from him and not go see him, wrap myself around him like a ribbon, and never let him go.

But I promised myself I would do this right. Or as right as I possibly could.

"I'm doing well," I say. "My calligraphy business is doing great. I'm actually designing a lot of hand-lettered tattoos for people, especially for Lukas's clients, and I'm selling a lot of the cookies I told you about."

I've been proud of the success of my artwork and baking ventures, but I can't help comparing my little budding career to those of Toren's ex-girlfriends, which include a famous rock star, a nurse, and a bank loan manager. Will a thirty-four-year-old man think my steps into adulthood are glaringly immature?

As much as I believe in us, sometimes small waves of doubt creep in—making me wonder if our age difference might cause bumps down the road.

"The cookies with the writing?" he asks.

"Yeah. A lot of brides have been buying them. And I just started making some for dogs that have cute words on them."

"Wow, that's really cool. I'm proud of you, Angel."

My heart flutters and I want to forget all this awkward small talk. This isn't us, and this isn't how I wanted our reunion to go. My chest aches with the need to touch his face, to feel his lips on mine and his muscular arms around me. I want to be alone with him—at his house or by our favorite rocks near the river—and have a *real* conversation.

"Thank you." I take a deep breath and continue. "I was going to call you once I got settled."

The tiny lines on his forehead furrow. "Why didn't you tell me you were coming home?" His voice is low and tinged with a painful disbelief that just about cracks my heart in two. My waiting was never, ever meant to hurt him. "Why were you waiting to call me? What if I hadn't run into you just now?"

Tears burn my eyes as I meet his, silently begging him to understand my need to come back home—to this town, to my friends and family, and to him—in a way that would do the least amount of damage.

"Because I wanted us to reconnect with me being on my own. Not living in my father's house. Even though he's doing his best to accept it, I couldn't have you coming over to see me in *his* house, or make him watch me leave his house to go to yours and then come back again later that night. That's the place where you were my uncle and I was your niece, and I think we need to stay away from those memories for a little while, at least in front of him."

Slowly, he takes in my explanation, then nods. "Okay. That makes sense, and I can accept that."

"I was definitely going to call you, Tor. Please don't think I wasn't. I just wanted us to start off right, and I wanted some time with my father, too. To make sure he's really okay. I just wanted to do everything right."

And that's the mountain I've been facing and trying my best to tackle: Is there any way to make falling in love with your father's lifelong best friend right for everyone involved?

He reaches for my hand and holds it tight in his. We stare at each other, taking careful breaths. It's the first time we've ever touched in public as a couple. I squeeze his hand and smile reassuringly.

This is right. We can do this.

"Can I take you to dinner?" he asks.

His question sends my heart into a spasm of frantic beats filled with long-suppressed hopes and wishes. "I'd love to. When?"

Tonight. Please say tonight. I can't wait another day or I might burst into a million tear-shaped pieces right here on the sidewalk.

Tor's boyish grin—my favorite—flashes across his full lips. "Is tonight too soon?"

A small laugh of relief and sheer happiness comes out of me. "Tonight is perfect." My brain is already mentally scanning my closet, trying to choose the perfect outfit.

"Can I pick you up?"

"Sure. Let me write down my address for you. Me and Rayne are renting a studio apartment in a converted barn in Amherst," I explain as I dig through my purse for a pen and a scrap of paper. "I know this is awful, but I keep forgetting the address." My fingers tremble with excitement as I jot the address. "I've only been there two weeks. I stayed at my dad's for a few weeks before I moved in with Rayne."

His fingers brush against mine when he takes the paper from my hand. I want to grab them and pull him closer. He stares at the note like it's a winning lottery ticket.

I have so much I want to say, but for right now, there's just one thing I need to tell him.

"Tor," I say softly. "The message in the bottle was amazing. It really made me see everything so clearly. I loved it. Every night before I go to sleep, I read it."

His chest rises and falls with a deep breath. "I was hoping you would."

"And I did make a wish that night. With the penny you sent." I close the space between us and take his hands in mine.

"You want to share it with me?" That subtle, sexy, teasing tone almost makes my knees buckle. He laces his long, rough fingers between mine and presses our palms together. His are warm and slightly calloused, just as I remember them. I've missed his touch so, so much.

"I wished for you. And us. And happiness."

He releases one of my hands to gently lift my chin. I stare up into the eyes of the man who has loved me, taken care of me, and been my very best friend without falter since the day I was born.

Sharing such an unconditional, timeless love and connection with him is indescribable. To me, it is the very essence of a fairy tale.

"I can make that happen," he whispers, lowering his lips to mine. I cling to his arm as he kisses me long, deep, and tantalizingly slow, his hand cradling the side of my throat, holding me to him. As if I'd ever think of breaking our kiss after waiting all this time. His possessive touch steals my breath and sends ripples of excitement through my veins.

Tonight can't come fast enough.

"I still love you the most," I whisper to him between kisses. "I never stopped."

He leans his forehead against mine and lets out a contented sigh. I can almost feel the weight of worry from the past year lifting from him.

"Neither did I, Angel. I never will."

READ TYLER'S STORY IN THE NEXT ALL TORN UP NOVEL

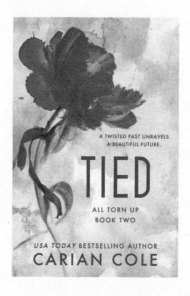

"An emotional novel filled with 'dark and delicious angst' between two broken souls connected by a dark, haunting past."

—L. J. Shen, *USA Today* and *Wall Street Journal* bestselling author

ACKNOWLEDGMENTS

I'm continually overwhelmed by how many people have helped me on my writing journey. I'm a loner by nature; I'm not used to talking to lots of people, or asking for help, or trying to get myself out there. So many people have reached out to help me, promote me, beta for me, share my posts, etc.—just to be nice, and to help me get noticed. That blows me away, and I am so incredibly grateful and appreciative. During the writing of this book, I had quite a blow to my personal life, and I had a very hard time finishing it. Once again, several amazing friends went above and beyond to make sure this book was as good as it could be, and to lend moral support when I desperately needed it. It means so much to me that people believe in my writing (and in me) enough to invest their own time and efforts.

So, huge heartfelt thanks to all of you—whether you read my books, chatted with me, left a review, beta read, edited, proofed, promoted, commented, liked, attended a takeover, or just listened to me—thank you!!!

Thank you to my husband, Eddie, because I wouldn't be able to write one word of love and heartache without you in my life. You have always been my biggest muse. xo

A LETTER FOR READERS

Dear Reader,

Thank you so much for reading Torn! *This was the first book that I really took a risk writing, as many friends told me that readers may not enjoy a taboo story that not only had a big age gap, but also the Hero knowing the heroine since she was a baby and having a close relationship with her as she grew up. I couldn't get the characters out of my head, so I put my whole heart into writing their story in the hopes that readers would fall in love with them and believe in their love as much as I had. I'm so glad I did because, years later, Kenzi and Toren continue to be favorites amongst my readers.*

I hope you enjoyed their love story. My goal for every book I write is to showcase an unconventional romance that will leave the reader closing the book believing in all kinds of happily-ever-afters.

I also want to give a special thank you to the fans in the list that follows who have given their support to this new edition of Torn.

Happy reading!
Carian

Hannah Abbott

Louisse Ang

Lori Apodaca

Shabnam Arora

Arlinda Baker

Emily Baker

Monica Bartsch

Emily Battilega

Kaytlin Bowen

Kimberly Brower

Frances Bullock

Tracy Burns

Debra Calhoun

Isis Cejas

Amber Christensen

Genene Clary

Carrie Cluster

Megan Cooley

Barbara Coon

Roseanna Cottone

Niki Cox

Kristi Cox

Dana Cuadrado

Tracy Harper Curtis

Yenny Dang

Karen-Nicole Darley

Vivian Diaz

Kaylah Dinsdale

Joanie Dupuis

Cindy Ehrlich

Michele Ellenberger

Michelle Villadelgado Ermita

Kristin Farley

Carla Fernandez More

Shannon Fissel

Sabrina Flemming

Katie Friend

Shaila Furtado

Loretta Gaines

Sally Gates

Nicola Geddes

Deborra Giavia

Colleen Gilchrist

Diana Gomez

Sara Green

Stacy Griffing

Estelle Hallick

Kara Hampton

Li Cai Haney

Rebekah Hatch

Lori Headley

MJ Heather

Noël Darling Hill

Rosemary Hollis

Nickiann Holt

Alisa Huntington

Molly Jaber

Daisy Jane

Cynthia Jeremica

Sharelly Johnson

Vedrana Jovanovic

Jess Jug

Meghan Katowitz

Korrie Kelley

Tara Kim

Stephanie Kluk

Kristen Kochis

Kyrstin Kuehn

Jill Kwochka

Maybelis Lopez

Amy Malek

Carolina Martin

Taylor Martin

Getsy Mason

Libby McCollum

Elizabeth McCollum

Raquel Mccoy

Shannon McCully

Cari McFarland

Daniela Medina

Marie-Eve Merliot

Autumn Miller

Marissa Miller

Candy Miller

Anne Milne

Ashley Mural

Danyelle Nelson

Sheena Nemecek

Amy Nestor

Haley Newport

Katy Nielsen

Bonnie Norton

Bria Oakley

Savannah Orr

Lorna Owens

Bethany Palmer

Ashley Panike

K. Partridge

Kayla Patton Willis

Kimberly Pickrell

Rebecca Pinquoch

Chelsea Plants

Tiffany Pledger

Danyel Pons

Debbie Ralph

Lisa Ray

Stacey Reid

Donna Marie Riani

Teresa Ricker

Brooke Rollins

Daniela Schilling

Kimberly Sciacca

Tina Sevison

Wendy Shouse

Darlene Simon

Melody Smith

Emma Smith

Natoria Strum

Cailin Svennes

Heather Swan

Karen Szakelyhidi

Mary Thamert

Anna Thoman

Theresa Thomas

Amy Tiffany

Angie Trumps

Angie Trumps

Charlene VanWinkle

Ana Volpentesta

Robyn Wallace

Samantha Westmoreland

Erin Wexler

Jessica White

Megan Wirth

Mandy Wolfe

Amber Yusko

ABOUT THE AUTHOR

Carian Cole has a passion for the bad boys, those covered in tattoos, sexy smirks, ripped jeans, fast cars, motorcycles, and of course, the sweet girls who try to tame them and win their hearts.

Born and raised a Jersey girl, Carian now resides in beautiful New Hampshire with her husband and their multitude of furry pets. She spends most of her time writing, reading, and vacuuming.

Carian loves to hear from readers and interacts daily on her social media accounts. To find out more or subscribe to Carian Cole's newsletter, visit:

CarianColeWrites.com
Facebook.com/CarianColeAuthor
Instagram @CarianCole_Author
X @CarianCole
TikTok @CarianCole.Author